STIRRING UP STRIFE

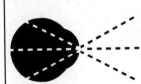

This Large Print Book carries the
Seal of Approval of N.A.V.H.

STIRRING UP STRIFE

JENNIFER STANLEY

THORNDIKE PRESS

A part of Gale, Cengage Learning

GALE
CENGAGE Learning

Detroit • New York • San Francisco • New Haven, Conn • Waterville, Maine • London

GALE
CENGAGE Learning

LIBRARY OF CONGRESS CATALOGING-IN-PUBLICATION DATA

Stanley, J. B.
    Stirring up strife / by Jennifer Stanley.
        p. cm. — (Thorndike Press large print Christian mystery)
    "A Hope Street church mystery"—Copyright p.
    ISBN-13: 978-1-4104-3036-6
    ISBN-10: 1-4104-3036-7
    1. Large type books. I. Title.
PS3619.T3655S76 2010
813'.6—dc22   2010023255

Published in 2010 by arrangement with St. Martin's Press, LLC.

Printed in Mexico
1 2 3 4 5 6 7 14 13 12 11 10

For Monica,
my spirited, beautiful friend.

ACKNOWLEDGMENTS

The author would like to thank:

Mary Harrison, for the invitation to attend Bible Study at Third Presbyterian Church, and to the kind-hearted ladies of Circle #2 for extending such a warm welcome.

Holly, Anne, and Mary, for sharing your gifts as sharp-eyed readers and honest friends.

Hope Dellon and Laura Bourgeois of St. Martin's, for shaping this stack of pages into something better than I'd dreamed possible.

Jessica Faust of Book Ends, for making me laugh and always being in my corner.

Jessica and Mark of the UPS store in Gayton Crossing, for answering a host of rather dull questions with patience and courtesy.

7

And last, but never least, my family, for letting me wander freely down these winding paths and then, just when I've had enough, bringing me home again.

Hatred stirs up strife,
But love covers all sins.
— Proverbs 10:12 (NKJV)

There should be no strife with the
vanquished or the dead.
— Virgil

1

Turn to me and be gracious to me, for I am lonely and afflicted.

Psalm 25:16 (NIV)

Cooper Lee was more comfortable with machines than with people. She drove all over the city of Richmond to fix them. By the time she got to these copiers, laminators, or fax machines as they waited in their offices, hospitals, or schools, they were broken. Broken and quiet. Cooper would arrive and meticulously lay out her tools, and as she did so, the machines didn't raise their brows in surprise or barely concealed amusement that a woman worked as an office-machine repairman. A thirty-two-year-old woman dressed in a man's uniform shirt didn't seem odd or funny to them at all.

Most importantly, they never stared at her eyes.

Her left eye wasn't worth a second look. It was a flat, almost colorless blue. No one would have dreamed of comparing it to sapphires or deep seas or cloudless summer skies. But the other eye, the eye Cooper had received through ocular transplant surgery after being smashed in the face with a field hock.y stick in junior high, was a shimmering green. It was exotic — invoking images of lush jungles flecked with firefly light or the green shallows of tropical waters, in which sunshine was trapped just below the surface.

That single moment at field hockey practice, when a girl on Cooper's own team had accidentally swung her stick too high as she prepared to hit the ball with incredible force, made Cooper more self-conscious than other teenagers. Still, she wanted what most people want. She longed to have one close friend, to be loved by someone she could grow old with, and for her life to have purpose. Cooper thought she had found all of those in her boyfriend, Drew. Until he dumped her.

Shaking off her gloomy thoughts, Cooper cut a piece of crumb cake for breakfast, wrapped it in a paper towel, filled her twenty-eight-ounce travel cup to the brim with milky, unsweetened coffee, and tossed a banana onto the passenger seat of her truck. She drove east on I-64, the sun blinding her most of the way. According to Bryant Shelton's weather report, there wasn't going to be a cloud in the sky this April Friday. For once, it appeared as though Bryant might be right, though it didn't matter much to Cooper. She'd be inside offices most of the day, but could enjoy brief moments of sunshine while driving the work van from one destination to another.

At ten minutes to nine, Cooper pulled into the parking lot belonging to one of a dozen corporate buildings resembling silvery LEGO blocks. The Make It Work! headquarters was on the fringe of an area called Innsbrook in which hundreds of different companies, replete with an abundance of office equipment, depended upon Cooper and her coworkers in order to operate smoothly.

" 'Mornin', Coop!" Angela called out a chipper greeting as Cooper approached the reception desk. Angela's smile, combined with a vase filled with plump, yellow roses, created a warm welcome. Few people visited the office as most of Make It Work!'s transactions were conducted via telephone, but Angela bought a dozen roses every Monday, claiming that a good workweek always began with fresh flowers. Angela was in charge of setting up appointments and billing. She was at her desk every morning before anyone else, wearing one of her vintage sweaters, a pencil skirt (both of which were always too tight), and a pair of sexy heels. Angela's platinum hair, powdered face, and fire-engine-red nails and lipstick were supposed to call to mind an image of Marilyn Monroe, but Angela was older and plumper than the late actress had ever been. Still, Angela was the heart and soul of their small operation. Filled with pluck and boundless optimism, even the frostiest customers thawed once Angela worked her magic on them.

"You've got an emergency waitin' for you, sug." Angela examined her reflection in a small compact that was never out of reach. "Some poor lady has gotten her weddin' ring jammed in the insides of a copier." She held out a pink memo pad and ripped off the top sheet with a flourish.

"Capital City, huh?" Cooper said, reading the message. "I have to go over there anyway. They've ordered half a dozen Hewlett-Packard 7410 multifunction printers and I've got to bring them to Building F and hook them up." She grinned at Angela. "A wedding ring, you say? I wonder how she got it stuck inside."

Angela shrugged. "You know folks like to try to fix things themselves. You've fished stranger things out of those machines. 'Member the bologna sandwich last year?"

"Do I?" Cooper laughed. "That mayo was *everywhere.* And that obnoxious executive tried to blame it on his administrative assistant. What a jerk."

"That's why I like workin' for Mr. Farmer. He's just as kind as he can be." Angela's eyes, beneath their curtain of long, fake lashes, twinkled as they always did when she mentioned the boss's name.

Cooper buttoned up her gun-smoke-gray Make It Work! uniform jacket and grabbed the keys to one of the company's two vans. Ben, the other repairman, was already off on his rounds. He came in an hour earlier than Cooper and was out of the door by 4:00 p.m. He was obsessed with developing his naturally thin frame into a walking mass of muscle, so he spent two hours at the gym before heading home to his wife — a woman no one from Make It Work! had ever laid eyes on. Ben never spoke about her either.

"Can you grab some Mexican from Casa Grande for lunch?" Angela asked as Cooper opened the front door, wiggling the van keys until they sounded like metal castanets.

"Sure. What would you like?"

"Chicken quesadillas for me, something for yourself, and a Pan Filo burrito for Mr. Farmer. He *said* he needed to be more like Ben and watch his weight but I told him that a little stuffing makes a nicer pillow." Angela giggled, placed a twenty-dollar bill on the desk, and pushed it toward Cooper. "Lord, he turned beet red when I said that!"

Cooper thought about her introverted boss being complimented by the effusive Angela. He was a man of few words and usually hid in his office, drooling over the latest issues of *Technology Review, Poplar Mechanics,* and *PC Magazine.* Cooper couldn't fathom why Angela found their short, balding, hermitlike employer so captivating. It was like having a crush on Danny DeVito.

"See you in a bit, Angela." Cooper saluted the other woman with her coffee cup and headed out to the van.

A Mrs. Brooke Hughes of Capital City, one of the nation's largest credit card companies, had placed the call regarding the lost wedding ring. Cooper could tell that Mrs. Hughes was either an administrative assistant or an investigative agent in the Fraud Protection Division by the fact that the copier in question was located on the

16

third floor in Building C. The Fraud Protection Division took up most of that floor, with the exception of a large filing room Cooper had never had reason to enter.

The second the elevator doors opened on the third floor, Mrs. Hughes leapt forward and latched onto Cooper's arm like a barnacle.

"Thank goodness you're here!" she exclaimed. Then, she looked down and realized she was clamping onto Cooper's arm with a viselike grip and that the younger woman was politely struggling to reclaim her limb. "Oh, I'm sorry!" Exhaling loudly, she released Cooper and then displayed her hands, which were coated with black toner. "I've really made a mess of things, I'm afraid."

Cooper could see that the woman had also smeared toner on her ivory blouse and berry-colored skirt. Mrs. Hughes, though agitated, had a friendly face and kind eyes. "Don't worry, ma'am," Cooper assured the woman and then introduced herself. "We'll get your ring back. Which machine is it stuck in?"

"Oh, please call me Brooke. The copier's right outside my office."

Although she wore a name tag, Cooper thought it only polite to speak her name aloud since her client had established a friendly rapport, despite her distress.

It turned out that Brooke Hughes was the head of the entire department. She had her own assistant and a full-sized six-thousand-dollar Sharp grayscale copier at her disposal. The chair at the assistant's desk was empty and her workstation was covered with mounds of wadded tissues and untidy stacks of paper.

"Cindi, my assistant, called out sick today. Again." Brooke's eyebrows shot up and down suggestively. "I've been trying to wrap up this case I'm working on and I just needed to pull together a few more documents." She gestured at Cindi's desk. "I was attempting to make sense of that mess when I came across a document that was *very, very* incriminating . . ." She trailed off, looking abashed. "I'm sorry to go on about all this to you." She lowered her voice to a whisper. "It's just that it was crucial for me to make multiple copies of this, ah, report so I could quickly store it in more than one location as soon as possible."

Brooke nervously picked at her cuticles and lowered her voice even further. "I'm concerned that the original document could suddenly *disappear.*" Her voice returned to normal as she continued. "But then the copier jammed and I was so desperate to make copies that I tried to fix it. When I reached under that panel" — she pointed inside the machine and Cooper noticed that the woman's finger was trembling — "and tried to rip out the paper, my ring slipped off my finger and fell down in there."

"Were you able to make any copies?" Cooper wondered, concerned about the woman's apparent anxiety.

Brooke shook her head and made a visible effort to pull herself together.

Wordlessly, Cooper rolled the copier away from the wall and scanned the carpet. She couldn't see the ring anywhere, so she knew that meant she'd have to unscrew the back panel from the machine. Retrieving a flashlight from her toolbox, she asked Brooke, "Has this copier been acting up lately?"

"I think so. Cindi's cursed quite loudly at it a few times. I also think she's given it a few solid kicks." Brooke winced as though she hated snitching on her assistant. "I'm afraid she's not too good at following directions. Mine or a machine's. But she's a single mom and I just don't have the heart to let her go." She laughed humorlessly. "I swear I do both our jobs most of the time."

Unused to being watched as she worked, Cooper began loosening the screws that secured the back panel to the main body of the copier.

"Unlike poor Cindi," Brooke rambled on, "I've been blessed. My husband is my best friend. We were high school sweethearts, raised a terrific son together, and are celebrating our thirty-year anniversary tonight. That's why I'm so desperate to get my ring back today."

Cooper glanced up at Brooke's face. She was gazing out a window beyond Cindi's desk, a small smile playing around the corners of her mouth. "Wesley, my husband, is picking me up after work today in a white limo. We're going out to dinner at this little hole-in-the-wall where we had our first date. He doesn't know that I know, but he also reserved the bridal suite at the Jefferson." She shook her head dreamily. "We couldn't afford anything like that when we got married, so I guess he's trying to make it up to me, but I wouldn't trade our first years of struggle for anything." She grinned at Cooper. "Are you married?"

"No, ma'am," Cooper answered without taking her eyes from her work. "My boyfriend of over five years left me six months ago. Really suddenly," she added and then instantly clammed up. People didn't usually speak to her once they had directed her to the machine they needed fixed so she was surprised to find herself sharing such an intimate exchange.

"I'm so sorry," Brooke answered sincerely. "Five years is a long time. Many marriages don't survive that long, so you two must have been doing something right."

"I thought so." Cooper sighed. "And I'd do anything to have my life with him back. All that time, he was my only friend, my whole world. I'm living with my parents again and just trying to figure out how to start again."

Brooke put her hand on Cooper's shoulder. "You're young and pretty and I can tell you must be awfully smart to be able to do what you do. Once time heals your wounds a bit, you're going to find that men will line up around the block just to take you out on a date."

"Really?" Cooper looked over her shoulder. "Where's the front of that line?"

Brooke smiled. "If you can laugh about your pain, you're on the road to getting the best of it. And I have an idea about a place that might help you in the whole recovery process. Hold on a sec." She pulled open a desk drawer, retrieved a marigold-colored brochure, and handed it to Cooper.

"This is the church I go to. I would love

for you to attend a service with me. Come as my friend. Any Sunday you'd like. Just walk on in and find me and we'll sit together."

Cooper stared at the yellow brochure. It was from Hope Street Church and simply had the church name, address, and the words *Welcome, Friends* on the cover. Brooke's invitation was filled with warmth and hospitality, but the idea of attending an unfamiliar church wasn't something Cooper could immediately agree to. "I'll think about it. Thank you, ma'am."

"Please do. And no more of this *ma'am* stuff. We're just two women trying to make our way in the world. Brooke and Cooper." She pointed at the brochure. "Take a look at that when you get a chance and feel free to call me if you have any questions. Now" — Brooke tugged on the bottom of her stained blouse — "*I* will stop blithering away like a chatty magpie and let you work your magic. I'll be in my office, so please let me know if you need an extra pair of hands — to hold the flashlight for you or something."

"Thanks, but I'm like an octopus when I'm working." Cooper grinned and watched the other woman walk away. She then folded the Hope Street brochure in half, tucked it in her pants pocket, and returned her focus to removing the bottom paper drawer so that she could get a better view of the copier's underbelly. After she detached the tray, she directed the powerful beam of her Maglite into the cavity and swept the light all around the base. A twinkle in one of the far corners alerted her to the presence of Brooke's ring.

Plucking the ring from the dark, Cooper cleaned it off using a fresh rag from her toolbox. A dozen tiny diamonds embedded in a band of yellow gold glistened as Cooper wiped away spots of toner and dust. As she rubbed the inside of the ring, she noticed an inscription. It read *Forever, I Corinthians 13:13.*

Cooper knew that I Corinthians 13:13 was a popular biblical quote to use for wedding ceremonies. Sitting on the floor of the quiet office, she called to mind the cover of her younger sister, Ashley's, wedding program. It showed the bride and groom as children inside a heart-shaped cut-out. Above the photograph were two doves flying toward each other and the words *And now these three remain: faith, hope and love. But the greatest of these is love.*

Folding the ring carefully inside another clean rag, Cooper set the precious package next to her toolbox and began the process of removing the jammed sheets of paper. She made a pile of torn strips of paper along with an anthill of bits and scraps that had likely collected inside the copier over the last few weeks. It only took her a few minutes to restore the machine to working order. She checked under the lid to see if Brooke's original document was still laid out on the glass. It was, so Cooper programmed the machine to make five duplicates in order to test the copier. It ran them through without a hitch.

Cooper didn't even glance at the pages that were so critical to Brooke Hughes. She had never examined the contents of a single document in her four years as a repairwoman and didn't plan to start now. Clearing her throat, she stood in the threshold of Brooke's office and unfolded the rag containing the wedding ring.

"Here's your ring, ma'am — um, Brooke. No harm done to it either."

Brooke plucked the ring from the rag, pushed it on her finger, and threw her arms around Cooper. "God bless you! I can't tell you how much this means to me!"

Though surprised by the woman's quickness, Cooper still managed to press the documents against her thigh so they wouldn't get crushed by Brooke's embrace.

"Your copier's back in order too," Cooper declared once Brooke had released her. "I made five copies just to test the machine, but you're good to go if you'd like to run off some more."

Brooke accepted the papers. The joy that had shone from her eyes upon seeing her wedding ring was instantaneously transformed into a mixture of worry and fear. "Thank you," she said softly.

The phone on her desk began to ring, and Brooke glanced in its direction. Once again, she began to pick nervously at her fingernails.

"I'd better get that." Her tone was regretful.

Cooper was accustomed to abrupt dismissals by busy and important people, or at least people who viewed themselves as busy and important, so Brooke's desire to linger was unusual.

"Have a nice day, ma'am," Cooper stated politely. She wished she could think of something more comforting to add but nothing came to mind.

Retreating toward her desk, Brooke gave Cooper a bright smile infused with warmth and then wiggled her ring finger. "I hope that one day a good man gives you a ring and a promise and makes you very, very happy. Maybe I'll see you at church some Sunday. I'll keep an eye out for you."

It took a moment for Cooper to move, as a vision of Drew bending down on one knee and offering her a velvet jewelry box had her so captivated that she almost forgot where she was. Finally, she blinked and Drew's handsome face and pleading eyes evaporated.

"Most folks don't talk to me when I'm working," Cooper found herself telling Brooke. "I kind of walk around as if I'm invisible. So . . . it was really nice to have done work for you today. Thank you."

"*No* one's invisible," Brooke replied firmly and smiled again. She then picked up her phone and her smile disappeared in a flash.

Sensing that Brooke needed privacy, Cooper returned to the restored copier and packed up her tools. Because the only trash receptacle in sight was the overflowing Rubbermaid can under Cindi's desk, Cooper folded the paper scraps she had removed from inside the copier into her rag and headed outside to the van. As she walked, she considered how her regular interactions with office workers were brief and impersonal and in general, she preferred it that way. Yet for the first time, she had met someone who had spoken to her openly, as

26

an equal, and it had felt really good. And though part of Cooper felt touched by Brooke Hughes's attention, the other part of her wished that she could have remained anonymous. That way, she could drive off into the sunshine without fretting over the welfare of someone she barely knew.

Heading toward another area of Capital City's mammoth campus in order to deliver the Hewlett-Packard 7410s, Cooper parked the van near the delivery entrance of Building F and turned off the engine. She felt like enjoying a cigarette beneath the plump buds of one of the lot's largest dogwood trees, but then remembered that she had smoked her last one that morning.

Cooper got out of the van and leaned against the tree trunk. She propped her leg against the smooth bark, enjoying the sun on her face as she opened a Ziploc bag containing two of her mother's homemade cookies. Suddenly, she felt an inexplicable urge to say a quick prayer before returning to work. She hadn't prayed for someone else for a long, long time. In fact, she couldn't remember praying much at all until Drew had left her, but now she said a nightly prayer that she might be reunited with him and soon.

Maybe I should focus on somebody else for

once, she thought, folding her hands together and closing her eyes.

"Lord," she began hesitantly and then felt words flow more easily from her mouth. "I hope that Brooke's husband is all that she says he is. I hope he rides up in his white limo and sweeps that nice woman away in a tide of happiness so powerful that whatever is troubling her will be completely washed away. Amen."

Not bad, Cooper thought and felt some of the tension she was holding on to ebb away. Chewing on one of her mother's chocolate pinwheel cookies, she got back to work.

2

In this same way, husbands ought to love their wives as their own bodies. He who loves his wife loves himself.

Ephesians 5:28 (NIV)

"I can't believe my only sister works as a copier repairman!" Ashley complained to their mother, Magnolia "Maggie" Lee, as Maggie finished up her daily baking that Sunday afternoon. "Do you know how weird that sounds when I tell people what my sister's job is?"

"Why?" Maggie momentarily paused in rolling out a ball of cookie dough for her Chinese almond cookies and gave her youngest child a perplexed look. "What's wrong with Cooper's job with Make It Work!? Your sister is *very* talented with her hands. She can fix most anything, just like her daddy. Though she's a whole lot prettier."

Ashley tossed a thick lock of glossy, radiant blond hair over her shoulder. "It would be one thing if she just did administrative stuff, but she actually gets *greasy* and wears a uniform with an embroidered *name tag!* What's next? Coveralls? Steel-tipped boots?"

Mrs. Lee shrugged. "Someone has to keep those complicated machines workin' smoothly. Lord knows how much folks seem to depend on them these days. And someone has to be strong enough to tell those stingy business owners when their machines have reached the end of their road and need to be replaced." She teared up. "Oh, now you've got me thinkin' about what I'm gonna do when Grammy is called by the angels!"

Ashley rolled a pair of captivating cerulean eyes. "There's nothing wrong with Grammy, Mama. Don't get all worked up. Besides, I don't think the angels are going to be able to handle her. She's going to be with us forever."

Maggie ignored that last bit and brightened. "You're right, dear. Grammy's plucky as a hen in springtime. Now" — she wiped her hands on the seat of her pants instead of her apron — "I've got to get these cookies ready for the folks at the Alzheimer's home." She glanced at her watch. "I want

30

them to have a special treat with their Sunday afternoon tea."

"Why?" Ashley's perfect lips screwed into a smirk. "They won't remember eating them."

"Ashley Elizabeth!" Mrs. Lee shook her rolling pin at her daughter. "Don't you say ugly things like that in *my* kitchen!"

"Sorry, Mama." Ashley shot Cooper a look to let her sister know that her apology was less than genuine, but Cooper wasn't paying attention. She had a mug of hot coffee in her right hand and was lost in the pages of the Sunday paper.

"Back to Cooper," Ashley persisted. "How is she ever going to meet a new man when her job is so . . . so macho?" She put her manicured hands on her narrow hips. "It's been six months since *he* left, ya know. It's time for her to start living again. She's pretty in that all-natural kind of way and has a body most girls would kill for, and what does she do with it? She just hides out above the garage like a nun. *Someone* will have to drag her out of there or she's going to turn into an old maid."

"Help me bag up these pinwheels while you're frettin' over your sister, Ashley."

Ashley obediently stuffed two cookies each into plastic bags decorated with gold stick-

31

ers reading *Magnolia's Marvels*. As she tied them using a small gold ribbon, she occasionally glanced over at Cooper, who was still engrossed in an article in the *Richmond Times-Dispatch* and had refused to respond to any of her sister's comments. Ashley, who was unaccustomed to being ignored, suddenly claimed the edge of Cooper's chair.

"I've got it!" she exclaimed as Cooper turned a mismatched but fiery gaze upon her sister. "Coop? You should start coming to church with me! There's tons of nice, single men at church. And they're your age too."

Watching her sister warily, Cooper reached out and folded the newspaper so that when her father got home from his weekly shopping trip to Wal-Mart, his paper would appear to have been unread. She got up from the worn and scrubbed farm table in her parents' kitchen, refilled her coffee cup, and helped herself to a cookie.

"Not gonna happen, Ashley," Cooper replied firmly. "Besides, I have plans of my own." She hadn't told anyone that she was thinking about attending Brooke's church the following Sunday. Wanting to reread the flyer on Hope Street alone, Cooper walked out the back door, down a short path, and entered the small greenhouse her father had built for her after the accident.

She inhaled the scents of her private refuge — a wheelbarrow filled with dark, rich soil, two aisles packed with seed trays bearing the first hints of green, a stack of terra-cotta planters, her bottles of pungent fertilizers, and a neat pile of gardening books on edible plants that Cooper had picked up from library and yard sales.

"*This* makes for a mighty nice church," she spoke to the air, delighting in the humidity and the dappled spring sunlight glinting off the glass roof. "There's plenty of proof of God right here." She looked around the cozy space, touching the plants flanking the center aisle. She then brushed some specks of dirt from the leaves of a seedling. "Grow well, my friend. You're going to help fill some hungry bellies come summertime."

Cooper spent the next few minutes flipping through a seed catalogue. She soon became so intent on deciding which tomato seeds to order that she didn't hear Ashley enter her sanctuary.

"I'm only trying to look out for you, Coop," her sister said as she watched Cooper straighten a group of seed trays on the potting table. Ashley held out her hand and wiggled the mammoth diamond of her engagement ring. The light caught the stone and shimmered along the row of smaller diamonds on her wedding band. "I'd like you to find someone as wonderful as my Lincoln." She sighed happily. "I know I'm just a bubbly newlywed talking, but the day I became Mrs. Lincoln Love was the happiest of my life. I know you thought you and Drew were gonna be like Lincoln and me, but it just wasn't meant to be I guess." Her long lashes fluttered as she surveyed her sister. "You're pretty, Cooper. You *could* catch a man and be happy again. I could help you."

Cooper crossed her arms and frowned. She felt no jealousy over her sister's ostentatious jewelry or the mention of her new and extremely wealthy husband, but she didn't like what she saw in Ashley's eyes.

"I don't want to be one of your charity projects." Cooper wiggled her index finger in irritation, knowing that Ashley saw herself as someone who had known no hardships in life and wanted to give something to those who were less fortunate. Cooper viewed these charitable works as Ashley's vain desire to appear in *Richmond* magazine and *Virginia Living* as often as possible, dressed in fabulous designer clothes, her arm draped around the mayor, the governor's wife, or another rich suburban do-gooder.

The trouble was, Ashley always distanced herself from the actual people she was purportedly bent on helping. She would organize builders, electricians, and plumbers to work for days constructing a house in the name of Habitat for Humanity, but she would never visit the site or meet the family. She would collect thousands of winter coats and Christmas presents for the children of area orphanages, but she would never meet any of the kids during the delivery of these gifts. Even her hospital volunteerism was conducted from a distance. Ashley would throw a dinner and raise funds for needed supplies or medical equipment, but she would never be introduced to one of the patients who had benefited from what the money had bought.

Everything Ashley did was self-serving to some degree, and Cooper didn't want to be a part of any of her sister's schemes. Suddenly, Cooper recalled Brooke's kindness and felt guilty over thinking such nasty thoughts about her sister.

"Look," Cooper told Ashley more gently and busied her hands tidying her pillar of catalogues. "I appreciate your wanting to help, I do, but I don't want to go to church to meet men. Isn't that what bars are for?" she quipped.

Ashley frowned. "Well, then go to church to pray. It doesn't look good that you're the only one of us that doesn't attend worship service."

"Doesn't look good to who?" Cooper demanded, getting annoyed again. She knew that Ashley wanted to chair some new committee at the large and powerful church she attended on River Road, a wealthy corridor composed of million-dollar homes and churches the size of college campuses. She was also aware of the fact that Ashley was embarrassed by her family.

Their father, Earl Lee, was in charge of maintenance at one of the area's private schools and their mother got up at 5:00 a.m. to bake cookies, which she sold to several Richmond sandwich shops. Except for Ashley, who resided with her husband in a mansion just off River Road, the Lees lived out in the country, a good twenty minutes from Richmond's West End subdivisions and endless strip malls. Cooper's parents were humble people who spent their money modestly but gave generously of their time. Their house was small, outdated, and yet incredibly cozy. Cooper lived in a minuscule studio apartment Mr. Lee had erected over the garage with the idea of moving his mother out of the main house, but Grammy Lee refused to budge.

Cooper shook her head, wondering for the millionth time how her parents could have spawned such entirely different children. She could only reason that during the one year, one month, one week, and one day that separated their birthdays, the world must have spun in the opposite direction. Looking at her sister as she turned the pages of a gardening magazine with complete disinterest, Cooper tried to keep her irritation in check. "No one outside of this house cares what I do, Ashley. Why don't you tell those snobby ladies at your church that your entire family was mauled by bears during a camping trip? Then you won't have to worry about how we make you look."

For a moment, Ashley turned Cooper's suggestion over in her mind. Suddenly, she scowled. "I can't say that! I've already talked about you all. Plus, it would be an outright lie and *that's* not going to get me elected."

Cooper began filling out the order form in the back of the seed catalogue. "Works for politicians all the time," she joked.

"Fine, Cooper. Rot away in this greenhouse, living with your parents until you're old and gray. Go ahead." Ashley turned to leave. "But you *should* go to church, even if it's to suffer through that awful choir at Mama and Daddy's church."

"Why?" Cooper paused in her writing to drink some coffee.

"Because it's a place where people go to try and better themselves. A place where hurt folks can find some healing and where lonely people can find friends." Cooper was surprised to see genuine concern on Ashley's face. "After all, without me living here anymore, you must not have any close friends. You and Drew spent all your time with each other."

Cooper had never considered her sister to be a close friend, but she nodded anyway. "I told you, I've got plans in the works, okay? Now, just drop the subject. Don't you have a husband to get home to?"

"I certainly do," Ashley replied with a satisfied nod. She then whipped her light-weight suede coat closed, cinched a crocodile belt around her shapely waist, and strutted away, her hair bouncing in a shiny wave of honey as she walked. Cooper studied her own athletic body and long, straight blond hair in the greenhouse glass, and, satisfied with what she saw, finished completing the order form.

Later that evening, she headed out to the

mailbox with a lit cigarette and her order form. She lingered for a moment at the end of the driveway, watching the sun sink into the spindly arms of the trees and listening to the excited chatter of bats as they fluttered above her head. Cooper blew a stream of smoke into the spring air, still tinged with some of winter's lingering coolness, and wondered if she was truly ready to put the pain of her broken heart behind her and begin living her life again.

She picked a piece of tobacco from the tip of her tongue and flicked it onto the ground. Her eyes became fixated on the glowing end of her cigarette. Bending down, she crushed it out in the gravel and spent several moments crouched there, observing the spent stub. "I really wish I could kick this stupid habit."

Searching in her pocket for a tissue in which to wrap the cigarette butt, Cooper instead removed the Hope Street brochure and gazed at the words of welcome printed on the front cover.

"Should I go?" she whispered to the first evening star. "Could you send me a sign?" When the only response she received was a tickle on the cheek by a momentary breeze, she slowly walked back toward the house.

■ ■ ■ ■

The workweek flew by and Cooper nearly forgot about Brooke Hughes and Hope Street. She and her mother spent most of the day on Saturday preparing the vegetable and herb gardens behind the house for planting. Together they weeded, tilled, and mixed compost with the soil, still damp from the previous evening's rain.

Earl Lee enjoyed the mild spring day by being outside as well. He mowed the lawn, replaced rotted posts on the split-rail fence, and tinkered around in the garage, undoubtedly trying to coax his '71 Chevy Malibu back to life.

When the family reconvened for dinner, Earl spoke a blessing over the food. As soon as they all finished saying amen, Grammy Lee launched a tirade over being served soft tacos with refried beans.

"What's this mush?" she demanded of no one in particular. "I still got my teeth, ya know." She plucked her dentures from her mouth and waved them around for everyone to see. "How about a nice piece of meat — one you gotta cut with a knife, not slurp up like pig slop?"

"We had rib eyes earlier this week,

Grammy," Maggie replied calmly. "You know we can't have steaks all the time. They're too expensive."

"At least tomorrow's Sunday," Grammy mumbled, glaring at her plate with her cataract-clouded eyes. "That'll mean ham or bacon." She took a bite of beans and grimaced. "You at least gonna make some cinnamon rolls?" she asked Maggie.

"From scratch," Maggie said, passing her husband a bowl of shredded cheese. Cooper was amazed by how her mother was able to handle Grammy's gruffness without ever getting ruffled.

"So I see you're goin' to church tomorrow, girlie." Grammy pointed her fork at Cooper. "What brought this on? You got a cravin' to listen to those tone-deaf songbirds with us, Granddaughter? I don't think there's a soul in that little church younger than fifty. You'd best go where the young folks are." She cackled and then went on to remind them that she had been married for twenty years, a mother for fifteen years, and the owner of her own farm stand for ten years by the time she turned thirty-five.

"How'd you know I was planning to go to church tomorrow?" Cooper asked in surprise. "I only made up my mind a little while ago while I was working in the garden.

41

I just got a feeling that it was time to try something new."

"How did I know?" Grammy guffawed, spraying the table in front of her with bits of refried beans. "Because, girlie, my room is right next to the washin' machine. You left the iron out to cool down and you haven't ironed anythin' since you graduated from high school." She took a sip of iced tea and choked down the rest of the beans. "I figured you were either goin' to church or on a date." She gave Cooper an assessing glance and made it clear that she didn't approve of what she saw. "I'm goin' with church."

Cooper opened the yellow Hope Street brochure and read it over for the tenth time.

"I wonder if Brooke's here today," Cooper said to her image in the rearview mirror and then retrieved her pack of Camel Lights from her faux-leather purse. She lit a cigarette and hung her arm out the window of her red Silverado, which she had affectionately dubbed Cherry-O.

Her reflection blew a veil of smoke from between her thin lips. "I know," Cooper said to the mirror. "You don't look very sexy doing that, despite what you may think." She scowled at the burning cigarette. "I'm going to give these things up. Time for a fresh start, right?" After staring at the weathered brick building for a minute, she straightened the collar of her freshly ironed blouse and said, "Let's go."

Cooper got out of the truck, put out her cigarette using the bottom of her shoe, and walked to one of the church's side entrances. She paused at the trash can positioned several feet from the double doors.

"Okay, if I can go in there, I can do this." She threw the nearly full pack of Camels and a plastic Bic lighter inside. The two items hit the bottom with a satisfying *thunk.* "I never smoked until I met Drew, so if I'm going to start over" — she dug around in her purse until she found a package of gum — "then I'm going to do it with a little help from Wrigley's."

Hope Street Church was unlike any church Cooper had ever experienced. She was accustomed to the small, white clapboard structures of country churches, the pealing of bells at every hour, and the captivating stained-glass windows to gaze upon should the sermon become a tad too lulling. Hope Street was an impressive brick building whose cornerstone had been placed over one hundred years ago. The original chapel had been expended after World War

I and a roomy wing had been built in the early eighties for the Hope Street Christian Academy.

Daydreaming students on the north side of the building were treated to the view of the church's lush garden, while those on the south side were stuck staring at the vast parking lot. When the bells called people to worship, the sound was like that of a symphony. The powerful melody carried far across the rooftops of the local subdivisions.

"This is some church," Cooper muttered to herself and looked around the deserted hallway. She noticed a bulletin board for Students Against Drunk Driving and a sign-up sheet for prom queen nominations. "I am *so* glad to be out of high school. I don't think I could survive it nowadays." Cooper tapped the bulletin board and listened to the sound echo around her. Where was everyone? She glanced at her watch. It was almost nine. Didn't the service start at nine? Which hallway would take her to the chapel?

Aware of the noisy *clip-clop* of her only pair of heels, which had lain dormant in the far reaches of her closet since the office Christmas party, Cooper made an attempt to walk on the balls of her feet. Tiptoeing, she glanced down every hall she passed, but didn't see another human being until she ran smack into a long torso clad in a blue-and-yellow-checked button-down.

"Sorry!" said a baritone voice somewhere well above her height of five foot six. After collecting herself, Cooper scrutinized the face of the very tall form she had collided with. She saw a pair of friendly brown eyes and a slightly bashful but kind smile. It was a pleasant face all around, though rather high in the forehead and sharp in the chin.

"Are you new to Hope Street?" the man asked softly, coming a step closer.

Cooper nodded. "Yes, and I'm totally lost." She laughed nervously. "This wing is like a rabbit warren, only I think their burrows smell less like Lysol."

The man's grin widened. "Come on, I'll show you where to go. I'm Nathan Dexter, by the way."

Pleased that she had an escort to the service, Cooper replied, "Nice to meet you. I'm Cooper."

"That's an unusual name for a woman," Nathan commented as they shook hands. "Must have been a barrel maker somewhere in your family history," he said as though the idea was fascinating. "I really like names that repeat in one family. Guess I admire the cyclical nature of old names. It's sort of

45

a way of uniting people from different generations, you know?" He cleared his throat, seemingly embarrassed. "That's my backward way of saying I think your name is cool."

"Thanks." No one had ever complimented Cooper on her name before. "It was my great-grandfather's. And you're right, he was named after his aunt — her last name was Cooper — and her father *was* a barrel maker. She didn't make any barrels, but she filled a lot of them with whiskey and dill pickles."

"Two of my favorites." Nathan grinned. "And don't be too impressed with my attempt at intelligence. I'm just a computer geek who likes crossword puzzles, so I've got my nose stuck in a dictionary a lot." He shrugged his shoulders and Cooper half-expected them to touch one of the exit signs. "We're in here, to your left."

Cooper hesitated for a moment, as the doorway appeared to lead into a classroom, not a chapel. She could hear the murmur of several voices, but not the rumble of dozens and dozens of parishioners getting settled for service. What was going on? With Nathan right on her heels and closing fast, she had no other choice but to enter.

All chatting ceased as soon as Cooper

stepped through the threshold. Four people were seated in a circle, their hands folded on top of student desks. Each person had a copy of the Bible opened in front of them, along with a few sheets of paper covered with notes, and a pen. Their postures were relaxed and they all smiled at her in welcome.

"Who's there?" asked a woman seated closest to the door. She had black hair, dark blue eyes, and unusually pale skin. She also seemed to be trying to figure out who had entered the room.

"It's Nathan, Savannah." Nathan called from the doorway. "And this is Cooper." Nathan gestured for Cooper to move nearer to where the woman sat. "Cooper," he said. "This is Savannah. She's the leader of our little group."

The woman held out a calloused hand speckled with colorful stains, like a child who'd used permanent markers and was only able to wash away the surface layer of pigment. Cooper placed her hand into the woman's. "Aha! Another woman who works using her hands!" the group leader announced enthusiastically.

As Cooper glanced around, wondering how to make a polite escape in order to locate the actual worship service, she noticed a white cane beneath Savannah's desk.

"In case you haven't guessed, I'm legally blind," Savannah said as if she knew exactly what Cooper had seen. "But I can still see shapes and, thank the Lord, colors. I figure out people by their outlines and their smell." She gave a series of sniffs like a bloodhound catching a fresh fox scent. "Let's see, you're Dove soap, aloe lotion, a little guava-scented shampoo, and . . ." She inhaled deeply and Cooper inched away even further. "Well, I'll be. I believe you might work on machines. Am I totally off the mark?"

"I repair office machines," Cooper answered in surprise, staring at the woman. "How did you know?" She pretended to check her armpits. "Am I giving off a whiff of toner? Maybe some grease? I use baby powder Secret every morning, I swear."

Savannah laughed.

"Okay, okay," a man who looked like he was in need of a haircut and shave quickly interjected. "Let the lovely lady get situated before we pry her open like a mussel and check out her innards." He held out his hand for Cooper to shake. "I'm Jake. Recovering Catholic, plumber and electrician, and Little League baseball coach. I'm here 'cause one of my buddies started readin'

Scripture durin' our lunch breaks and I felt called to learn some more. Come sit by me and I'll get you some coffee."

Cooper gave him a grateful nod but didn't settle into the empty desk he pulled over. "Actually, I think I'm in the wrong place," she stated and smiled politely.

"We're the Sunrise Bible Study Group," a woman wearing gobs of makeup beneath a helmet of copper hair explained. "I'm Trish Tyler. I'm here because my husband's one of Hope's elders," she said importantly. "And I'm sure you know *my* name because you've bound to have seen my billboards. My assistants tease that I'm trying to get as many as South of the Border!" She leapt up and placed a business card on Cooper's desk. "No cacti or sombreros on mine, though. Anyway, welcome to Hope Street."

Cooper had heard of Trish Tyler, as she was a well-known face in real estate. Her picture was plastered on billboards, moving vans, and on the hundreds of Tyler Realty FOR SALE signs across the city. Trish was seated next to another well-known Richmonder. Bryant Shelton was the meteorologist for Channel 6 news. He was notorious for being incredibly vague in his forecasts, for his string of marriages to women much younger than himself, and for raising funds

49

for poverty-stricken senior citizens.

Bryant offered Cooper his best TV smile, nearly blinding her with the stark whiteness of his porcelain veneers, and said, "I'm new as well. Just joined a few weeks ago." He pointed at Trish. "She gave *me* a business card within the first ten seconds of my arrival too. Personally," he said, raising his voice as he winked playfully at Trish, "I think she puts them in the offering plate so that everyone can see them as it gets passed around."

"That's not a bad idea, Bryant." Trish pretended to count her business cards. "Do you think I have enough?"

Bryant gave Cooper a flirtatious smile. "I like the young and hip feel of this church. It might look old school, but this church is hi-tech." The light in his eyes dimmed slightly. "Ever since my wife left, Sunday mornings were getting kind of lonely, so I came here to meet some new friends. The band is *really* good too. I never knew that church could be so much like a party. We really rock out during the service."

"That sounds cool," Cooper replied, trying to visualize the combination of a church service and an Aerosmith concert.

"We haven't started our morning's lesson yet, so don't worry about missing anything,"

Trish said to ease Cooper's mind. "We're waiting for another member to arrive."

"That would be Quinton," Jake added. "Big-time banker dude and the best cake baker you ever met. He's probably late because he's frostin' the tenth layer of some awesome chocolate fudge cake." He grinned smugly. "That's why *our* study's better than everybody else's. We've got the best food."

Nathan was still blocking Cooper's path to the door. He cast an amused glance at Jake. "Well, that's all of us."

Savannah nodded. "Let's begin so we're not late for worship. I hope Quinton will join us shortly." She turned toward Cooper. "It's a good day for you to jump in, since the theme we're discussing is 'beginnings.' Next week we're going to start a study on Paul's letters called 'Dear Church: Paul's Letter in the Book of Ephesians.' "

Trish held out her workbook. "Cooper, you can just run over to LifeWay Christian store and buy one of these there. Then you'll be all set to join our little group."

Cooper was slightly baffled by what Savannah and Trish had said. She knew that Ephesians was one of the books in the Bible, but she'd never read it before, and though she'd driven by a LifeWay store on Broad Street, she'd never gone inside. "Sorry, but you've totally lost me. I don't even have a Bible." Feeling that was the wrong thing to say, Cooper quickly amended her statement. "I mean, with me. I've got a Bible at home, but I'm pretty sure it's a kid's Bible. It's full of colored illustrations and I think my name's written on the first page in purple crayon."

"My favorite color." Savannah patted the empty desk beside her. "Have a seat, honey. You can share my Bible. Shoot, I can't see it anyway!" She laughed and then waited patiently until Cooper sat down.

Savannah pushed a small Bible with a worn red leather cover toward Cooper's side of her desk and said, "I've had this since I was confirmed, so it's kind of like an old friend. I take it everywhere and it's never led me astray. It's my own version of a Seeing Eye dog."

"Hey, why don't you have one of those dogs anyhow?" Jake wondered. Cooper thought his voice sounded as if he were gargling gravel.

"I told you before. I don't want my blindness to come before *me.*" Savannah held out her multihued hands. "And I don't want people to buy my paintings because I'm blind. I'd like the paintings to speak to something inside of them."

"Anyway," Trish interjected gently, "we're talking about how the book of Mark starts and how it's similar to Genesis." She elaborated for Cooper's benefit. "We were all going to kick off the study by sharing a significant 'beginning' in our own lives. *I was going to share the ups and downs of starting my own business.*"

"I wish you'd tell me the secret," Jake answered as he handed Cooper a mug filled with coffee and a small pitcher of cream. "I'm tired of workin' for The Man."

Smoothing her straight, copper-hued bangs, which looked as though they had been sprayed with polyurethane and wouldn't budge an inch during a Category Five hurricane, Trish turned an intense pair of violet eyes (which were likely the result of contacts) on Jake. "Is that your new beginning? To start your own plumbing company?"

Jake shook his head. "Nah. I'm not ready to make that big a move just yet. Besides, my boss has always played straight with me and I like the other guys in my crew. Actually, my most recent beginning is this." He pushed up the sleeve of his long-sleeve crewneck with a flourish. Cooper noticed an enormous tattoo of a Celtic cross on his bulging bicep. An inch above the top of the cross was a square of flesh-colored material resembling a Band-Aid.

"Oh my." Trish put her hand over her lips as she stared at Jake's tattoo.

Savannah leaned closer to Cooper. "What is he showing us?"

"I'm wearin' a patch," Jake replied proudly. "I'm gonna quit smokin'. This patch is supposed to help me keep from wantin' to drive over to the nearest Wawa and buy a pack." His gaze remained fixed on Savannah's face as he awaited her reply.

"Good for you, Jake!" She clapped her hands together happily. "How many years have you smoked?"

Jake rolled his sleeve back down. "Started sneakin' the ole cancer sticks in junior high. All my friends did. It made us feel like men." He shrugged. "But now I know I don't need 'em to feel like a man and I'm damned tired of how they've got such a powerful hold over me."

"It won't be an easy struggle," Savannah said seriously. "But I have faith in you, Jake. You can do this and we'll encourage you in any way that we can."

Buoyed by her warm response, Jake's face broke into a smile and he seemed to grow an inch taller in his chair. Cooper noticed for the first time that he was a fairly attractive man behind his stubble and slightly unkempt hair.

"Hey, you've got a partner in withdrawal," she whispered to him. "I just threw a full pack of Camel Lights into the garbage can outside the back door."

Jake gave her a high-five and offered her a piece of nicotine gum, but she brandished the package of Wrigley's within her purse and, after exchanging collaborative grins, the pair returned their attention to Bryant.

"My best beginning was the day of my wedding," the meteorologist stated, pushing a wave of blond hair off his forehead. Cooper thought that Bryant looked like he should be on a beach in California instead of in a Bible study group in Richmond.

"I'm not trying to sound crass, but which wedding?" Savannah inquired.

Everyone giggled and Cooper took the opportunity to peek over at Nathan. He was refreshingly quiet. He simply listened to the others and sat in his chair with an aura of calmness that Cooper found appealing. She noticed that he tucked his feet under his chair as far as they would go and wondered if he was self-conscious about his height or his incredibly big shoes.

"The first one," Bryant answered without ire. He was undoubtedly used to answering questions from the local media about his marriages and divorces. Cooper realized that he was probably closest to her in age. Everyone else seemed to be in his or her late thirties.

How many marriages could the guy have and barely look a day over thirty? she wondered to herself.

"The wedding most people don't know about because the marriage was annulled the next day," Bryant continued.

"Sounds like Britney Spears." Trish looked at the others. "Wasn't her first marriage some kind of Vegas hoax?"

No one seemed to know the specifics of Britney's marital past. "I loved my first wife more than I've ever loved any woman," Bryant declared with feeling. "But she was pregnant when we got married and it turned out I wasn't the father. She left me for *him* the day after our wedding."

"That's awful!" Trish cried, while the rest of the members nodded in sympathy.

Savannah turned her face toward the seat where she thought Nathan was sitting. Nathan was actually in the next seat over, so when she said, "What about you, Nathan?" he waved his arms to indicate where he was in the room. Savannah adjusted her nearly blind gaze.

"Um." He tucked his feet a few inches farther under the chair. "This is a bit embarrassing, but my beginning is that I've joined an online dating service."

Trish licked her shellacked lips and leaned forward eagerly in her seat. "Which one?"

Nathan scratched his hair in agitation and mumbled, "RichmondMatchmaker.com." He then shrugged and looked over at Cooper. "I'm a Web designer and developer, so I spend most of my time in front of my computer. Figured I may as well date on the computer too." He clasped his long fingers together and raised his eyebrows. "Your turn, new girl."

Cooper traced the rim of her coffee cup. "I met a woman who's a member here. She invited me to come and it felt like something I wanted to do."

Jake leaned forward. "You lookin' for a church to join?"

The Sunrise members gazed at her expectantly. "I'm not sure what I'm looking for," Cooper answered truthfully.

"Today is a beginning," Savannah said and reached out until her hand brushed Cooper's fingertips. The blind woman then whispered, "No one will judge you here. You are among friends. Whatever you may be trying to rise above, you are already on your way up. You're here because God brought you to us. You are already loved, my dear."

Cooper felt unwelcome tears fill her eyes as Savannah spoke. The kindness and sincerity of her words penetrated the layers of doubt Cooper felt. "The man I always expected to marry broke up with me. I'm trying to get over him — to move on."

"What happened?" Nathan asked sympathetically.

Encouraged by his tone, Cooper continued, pushing the words out rapid-fire. "My boyfriend was a home inspector. He liked to drink beer and toward the end of our relationship, he was drinking a lot of it. He started showing up to work late or sometimes not at all. One day he went to a home inspection totally drunk and that didn't work out so well."

Trish made a disapproving *tsk-tsk* noise with her tongue.

"Exactly," Cooper said to Trish. "Drew threw up all over the client's antique Oriental rug. Drew and the guy called each other some ugly names, punches were thrown, and finally a neighbor called the cops. Both men spent the night in jail and when it was time for their bail to be posted . . . ah, now I'm at the hard part . . ."

"You're doin' great," Jake coaxed. "Go on.

Get it out."

Nodding her gratitude, Cooper rubbed the smooth surface of the desktop. "This gorgeous redhead named Anna Lynne White came to bail out the homeowner — her brother, Trent." Cooper fought to keep her voice even. "She also paid for Drew's bail and announced to both guys that the price for her having sprung them was that they would both have to go with her to church and ask for forgiveness for their unchristian behavior. They had to go right then and there. That was her deal. Trent followed his sister's instructions to the letter but the big surprise was that Drew did too. Apparently, Drew fell in love with Anna Lynne White the second he laid eyes on her. That spelled the end of us, all right."

The room was silent for a moment.

"Thank you for sharing that with us," Savannah said after several moments had passed and some of the other group members echoed their gratitude. "We welcome you to our group with open hearts and open hands. If you're ready for a new beginning, then we'll do our best to praise and support you as you step onto this unfamiliar road. Friends," — Savannah held out her hands — "let us pray for our friend Cooper."

Cooper watched as the other Sunrise

members bowed their heads and closed their eyes.

They're doing that for me, she thought, amazed.

Just as the group finished praying, a plain-faced man in an expensive but rumpled suit and maroon loafers that didn't quite match the rest of his ensemble entered the room. Everything about him spoke of excess, including the gold rings stuffed onto his sausagelike fingers, the loose double chin, and the swell of an overfed belly that strained the rich material of his double-breasted blazer. But his face looked kind, though it was drained of color. The large man gripped a Tupperware cake holder in his free hand as if it offered protection. Cooper could detect smudges of chocolate frosting shadowing the inside of the lid.

"Quinton?" Savannah lifted her nose in the air. "Is that you?"

"Yes," Jake confirmed, his rough voice sounding worried. "What's wrong, big man?"

Staggering toward the closest empty seat, Quinton fell into the chair heavily, as though being shoved down by the force of a great burden. Cooper felt the atmosphere in the classroom transform. Gone was the light-spirited talk and the intimate banter. Every set of anxious eyes was glued to Quinton's troubled face.

"Savannah," he murmured in an anguished tone, "a member of our congregation has been killed." He put his face in his hands and, without looking up, said, "And Wesley Hughes has been arrested . . . for murder." As a collective, the group gasped.

Quinton stared down at his doughy hands, which were trembling, and tried locking them together. His eyes shifted around the room, as though seeking a point upon which to fasten. They alighted on Cooper. "Forgive me." He spoke directly to her. "I'm afraid I'm still in shock."

Jake rose and left the room, returning seconds later with a paper cup filled with water.

"Who's been killed?" Jake asked, holding on to his friend's shoulder.

Quinton took a sip of water and seemed to draw strength from the cool liquid. He put down the cup and sighed. "I don't know how to tell you this, because she was such a sweet and generous woman. Simple and lovely and . . ." he trailed off and dropped his gaze.

Cooper felt a deep sense of dread creep into her belly and rise inside her chest. She could not tear her gaze from Quinton's pained face, even when the anguished man looked up and stared at Cooper's peculiar eyes.

"Oh, my friends." He sighed. "Wesley Hughes is being accused of murder. It's . . . you see, it's Brooke. Brooke's the one who's been killed."

Trish closed her gaping mouth and then opened it again to speak. "Brooke! But, I just saw her at the Women's Fellowship luncheon last week. She was happy, healthy. This is insane. She can't be dead!"

Quinton nodded, reluctant to confirm what he knew. "One of the officers who responded to the 911 call goes to church here at Hope Street. I just overheard him in the teacher's lounge telling Pastor Matthews what he knew. Brooke is gone and Wesley's suspected of . . . ." He pressed his fingers into his eyes to stop his tears from escaping. "Sorry. But they think he's to blame. They think he murdered Brooke."

"Murdered his own wife!" Jake sprang to his feet, his face filled with fury. "Wesley Hughes wouldn't step on a snake even if it bit him. He's been an elder at this church for years. Those idiot cops have got the wrong man!"

"Friends, friends!" Savannah called out urgently, silencing Jake and causing everyone to turn to her. "Reach out to one another. Hold on tight. Now is the time for prayer."

Automatically, the Sunrise Bible Study members grasped one another's hands. Cooper hastily closed her eyes and took the hands of Jake and Savannah. They squeezed hers firmly and she took comfort from the warmth of their skin.

"Our Heavenly Father," Savannah whispered with her eyes shut against the fluorescent classroom lights. "Give us strength as we receive the terrible news of the loss of one of our sisters. Brooke Hughes had a compassionate heart and her soul was filled with grace and generosity. Place hands of comfort upon us as we try to absorb the idea of her being gone, even though she's left us to reside with You in a better place. And please look after one of your children this day. Look after Wesley. A good man has been arrested for a trespass I am *certain* he did not commit. Lend him your strength and let him feel the love of his friends during his time of great need. Amen."

Everyone, including Cooper, whispered a resolute "Amen," and then remained totally still. They did not release one another's hands, as if keeping their circle intact could somehow prevent the force of Quinton's words from penetrating into their hearts and lives. In the silence, no one let go.

3

He who finds a wife finds what is good and receives favor from the LORD.

Proverbs 18:22 (NIV)

Music began to float through the halls of the school wing. It had an uplifting and slightly frenzied beat, as though hurrying its listeners to quickly find seats in the chapel before its melody ended.

Trish raised her head in the direction of the muted strains and dropped her friends' hands. "The band's started playing. I was supposed to leave our study early today so I could greet people at the front door and distribute programs, but I don't think I can go out there right now."

No one moved. They all seemed paralyzed by the weight of Quinton's news.

Cooper felt as though her own limbs had turned to stone. Brooke Hughes was dead? How could it be possible? She recalled the elation on Brooke's face a little over a week ago as the married woman envisioned celebrating her anniversary with her beloved husband. Her state of marital bliss was utterly genuine, of that Cooper was certain. And yet, Brooke had been upset too. She had behaved like a person on the verge of a significant and possibly dangerous act. Still, Cooper was certain that Brooke's agitation was work-related and that her proclamations about her wonderful relationship with her husband were true.

How could anyone harm such a caring and delightful person? Cooper felt the heaviness of grief spread through her body as she fixed her eyes at a spot on the floor and listened to the other members vocalize their feelings.

"I've only met the Hugheses a few times," Nathan spoke into the silence, clearly trying to distract Quinton from sinking further into a state of shock. "But I got the impression they were both really involved with Hope Street. I know that Brooke was devoted to our mission trips, and isn't Wesley one of the church's stewards?"

Savannah nodded. "Yes. He's been on our Leadership Team for years." She offered Nathan a small smile. "You haven't been with us long enough to completely know what a giving and inspirational soul resides within Wesley Hughes. He and Brooke and I were in the Newcomers' Class together many years ago. We've shared many experiences since then, and I have cherished their friendship as one of the great gifts of my life."

Turning to Cooper, Savannah said, "Forgive me, my dear. I haven't introduced you to Quinton. It just didn't seem like the right time and oh, I'm sorry that your first experience with our church has been . . . marred."

"I'm Cooper." She tried to muster a slight smile for Quinton, but failing to do so, returned her gaze to Savannah. "And you have nothing to apologize for," Cooper assured the group leader while thinking that she had never wanted a cigarette so badly in her life. "I just wish there was something I could say or do."

"Yeah, me too." Jake twisted his hands together on his lap. Cooper noticed that his nails had been chewed right down to the beds. The skin on his hands looked raw and the palms were covered with tough, discolored calluses. He picked at one of these and then his eyes flashed with anger. "This is crazy! Wesley wouldn't harm a hair on Brooke's head."

"It's true." Bryant sighed. "Unlike me,

those two knew how to make a marriage work."

Trish shot him a surprised look. Then she smoothed her skirt and tugged on her form-fitting blazer as her face took on a determined expression. "Well, we can't help unless we're more informed. Do you know any details, Quinton? Did you hear exactly how Brooke was . . . taken from us?"

Quinton clutched his thick study Bible as though he could draw strength from simply touching its worn and supple cover. "I overheard Jack Burgess — the policeman I mentioned before — telling Pastor Matthews that Brooke was shot. Wesley's prints were on the gun, though he swears they never owned one. He said he was the only one in the house with her. There were no signs of a struggle or a burglary or anything indicating that a stranger was involved."

"Where was Wesley?" Bryant asked.

"He was upstairs taking a nap and he slept very deeply because he had a cold and had taken a dose of Benadryl. When he woke up, he went downstairs for a cup of coffee and found Brooke." Quinton paused in order to control the tremble in his voice. "Wesley saw the blood around her head and the gun near her hand and he pushed it away — said it was like the feeling you get when you're near a snake or a rat. You just have to get it away from you. That's why he touched it."

Trish shook her head. "I can't see Wesley having a gun within miles of his home." She turned to Cooper. "He owns a store for wild birds. It offers all kinds of food, baths, houses, and ornamental things for the garden," she explained. "He's a really gentle man who loves nature."

"He's always reminded me a bit of Francis of Assisi," Savannah added, her voice laced with sadness. "I remember having a meeting of church leaders at their house last summer. We could barely hear one another over the birdsong."

"And now he's in a cage," Quinton said mournfully.

Cooper glanced around the circle of somber faces and felt at a complete loss. She was a stranger in the midst of a group of people suddenly stricken with pain and couldn't think of anything to say.

"We should go see him," Jake suddenly suggested. "He's gotta be sittin' in that jail right now, feelin' like he hasn't got a friend in this world."

Trish clucked in approval. "Yes! I think we should take action! Obviously, the evidence found at the scene is determining the action of the authorities. Wesley's were the only prints found on an untraceable gun and he was the only one in the house with Brooke when she was killed, but *they* don't know the soul of this man. *They* don't realize that he is simply incapable of such an act of violence."

Nathan rose from his chair. "Instead of attending service, why don't we bring Fellowship Hour to Wesley?"

Quinton gestured to the cake holder on his desk. "I've got this triple chocolate praline layer cake just waiting to be sliced. We can fill up a Thermos of coffee for him too."

"What a wonderful idea." Savannah smiled. "If someone wouldn't mind dropping me off at home afterward, I'd love to join you all."

Jake practically leapt from his chair. "I'll take you! That is, if you don't mind riding in my work van."

Savannah reached out and grasped Jake's hand. "It will make a fine chariot, I'm sure."

Jake's entire being became illuminated under Savannah's touch.

As the group organized themselves for the trip to the jail, Cooper softly made her excuses and headed for the door. Before she was able to cross the threshold, Nathan stopped her by holding out his business card.

"Here's my card," he said. "Call me if you have any questions about the workbook assignments or anything else. We really hope you come back next week. We'll all be starting on the first assignment then, since . . . since we didn't get to it today, so you won't need to play catch-up or anything." He shifted on his big feet, clearly searching for the appropriate words. "Sorry about everything. It must have felt . . . strange for you."

Again, Cooper thought about her encounter with Brooke. She should say something about the experience to Nathan. The other members of the group were out of earshot and she could quickly and quietly confide in him and then let him handle the information. She knew telling someone was the right thing to do, but she couldn't seem to get her tongue or lips to move. All she wanted to do was go home. She wanted time to absorb the stunning news inside her greenhouse, where she could run her fingers through some soil while listening to the resonating strains of Bob Dylan. She wanted home, where her parents were close at hand — her mother humming hymns and cooking while her father drank coffee and did the puzzles in the Sunday paper.

71

"Thanks," she said, accepting Nathan's card. "I hope the group can bring Mr. Hughes some comfort." She smiled briefly, pivoted awkwardly on her wedge-shaped heels, and hastened down the hall.

As she shoved the doors to the outside open, the sound of the congregation lifting their voices in the opening song of worship seemed to explode straight through the walls of the building. Cooper froze and leaned against the aged bricks. It was not a song she knew, for she was only familiar with traditional hymns, but the melody washed through her. The voices singing *Holy, holy, holy* in beautiful unison restored some steadiness to her step. After absorbing some courage from the repetitive lyrics, she walked slowly away from the jubilant music and toward her truck.

Sunday suppers around the Lee table were normally boisterous affairs. Ashley and her husband Lincoln often joined the family for the large midday meal and Maggie always outdid herself preparing a feast reminiscent in its bounty of a Thanksgiving celebration.

That Sunday, however, Ashley called to say that she and Lincoln had been invited to his father's golf club for lunch following their church service and she wouldn't be coming over. Maggie was disappointed by the news, but both Earl and Grammy seemed secretly pleased. Now there would be more helpings of Maggie's honey-glazed ham for the taking, with plenty of leftovers for biscuits the following morning. In addition, no one would have to worry about whether the Lees' table manners would be offensive to Ashley's blue-blooded husband.

After Cooper passed the dishes containing lima beans, onion rolls, and scalloped potatoes smothered in cheese down the table to her father, she stared at the food on her own plate as though she didn't know what to do with it.

"You're awful quiet, Cooper," Maggie commented as she slathered butter on an onion roll. "I saw the flyer you left us on Hope Street. Did you enjoy the service?"

Grammy pointed her ham-laden fork across the table at her granddaughter. "What went on at that newfangled church of yours? Their rock and roll music addle your brain? I heard folks dance in the aisles at those modern churches."

Cooper pushed her pile of limas back and forth on her plate. "I accidentally found myself in a Bible study meeting. This group is starting a discussion on Ephesians."

"Bet you felt like a schoolgirl who hasn't

done her homework," Grammy cackled and pushed such a large spoonful of potatoes into her mouth that Cooper felt sure bits of the starchy vegetable would come out of Grammy's ears.

"You liked them Bible stories when you were little," Earl said in his soft voice. "I remember reading the story of the Flood to you over and over. You always loved the part when the dove came back to the ark with the olive branch."

Cooper cut into a piece of ham with the side of the fork and then tapped on its pink surface with the tines. "I still love those stories, Daddy. But that's all I know. The big stories. The ones everyone knows. The Garden of Eden, the Flood, the Tower of Babel, Moses parting the sea, and Jesus's birth and death. Other than that, I don't know anything. But they asked me to come back. I'm going to buy a workbook and a study Bible and stuff, because I like the people in this group. It felt good to be with them."

Maggie pushed the plate of rolls toward Grammy, who grabbed one greedily and covered the golden top with a thick layer of butter. "Seems like you've got a chance to learn a whole mess of new things. You've always loved reading and learning, Cooper.

74

This sounds like just the thing for you," Maggie said.

"Yeah, but it's not just the Bible study that's preying on my mind," Cooper began. "Something else happened at church." She told her family about Brooke's murder and Wesley's arrest. She then explained about her visit to Capital City two Fridays ago and about meeting Brooke Hughes.

"See? Even though I met Mrs. Hughes, I don't know anything important about her. Nothing worth talking to anyone about," she added once she had finished. "This is all police business now, I figure. Nothing I can do will change the situation."

"Then you shouldn't feel troubled," Grammy answered decisively and pushed her dinner plate forward an inch, signaling that she was ready for someone to clear it away. Settling back in her chair, she noisily shifted her teeth around inside her mouth and sighed with contentment as Cooper wrestled with her conscience.

Casting a sideways glance at her granddaughter, Grammy seemed satisfied with the result of her statement. Settling her teeth back on her gums she asked, "What's for dessert, Maggie?"

After a lemon yogurt pound cake drizzled

75

with a sugary lemon glaze, Grammy commanded Cooper to help her feed the animals. Cooper first assisted in cleaning up after their large meal and then left her parents to dry dishes side by side exactly as they had done for the past thirty-eight years. She grabbed a pair of heavy leather gloves Earl kept hanging next to the fireplace and made her way to her grandmother's room.

Grammy needed no help in feeding the stray tomcat she had taken in two summers ago. Her twenty-two-pound bedfellow was given the name Little Boy when he had first appeared, soaking wet with a blood-encrusted stump of a tail, at the Lees' back door. Grammy miraculously heard the kitten's mewling over the pounding rain. She fetched the ragged animal inside, carefully dried the little orange cat's matted fur, and tended to its wound. It was likely that a car had crushed the yearling's tail.

The next morning, having been fed and doctored, the newly named Little Boy had curled up on Grammy's pillow as though he planned on staying in that exact spot for the rest of his days. Typically, Grammy cared for strays only until homes could be found for them, so she never named the animals, but Little Boy clawed his way straight into the old woman's heart. As the months passed, she snuck table scraps back to her room and fed Little Boy choice tidbits until his stomach was a centimeter shy of sweeping the ground. Whenever the massive tabby saw Grammy coming, his purrs would echo like a waterfall and he'd wave the stump of his tail back and forth like a dog.

Ever since Cooper had been a child, cats, dogs, birds, opossums, raccoons, and rabbits had made their way to the back door of their house. At first, strays arrived sporadically, but once Grammy came to live with her son and his family, more and more animals began to seek refuge with the Lee clan. Grammy wasn't much of a people person, but the animal kingdom must have been aware that she had a soft spot for any creature with fur or feathers.

At the moment, she was caretaker to an injured turtle, a baby squirrel, and a three-legged dog. Those were temporary residents, however. Over the years, the only permanent additions to the Lee family had been Little Boy and Columbus the Hawk.

"Got your gloves?" Grammy asked when Cooper entered her room and handed her lettuce and carrots for the turtle's supper. "You handle Columbus's snack and I'll take care of the other critters." She turned away and stroked Little Boy. "Mama's got some juicy ham for you, my precious. Why, you're practically wastin' away!"

The cat purred and arched his back expectantly. Smiling at the pair, Cooper went out to the backyard, approached a birdcage large enough to house an ostrich, and pulled on her gloves.

"Like to go for a walk, big fellow?" she asked the magnificent red-tailed hawk perched inside. The raptor gazed at her with its piercing yellow eyes and then blinked three times, as though to signal his readiness to be released from captivity. Cooper opened the door to the aviary Earl had custom-built and held out her arm. Columbus shook his head, ruffled his white and tawny feathers, and uttered a brief squawk as he alighted onto her right forearm.

Columbus had been shot through the wing during his days as a working bird at the county airport. Like a dozen other hawks and falcons, Columbus was encouraged to establish a territory around the runways. The birds of prey feasted on the less intelligent feathered inhabitants living near the airfield. In the past, several pigeons and doves had been known to fly right into the engine of a plane, and when pesticides and owl decoys failed, birds of prey were hired in their place. The hawks, beloved by all the airfield pilots and employees, had successfully prevented an accident since 1972. Columbus was one of the program's finest hunters and had performed his duty perfectly until someone decided to use him as target practice.

Columbus's plight was written up in the *Richmond Times-Dispatch,* and within the hour, Grammy was on the phone with the airfield and Earl found himself buying supplies with which to build a home for the feathered hero. Even though Grammy fed him rodents caught in traps Earl set out around the perimeter of their property, the mighty hunter preferred to catch his own fare several times a week. Due to his injury, he couldn't fly for long, but Columbus enjoyed his romps in the open air, and Cooper always took pleasure in seeing him soar above the fields.

She walked him to the split-rail fence and then thrust her arm upward, providing him with a little momentum so that he could begin his circled ascent. As she methodically traced a splinter of wood on the top fence rail, Cooper watched Columbus climb higher and higher, his white breast gleaming against the cobalt sky. She held her breath as the sun illuminated his tail feathers and they glowed russet-red against a backdrop of chalk-dust clouds.

Cooper observed his graceful flight for several minutes and then let her eyes drift to the swaying tips of the pine trees. Looking back toward the earth, she noted the bold and brambly forsythia and a collection of robins rooting around beneath a loose blanket of dried leaves. Spring had arrived and Cooper should have been elated by the new season of growth. Instead, she found that she was weeping.

Swatting the tears away in annoyance, Cooper's attention was distracted by Columbus as he abruptly dove into the center of the field, his talons curved in preparation to strike. When the hawk rose above the tall grass seconds later, a squirming gray shape wriggling in the prison made by his left foot, Columbus seemed to wink at her with pleasure. He then alighted on the fence rail and consumed his meal in under a minute.

"Well, that's one less shrew for the taming," Cooper commented wryly as she held out her arm.

Just as she was returning a reluctant Columbus to his cage, Grammy appeared, wearing her Sunday afternoon tracksuit. She must have changed out of her church clothes while Cooper and Columbus were visiting the field. Grammy had a different color tracksuit for every day of the week. Sunday's was a deep purple and like all the others, was made out of the type of shiny polyester that made *swish-swish* noises with every step.

"You got something weighin' on your mind, girlie. I can just smell it." Grammy stuck a bony finger into Columbus's cage and stroked the feathers on the top of his dignified head. "What's eatin' you?"

Cooper marveled time and time again over her grandmother's intuitiveness. She decided to be honest. "That woman who was killed . . . I saw her a little over a week ago. I mean, she talked to me while I was working on her copier. Something was troubling her, but I don't know if telling anybody what she said to me will matter a lick." Cooper quickly went on to explain how certain the members of the Sunrise Bible Study Group were that Wesley Hughes hadn't killed his wife.

Grammy gave Cooper a sharp look. "Those folks you met today are hurtin' somethin' fierce. If you can do anything to grant that woman justice and to help an innocent man from being branded with a wrong he didn't commit — and you keep in mind that he might damned well have done his wife in, no matter what those Bible folks say — then you gotta share what you know." Grammy bent over and pulled up a drooping sock covered with polka-dotted Easter eggs. She never wore any jewelry or makeup, but she loved socks — the more garish the better.

"I know you've turned into a bit of a hermit since your man took up with another woman, Granddaughter, but there comes a time" — she wiggled her finger at Cooper — "when you need to dust yourself off and get back to the land of the livin'. You gonna spend the rest of your life puttering around this house, your nose stuck in some Time Life fix-it book and your hands buried in dirt when you should be changin' diapers and makin' supper for your husband?"

Cooper squirmed and began sweeping at the dirt with her left foot. Every conversation with Grammy ended with a similar lecture. Before her grandmother could get too warmed up to the subject, Cooper placed a hand on the old woman's twiggy arm. "I'll call one of the Sunrise members tomorrow and tell them all I know. Maybe figuring out what happened to Brooke is like figuring out what's wrong with a broken machine. I can probably be of some help to them."

"That's my granddaughter." Grammy

seemed satisfied, but as she moved to return inside the house, she hesitated long enough to say, "But make sure you call one of the available male members in that group. If there *are* any. Now, *that* would be somethin' to pray for, girlie!"

4

The words of the wise are like goads, their collected sayings like firmly embedded nails — given by one Shepherd.

Be warned, my son, of anything in addition to them. Of making many books there is no end, and much study wearies the body.

Ecclesiastes 12:11–12 (NIV)

Monday was a run-of-the-mill day for the employees of Make It Work! Angela arranged a fresh bouquet of peach roses on the corner of her desk, Ben complained about his sore muscles and rubbed his left bicep on the way out to his van, and Mr. Farmer tried to reply as politely and succinctly as possible to Angela's scores of enthusiastic and unnecessary questions. Cooper wondered why her boss didn't ask Angela why she refused to use her state-of-the-art intercom system instead of sashaying back to his office with every new phone message, mail delivery, or interesting bit of gossip. He and Cooper were content to communicate through friendly waves and brief e-mails, especially since Angela seemed determined to fill all moments of silence with her bubbly chatter.

Cooper had spent the day emptying shredder receptacles around Innsbrook's office park. Make It Work! was one of the few shredding companies in Richmond. Ben, Cooper, and a part-time employee named Stuart had a rotation so that no one was routinely stuck with the monotonous task of collecting the green bags stuffed with minuscule pieces of paper. Mr. Farmer charged his clients reasonable fees for this shredding service and then sold the destroyed paper to a recycling company for another tidy profit. Thus, the account statements, tax forms, and other confidential documents of Richmond's top companies were reborn as rolls of paper towels and toilet paper.

Just once, when the shredding business was first getting underway, their boss purchased the recycled products for use in their own office. After one week, Angela threatened to quit if he continued to force them to use "paper as prickly as a thornbush." Mr. Farmer quickly relented and gave Angela permission to go on a shopping spree at Sam's Club with the company credit card. Even when she returned with an enormous bouquet of pink roses, a van-load of Charmin, and enough microwave popcorn, soda, Slim Jims, and chewing gum to supply the employees with snacks for months, he did nothing but graciously thank Angela for her thoughtfulness.

Cooper laughed as her memory re-created the image of Angela, in a pencil skirt that threatened to burst apart at any moment, using a dolly to wheel in packages of Charmin.

Filling up her coffee Thermos from the supply in the break room, Cooper resumed her accustomed sense of anonymity as she entered office building after office building, inserting a master key into the locked shredder receptacles. She replaced stuffed green bags with new empty ones, checked to make sure that the shredder was functioning properly by destroying a thick packet of papers held together with both staples and paperclips, and then moved on to the next site. No one spoke to her or showed her a fraction of the friendliness Brooke Hughes had.

After an uneventful day, Cooper hopped into Cherry-O and drove home. She made herself a tuna melt and a Caesar salad for dinner. As she ate, she stared at Nathan's business card. His company was called Spider Web Designs & Hosting. The card was printed on heavy gray card stock with a graphic showing an industrious spider spinning the letters *www* in a thin, silky-looking font. It was a simple yet striking card. Cooper thought that Nathan must be quite talented at designing Web sites if his business card made such a favorable impression.

Taking the last bite of her tuna melt, Cooper eyed the thumbprint cookies that Maggie had left on her kitchen counter. The strawberry and apricot jam in the center of each cookie glistened in the amber light of her cheap brass chandelier. She knew the cookies were rich and buttery and would be the perfect accompaniment to a cup of decaffeinated French vanilla tea followed by one or two cigarettes.

"No. I'm done with those," she reprimanded herself. "I can call a guy without needing a smoke."

In fact, Cooper was much more interested in finding out what had happened when the Bible study members visited Wesley Hughes in jail than submitting to her nicotine craving, so she pushed the plate a few inches away and picked up the phone. It had been a long time since she had called a single man at home and her fingers hesitated over the number pad. She couldn't help but experience a sharp pang that Drew's voice wouldn't be at the other end of the line, and Cooper tried not to think about the last time she had spoken to him, but the memory surfaced all the same.

Drew had returned to the two-bedroom apartment they had shared for more than four years — a hastily built yellow tower within walking distance of a grocery store and Home Depot — with a U-Haul van and his new girlfriend's brother.

"Trent's here to help me pack up my things," Drew had explained to Cooper three weeks after his arrest. "I'm going to live on my own for a while."

Sitting at her kitchen table nearly six months after this event, Cooper felt a flush of shame as she recalled how she had cried and begged Drew not to leave her. She remembered how Trent had carried out the last box without meeting her eyes and how Drew had kissed her on the cheek for the last time, whispering that he was sorry and that he hadn't planned on falling in love with Anna Lynne.

Reaching up to touch the smooth skin of her cheek, as though the flutter of Drew's lips still lingered there, Cooper dialed Nathan's cell phone number.

"I'm so glad you called!" Nathan exclaimed after Cooper identified herself. "We all thought you might have been a bit freaked out after yesterday."

"I was wondering how Brooke's husband is doing."

"We weren't able to see Wesley." Nathan sounded dejected. "He was meeting with his lawyer all afternoon but we wrote him a note that said we'd be back and to hang in there. I can't even begin to imagine what that poor guy is going through. It's hard enough that he's lost his wife, but to be accused of killing her too . . . Well! Our little group is not going to sit on our hands and let him go to prison or allow Brooke's real killer to go free."

"No offense," Cooper said tentatively, "but what can you guys do?"

"I believe there's power in numbers. We're going to do a little snooping and a whole lot of praying. Savannah was able to visit him today and he told her where he has a spare house key hidden, along with his blessing to search everything once the police are out of there. We're meeting at Trish's house after church next Sunday to come up with a plan."

"Why wait so long? Shouldn't we . . . you guys get in the house right now?"

"We can't. Cops don't want anyone in there this week. They were pretty firm about that and we don't want to do anything to antagonize them or worsen Wesley's situation. Believe me, we're all frustrated by having to sit on our hands."

"At least you've got a plan," Cooper said soothingly.

Nathan hesitated and then said, "I hope you'll join us. You're coming to Bible study, right?"

Cooper had a strong feeling that she had something to offer in the group's efforts to assist Wesley, so she quickly said, "Yeah, I'm in."

"Good." Nathan sounded pleased. "We could use all the assistance we can get. And speaking of help, did you need some guidance getting started on your workbook?"

"I haven't bought it yet, but it's on the top of my list of things to do." She took a cookie off the plate and inhaled its sweet aroma.

"Listen, I know it must be awkward for us to be recruiting you in the midst of our concern for the Hughes family, and even though I've only met them a few times, they were so warm and generous of spirit." He paused. "It's hard to explain. If only you could have talked to one of them, you'd understand."

Now Cooper knew she couldn't remain silent about her encounter with Brooke for another second. "I actually called to tell you that I met Brooke Hughes two Fridays ago."

"What!" Nathan's gentle voice turned urgent. "How? Why?"

She hesitated again. "Well, I install and repair office equipment and she had a problem with one of her machines."

"Whoa, cool job. Go on."

Relieved that Nathan hadn't passed judgment on her unusual career choice, Cooper told him every detail of her encounter with Brooke.

"There's got to be something incriminating about that document she needed to copy." Nathan sounded excited. "But you didn't look at it? Not at all?" His hopeful tone deflated somewhat.

"No. I make it a point not to look at the content of any documents," Cooper replied firmly.

"Right. Of course." Nathan grew quiet as if he was thinking hard. Cooper could hear his breath on the other end but found his silence rather disconcerting. She noticed that she had unconsciously ripped her napkin into little shreds during the latter part of their conversation. Suddenly, as she gazed at the mess she had made, she remembered the scraps of paper wadded up at the bottom of her toolbox. "Nathan?" She jerked upright. "I don't want to make any promises, but I might have part of that document at work."

"How?"

Cooper described the chaotic state of Cindi's desk and overflowing garbage can. "There was no place to throw out the pieces that were jammed inside the copier, so I put them in my toolbox."

"Can you tape them together?" he asked eagerly.

"It's going to take a couple of days. Some of the pieces are the size of cupcake sprinkles. Plus, I still don't know if anything is readable on there. Most of it's probably full of smeared ink."

"Will you give it a try anyway?" Nathan persisted.

"Yes, of course!" Cooper promised with feeling, wishing that she hadn't been so pessimistic. After all, she might actually be in possession of a clue relating to Brooke's death.

"Listen, since you met Brooke, you'll probably want to attend her funeral," Nathan said. "We're all going to mourn Brooke, but also to show our support for Wesley. Savannah says that he'll be there, under guard, of course." He paused again. "I'm sure their son, Caleb, will be there too. Can you imagine what that poor guy is going through? I mean, he's not a little kid or anything. He's in grad school, but I'm sure he's a wreck with one parent killed and the other in jail." Nathan sighed sympathetically. "If he sees how many people believe in his father's innocence, it might lessen his pain by the smallest bit, ya know?"

"Does he have any other family?" Cooper hated the idea of Brooke's son dealing with such a tragedy on his own.

"According to the church grapevine, he's staying with his grandparents. A lot of folks from Hope Street have been visiting him since his father's arrest."

"That's good. And if nothing else, the church women won't let him go hungry," Cooper replied, stalling for time. She was reluctant to attend Brooke's funeral. After all, she was still only on the periphery of both the church group and the Hughes family and was certain she'd feel extremely uncomfortable. Still, Brooke had gone out of her way to show Cooper kindness, and she owed it to her to show up and pay her respects. "When is the funeral, Nathan?" she asked.

"Saturday at Westhampton Memorial Park. It's just a graveside service at ten. I guess Wesley wasn't allowed to plan a church memorial," he added glumly.

"I'll be there," she responded decisively.

"And the document? Can you bring it with you on Sunday?" Nathan asked with renewed hope. "Maybe we can make some sense out of whatever we *can* read. I'll let Trish know you'll be coming to lunch at her place after the worship service. If we all put our heads together, I'm sure our purpose will be made clear." He took a breath, as though unused to speaking that many sentences in a row. "So you'll join us for both the study and the lunch, that is, if you're free?"

"Hmm. Let me check my calendar," Cooper joked. "I've got dinner with the governor on Tuesday, a spa treatment with Jessica Simpson on Wednesday, and Oprah and I are reviewing her latest book picks on Thursday, but Sunday's wide open. I'd love to join you guys, thank you." And just like that, Cooper officially became a member of the Sunrise Bible Study.

It was with regret that Cooper told Angela she would pass on their weekly takeout order from the Curry House. She never grew tired of chicken curry served over basmati rice with a side of warm *naan*. Instead, she ordered a Quarter Pounder with Cheese and extra pickles, large fries, and a Diet Coke at the McDonald's drive-thru. She then drove to the LifeWay Christian store and parked so that she could eat and complete her bookstore errand within her lunch hour.

After she'd wolfed down her food, Cooper wiped away a smear of ketchup from her chin, tucked a strand of blond hair behind her ear, and entered the store. Inside, her senses were instantly assaulted by shelves of glitzy giftware. Dazzling displays showcased crosses on stands, plaques, candles, angels, throws woven with lines of Scripture, and spinner racks of bookmarks. Cooper cast her eyes around in search of signage. Noting that the books seemed to be in the center section of the store, she navigated through aisles of inspirational reading, self-help books, and journals until she ended up in the children's section, where she flipped through a coloring book on Moses just to appear as though she weren't completely lost.

"Can I help you find anything?" asked a young, pretty salesgirl as Cooper replaced the coloring book.

"Yes, please." She unfolded a piece of paper from her coat pocket and handed it to the girl. "I'm looking for this workbook."

"Okay. Our study guides are in the back of the store. Would you like to follow me?"

"Only if you promise to leave a trail of bread crumbs," Cooper joked. "This place isn't big, but I'm feeling overstimulated. It's like a scene from *Charlie and the Chocolate Factory,* only instead of candy everywhere, there's books and crosses."

The salesgirl laughed. "We've got candy too. Up at the register. I recommend the chocolate peanut-butter meltaways." She led Cooper to the back of the store. "Here's the Ecclesiastes workbook. Do you need the leader's guide or the student guide?"

"Oh, I'm definitely *not* the leader!" Cooper laughed at the idea. "To tell the truth, this is my first Bible study and I'm a little nervous about the whole thing. I haven't cracked open a Bible since the *other* Bush was in office."

The girl smiled. "I just started my first

one in the fall. We're doing a Beth Moore study called Breaking Free and I totally love it. Don't worry, it'll be awesome. Let me know if you need anything else."

Cooper thanked the enthusiastic young woman and surveyed the different workbook titles. She then meandered over to a wall filled with shelf after shelf of assorted Bibles. Though she had an illustrated children's Bible at home as well as a King James Version given to her as a confirmation gift almost twenty years ago, she was hoping to find a Bible that presented Scripture in plainer language.

She flipped through a hardcover adult study Bible, but decided that it was too cumbersome to carry to class. A New Living Translation with a smooth brown leather cover appealed to her, but the print was way too small. Another New International Version seemed like the perfect size, but the pages were so thin Cooper feared she'd tear them each time she searched for a passage. Having no idea what an amplified version was or the difference between a 21st Century King James or an American Standard Bible, Cooper sank back on her heels, a pile of Bibles strewn out around her on the floor.

"You look like you're building yourself a Bible enclosure," a man standing behind her said. "It can be overwhelming to choose one, I know." He squatted down next to her and chuckled. "My wife said it was harder for her to shop for a new Bible than it was to find a husband. Lucky for me, she's stuck with both her Bible *and* me for over twenty-two years."

Cooper looked for a name tag on the man's polo shirt, but didn't see one. He carried a white LifeWay plastic bag weighted down with purchases in one hand and his car keys in the other. She held out her workbook so that he could read the cover. "Any idea what would be the best Bible to go with this book?"

The man flipped the workbook open. "Looks like the author refers to passages in the NIV." He gestured at the wall and grinned. "Well, that at least narrows your search to a few hundred. I'm the manager here and I'm late pickin' up my daughter from dance class, but I know the right Bible will find its way to you. And if you're still here in the morning, I won't be a bit surprised." Smiling, he saluted her playfully and walked away, leaving Cooper alone with six rows of the New International Version before her.

Passing on the illustrated, large print, daily, and study Bibles, or those geared toward a specific gender or age group, Cooper's fingers brushed against the caramel spine of a novel-sized Bible with a soft leather cover. As she opened the pages, she was pleased by the font size and the summaries presented in the front of each book. She liked the chocolate-colored ribbon that would help her mark her place and the manner in which the Bible was fastened with a slide-tab closure in the same dark walnut hue. Everything about the Bible felt right. Just holding on to it seemed to instill Cooper with a sense of strength and hope.

Gathering her two books, Cooper made her way to the register feeling excited about her new adventure. She added three peanut-butter meltaways to her pile and handed the cashier her Visa card.

"I hope there's enough room on there for this stuff," she told the young male cashier ruefully.

"Almost maxed out, huh?" he inquired kindly.

"Yeah. I used to split the payments with my boyfriend, but now I've just got memories of happier times and a whopper of a Visa bill."

"Well, from where I'm standing, that guy's crazy." The cashier grinned and handed Cooper her purchases. "Pretty lady like you.

With those super-cool eyes?" He stopped as Cooper blushed. "Sorry. But if you want someone to compliment you some more, you know where to find me."

Cooper gave him a grateful smile and left the store.

Inside the cab of Cherry-O, she sank back against the charcoal gray seat, popped one of the candies in her mouth, pulled her new Bible out of the plastic bag and began to finger its gilt edges.

"Okay, Lord. Let's see what you have to tell me." Cooper closed her eyes, opened the Bible, and placed her index finger onto a random line of text. Opening her eyes, she read aloud, *The LORD watches over you — the LORD is your shade at your right hand."*

Cooper glanced at her empty passenger seat and immediately, an image of Brooke's face appeared in her mind. She was surprised, because she always expected to see Drew waiting in the recesses of her cerebellum. Cooper looked back at the verses of Psalm 121. "I hear what you're trying to tell me, Lord, and I'm going to go right home and work on that paper from Brooke's office. You've got a job for me to do, and I'm on it."

The moment Cooper got home she retrieved the rag containing the remnants of Brooke's document from her toolbox. After taking a refreshing sip of cold sweet tea, she steeled herself and unfolded the rag. Just as she feared, there were dozens of paper scraps lying inside.

"Good thing I love puzzles," Cooper said to the rag and then cleared a space on her kitchen table. She set out two sheets of black construction paper side by side and dumped the bits of paper onto the sheet on the right. Her plan was to reconstruct the document and use tape on the connecting pieces in order to secure them to the sheet on the left.

Cooper began by sifting through the litter and pulling out the biggest scraps. She examined each one through a magnifying glass and then laid them out on the black paper. Unfortunately, she had been right to assume that many of the pieces would be covered by smeared ink, but she could also see legible, typewritten letters here and there.

"This is going to take a miracle," she said as she stared forlornly at the seemingly impossible task, but she was determined to succeed in re-creating the document. Somehow, she felt that Brooke was looking over her shoulder, willing her to solve the riddle of her death.

"Yoo-hoo!" Ashley's voice interrupted Cooper's work. Her sister swept in the room with a stuffed Nordstrom bag in each hand. "Here you are, hiding up in your tower like Rapunzel!" she exclaimed and deposited the bags on the empty chair across from Cooper.

The action caused several tiny fragments of paper to flutter off the table and onto the floor. "Ashley!" Cooper held out a hand to prevent her sister from moving again. "Watch out."

Ashley pouted. "Well, that's a fine way to greet me, especially when I've got goodies for you."

Cooper eyed the bags warily. "Are you going to try and gussy me up again? I'm busy right now."

"Doing what?" Ashley put her hands on her hips. "You're going to that new church and you've joined a Bible study. Next on your list is to meet some nice man with a big heart and the type of career that would make him an excellent provider." She gave Cooper an appraising look. "But first you really need to get a haircut. Your hair has hung long and straight to your shoulders since you were ten. And how about just a *little* makeup? I know you've got that natural look going on and you can pull it off better than most, but you could *enhance* that pretty skin of yours and those nice, symmetrical lips with a bit of color. I'm not talking anything rash —"

"Speaking of rashes," Cooper interrupted, trying not to think about how Drew had liked her to wear her hair long and straight or how he had always insisted that she was attractive without the aid of makeup. "Why is your face so splotchy?"

Ashley gave a little squeak as she touched her cheek and then rushed to examine her reflection in the toaster oven. "Oh yeah! I had a glycolic peel at the Red Door Spa this afternoon. They told me I might be a little discolored for a few hours, but that my skin would be smooth as a baby's butt afterward. Lord, is it! Wanna feel?" Ashley rushed back over to Cooper's side and held her face out to be touched.

Curious, Cooper reached out and stroked her sister's face with her index finger. "You're right. Your cheek feels like velvet."

"I hope Lincoln notices," Ashley said with a slight frown. "I do all this stuff to make myself pretty for him and half the time he can't even tell the difference."

"I'm sure he's good and aware of it every month when the mailman drops off your credit card bills," Cooper replied caustically.

Ignoring the jibe, Ashley removed the shopping bags and sat down at the table. "Mama told me *all* about the murder." Her sapphire eyes sparkled. "That must have been *some* first day at church for you! Go on now, give me the dirt."

"It's not dirt, Ashley, it's someone's life," Cooper retorted and then softened her tone. "Fine. If you promise to return whatever's inside those bags." She pointed at the silver Nordstrom bags. "I can't afford their clothes no matter how fab they might be."

"But it was all on sale," Ashley persisted.

Cooper silently got up from the table, removed a bill from a basket on her kitchen counter and handed it to Ashley. "I can't afford it, Ashley. Here's my Visa bill to prove it."

Her blue eyes springing open, Ashley glanced from the bill to her sister and back again. "This is a lot of money, Coop! How did this happen?"

"When Drew moved out, I was left with that green contact he liked me to wear and about five grand in debt," Cooper confessed. "Together we'd picked out our coffee-table-sized plasma TV, that silly karaoke machine, a cappuccino maker that required NASA scientists to operate, and a superhip living room set from Ikea. See, Drew really wanted to start his own home inspection business and he was saving money for that and I really wanted to support him, so a lot of the day-to-day expenses *and* all those big ticket things ended up on my Visa card."

"I always thought you guys split all your bills down the middle," Ashley said. "And Drew . . . he was always such a gentleman. Have you asked him for money?"

Cooper shook her head. "Drew *was* a gentleman, Ashley, until the very end. He treated me like a queen, told me I was beautiful every single day, and . . ." She folded the bill and returned it to the basket, fighting tears. "We laughed together, Ashley. We had fun together. I thought we were happy."

"We all did too," Ashley responded. "The whole family was waiting for you guys to announce your engagement any second. I never imagined I'd be marching up the aisle before my big sister."

"I didn't realize until those last few months we were together, when he started drinking three or four beers a night that he wasn't happy anymore. I thought it was work stuff and that he'd sort out what was eating him and we'd move on. Well, he didn't sort it out. He blew up and Anna

105

Lynne was there to help him pick up the pieces." Cooper sighed. "I still love him, Ashley. I've loved him for over five years. It's so hard to just . . . stop. And there's no way I'm asking him for money."

"I'll give it to you," Ashley whispered and took her sister's hand.

Deeply moved by the offer, Cooper squeezed Ashley's hand and tried not to cry. "That is so sweet, thank you, but this is my mess. I'll take care of it. And I know you're going to offer to pay for those Nordstrom clothes too, but I don't want you to, okay?"

Ashley pretended to sulk. "Suits me, but you're missing out. I had a really pretty outfit for you to wear to church this week so you could dazzle all the eligible men."

"I'm not interested in any of those guys, but even if I was, I'd like to think they're not that shallow." Cooper returned her focus to Brooke's document.

"Oh, please!" Ashley dismissed the idea. "Everyone judges a book by its cover for at least the first few minutes. You ever want someone *else* to open up your cover and peer inside, then you better do something, 'cause right now your book title is *Thirty-Three and Heading Down the Road That Leads to Spinsterhood.*"

Cooper scowled. "I'm not thirty-three *yet.*

Now, do you want to hear about my experience at Hope Street or not?"

Ashley nodded and Cooper got up to brew some decaf coffee. As the girls ate several of their mother's raspberry squares, she filled Ashley in on the death of Brooke Hughes.

When Cooper was done, Ashley gestured at the scraps of paper. "So this mess is what you pulled out of the copier?"

Cooper smirked. "Yep. And this *mess* may actually contain some kind of a clue. It's really important for me to piece it back together. I'm not going to do anything else other than my job until this is done." Staring at the minute progress she had made, she sighed. "So far, the only word I've been able to make out is *Hazel.*"

"Hazel? What's that?"

"I'm guessing it's a woman's name, but who she is and how she ties into this whole thing is a mystery to me."

"You're lucky, Coop. You're right in the thick of it all." Ashley folded her manicured hands and rested her lovely chin on top of them. "It's *so* exciting!"

Cooper frowned at her sister. "I don't think Mr. Hughes is feeling all too *excited* about what's happened. If it weren't for him and the fact that his wife was so nice to me, I'd be watching HGTV with a pile of gardening catalogues on my lap."

"Then thank God for small favors," Ashley declared. "Here you are with a real, live murder case that you could help solve. I mean, maybe you were *meant* to meet Brooke and these Bible study folks." She sighed. "See? You're lucky to have such an important role to play!"

Cooper watched her sister pout. "Aw, cheer up, Ashley. Maybe someone will meet their Maker by getting wrapped too tight in seaweed during your spa visit."

Ashley picked up the shopping bags and fluffed her radiant blond locks. "Well, it *could* happen! But for now I'll just have to settle for exchanging these clothes for some of those darling summer sandals I saw on display. Bye now!" She wiggled a few of her fingers in a lazy wave and then marched out the door. Cooper could hear the *clomp-clomp* of Ashley's designer heels as her sister made her way downstairs.

Shaking her head, Cooper got back to work. She was determined not to go to sleep until she had something to show her new friends at Hope Street.

5

The nations will see your righteousness,
and all kings your glory;
you will be called by a new name
that the mouth of the LORD will bestow.
                                    Isaiah 62: 2 (NIV)

The morning of Brooke's funeral arrived
and the weather seemed completely out of
sorts for such a sorrowful event. A bright
sun rose in a cloudless sky and the temperature climbed to a delightful sixty-five degrees by the time dark-clad mourners had
gathered around Brooke's grave.

Cooper spotted the members of the Sunrise Bible Study Group clustered behind a
tall man in a gray suit flanked by officers
from the sheriff's department. Instead of
joining them, she took a seat on a memorial
bench several yards away.

As the minister spoke in a voice filled with
gentle conviction, Cooper studied Wesley

Hughes. He was thin and balding but still very attractive. His drawn face was splotched by tears and he kept his eyes riveted on his wife's casket. When it was time for him to sprinkle dirt into Brooke's grave, he fell to his knees, sobbing, and had to be supported by his two guards. A young man in his early twenties with closely cropped blond hair and broad shoulders embraced Wesley with a desperation that tore at Cooper's heart and she had to assume that he was Caleb, the Hugheses' son.

After the final benediction was spoken, the deputies led Wesley toward Cooper's bench and she realized that their brown cruiser was parked directly in front of her truck. A police officer with a grim face joined the threesome, but kept a respectful distance behind Wesley. At one point, Wesley stumbled. Instantly, Caleb surged forward and caught hold of his father's arm, which he held on to with a desperate possessiveness.

As the group drew closer to the sheriff's department cruiser, one of the deputies reached out for Wesley, but Caleb inserted himself between the guard and his father. His young face was etched with anger and pain, and he balled his hands into fists and clenched them helplessly at his side.

"Why isn't my dad out on bail?" he shouted to a man in a dark blue suit who had also detached himself from the mourners in order to bid Wesley good-bye. When the man did not respond, Caleb's voice grew shriller. "What kind of lawyer are you?"

The solitary police officer turned to the young man. "Son, we're doin' all we can to look out for your father. Don't make things harder on him than they already are."

"What do you know about him?" Caleb seethed. "I don't want advice from anyone unless you can help me get my dad out of jail! He didn't do this!"

"I'm Investigator McNamara," the burly officer replied and handed Caleb a business card. His voice softened as he studied the grief-stricken young man. "You can call me anytime, son, to check up on your dad."

Caleb stared at his father and Cooper almost winced. The young man's vulnerability was so poignant that she longed to comfort him. It was apparent that Wesley Hughes had no solace to offer his son. He looked like an empty shell. Sorrow and hopelessness had slumped his shoulders and his eyes were dull. He mechanically squeezed Caleb's hand and slid into the backseat of the sheriff's cruiser, as mindlessly as a cow being sent to slaughter.

Investigator McNamara clapped a strong arm around Caleb's shoulders and held it there a moment. "You'll be all right, son. I know this day seems as dark as they come, but you'll be all right."

Caleb wriggled away from McNamara's touch. "Will you swear to me that you'll look for the real killer, even though you've got my dad in custody? Swear to me that you won't take the easy route and let an innocent man suffer! That man" — he jabbed his finger toward his father — "loved my mother more than life!"

McNamara never took his eyes off Caleb. "I understand, son. Now, let's not put your father through any more grief."

As Caleb slumped off, McNamara's and Cooper's eyes met. He studied her for a moment and she felt the heat of his penetrating stare. She finally averted her gaze and, without saying good-bye to the Bible study members who were engaged in conversation with the other mourners, walked off to her truck. Once inside, Cooper spent several minutes rubbing the leather-wrapped steering wheel as the image of Caleb's anguished face swam before her eyes. Once again, her longing for a cigarette almost seduced her into driving straight to the nearest convenience store.

"I must help Brooke's son," she muttered, shaking off the temptation. "We've got to get his daddy freed."

Back at home, Cooper settled down at her kitchen table, picked up her magnifying glass and a scrap of Brooke's document, and prayed, "Guide my fingers, Lord." And then she got to work.

Cooper was so engrossed that she forgot she had wanted a cigarette a few hours earlier. She forgot to drink her afternoon coffee or dig around in her parents' kitchen for her daily dose of her mother's cookies. She didn't think to take Columbus out for a meal or water the plants in her greenhouse. She forgot about everything but the grief-stricken visage of Brooke's son.

"You got such a long face on, I can't tell if you're goin' to church or to a hangin'," Grammy remarked the next morning as she and Cooper crossed paths in the backyard. Grammy used a tissue to toss a stunned mouse into Columbus's cage. Once the hawk had swallowed his breakfast, Grammy blew him a kiss, shuffled through the house, and stood impatiently by the front door. Cooper followed behind, knowing that Grammy's balance wasn't what it had once

been and that she might require help nego-
tiating their gravel driveway. Grammy
checked her reflection in a cracked compact
and then gave her granddaughter the once-
over. "What's that you got in your hand?"

"My workbook for Bible class." Cooper
realized that she was unconsciously curling
her book into a tube. "I was just reading
over my notes again."

"Listen. There's no right or wrong answer
to these things, girlie." Grammy hitched up
her navy blue knee-highs and licked her
finger in order to rub a spot of dirt from
her shoe. "This is about bein' *on* a path —
not gettin' to the end of it."

Cooper nodded. "I like that. You know,
you're pretty smart, Grammy."

"Used to be, anyways." Grammy held out
her scrawny arm. "How about walkin' an
old lady to your daddy's car?"

As Cooper guided her grandmother to the
backseat of her father's rusty Oldsmobile,
her parents stepped outside and, hand in
hand, promenaded toward the car as though
they were marching down the aisle for the
first time after being pronounced man and
wife. Cooper smiled. Few days passed when
she didn't yearn for a love like the one her
parents had. It wasn't so long ago that she
felt that she and Drew would become just

like her parents. She had even envisioned what their babies would look like.

Earl and Maggie exchanged morning greetings with their oldest daughter while Grammy settled herself inside the car and rummaged around in her canvas purse. Just as Cooper was about to shut the door, Grammy sprayed Cooper's entire torso with a liberal dose of her powerful perfume.

"That'll get ya some male attention!" she announced triumphantly.

"Ugh!" Cooper managed to splutter in between indignant coughs, swiping frantically at the beads of scented mist plastered on her shirt. "Grammy! What is this stuff?"

Grammy slammed the door closed and rolled down her window inch by tedious inch. "I got it at the Dollar Tree. Came in a real nice pink bottle. Have a fine time at church, Granddaughter. Let's go, Earl!" She directed her son. "I wanna get my usual seat up front."

"I smell like a PEZ factory!" Cooper called after the retreating car and then checked her watch. There wasn't enough time to change her peach blouse, so she sped to Hope Street Church with both of Cherry-O's windows down, goose bumps blooming on her arms. By the time she reached the classroom where the Sunrise

Bible Study met, she could only hope that no one would notice the perfume.

Unfortunately, Jake started sniffing the air the second Cooper entered the room. "You wearin' perfume?" he asked her. "It's nice. Smells like . . . I don't know, cotton candy?"

Savannah inhaled as well, waving her hand in Cooper's direction. "Hello, Cooper. My, it *is* a sweet scent. Reminds me of those candy necklaces. I loved those things, but once I'd eaten the candy beads, my neck would be all kinds of sticky." She smiled at the memory. "Speaking of eating, dig in, my friends. We've got two lessons to cover today, so let's fill our plates and then open our books. I know everyone's mighty eager to talk about our plans to help the Hughes family, but that'll keep until we've fueled ourselves with a generous helping of spirit."

Quinton gave Cooper a gallant bow and gesticulated at a square table laden with aromatic baked goods, sliced fresh fruit, and a coffee urn. "I'm so glad to see you this morning. Come grab a plate. Or two. They're kind of small." He grinned warmly. "Did you have any trouble finding the work-book?"

Cooper helped herself to a cinnamon roll and five slices of crisp Gala apples. "I had to ask for help," she admitted as she poured herself a cup of coffee into one of several mugs showing Moses parting the Red Sea. A brilliant sunrise sent its rays over the mountains of water and ignited Moses's long, white beard and his wooden staff with rosy yellow light.

"We all need help sometimes," Savannah said from her seat. "Speaking of which, would someone be good enough to get me a few pieces of fruit? And I believe my nose is detecting Quinton's blueberry coffee cake, so I'll just have to add that to my order, please."

Jake leapt out of his chair. "I'll get you a plate, Savannah. Let's see, you like strawberries and take milk in your cuppa joe but no sugar, right?"

"You've got a great memory, Jake. Thank you."

Jake beamed as he cut a mammoth square of coffee cake and took every last strawberry from the fruit bowl before placing Savannah's plate on the desk in front of her.

Once everyone had gathered refreshments and returned to their seats, Savannah cleared her throat. "This study focuses on the apostle Paul and the letter he writes to the church in Ephesus. Now, Paul was actually Jewish and his name was really Saul, but since he was writing to a Roman audience — to those living in Asia Minor — he adopted the use of a Roman name."

Pushing a piece of black hair away from her eyes, Savannah's face creased into a self-effacing smile. "When I first began selling my paintings, and that was some years ago, I decided that I needed a more cosmopolitan name than Savannah Knapp. So I chose Alexandra Van Briggle. Can you believe that?" She chuckled and the group members joined in. "I didn't sell a single painting until I began using my real name. Turns out folks were willing to buy art from a simple Southern gal after all." She made a sweeping motion with her arm, encompassing the group members. "Have any of you ever changed your name to suit your audience — to fit in better?"

"I did," Nathan volunteered and gave a slight shrug of embarrassment. "Once, I went to a frat party in college just to impress a girl. She was in one of my classes but always hung out with the jocks, so I got one of them to invite me and then I introduced myself to her as Nate the Great. We talked for a bit and I was ready to ask her out. When I admitted that I didn't play any sports, she started flirting with the guy standing right next to me!" He laughed. "I guess it was a good thing in a way, 'cause if she had asked me what I was *great* at, I wouldn't have had a clue what to say."

Jake spun his coffee cup around and around in the bowl of his rough hands and said, "Bein' a Jake automatically gets you called Jake-the-Snake at some point in your life. Since I have a particular bad feeling toward snakes, I *really* hated that nickname. When I was in the fifth grade, my family moved to another town. I told everybody in my new school that my name was Jack. You should have seen my mama's face at the parent–teacher conference. The teacher was goin' on and on about her son, Jack Lombardi!" He slapped his knee. "Finally, Mama told her that my name was Jake and the jig was up."

Quinton nodded his head in sympathy, the spare flesh on his neck rippling like shallow water in the wind. "Well, I come from a family of big-boned people." He paused and twisted a gold ring on his right pinky. "Even as a kid, I was big. The other kids used to ask me when I was due with my quintuplets and they'd poke me in the belly. It got worse when they started calling me Quinton Five Chins in Junior High. That one really stuck." He sighed. "In high school, I tried to go by the name Quinn instead, but I never graduated from Quinton Five Chins."

"That's terrible," Savannah said softly. "Kids can be very cruel. I think your name is very dignified, Quinton."

"Downright stately," Nathan added.

"I don't have much to chime in here, folks." Bryant threw up his hands in supplication. "I've always liked my name and I try to spread it around as much as possible. It's good for my career to become a household name in Richmond. Gets me more appearances at the car dealerships and stuff. It also helps me raise money for my campaign to help senior citizens find housing." He straightened his tie in a pretense of importance. "And my mama just loves it when she sees my name on the TV."

"I like my name too! And I'm sure you can tell that I do my best to make sure that *everybody* knows that Trish Tyler is the name to remember when it comes to real estate!" Trish threw out her hands as though she expected a smattering of applause. Cooper thought of the hundreds of Trish Tyler real estate signs propped up on the front lawns of homes across Richmond, Trish's face plastered on each one and her name highlighted in bold, red letters. She certainly had succeeded when it came to name recognition.

Cooper realized that all the other members

had said something and were now waiting for her to speak. They turned to her with looks of kind expectation. She grinned with embarrassment and said, "I probably don't have to spell out what 'Cooper' rhymes with." A few of her study members sniggered as they made the connection. "See? That's what some of the mean kids called me, but only in grade school. When I was a senior in high school, they had more to work with besides my name." She pointed at her right eye.

"Well, I think our group is filled with lovely names," Trish declared.

The group took a short break in which several members refilled their plates or their coffee cups. As Cooper sat back down at her student desk with a fresh cup of coffee, she thought about how much she was enjoying herself.

"Last discussion point for today, friends." Savannah closed her Bible and rubbed its cover affectionately. "Paul mentions the phrase 'heavenly realms' several times. What does that mean to you?"

"Here's my idea of heaven." Trish ran an acrylic nail down her lacquered hair. "All the chocolate you want with no guilt." Then, more somberly, she added, "In fact, there'd be no guilt at all. Only forgiveness."

"I think we're going to recognize some of the angels we see in heaven," Bryant stated, his white teeth flashing as he spoke. "I bet some of them have lived around us the whole time — down the street, at the next cubicle at the office, serving us cups of coffee, or bagging our groceries. A complete stranger has helped me in a time of need more than once. It was like they were put there, in my path."

"I like that idea," Nathan said.

Quinton spoke up in a soft voice. "There's no pain in heaven. And nobody's ever, ever lonely. No matter what you look like."

"I reckon there's music there too," Jake said and then cleared his throat. "A kind we've never heard before, but it's so beautiful that it fills you up inside."

Savannah picked up her white cane and waved it in front of her. "I love how Paul says that he is going to pray for us. In chapter one, verse eighteen, he says that he'll pray 'that the eyes of your heart may be enlightened.' " She tossed the cane to the floor, put her hands over her heart, and smiled. "To me, that's heaven. When you see others with the eyes of your heart."

"Amen to that!" Nathan stated with feeling and took Savannah's arm.

The blind woman put her belongings in a

leather tote and shouldered the bag. "Trish, can you pass out directions to your house and then let's all head to worship. They're playing our song."

As the music filled the school wing, the Sunrise members sat down together in the auditorium. Cooper was amazed by the number of people in the congregation. Surrounded by at least three hundred men, women, and teens, she was grateful to be sitting with her new friends.

"What's this?" she asked Quinton as she pointed at the large screens poised above the stage. "A PowerPoint presentation?"

"No." He laughed. "They post the song lyrics and Scripture passages up there. It helps folks follow along and keeps our eyes from being stuck in a hymnal. This way, our words flow outward and upward, not down into our books."

The service began when the band onstage ceased their instrumental music and began playing a loud and uplifting contemporary worship song. The lyrics were projected onto the white screens and people lifted their hands into the air or clapped in time to the music. Half of the congregation swayed their hips or shoulders as they sang their hearts out. Cooper had never heard the song before and was too surprised by the rock-concert feel in the chapel to do more than stare.

"Is it always like this?" Cooper interrupted Quinton, who was singing sweetly — sounding more like a young boy than a man in his thirties. Nathan sat right behind Cooper and she couldn't help but grin over his singing, which was enthusiastic but entirely off-key.

"Hallelujah!" Quinton shouted over the voices. "Isn't it great?"

Cooper thought about his question for a moment and then realized that the people around her weren't singing mechanically as they did in some churches, but with a genuine joy she found truly moving. Allowing herself to be gathered into the arms of the music, Cooper did her best to follow along. Before she knew it, she was clapping in time to the beat.

After three or four songs, the spotlights illuminating the band fell dark and Pastor Matthews stepped forward to greet the congregation. He removed his round, silver glasses and then proceeded to clean them on his sweater vest as he made several announcements about church finances and charitable missions. He then welcomed all newcomers and led a prayer for the offering. His sermon, which focused on procrastination, was peppered with several humorous anecdotes, and Cooper felt completely engaged by his words. Though he was likely in his late sixties, he had a youthful exuberance and an openness she found appealing. He made fun of himself, cited several examples from Scripture, and then grew serious as he reminded his flock that they needed to go out into the community and make positive changes without further hesitation.

"Be a light in this world!" he commanded them and then surrendered the stage to the band.

As the final song died away, the congregation filed out to begin their Fellowship Hour in the annex adjacent to the chapel. The Sunrise Bible Study members waved at acquaintances but didn't pause on the way to their cars. They were all in a hurry to begin their discussion on what they could do to solve Brooke's murder.

Inside Cherry-O, Cooper examined the map Trish had drawn. The real estate queen lived in a very posh neighborhood off River Road, not far from Ashley's sprawling home. Cooper was very familiar with the area, as her father worked at a large private school almost across the street from Trish's exclusive development. The school's parking lots were empty and the swings tilted slightly in the breeze, but Cooper glanced at the carefully tended grounds with pride. Her father was responsible for every building, tree, bush, and blade of grass on the school's campus, and she knew that he worked extremely hard to keep the place in top form.

Turning south off River Road, Cooper pulled into a circular driveway right behind Quinton, who drove a cream-colored Cadillac. A three-story brick monster, the house had an enormous entry with two sets of thick white columns stretching from the ground to the second floor. Through a giant second-story window set above the front doors, a chandelier the size of Cooper's kitchen table sparkled through the panes. Meticulously pruned ivy topiaries in heavy cast-iron urns flanked the doors. As she faced the polished front doors of the house, Cooper wondered if Trish's life was as perfect as it seemed from the outside. Just then, Trish opened both doors with a flourish.

"Come in!" she trilled and backed away so that everyone could enter and simultaneously *ooh* and *aah* over her house.

The group stood in the entranceway for a moment, trying to take in the bold colors, the busy patterns on pillows and window treatments, the heavy wood furniture, and the dozens of gilt-framed portraits of Trish and her family. Cooper was surprised to realize that Trish was the mother of two daughters. It seemed that Trish talked about her business all the time but had never mentioned her children in Cooper's presence.

Their hostess led them into a formal dining room with crimson walls, white trim, and a wall of mirrors of all different sizes and shapes set in gold frames. As Cooper sat down, the room's calm was erupted by the sound of frantic yipping. A pair of small, fuzzy dogs burst into the room and began dancing around Trish's legs.

"My babies!" Trish covered her dogs' faces with kisses, which they returned with fervor. "Everyone, these are my darlings, Donald and Ivana."

"They're *little* things," Jake commented. "Never seen dogs like that. They mutts?"

"I should say not!" Trish bristled. "These are miniature cockapoos."

Jake laughed. "Cock-a-whats?"

"A cockapoo is a cross between a poodle and a cocker spaniel," Trish explained rather haughtily. "They're the perfect pets because they're sweet and cute and, most importantly, they don't shed."

It was quite obvious that Trish liked things to be orderly and pretty. Cooper could see through the open door opposite from her into the immaculate kitchen, which had blue-black polished granite countertops, a crystal vase filled with irises, and a selection of gleaming copper pots hanging from a ceiling rack. As Cooper examined the dining room table laden with plates of hors d'oeuvres, a bowl of spinach salad, tea sandwiches, a tomato and mozzarella quiche, and vegetable crudités, she wondered if food was ever prepared in such a pristine kitchen. Taking note of a platter of delicate pastries that were spaced precisely half an inch apart, Cooper doubted Trish had cooked their lunch, but she was certain that it had been arranged to resemble a *Southern Living* cover.

"This is quite a spread," Nathan complimented their hostess as Bryant described the dishes to Savannah.

"Oh, it was nothing. I just called a caterer," Trish answered. "*I* don't have time to mess around in the kitchen." She gestured at the heaping plates. "Shall we get started?"

Cooper looked down at the five pieces of gold-plated silverware surrounding her white china plate. There were two forks, two spoons (a teaspoon and a long, thin spoon for iced tea), and a knife.

"This is more silverware than I use in a week," she joked. Trish smiled, somehow pleased by the remark, and picked up her salad fork.

"Let's talk about the matter that's weighed on our hearts all week," Savannah began once Trish had carefully placed a selection of food upon her plate. "As most of you know, one of the elders took me to visit Wesley this week. The time he is allowed to see visitors is very short, but he told me where his spare house key is hidden and asked that I arrange for someone to care for his birds and get the mail. He has also given our group permission to go through the house." She sighed and absently pushed at a wedge of quiche on her plate. "He told me that he had no secrets from his wife, the police, or any of us and he accepted our offer to do what we can to find out what happened to Brooke."

"How's the poor guy holding up?" Bryant asked, his handsome brow creased in concern.

"I won't bend the truth," Savannah answered. "He sounded utterly defeated. He told me that without Brooke, he doesn't care what becomes of his life, but he's trying to hold it together for Caleb's sake."

Trish dabbed at her lips with her napkin. "Oh dear."

"Were you able to ask him any . . . personal questions?" Quinton wondered.

Savannah folded her hands together as if considering how to reply. "Yes. According to Wesley, their marriage was strong. He and Brooke had their ups and downs like any other couple, but they loved each other and were very committed to their vows."

"There goes the jealousy motive," Jake said as he inspected the contents of the pastry tray. He stuck his fork into the center of a pecan pie the size of a yo-yo and unceremoniously dropped it on his plate.

"There are tongs for that," Trish admonished gently.

Jake scowled. "Sorry, Miss Manners, but I'm not used to dining fancy-like for Sunday lunch. I usually fill up at church and then open a can of stew for dinner."

"One of Brooke's closest friends works at the Tuckahoe library," Savannah continued quickly, before Trish could give Jake a friendly lecture on the nuances of fine dining. "I take the bus there a lot to check out audiobooks. I could speak to this friend — find out if there was anything out of the ordinary going on in Brooke's life."

Nathan caught Cooper's eye. "I believe something *was* bothering her," he stated. "At work. But Cooper can tell you more than I can."

Taking a breath, Cooper told her tale about meeting Brooke yet again. When she was finished, she could practically hear the gears turning as the Bible study members tried to discern the significance of Cooper's story.

"And the pieces of the document were from inside her copier, right?" Nathan prodded. "Were you able to tape it back together?"

"I'm about half done." Cooper wound her napkin around her index finger. "I've been working on it every night and now my daddy's helping me too. A lot of it is unreadable and all I could figure out so far were some numbers, the name *Hazel* followed by the letter *W,* and what might be a date on the upper left corner."

"You think Hazel is a name and not a color?" Savannah wondered.

Cooper shrugged. "It's capitalized."

"Wasn't one of the rabbits from *Watership Down* named Hazel?" Quinton asked and everyone looked at him with astonishment. "It's all I can think of. I read kids' books a lot," he added sheepishly. "I've got four

131

nephews."

"Julia Roberts named one of her twins Hazel," Trish suggested. "That's the only Hazel *I* know of. I've never ever sold a house to a Hazel and I would have remembered if I had."

"Well, I'm a media guy, so I can tell you Shirley Booth played a maid named Hazel on a TV show in the early sixties," Bryant said and then quickly shook his head. "But these thoughts aren't really helpful. Hazel must have been someone Brooke knew."

"She could have been a client," Quinton offered as he loaded his plate with a second helping of lunch. "Brooke was the head of Fraud over at Capital City. Maybe Hazel's account was being investigated."

"Would someone commit murder to keep their fraud from being discovered?" Trish asked Quinton, who consumed a crustless egg-salad sandwich in two bites before answering.

"Depends. You can go to jail for a long time for credit card fraud. Banks don't think too highly of people who try to get away with it and they've gotten better and better at recognizing the difference between fraudulent charges and real ones." He swallowed some sweet tea and reached for a ham-and-cheese sandwich. Cooper noted that though he ate voraciously, Quinton was very tidy. There wasn't a crumb on his silk tie or a single spot on his starched dress shirt. "Plus, they've got people on the lookout for fraud all the time. In most cases, a credit card has been stolen and the thieves will use it for a couple of quick purchases and then ditch it, but sometimes thousands and thousands of dollars are at stake."

"Computer hackers can gain access to credit card information too," Nathan informed them. "If you've ever ordered anything online, your numbers can be discovered and used fraudulently. The possibilities for financial theft are out there in cyberspace, that's for sure."

Trish swallowed hard. "I'd better stop buying stuff from Overstock.com. My credit card number has been sent to them so many times that I think everyone in their company must have it memorized by now."

"So Hazel might have been involved in credit card fraud." Bryant got back on track. "How are we going to find out who she is?"

The group fell silent. It was as if the problem was too large for them to wrap their minds around. It was one thing to hunt for Brooke's killer, but having a single name as the only clue was a different matter entirely.

"So what are we gonna do?" Jake asked. "I feel like we're doin' a whole lot of talkin', but not plannin' on much action. We can't just go on with our lives like someone else will take care of makin' sure right is done."

"I think we should all go to the Hughes house over the next couple of days. And no one's standing idly by, Jake, but we need to address this problem with more logic than passion." Savannah's voice was determined.

Cooper had a suggestion as well. "Maybe we should go in pairs. One of us might spot something that someone else might not notice. We all look at different things inside a person's house," she continued. "Trish might notice the curtains while I might fix my sights on their answering machine or security system. You know?"

"That's a terrific idea," Savannah stated. "And I'm not any good as a pair of eyes, so I'll concentrate on Brooke's librarian friend."

"I can swing by Wesley's store — see if I can pick up any gossip from the women working there." Bryant smirked. "After all, the ladies *do* like to talk to me."

Nathan frowned and then glanced at Cooper. "I'm pretty decent at puzzles. Do you want some help on the document? I could come to your —"

"That's okay!" Cooper quickly exclaimed. "I don't think more than two people can work on it at once and I'll have it done in the next two or three days. It's not at all like a regular jigsaw puzzle." She smiled weakly at Nathan, regretting that she had interrupted him, but she wasn't ready to introduce him to her parents or to let Grammy get her hooks into him. If Cooper dared to invite him over, Grammy might have Earl build a man-sized pen and only agree to release Nathan if he swore to marry Cooper by sunset.

Nathan shrugged and smiled. "It's all you, then."

"Okay, friends." Trish went into the kitchen and returned with a calendar. "Let's pair off and pick a day to look through the house. I've got a mammogram tomorrow, but I'll reschedule it for another time, so I'll put myself down for Monday."

"A mammogram?" Savannah asked gently. "Is everything all right, Trish?"

Trish pushed the calendar to the center of the table. "Oh yes. There's a history of breast cancer in my family so they want me to get checked out early." She shrugged. "But I'm not worried about it and I know how to examine myself."

The men shifted uncomfortably except for

Jake, who pointed his pie-encrusted fork at Trish. "Just make sure to reschedule, lady. We don't want anything happenin' to you."

Looking flustered by Jake's friendly scolding, Trish handed Quinton the pen and asked him which day he was free.

The group divvied up the days of the week, and Cooper noted that she and Nathan were paired up for Wednesday night. Of course she was free every evening of the week, but was relieved that they were heading to the Hughes place without delay.

"Partners?" Nathan grinned at her and then held out his hand for a high-five. She returned the gesture and nearly spilled her glass of tea.

Jake's hand shot across the table and steadied her tumbler. "We gotta cut you off, girl." He then looked around at the rest of his tablefellows. "So are we gonna have another lunch powwow after we all check out the Hughes place? 'Cause no offense, but I don't have digs like this and I don't wanna even try to cook for y'all. Can we meet at a pizza place or somethin'?"

"How about Cheesecake Factory?" Trish suggested. "I love their salads."

Savannah shook her head. "It's too loud in there."

"And too pricey for some of us," Jake added.

"How about Panera Bread on Broad Street?" Quinton recommended. "It's close to church and the food is good."

Everyone agreed, thanked Trish for her hospitality, and headed outside. As she walked to her truck, Cooper noticed that there wasn't a flower in sight. The whole front yard was composed of stunted creeping junipers and tamed red-tip bushes. Despite the fact that the lawn was almost an electric green due to regular doses of powerful chemicals and that there wasn't a stray twig in sight, the landscaping was utterly devoid of personality.

"I bet it takes a whole staff to take care of this place," Nathan commented in a low voice as he walked behind Cooper. "Must be nice, huh?"

"I don't know. This landscaping looks the same as all the office buildings I visit. A bit bland. I prefer a yard to be a little less perfect, but with more personality." Cooper thought about her greenhouse and her cluttered studio apartment. "Plus, I like to do things myself."

"Yeah, I get that sense about you," Nathan replied and then let his gaze linger on her face until she looked away. "By the way, your eyes are really cool. Both of them," he added and then, after touching the tip of her chin with his fingertips, turned and got into his truck.

Cooper stood in the driveway as though she had forgotten how to move her body. It had been months since someone had touched her with such tenderness and she felt both elated and confused. Although she liked Nathan Dexter as a friend, the brush of his fingers against her skin reminded Cooper of her last romantic moment with Drew and that memory provoked a renewed feeling of loss.

She and Drew had driven to an apple orchard in the western part of the state, hoping to collect apples for pies, strudels, and apple cakes. After filling several brown bags with luscious, ripe fruit, Cooper and Drew had spread out a blanket and shared a picnic lunch right in the orchard.

"Can I tempt you with my apple?" Cooper had teased, playing Eve.

"You can tempt me anytime, baby." Drew had grabbed the apple, taken a vicious bite, and laughed as a trickle of juice ran down his chin.

Cooper had leaned over to kiss his sticky face as the sun seared the leaves above them into golden russet and pumpkin orange. She remembered feeling so secure, so loved, so utterly content.

Standing in Trish's driveway, she prayed that she might someday feel that way again.

6

Who of you is left who saw this house in its former glory? How does it look to you now? Does it not seem to you like nothing?

Haggai 2:3 (NIV)

By Wednesday evening, working at a feverish pace in all of their spare time, Cooper and her dad had finished piecing the document from Brooke's copier together. It was a mess of tape, jagged tears, and ink smears, but here and there a word or group of words had emerged. There was an unreadable signature on the bottom made with a blue pen and some kind of company insignia on the very top of what Cooper suspected was once a formal letter. The insignia, which was covered by a thick stripe of black toner, simply appeared as a darker blob beneath the layer of ink that cruised the length of the paper like a newly paved highway.

As Cooper sat in Cherry-O waiting for Nathan to join her outside the Hughes home, she studied the document as she had countless times. The letter hadn't provided any kind of revelation to Cooper, but she hoped someone else in the Sunrise group would be able to shed some light on the few readable words. Tucking the reconstructed paper into her purse, she closed her eyes and prayed that she and Nathan would find a tangible clue inside the Victorian-style home. Painted butter yellow with gray shutters and a dark purple door, the large home had wraparound porches, wicker rockers with plump floral cushions, and a rolling lawn graced by ancient magnolias, live oaks, and dogwoods. Checking her watch, Cooper decided that she had time to wander to the backyard.

After opening the gate of a waist-high picket fence, Cooper stepped into an English cottage garden ornamented by benches, fountains, birdbaths, and a dozen different birdfeeders. Bluebells, wild pink geraniums, chickweeds, and perky white forget-me-nots were amassed among lavender and fuchsia azalea blooms and a stunning crimson barberry bush. Above her head, a vibrant redbud tree provided shade for the wide, serrated leaves of several hydrangeas. Cardinals, blue jays, finches, and sparrows darted about the yard, making the most of the remaining daylight to feed and splash about in the shallow baths.

"This is really nice!" Nathan's voice suddenly cut into the silence.

Cooper swiveled around as dozens of startled birds flew off to seek safety in higher perches.

"Sorry," Nathan lowered his voice to a whisper. "Man, what a tranquil place. I'd love to live in a home like this." He plucked a brass house key from its hiding place beneath a ceramic squirrel statue on the front porch and twirled it nervously around in his right hand. "You know, I feel really weird about rifling through their house. I barely knew them and what, now I'm going to be sifting through their drawers? It feels wrong, even though I know it's to help and all."

"Tell me about it," Cooper agreed. "I only met Brooke *once,* but she was very kind to me. If it wasn't for that, I wouldn't be caught de—" She stopped herself and turned away from the garden. As she gazed up at the back of the house, she noticed that shadows from the trees had begun to fall in jagged lines across the yellow boards.

"Come on." Nathan gestured toward the

142

garden gate. "We just need to keep in mind that we're entering their home in order to bring about peace. Peace for Wesley and, well, hopefully for Brooke too. If we keep reminding ourselves about that, our job should be easier."

As Cooper followed Nathan to the cobblestone front path, she observed that he walked with his torso slightly tilted over his large feet. Even though he lunged forward, his stride was still brisk and Cooper had to increase her own pace in order to keep up with him. Without pause, he marched up to the door, fit the key into the brass lock and swung the massive piece of oak inward.

Once inside, he said, "I think we should see if Brooke had a home office. Maybe she hid something in the house that would give us an idea of what made her so anxious at work."

Together, they entered a spacious hall with wide-planked pine floors covered by a wool runner in deep blues and golds. To the left, the opening to the large, bright kitchen had been roped off with electric yellow crime-scene tape, but it looked as though the authorities had already pored over every inch of the room. Black smudges where fingerprints had been lifted spotted the pale lavender walls, beige granite counters, and cherry cabinets. Even the stainless steel appliances were smudged with powder.

Cooper stared at a red-black stain on the pine floor and shivered. Trying to block the image of Brooke's body splayed upon the polished wood, she lifted her eyes to the lovely hand-painted border of African violets that ran along the perimeter of the walls. The delicate flowers seemed in defiant juxtaposition to the ink smears and disheveled drawers, some of which were stuck open — spatulas, knives, cheese graters, and tongs poking out at odd angles. Cooper stared at the utensils and the overturned trash can and then turned away from the room where Brooke Hughes had been shot to death.

"What a mess," Nathan remarked. "Looks like the cops have left no stone, fork, or spoon unturned." He shook his head sadly. "I guess we'd better not go in there."

Grateful to avert her gaze from the once-cheerful kitchen, Cooper trailed behind Nathan as they walked past a sophisticated living room done in salmon and forest greens, opened the door to a downstairs bath, a book-lined reading room, and a sun room filled with comfortable chairs and mammoth potted ferns. The room faced the back garden and looked like a heavenly place to sit and while away an afternoon with a good book and a cup of coffee. There was a formal dining room with filmy draperies floating from ceiling to floor in romantic folds of ivory silk. Cooper ran her finger over the upholstered chairs and thought about how the window treatments resembled the train of a wedding dress.

"This is really hard," she whispered, gazing out a bay window into the side yard. "I feel like I'm spying on them and we haven't even gone through any of their things yet."

As they moved upstairs, Cooper tried to shake off the feeling that she was moving through a place that had been permanently marked by tragedy.

Focus, she told herself firmly. *People are a lot like machines. There are always clues that something isn't running right. I just need to keep my eyes open and look for the little details — the thing that's out of place.*

Once Cooper and Nathan reached the top of the stairs, the hall split into a T. Cooper turned to the left and entered a small bedroom with a set of twin beds. She then poked her head into a laundry room, guest bath, and a room that clearly belonged to Caleb, the Hugheses' son. Cooper was taking in the bookshelves filled with trophies, CDs, and books when Nathan called out,

"The office is down here!"

The Hugheses had a large master bedroom suite, complete with his and hers walk-in closets, a sitting room with a fireplace, and a bathroom featuring a deep claw-foot tub. A door next to a massive Victorian chest of drawers led into a small office. The only furniture within was a desk, a side table, a straight-back chair, two sets of filing cabinets, and a narrow bookshelf bearing business and legal books, a dictionary, and photographs of the Hughes family.

There was a single window in the office, flanked on one side by a framed print of Van Gogh's *Irises* and on the other by a framed letter and a dry-mounted newspaper article. Cooper read the title of the article and studied the photograph. It was a short piece in the *Richmond Times-Dispatch* announcing the promotion of three Capital City employees. Cooper immediately recognized Brooke Hughes, though her hair was noticeably shorter, as the new head of Fraud. On her right, standing a few inches away from her shoulder was a dark-skinned man with a thick mustache. Cooper assumed he was Jay Kumar, who had been named as Capital City's new project manager.

The third proud employee was a man named Reed Newcombe, who had been promoted to head of IT. Reed had a large, square head, a sparse goatee, and thinning hair. He had a slight build with a light paunch and was captured in time in the photograph shaking the hand of the man standing next to him. Listed as Vance Maynard, executive vice president of Capital City, the man in the center of the photo seemed close to Reed's age, but was more attractive than his employee and had a leaner, more athletic body. He was also noticeably taller than Reed. Vance wore tinted glasses and a practiced smile.

"Good for you, Brooke — breakin' into the boys' club," Cooper complimented the dead woman's image.

"Boys' club?" Nathan raised his eyebrows.

"Believe me, I know about being good at something most folks think only men can do." She gestured at Brooke's photograph. "She was in a white-collar world, but I bet plenty of Capital City folks still doubted whether Brooke could do what they considered to be a man's job. It took me two years of going to the same offices before those folks realized I was as good, if not better, at fixing machines than my male coworkers."

"Remind me never to doubt your skills,"

Nathan quipped. "What's that typed note about?"

Cooper examined the framed letter, which had been written to Brooke by Vance Maynard, the same executive vice president from the newspaper article. She then read it aloud for Nathan's benefit. The letter formally announced Brooke's promotion but went on to compliment Brooke on her devotion, hard work, and adherence to good ethics. It was a very personal and flattering letter.

"Mr. Maynard must be a cool guy to work for," Cooper remarked before turning her attention to Brooke's desk.

The desk was covered with two paper trays, a coffee mug stuffed with pens, and several books. One was open, and a sticky note had been fastened near the top gutter of the left page. The garbage can was full of papers and piles of documents filled the out-box while only one sheet lay within the in-box. Cooper turned to the piece of office equipment perched on a small table beneath the window.

"A Brother MFC-8860 laser flatbed all-in-one." Cooper admired the machine. "Nice."

An orange light was flashing on the machine, indicating that it was out of paper.

Cooper's mind immediately leapt into repair mode. Nothing was sitting in the printer tray and Cooper saw no signs of jams. Based on years of experience, she pulled the machine slightly away from the wall, hoping that the last print job had fallen behind the machine. "Aha!" she exclaimed as a sheet of paper, freed from where it was pinned against the wall, slid onto the floor.

"What's that?" Nathan asked.

Cooper knelt down and grabbed the paper. Bringing it back into the light, she examined the letters and numbers printed on the top. "It's a fax. There's a phone number here, followed by a code that identifies a specific fax machine." She held the paper out for Nathan to examine. "I have a feeling the police never saw this. It's all covered in dust."

Puzzled, Nathan looked at the sheet and read:

FORGET ABOUT HAZEL

"Nathan, this seems an awful lot like a threat." Cooper reclaimed the letter and placed it on the desk, warily, as though it still had the power to harm. "The name Hazel was also mentioned in the document jammed in Brooke's work copier. We should show both papers to the police right away. Maybe they can find out who this Hazel person is."

His brow creased in thought, Nathan began searching through the papers in the garbage. He dug out a sheet of paper from the bottom of the trash can and sat back on his heels, his eyes wide. The paper repeated the same text as the fax Cooper had found. Nathan turned the trash can upside down and shifted through assorted pieces of junk mail and clothing catalogues. Apparently, the weight of the other mail had pressed downward so that the faxes had formed a compressed pile on the bottom of the can. It was easy to imagine Brooke trying to hide the notes from sight, but Cooper and Nathan could see that someone had gone out of their way to get their point across to her.

Nathan laid out sheet after sheet on the surface of Brooke's desk. "They all say the same thing."

Cooper examined the copy in her hand more carefully. Next to what appeared to be a local number identifying the fax machine sending the message, there was a date. The fax had been sent the Friday Cooper had met Brooke Hughes at Capital City. Cooper compared her copy to those Nathan had taken from the trash. They were all dated the same Friday, which, according to Brooke's wall calendar, was April 6.

"There must be twenty copies here," Nathan observed aloud. "But who sent them?"

"Only one way to find out." Cooper reached for the phone and pressed the speaker button. The blare of the dial tone in the silent room caused her heart to skip a beat. As she punched the numbers into the keypad, she couldn't help but wonder if, in a matter of seconds, they'd be listening to the voice of Brooke's killer.

After a single ring, a recorded voice alerted them that it was necessary to add an area code when dialing that number. "Looks like the number's not as local as I thought." Cooper took a deep breath and then redialed.

"JessMark's Shipping of Chesterfield. This is Mark. How can I help you?"

"Ah, hi." Cooper quickly gathered her thoughts. "I received a fax here at work and I don't know who sent it. Do you folks keep records of your outgoing faxes?"

"For a month, yes. But we don't keep cover letters or anything like that. Just a receipt showing the fax was received and the time and date it was sent." A pause. "In case someone says that it didn't go through.

151

That happens a lot," Mark added with a hint of ire.

"I'm sure you get questioned all the time," Cooper sympathized. "See, my boss thinks that I've misplaced this fax she received on Friday, April 6 at 5:43 p.m., but I wasn't even in the office at that time. Is there any chance you can check the records for me and make sure it actually got here? I've never lost one before and to tell you the truth," — she lowered her voice to a conspiratorial whisper — "I think the temp who's been working here in the evenings is reading all the faxes and deciding which ones are important before my boss gets a chance to look at them." Cooper cleared her throat nervously. "Thing is, my butt's on the line over this whole thing and I can't afford to lose this job."

"Well, we can't let that happen," Mark responded kindly. "Let me put you on hold and I'll ask my wife to check our report for the beginning of the month. She's better at all the tech stuff than I am. What's the number where you received the fax?"

Nathan and Cooper exchanged panicked looks. "Um . . ." Cooper lifted the phone from its cradle in order to see if the number had been written underneath while Nathan frantically read over the numbers listed on a bulletin board tacked to the wall next to the door. When he spotted the words *Home Fax,* he elbowed Cooper and she hastily repeated the digits to Mark.

Putting the phone back on speaker mode, Nathan and Cooper continued to search Brooke's office as Etta James kept them company through the phone line.

"Mark's got good taste," Nathan said as he opened desk drawers. "Usually you hear elevator music when you're put on hold. This is refreshing." Flipping through a stack of papers in the out-box, he looked up at Cooper. "What kind of music do you like?"

Cooper opened one of the file cabinets and began to read the printed labels on the file folders. Brooke had created folders for medical and tax records, bank statements, insurance documents, appliance warranties, and the like. Nothing in the file seemed connected to Capital City. "I like the Beatles," she answered, sliding the top drawer shut. She then thought about the songs Drew had always chosen on the jukebox at their favorite bar and added, "I also like Elvis, Simon and Garfunkel, U2, Bruce Springsteen, Billy Joel, Fleetwood Mac, and a bunch of country singers. You?"

"I like real musicians. I don't care what the genre is, but I like people who write and play their own music and aren't just a pretty face backed by computers." He gestured at the fax machine. "Ms. James could sing, yessir. But as far as contemporary stuff goes? My two latest CD purchases were Norah Jones and Josh Groban. If those two don't sound like a pair of angels, then I don't know who does."

"You still there?" Mark's voice cut off Etta's crooning.

"I sure am. Just enjoying your hold music," Cooper answered.

Mark laughed. "That's my wife Jessica's doing. I was all for ordering Muzak and she said we'd lose customers by the fistful. Guess she was right *again.* Anyhow, I've got the reports and am sorry to say that I've only got bad news for you."

"Oh?"

"Not only did the fax go through to your number, but it would have been mighty hard to miss when it arrived."

Cooper frowned. "I'm not following you."

"According to our report, that fax was twenty-five pages long." He hesitated. "I think you might have to talk things out with the temp."

"Yeah, I guess so," Cooper said, nodding. Then, her head snapped up and she asked, "Does anyone else work there besides you

154

and your wife? I mean, do you think you'd remember who sent this fax? Maybe that would help me figure out what it was about."

"It's just the two of us on the weekdays, and we close at six. I haven't sent a fax that long in ages, so it must've been Jess. I'll put her on."

"I feel really bad about lying to the guy," Cooper whispered to Nathan. "He's gone out of his way to be helpful."

"I know, but we've got to find out every detail." Nathan picked up the calendar from Brooke's desk and glanced at it briefly.

"Hello?" A perky voice picked up the receiver. "We've got a rush of folks in here now, so I've got to be quick. I only remember that a man wearing mirrored sunglasses and a baseball hat sent that fax. The only reason I can even call him to mind was that he acted weird. Yep. Odd and rude. He just gave me the papers, ordered me not to look at them in this bossy tone, and then turned his back while they went through. When I handed him the original copies and the receipt, he shoved them all in our shredder and walked out without another word! No 'Thank you' or 'Bye now.' Nothin'!"

"So there wasn't anything unusual about him like . . . his height or weight or" —

Cooper looked down at Nathan's shoes — "big feet or ears or really yellow teeth or something like that?"

"No, 'fraid not. Only thing I noticed was that he had a bunch of curly blond fur stuck to his jacket sleeve, like he'd pet a dog with that hand and the dog hair had gotten all over his coat. I doubt it was human hair, unless someone was *really* stressed and was shedding like crazy. Working here, I could kind of see how that could happen!" She laughed. "I'm sorry I can't be of more help, but if you leave me your number, I'll let you know if anything comes back to me."

Cooper gave Jessica her phone number, thanked her for her time, and asked her to extend her gratitude to Mark as well.

"The shipping store's in Chesterfield, huh?" Nathan said after Cooper hung up. "That's about thirty minutes south of here. Some guy with a dog in Chesterfield." He stood still and thought for a moment and then shrugged helplessly. "I can't come up with anything. Let's finish up in here. It's getting late."

Cooper's stomach grumbled as she checked her watch. It was dinnertime, all right. As Nathan shifted through the other file cabinet, she took a closer look at the text on Brooke's desk that had been marked with the Post-it note. The title of the book was *Offshore Accounts: Tax-Free, Private, and Profitable.* Cooper scanned the marked page, which focused on Swiss bank accounts, but couldn't comprehend what she was reading. She had no business background and the terms seemed utterly foreign to her. She pointed the page out to Nathan, but neither of them could determine how the passage might be relevant to their search, so Nathan began to sift through the file cabinet as Cooper focused her attention on the photographs of the Hughes family.

There were a half dozen altogether, taken at various birthday celebrations, in front of the Christmas tree, at Easter egg hunts, and during graduation ceremonies. In all the photographs, the three family members looked happy and relaxed in one another's company. There was the lovely Brooke, with her kind eyes and warm smile, who stood side by side with her husband, Wesley, who was slim, but not as thin as he had appeared at the funeral. Wesley had an uneven smile and a pair of appealing dimples that Caleb had clearly inherited.

"That's Caleb, their son. Did you see him at the funeral?" Nathan asked.

"Yes. It was gut-wrenching to watch him as his father was taken away by the cops,"

Cooper replied somberly and glanced out the nearby window. "I wonder if he's going to ever want to come back to this house."

"He's with his grandparents in Norfolk, so at least we're not invading his privacy." Nathan gestured at a row of manila file folders. "Most of these documents are related to him. This whole cabinet is filled with his school records, class photos, health information, award certificates, letters written to his parents, and drawings from kindergarten through college. I think everything from this kid's life has been saved."

Cooper traced the young man's radiant face in what must have been the most recent photograph of the Hughes family, taken just a few months ago at a New Year's Eve party. She studied their laughing faces as Caleb pointed at the sparkling pink tiara on his head while Brooke touched the top hat perched rakishly on hers. Wesley held up a fistful of noisemakers, and confetti fell about the threesome like fairy dust.

"That poor kid," she said and felt her eyes watering again.

Nathan joined her at the bookshelf. "Caleb's in a graduate program in DC, but I've seen him once or twice when he came to church with his parents." He stood and lightly placed a hand on her shoulder. "We found a clue today, Cooper. We've got to see the positive side of things if we're going to help Caleb get his father back and discover the truth about Brooke's death. Let's leave it at that for now."

Nodding, she sniffed and took a last look at the picture, more determined than ever to exonerate Brooke's husband and reunite father and son.

"You know," Nathan whispered once they were back downstairs. "I'm feeling pretty down right now. It'd be nice to have some company for dinner. Do you like sushi?"

Cooper hated sushi, but she'd eat raw octopus by the forkful if it meant postponing going home for a little while. It wasn't that she didn't like her home — she had grown used to living by herself — but she also knew that as soon as she turned off the TV, closed the book she was reading, and lay down in the dark, either her memories of Drew or the faces of the Hughes family would haunt her. She would see their smiles, hear their laughter, albeit distantly, as though from a far-off place, and ache over the joy they had clearly given one another. She would fantasize about sharing that kind of joy with Drew, visualizing their reunion in which he regretted leaving her for Anna Lynne White and begged for forgiveness with tears in his gray-blue eyes. And after all that, she'd have to fight off her desire for a cigarette.

Glancing askew at Nathan, Cooper decided that having a meal with a friend from Bible study wouldn't in any way be a betrayal of the feelings she still harbored for Drew.

"Dinner sounds great," she said, "But I'm not eating anything that has the consistency of a jellyfish. Just tell me they've got something that's been *cooked* for a good long time on their menu."

7

What do you think? If a man owns a hundred sheep, and one of them wanders away, will he not leave the ninety-nine on the hills and go to look for the one that wandered off?

Matthew 18:12 (NIV)

On Saturday afternoon, Cooper asked her mother if they could bake some cookies to bring to the Sunrise Bible Study members the next morning.

"If visiting the Hughes home was rough for you, hon, it must have been powerful hard on the folks who knew them," Mama had replied, tying on a frilly apron and reaching for her recipe box. "This is gonna take one of my *special* cookies."

As Maggie rummaged through index cards, shaking her head and occasionally lifting one to the light before dropping it dismissively back into the box, Cooper took

161

Columbus to the field for a snack.

As she watched him soar overhead, she mused over her dinner with Nathan Wednesday night. She pictured his pleasant face, his gentle eyes, and the way in which he cocked his head slightly to the side as he listened. Thinking about how at ease she felt in his presence, Cooper couldn't help but smile. She had tried not to notice the freckles scattered on his cheeks, the way a wave of his hair fell over his forehead, and how his fingers nimbly clasped a piece of sushi and then delicately dipped the seaweed-wrapped morsel into a bath made of soy and wasabi sauces, but she had. And while Nathan wasn't Drew, and she didn't think she felt romantic toward him, it was nice to be out on the town again.

Cooper was so busy reminiscing that she didn't hear Ashley's approach through the tall grass.

"You look like a cat that's just caught the canary," Ashley marveled. Draping her arms languidly over the top rail of the fence, Ashley surveyed her sister. "Something's up with you."

Cooper felt her neck grow warm and knew that spots of red were prickling her skin. Hoping to disguise her telltale embarrassment, she pointed at Columbus. "Looks like he's caught two mice. There's one in each talon."

"Eww," Ashley squeaked, but wasn't about to be put off so easily. "You were thinking about a guy, weren't you? Look at your neck?" She elbowed Cooper playfully. "Praise the Lord! Finally! We're all so sick of you moping over Drew. Now, spill it. He's in your Bible study, right?" Without waiting for an answer, she put her hands on her hips and gave Cooper a smug grin. "I *told* you church was a good place to meet men."

"I just went to dinner with this guy to talk about the Hughes case," Cooper replied, feeling a bit silly for using such an official-sounding term when in truth all they were doing was blindly nosing around. "It wasn't a date," she quickly added, and began to peel apart a piece of grass. "Nathan's involved with some kind of online dating service and I don't think I'm interested in him that way."

Ashley scowled. "You don't think you're interested? Well, *that's* going to have to change. Nathan, huh? I like that name." She paused. "Seriously, Coop. *I* can tell you like him, even if you can't. Are you going to do anything about it, like exert some feminine charm?" She took Cooper's elbow. "I'm really not trying to be mean. I want you to

163

be happy. I think you should go for this Nathan guy." Ashley's eyes flashed a brilliant blue beneath the clear, bright sky. "You're making some changes in your life already. Going to a new church, giving up smoking, becoming a freelance detective — what's a few more?"

Cooper held out her arm for Columbus, and the hawk returned to her, issuing a squawk of triumph over his productive hunt. Stroking the magnificent bird, she shrugged. "I guess I'm about due for a new hairstyle. Nothing crazy," she warned. "With my Visa bill being what it is, I can't spend hundreds of dollars on beauty treatments."

Ashley rubbed her hands together with glee. "I know, but if you'd add some layers and get some highlights, then we'd really be talking."

"No way am I coloring my hair," Cooper objected. "Too much expensive maintenance."

"Fine." Ashley pretended to pout as they walked back to the house. "But at least get those tumbleweeds you call eyebrows waxed. They are so out of control Columbus is going to start hunting for mice in there." She playfully flicked Cooper's left brow.

Cooper gazed at her reflection in the glass

of the back door. "Are they really bad? I tweeze them twice a month."

Ashley stood next to her sister. "But you're not *trained* in the art of plucking, Cooper, and it shows. Look at mine. They're nice, subtle arches. You can actually *see* my upper eyelid. Now, compare yours."

After glancing at the gentle curve of her sister's blond brows, Cooper examined her own. Ashley was right. Hairs grew well below her natural arch and several stuck out too far above the bridge of her nose as though one day planning to form a unibrow. They were a bit unkempt, but Drew had never commented on her eyebrows. He had always said that he could only focus on her beautiful green eyes. Of course, at that time, she'd worn her green contact so that her eyes matched.

Ashley seemed to have read her mind. "Ever since you ditched that contact, which I think was wonderfully brave, you've looked so much more like *you*." She slid an arm around Cooper's waist and squeezed — something she hadn't done for a while. "Let people see all of you, Coop. You're lovely — a natural beauty. You really are. Let them see you."

Cooper nodded, pleasantly surprised by her sister's display of affection. "I stopped wearing that contact because I want people to take me as I come, but I haven't really been putting my best face forward. Okay, then. Where should I go, Ms. Yellowbook?"

"Leave it all to me," Ashley declared, reaching for her fuchsia cell phone.

"You look different," Jake said and then his gaze immediately fell upon the basket in Cooper's hands. "What are those and are they for us?" he demanded, licking his lips.

Cooper smiled at his eagerness, trying not to allow her fingers to touch the blunt layers of her new, shoulder-length bob or rub the sensitive skin above her eyes where hair had been ripped away using hot wax and strips of white cloth. She had barely recognized herself in the mirror when the beautician swiveled her chair around, revealing stylish hair with movement and body. Cooper also saw that her eyes, though rimmed with smarting skin, seemed more willing to welcome their own reflection. Even the beautician's declarations over the different shades of her client's eyes hadn't put a damper on the final result.

"I'm smelling butterscotch," Savannah said from her chair. "Definitely homemade baked goods. Did you make us this treat? Aren't you nice."

"Mama did most of the work," Cooper admitted. "She's a master baker. She makes cookies for a lot of the local sandwich places."

"Not Magnolia's Marvels?" Trish inquired, her interest clearly piqued.

"Actually, yes." Cooper handed the basket to Savannah and placed her travel mug on the surface of an empty desk. "These are her butterscotch cheesecake squares."

"Come on, Savannah. Grab one and pass the basket my way!" Trish ordered. "I am addicted to everything that woman makes. If I didn't have a treadmill *and* a StairMaster in my house, I'd be a thousand pounds because of those cookies!"

At that moment, Nathan, Bryant, and Quinton stepped into the room.

"Hey, you got your hair cut," Bryant observed, giving Cooper elevator eyes. "It looks really good."

Nathan smiled. "Yeah, you look . . . I don't know. Younger, more energized."

"Whoa, *that's* a great haircut," Trish said once her mouth was empty. "If it can turn back time, it's a winner. I like all the layers around your face. Makes you look softer, more feminine."

Shaking his head, Nathan said, "No, that's not what I meant." Still staring at Cooper,

167

he continued, "You look refreshed, um, ready for —"

"Like you're ready to take on the world!" Savannah completed his sentence for him. Nathan looked at the blind woman gratefully.

"Did you bring that document from Brooke's copier along with these *unbelievable* cookies?" Quinton brandished a cookie in each hand. "I know we're supposed to talk about this stuff at lunch, but I can't stop thinking about a way to help the Hugheses."

"Me either, Quinton." Cooper passed him the taped paper. "I hope you can make some sense out of it."

As Quinton scrutinized the document, the rest of the group took their seats and opened their workbooks. When everyone was clearly prepared to start, Savannah asked the Sunrise members to join her in a prayer for those feeling sick, lonely, or lost.

"These cookies are divine," Savannah said to Cooper afterward. "I've got to get the recipe. We're starting to eat the same old boxed cookies and crackers at my couples group. These would certainly perk us all up." She dusted some crumbs from her fingertips. "Does anyone have anything to share before we dive in?"

"When I was doing the exercises on Ephesians this week, I thought of a strange coincidence between our study and our investigation." Bryant held out his workbook. "Paul was in prison when he wrote this letter to the church, and yet it's still full of praise, worship, and love."

"And here we've got Wesley in prison, but he doesn't seem to be feeling anything but sorrow and hopelessness. He doesn't seem able to display Paul's optimism, isn't that right?" Trish directed her question at Savannah.

Before Savannah could answer, Jake slammed his workbook on his desk. "I wish a little bit of that wrath Paul talks about in chapter two, verse three would fall on the head of the lowlife who *should* be in prison for this crime."

"I don't know about that," Savannah countered with extreme gentleness. "I think we need a little more of God's grace and mercy, as mentioned in Paul's next two verses, in this crazy, mixed-up world."

Jake hung his head, obviously concerned that he had disappointed their leader. Cooper quickly passed him a butterscotch cheesecake square to perk him up again.

The group spent the remaining thirty minutes discussing their homework answers and then headed to worship service.

During the offering, Quinton pulled out a check from the inside pocket of his shiny suit coat and deposited it in the brass plate Bryant passed him. Cooper noticed Quinton drop a piece of paper while removing his check from his pocket, but she couldn't mention it to him, as the entire congregation was engaged in singing a boisterous praise song. During the brief pause between the offering and the commencement of the sermon, Quinton was preoccupied with blowing his nose, so Cooper decided to wait until the service was over to hand him the paper.

However, immediately following the last note of the final song, Quinton fell into conversation with a man seated behind him. As she had no particular desire to be introduced to the man, his wife, or their six rambunctious children, Cooper reached under the seat, grabbed the paper, and headed out to the lobby.

She only took a momentary glance at the sheet, but it was enough to recognize that the words written in neat penmanship were those of a poem or possibly song lyrics. It was completely out of character for Cooper to read any document that did not belong to her, but having already scanned the first line, she felt compelled to finish it. Ducking behind a pillar, she absorbed the words as quickly as she could.

Sunlight, Moonshine

Sunlight, moonshine,
The deep and swelling sea,
My God, mighty and tender,
He made them all for me.

His fingers forged the mountains,
Stretched clouds across the sky,
My God, mighty and tender,
gave life to you and I.

(Chorus) My God, mighty and tender,
My God, timeless and true,
My God, mighty and tender,
I give myself to You.

The fragile wings of butterflies,
The stars burning above,
My God, mighty and tender,
I give to You my love.

"It must be a song," Cooper said to herself and then finished reading the lyrics, allowing the words to spread a warm calm through her. She also felt a flush of guilt at her surprise over the idea that Quinton, the wealthy and rather gluttonous financier, could have crafted such simple yet moving images. Then again, Cooper reminded herself, he was also sweet, funny, aching to please, and a fantastic baker.

"I don't want people to judge *me* like a book cover, but that's just what I've been doing with the Sunrise members," Cooper mumbled to herself. She though about how she had scrutinized Trish's home with such a critical eye, her assumptions that Bryant was a womanizer, that Jake only looked handsome when he was freshly shaved, and that Nathan's feet reminded her of Sasquatch. Ashamed, Cooper hoped she could find a way to make up her inaccurate judgments to Quinton and to the rest of her new friends.

Tucking the paper in her purse, Cooper looked around for the large man and then realized that her friends had probably all left for their lunch meeting, so she hurried outside to her truck.

By the time Cooper pushed open the front door of Panera Bread on Broad Street, she saw most of the group already inside collecting their orders from the counter, filling cups with beverages, and distributing brown paper napkins around the tabletop. Cooper ordered a portabella and mozzarella melt with a small Greek salad and joined her friends.

"I know we're waiting for Bryant and Savannah," Quinton said after swallowing a mammoth bite of roast beef, cheddar, and all the fixings served on toasted Asiago cheese bread. "But I took a look at the paper Cooper put back together." He reached across the table and covered her thin hand with his meaty one. "Good job, by the way." He then pointed at the numbers on the top of the paper. "These are someone's credit card numbers. I believe that because credit cards are all assigned sixteen digits. Check it out." Everyone leaned over in order to view the numbers. "It seems like there are only fifteen here, but there's actually another digit beneath this ink smear. If you stare at it long enough, you can see a shape, but I'm not sure what it is."

Jake was skeptical. "Lemme see that." He plucked the paper off the table and peered at it while rubbing at the dark stubble on his chin. Cooper noticed that his foot was shaking back and forth beneath the table and wondered if he was exhibiting signs of nicotine withdrawal. When she'd stepped on the scale that morning and found that she had gained five pounds, she knew that she'd been eating twice as many Magnolia's Marvels in an effort to answer her own nicotine cravings.

"You're right, big man," Jake said to Quinton. "But it could be a four or a nine. It's too blurry to tell."

"Do you think the account is this Hazel person's?" Trish asked, poking at her Asian sesame chicken salad.

Quinton nodded. "I do. The numbers are written right after her name. We just can't tell what her last name is because of this hole here."

Nathan finished the final spoonful of his French onion soup and turned to Cooper. "This might be a crazy question, but is there any way this teeny tiny missing piece of paper could still be in the copier?"

Cooper looked thoughtful. "Maybe. I thought I got all the scraps, but I could check. I have a routine maintenance schedule at Capital City. They wouldn't pay me any mind if I poked around in Brooke's copier." She glanced at her friends, her mismatched eyes glimmering. "I might be able to nose about in her office too. There might be a clue in there."

"And what about the assistant you mentioned?" Trish added. "Cindi? Was that her name? Maybe she knows something."

As Cooper chewed, she tried to visualize herself prowling around Brooke's office after hours. She imagined finding a clue that would instantly exonerate Wesley and identify the real murderer. She saw herself shying away from camera lights and pictured Drew watching her on TV. However, that fantasy was quickly replaced by the visual of being caught by Capital City's security guards, roughly questioned by the police, and being fired from Make It Work! After that, the bank that had issued her Visa card would start calling, demanding to know why she hadn't made her payment against her staggering debt.

Turning over all these thoughts within seconds caused Cooper's throat to tighten, and a bite of her sandwich lodged in her windpipe. She began to cough, unable to swallow the congealed ball of mushroom, bread, and cheese.

"Are you okay?" Nathan inquired and then proceeded to thump her roughly on the back, which only caused her to stiffen further.

"Give her some water," Trish ordered. "Stop smacking her, Nathan. That doesn't help at all. I don't know *why* people always do that."

Jake put his hands out to stop his friends

from further action. "Just leave the woman alone!" he barked. "Jeez, y'all hangin' all over her is just gonna embarrass her."

As Jake spoke, Cooper gulped down some Dr Pepper and managed to inhale a decent lungful of oxygen. "I'm sorry," she spluttered when she could speak again. "But I don't think I make a very good detective." She wiped her mouth with her napkin and dabbed away the tear that had inadvertently slipped from her blue eye during her choking episode. "I couldn't talk my way out of a paper bag. If I got caught, I'd need someone there who could think fast and tell a good tale. You know, in case we get in a bind."

"Yeah! You need to take someone with you, like, in disguise!" Jake looked expectantly at Cooper.

"Not Mr. Meteorologist Bryant. He's too famous!" Trish fluffed her coppery hair. "Me too."

"And you probably don't have a uniform my size," Quinton said glumly.

Jake elbowed Nathan in the side. "That leaves you and me, man."

"Maybe I could go with Cooper and check out Brooke's computer files," Nathan said, after a moment's hesitation. "As long as you're cool with this." He met Cooper's eyes and held them. "You'd be risking your job by sneaking me in the building."

"I know the risks," Cooper answered. "But it's a gamble I'm willing to make."

Nodding briefly, Nathan pulled out a copy of the fax they had discovered at the Hughes home. "Cooper's a better detective than she thinks, folks. She found this during our search Wednesday night." He placed the paper on the center of the table alongside the battered document from Brooke's copier.

"Hazel again!" Trish exclaimed.

"Well, *we* certainly didn't find anything." Quinton gestured at Trish. "Seemed like a nice house belonging to a close, loving family. No skeletons in any of their closets. Except for Hazel. Someone wanted Brooke to keep *her* a secret."

The group fell silent, absently picking at the remnants of their lunches as they pondered over the meaning of the threatening fax.

"I think Cindi could be important. All assistants have the inside scoop on their bosses," Quinton said as he examined the glossy surface of the red apple on his tray. "*Someone* needs to talk to her and someone also needs to get into the computers at Capital City and enter in this account number. We need to know who Hazel is — and since Capital City has over forty million customers, I don't think we're going to find one of them without bending some rules."

"What about the police?" Trish countered. "We're a little out of our league here, and I think we need to leave this matter to the experts."

Nathan shook his head. "I called them about the faxes. They said they would look into it, but they were more concerned about me being in the house than anything else. I think we need some concrete evidence to show them before they're going to take action."

"Yeah, they've already bagged their bird and put him in a cage," Jake said with a snarl. "Why should they do more legwork on an open-and-shut case?"

"I don't think we should judge the police too harshly," Trish's voice was firm. "Think about what they're dealing with these days. That little boy who was kidnapped, those drug-related killings last week, and now an arsonist at work downtown . . . I think they need our support for *all* of these unresolved cases."

Abashed by Trish's uncharacteristically empathetic statement, Jake nodded. "You're right. I just hate sittin' and twiddlin' my thumbs while Wesley loses hope with every passin' day." He looked around. "Where on earth is Savannah?"

Quinton cleaned up his tray and went to order a caramel latte. Cooper was about to join him at the counter so she could return his song without the others overhearing their exchange, but Nathan wanted to talk over details of how and when they would go to Capital City together. By the time Quinton returned with a whipped cream mustache dripping down onto his upper lip, the others had finished clearing their lunch trays and Bryant and Savannah had finally arrived.

"I'm having a strong feeling of déjà vu," Trish said glumly as she gazed up at Savannah's drawn face.

"I don't know what's happening to our congregation." Bryant helped Savannah sink into a chair as she allowed her purse to drop to the floor with a thud. "First Wesley, and now this." She paused to catch her breath. "You all probably know or have heard of Jed Weeks. He coordinates home visits for the members of our congregation who aren't able to attend worship service."

With the exception of Cooper, everyone nodded.

"What you may not know is that he started the program because his wife, Eliza, is unable to make it to church," she continued. "Eliza asked Pastor Matthews to take over last week's duties as Jed was heading out of town for a weeklong fishing trip." She sighed and placed her hands on either side of her temple. "Eliza called Pastor Matthews last night and asked him to take over Jed's duties for another week."

"What happened to Jed?" Quinton asked, his eyes fearful.

Savannah shrugged. "Eliza called both sets of neighbors at their river house. According to those folks, Jed never showed up." She wrung her hands together. "Eliza fears that he might be having an affair and has run off with another woman. I pray that she's wrong about Jed, but either way, Eliza is going to need some help until her sister can fly in from Alabama as the poor soul is wheelchair-bound. I know I keep placing weight on your shoulders, but can I count on you to help me share in this burden?"

"Of course!" Nathan answered for all of them.

"Now, fill me in on what I've missed," Savannah said as she composed herself. "We've got to get Wesley out of that jail so that we have time to chase down wayward husbands." Inhaling deeply near the vicinity of Jake's ceramic mug, she said, "Just one more indulgence, friends. Can someone lead me to the counter? I can't go on another second without a jolt of caffeine."

a time to search and a time to give up,
a time to keep and a time to throw away,

a time to tear and a time to mend,
a time to be silent and a time to speak.

Ecclesiastes 3:6–7 (NIV)

"They're a little short," Nathan said as he jumped out of the Make It Work! van. He pulled at the black uniform pants Cooper had borrowed from a part-time coworker's locker. Cooper had also brought one of Earl's extra toolboxes from home so that Nathan would resemble a copier repairman. At this point, however, he had only succeeded in looking awkward in pants that displayed two inches of white tube sock and a shirt that kept popping out from beneath his black belt.

Despite her nervousness, Cooper smiled. "I think the shirt's a bit short too. Sorry, but that uniform's actually got a few more inches than my other coworker's, so it was our only choice."

Nathan grabbed the toolbox and as he did so, he took a second glance at his long, smooth fingers, which spent most of the day flitting over a keyboard. "Guess when it comes down to it, I don't really look the part, do I?"

"Just keep your head down and remember to answer to *Stuart*," Cooper pointed at the name tag on his uniform shirt. "If you don't make eye contact, no one will pay any attention to you. Trust me. I've been servicing these machines for years, and no one knows my name."

Nathan puffed up his chest. "Well, I'm disappointed. I figured a bunch of gorgeous office workers would be sitting around, waiting to drool over the UPS man, but as soon as they saw me in my studly uniform, they'd forget about all the men in brown."

Cooper laughed. "The UPS *man* is a *woman* called Esmeralda, and she's built like a brick house, so you can forget about stealing her thunder, her spotlight, or anything else." She chuckled. "Besides, I don't think our uniforms can compete with those sexy UPS shorts. Come on, Studly." Cooper began walking toward Building F, gazing around the Capital City parking lot for signs of anything out of the ordinary that would cause her to abort their risky mission. Cooper cast a sideways glance at Nathan, thinking that he did look appealing as he gripped his toolbox with a determined expression.

"Speaking of attractive secretaries and the like," Cooper said softly as they entered the building, "how's that online dating service going?"

Nathan shrugged. "I don't seem to be finding any matches on there." He nodded to the receptionist in the lobby, but she smiled without actually looking at him and immediately went back to typing on her computer.

"Do you have to post a picture of yourself?" Cooper inquired, inwardly shuddering at the thought.

Nathan followed her into the elevator. "Yeah, but I think some of the photos I've looked at are about ten years old. I did read one profile that I thought was a terrific fit for me, but when I met the woman for coffee last week, she looked nothing like her photo. I think it must have been taken when she was still in high school."

"Did her looks matter *that* much to you?" Cooper teased. As the elevator doors opened, she walked briskly down the hall toward Brooke's office.

"No." Nathan bristled behind her. "I was just surprised by the difference, but I was still willing to see what she was like as a person." He suddenly stumbled on a snag in the carpet and nearly dropped his tool-box. "Sorry, I never quite grew into these feet. Anyway, in this woman's profile, she claimed to be into the outdoors and enjoyed helping people et cetera, but in person, she said that her great loves in life were shopping for shoes, sitting in the sauna with a copy of the *Enquirer,* and sleeping late." He stopped abruptly as Cooper gestured at the copier near Cindi's desk.

"This is it," she quickly whispered. "And that mess over there is the assistant's desk. It doesn't look like she's moved so much as a paper clip since I was here last, though at least the garbage has been emptied."

"Let's try to find the scraps from the Hazel document first," Nathan suggested, shoving his untucked shirt back into his pants.

Together, they pulled the copier away from the wall. Cooper unscrewed the back panel and then asked Nathan to position himself on the opposite side of the machine and hold the flashlight steady while she searched around on the ground for a shred large enough to reveal Hazel's last name.

"What are y'all doin'?" a raspy female voice behind Nathan's left shoulder demanded.

Nathan nearly dropped the flashlight. "Routine maintenance, ma'am. Has this machine been acting up on you lately?"

"Piece of junk. It gets jammed all the time, but I wouldn't spend too much time on it if I were you. It's probably getting moved somewhere else soon." The woman's tone indicated her disinterest.

From her vantage point on the floor, Cooper couldn't see the woman, but she had a clear view of the dazzling smile Nathan had turned on for her benefit. He shoved the flashlight into Cooper's hand and moved away from the copier.

"Aren't you ready to go home, ma'am?" he asked the woman. "It's five o'clock on a Friday afternoon, after all. You *must* have a date to get ready for."

"Pfffah!" the woman snorted playfully. "I've got two kids. I'm not exactly anyone's idea of a dream date."

The woman must be Cindi, Cooper thought. She gave Nathan a thumbs-up gesture, encouraging him to continue flirting.

"I love kids," Nathan replied genuinely. "Got any pictures of yours? I bet they're supercute."

"On my desk over here," she answered, leading Nathan away from the copier. "I'm getting transferred to the IT division next week and I'm supposed to pack up my things. I know it's kind of a jumble, but I just can't focus on work ever since . . ." She began to sniffle.

"Are you okay?" Cooper heard Nathan ask sympathetically as he moved around Cindi's workspace. "Here, let me get you a tissue."

After several sniffs, Cindi said, "You're sweet. I don't think I've ever seen you here before." Her voice held a trace of suspicion.

"No, ma'am. I'm new. I used to fix computers, but that field's getting overcrowded, so I decided to branch out a bit."

"Well, then you wouldn't have met my former boss, so you don't know what I've been dealing with, but you probably saw her name in the papers." She paused for effect. "Brooke Hughes?"

"The woman who was shot by her husband?" Nathan pretended to be mortified. "She was your boss?"

"Yeah, that's her." Cindi blew her nose with a shrill toot. "That *was* her. She was real good to me. I can't believe Wesley . . . Well, I shouldn't dwell on it. It won't bring her back and now I need to move on." She paused. "I just got so used to my little corner of the world here." She rustled some papers. "Now I've got to work for some guy and can only hope he's half as nice as Mrs. Hughes was." She honked into the tissue again. "She was so understanding about my challenges . . . bein' a single mom and all."

During this exchange, Cooper had collected several scraps that turned out to be of no use, but as she leveled the flashlight beam on the metal shelf closest to the floor, she noticed two small scraps bearing black letters. Tucking them into a tiny Ziploc bag, she completed her search and then began to slowly replace the back panel, as she wanted to give Nathan plenty of time to chat up Cindi.

"Poor you," Nathan was saying. "I can't imagine how stressed you must be. Have the police been crawling all over here too?"

"Not really. I mean, they came by, but none of us could help them. We were as shocked and upset as everybody else who knew her. The whole environment around here is creepy and sad. None of us talk about her or what happened. We're all trying to move on." Cindi sounded as though she was reluctant to discuss the subject any further.

"I bet you two were close." Nathan continued gently. "I can just tell you're the kind of person people can rely on and trust. *You'd* have known if she was upset or scared before . . . the awful event, even if no one else did."

As Cooper tightened the last screw of the back panel, she longed to give Nathan an indication that said he was laying it on too thick, but as she stood erect, she noticed that his back was to her and that he was replacing a framed photograph on the only square foot of uncluttered space on Cindi's desk.

Preening as a result of Nathan's praise, Cindi declared, "I *do* get gut feelings about people close to me. I don't mind telling you that Brooke seemed kind of rattled the last few days before she died, but I don't know *exactly* why." She lowered her voice conspiratorially. "I didn't tell the cops this, 'cause it's none of their beeswax, but Brooke and her husband had a fight over the phone a few days before he killed her. I mean, they already had him locked up, so what was the point? And anyways, I didn't listen to her private conversations, so I don't even know what their tiff was about."

Cooper placed her screwdriver in the tool-box and began to make minor adjustments to the copier. As she did, she checked out Cindi from the corner of her eye. Brooke's assistant was a trim vision of jet-black hair, tanned skin, and a form-fitting pink leopard skin skirt. Cooper noticed her muscular legs, which were encased in knee-high riding boots, and her unusually high bosom, which threatened to spill out of the low V of her black blouse. She flicked a pair of silver-blue eyes to Cooper and then instantly returned her attention to Nathan.

"I'd better get going. Fridays are pizza night for us and if I don't get Bottoms Up Pizza by six, I'll have a mutiny on my hands." She put a hand with bubble-gum painted nails on Nathan's sleeve and let it linger there for a moment. "It was nice talking to you. I'm Cindi Rolfing, by the way."

"And I'm, ah, Stuart. It was a pleasure to meet you, Ms. Rolfing." Nathan gave a gallant bow, which looked slightly awkward coming from someone of his height. His shirt immediately popped out from his pants and he frantically pushed it back into place. "Um, I know this is a bit forward, but would you like . . . um, could I have your number?"

Cindi giggled. "I'm sorry, sugar. I'm kind

of in an exclusive thing with someone right now, but if that doesn't work out" — she touched the place on Nathan's uniform shirt where the company logo was embroidered — "I know where to find you."

As she pulled on a cropped black leather jacket, Cooper noticed Cindi's gold bracelet. It was a chain bracelet with a heart charm hanging from the middle and had been engraved with a message too small for Cooper to read from such a distance. Cindi blew Nathan a kiss and strutted off to the elevators, while Nathan waved at her until she disappeared inside and then quickly canvassed the rest of the floor.

"There's only one guy left at his workstation and he's listening to his iPod and playing Tetris on his computer on the opposite end of the room." Nathan's eyes were bright with excitement. "Keep a lookout while I hack into Brooke's computer, okay, partner?"

"Were you serious when you asked her out?" Cooper whispered in surprise as Nathan booted up Brooke's computer and Cooper began to examine the surface of Cindi's disheveled desk.

"Lord, no!" Nathan hissed from inside Brooke's dark office. "But I believe that woman listened to every phone conversation Brooke had and that she knows every word exchanged in Brooke's argument with Wesley. I wanted to discover what that fight was about. It could be important."

"Nathan. What if the police are right?" Cooper's throat turned dry as she offered up this theory. "They were fighting a few days before she was killed."

Nathan swiveled around on his chair. "People argue. Even people who love each other deeply. Remember that *you* said Brooke was really happy talking about her marriage, so they had already worked out their problems."

Feeling like a louse, Cooper fell silent as she carefully shifted through interoffice memos, old faxes, and other work-related documents that didn't raise any red flags. She then flipped through the pages of Cindi's phone message pad, which was the same pink pad Angela used to deliver notes to the employees of Make It Work! Several messages had been written down, but not delivered to Brooke. Cooper assumed this was normal protocol. One of Cindi's jobs was likely to screen calls and handle some of the less complex requests so that Brooke could concentrate on more important tasks.

Cindi was a prolific doodler and had drawn hearts, martini glasses with olives, dollar signs, and striped beach umbrellas propped on a sand dune on dozens of pages. Sometimes she was an efficient assistant, writing the date and time of each call. Other times, she simply wrote down a name and then surrounded the letters with stars or smiley faces or childish flowers, probably while she listened to the caller speak. These memos made it clear that Cindi didn't always find her job too exciting. Turning over the pages, Cooper was surprised at the number of messages from repeat callers that Cindi never delivered to her boss and could only assume that she'd told Brooke about the calls in person.

The pad dated back to mid-March. It was on the last few pages that Cooper spied a familiar name: Hazel. There were three calls from Hazel in March, but no last name or return number was listed. On the second to last page, it looked as if Cindi had begun to write Hazel's number down, but had scratched over the first two digits as though Hazel wasn't significant enough to tell Brooke about. The last page had been torn from the book. Two inches of pink paper remained attached to the spine of the pad, but there was nothing written upon it.

Cooper popped her head into Brooke's office, where Nathan was shutting down

Brooke's computer.

"I didn't see any files with any unusual content," he said, sounding dejected. "There are no documents in code or hidden folders. Her stuff is organized and totally straightforward. Anything interesting on Cindi's desk?"

Cooper brandished the pad. "Hazel strikes again." She showed him the messages from March. "Nathan, I think you need to talk to Cindi some more."

"Based on that torn page at the end, I wonder if Cindi got rid of even more messages from Hazel." Nathan scrutinized the two digits hidden beneath concentrated scribbles of purple ink. "I think it's an *eight* and a *zero.* Cindi was probably going to write 804 and then realized Hazel was giving her the same area code we all have, so she didn't bother writing any more."

"This is so frustrating!" Cooper declared. "Every clue leads to the same thing. Hazel, Hazel, Hazel. I'd give my left lung to know who this woman is!"

"Cindi knows who she is, but how are we going to get more info out of her?" Nathan sighed. "Since she has a boyfriend, flirting isn't the answer. I think another one of the Sunrise members is going to have to approach her."

"Maybe Trish can give her a free home assessment," Cooper half-teased as they exited the elevator.

Nathan mulled this over. "That's not half bad, actually." He nudged her in the side and Cooper let out a small shriek. "Wow, not only are you ticklish, but you *do* have the makings of a real detective."

Cooper's neck turned pink.

Out in the parking lot, Nathan climbed into the back of the van in order to change into a sweatshirt and jeans. As Cooper settled herself in the driver's seat, she saw a flash of pink leopard print. A few rows in front of the van, Cindi was making a graceful exit from the passenger side of a black Acura SUV. After shaking her bottom as she threw a kiss back over her shoulder to the car's occupant, she unlocked the door to her own car — a ten-year-old Civic — and sped off.

Cooper had enough time before the SUV drove away to observe two things. The first was that the vanity plate read HRD DRIV, so she assumed the car owner must work for Capital City's IT department. The second was far more interesting. When the driver put his arm out the window in order to feel the crisp late afternoon breeze as he accelerated, Cooper saw the glint of a gold

195

band on his ring finger. Cindi had been shimmying her rear and sending air kisses to a married man.

9

"Can anyone hide in secret places
so that I cannot see him?"
declares the LORD.
"Do not I fill heaven and earth?"
declares the LORD.

Jeremiah 23:24 (NIV)

Cooper brought the uniform Nathan had worn home to be washed and ironed. As she was erasing the final crease from the black pants early Saturday morning, Grammy appeared in the doorway to her bedroom wearing her teal tracksuit with a pair of white socks embroidered with multi-colored tulips. She gave the pants on the ironing board an appraising look and then searched her granddaughter's face.

"Where'd those come from?" She pointed at the garment, her wrinkled face animated with curiosity. "You don't have a man up in that apartment of yours, do ya?"

"No, Grammy," Cooper replied as she made another sweep with the iron.

"Too bad." Frowning in disappointment, the older woman shuffled off to the kitchen. Minutes later, Cooper followed her and joined her father by the coffee carafe. Silently, Earl poured his daughter a mug, settled himself at the scrubbed farm table, and began to work the puzzles in the *Times-Dispatch*.

"You doing a cryptogram?" Cooper asked him as she took a sip of coffee that always seemed significantly more rich and flavorful than the stuff she brewed in her own tiny kitchen.

Earl nodded, rubbing a hand over his hairless head. He removed his reading glasses, cleaned an imaginary spot from the lenses, and clicked the point of his pen in and out. This was a sign that he wanted to talk about something, but wasn't sure how to broach the subject. In a household filled with so many women, Earl was a taciturn rock weathering three generations of estrogen-induced tempests. He normally waited for his mother, wife, or daughters to initiate conversation, and as there was rarely a stretch of silence in his house, he didn't go out of his way to encourage more prattle. However, the morning seemed unusually quiet and Earl decided to take advantage of an opportunity to begin a discussion of his choosing.

"You seem to be mighty busy these days, my girl," Earl commented. "You makin' any headway in findin' out what happened to that nice lady?"

Cooper idly flipped through the Metro section and shook her head. "More questions than answers at this point." She raised her eyes to meet her father's bright blue ones. "The more we dig, the more dirt we're finding on other folks. First, it was Brooke's death. That led to trying to keep an innocent man from a lifetime in prison. Today, I'm going with some of my Bible study friends to visit a woman whose husband's run off." She sighed. "I thought going to church would make me feel . . . I don't know, more sure about life, but I'm more uncertain of things now than when Drew left."

Earl nodded, digesting his daughter's words. "Well, you've been hidin' a bit too long in our back yard. You've done a lot of good for hungry people by growin' fruit and vegetables for the food bank, but that's been a safe pastime for you. Now you're out there, mixin' with folks and seein' the good and the bad. It takes some kind of courage to take on new hardships, but you can tackle 'em."

"And hopefully tackle a new man while you're at it!" Grammy added from the next room.

Earl grinned. "Her ears are right keen for someone her age."

"I heard that!" Grammy hollered as Cooper laughed into her hand.

"So." Earl clicked his pen repeatedly. "Your mama said you went out to dinner with a fellow a few nights back. Is he your . . . is he someone you've set your cap on?"

Cooper's neck grew pink, though she didn't know why. "His name's Nathan Dexter." She then told her father all she knew about the tall Web site designer with the pleasant face. "He's a great guy, but he's just a friend. I still love Drew. I've loved him for such a long time that I don't know how to stop, Daddy."

Earl put down his pen and took Cooper's hands in his. "Listen here, my girl. That boy is gone. Let him go. He was a nice boy and we liked him, but he slid off the edge and took a piece of you with him. You're on a new road now and it's gonna be rocky, but I think it's leadin' you toward a good place and to fine people like this Nathan fellow."

He squeezed her hand. "I know this is not what you wanna hear, but I don't think Drew belongs where you're goin'. Let him go."

Cooper felt the truth of her father's words sear her heart. She put her hands over her eyes and pushed back the tears.

"Why don't you try spending time with Nathan? You could fix him something to eat and just get to know each other more," Maggie suggested softly, having stealthily tiptoed into the kitchen during their conversation. "I won your daddy over by feeding him. Never met a man that didn't fall for a girl once he had gotten a taste for her cooking."

"That's some wise counsel!" Grammy called out her two cents from the other room. She had turned the television volume down until it was barely audible and Cooper was certain her grandmother could no longer hear the dialogue between Ellen DeGeneres and the handsome young actor Orlando Bloom.

Ignoring her mother and grandmother's advice, Cooper examined the crossword, which her father had filled out in record time. "How'd you get so good at puzzles, Daddy?" she asked him in an effort to change the subject.

He shrugged. "Just like figurin' them out, same as I like workin' on that old Malibu or changin' a tractor blade. Feels good to see how things fit together, to come to the end of a problem." He patted her hand. "But you gotta stick with things, my girl. No quittin' when you hit a rough patch. You're gonna help solve your murder case and then you're gonna have to solve the mystery of who you wanna be."

Cooper smiled fondly at her father and he gave her a little wink as he pointed at her mother. Maggie had her box of recipe cards in her hands and was holding her greatest treasure out for Cooper to take. "Meat's always a good place to start when it comes to men. Maybe a pot roast?"

Relenting, Cooper accepted the box. "Well, I kind of do want to get to know Nathan better, so I'll invite him for dinner. I'll be seeing him today because we're going to visit that wheelchair-bound lady I told you about last Sunday." She opened the freezer. "Do you have some cookies I could take her, Mama?"

Maggie smoothed her apron, her face all business. "Lord have mercy, Cooper. I can do better than that! The woman's husband has gone missing! She needs more than a few cookies." Maggie began whipping cupboards and drawers open and piling bowls, utensils, and ingredients on the counter. "I'm going to fix her up a nice turkey rice casserole, a fresh loaf of honey wheat bread, and a chocolate chess pie. Go on now. Get out of my kitchen. I've got work to do." Smiling, she gestured at the back door.

"Don't let her go without that pot roast recipe!" Grammy yelled out. "I expect to hear of a supper date by this time next week. That Ashley's too busy bein' a socialite to give me great-grandchildren, so you may as well try to catch up, Granddaughter!"

Cooper was relieved to be alone in her greenhouse. She watered her seedlings and tried not to think about how much she would like to fulfill both of Grammy's wishes. She was ready for marriage and for children. She had always wanted both, but for the last five years she had wanted them with Drew.

"I've got to start picturing the future without Drew in it," she murmured as she spritzed water on a young parsley plant. "I wonder if Nathan will start appearing in my dreams instead."

The plan was for Cooper to drive to Nathan's house in the Fan district and from there, the two of them would pick up Savannah and head north to Ashland, to the home of Eliza and Jed Weeks.

Nathan lived in a blue row house on Floyd Street in Williamsburg. His tiny front garden was comprised of a bed of crabgrass speckled with chickweed. The weed-filled lawn was edged with a row of dwarf euonymus desperately in need of water and a good pruning. Despite the lack of curb appeal, Nathan's small porch was swept free of leaves and dust, and he had placed a straw welcome mat with an ivy border at the foot of his front door.

Cooper hustled up the stairs and rang the bell, using three short jabs of her index finger. She could hear Nathan's large feet bounding toward the door like an eager dog. As he pulled it open with a smile, smells of tomato sauce and crushed basil floated across the threshold.

"Are you cooking something?" she asked as she stepped inside and peered around his sparse living room.

Nathan followed her gaze as she took in the solitary club chair and end table placed near the brick fireplace. "I haven't done much with this room," he said, indicating that Cooper should continue walking toward the back of the house. "I pretty much live in the kitchen and my office."

In the kitchen, which was painted a deep cranberry red and had amber-colored countertops and blond cabinets, the delicious aroma that had greeted Cooper at the front door was even stronger. "Are you part Web designer, part Iron Chef?" she inquired, grinning at the sight of his lobster-shaped potholders.

"Not me!" Nathan exclaimed. "I can grill a decent steak and open a mean can of tuna fish, but that's about it. Oh, and omelets. I'm good at omelets." He pointed at the oven. "That's a lasagna I picked up from Meal Makers. It was frozen, so I'm just cooking it before we visit Eliza. And I couldn't resist their Greek chicken and pasta, but I grabbed the family-sized bag by mistake, so unless you're willing to stay for dinner, I'm going to be eating that for the next four days. Are you free tonight?"

It took a moment for Nathan's last line to sink in. "Um, sure," she replied rather ungraciously, surprised by the invitation. "I mean, that sounds great," she hastily added. Her neck began to grow warm and she turned toward the window in search of a distraction, but couldn't see much beyond the plantation shutters. "So where's your office?"

Nathan began to fidget. "Ah, it's across the hall." He gestured at the closed door just as the oven timer began to beep. "Go ahead and look while I take this out, but I'm giving you fair warning, you might find it a bit bizarre. Most women do."

Her curiosity piqued, Cooper opened the door to what appeared to be a shrine filled with *Star Wars* toys. Spaceships hung from the ceiling, action figures stood on every inch of available shelving, and framed posters, decals, ticket stubs, cereal boxes, and trading cards vied for breathing room on the crowded walls. The room had been painted a deep blue and Nathan had placed adhesive stars over every surface, so that the daylight streaming in through the floor-to-ceiling bay window in front of his desk illuminated the stars until they appeared to be twinkling.

"I'm a bit of a *Star Wars* fan," Nathan said sheepishly as he came up behind her.

"I can see that," Cooper answered with a laugh. "How many items do you have in your . . . collection?"

Nathan removed a Han Solo PEZ dispenser from the nearest shelf. "Over two thousand."

Cooper vaguely remembered seeing the movie as a child, but couldn't see why a grown man would fill an entire room with *Star Wars* memorabilia. "What got you started on all this?"

Shrugging, Nathan replaced the candy dispenser and removed a comic book from a bookrack near the door. "I wanted to be a comic-book artist after I saw the movie. I was so inspired that I began drawing scenes and characters from *Star Wars* in my spare time. Eventually, I holed up in my room, creating my own galaxies, heroes, and villains. I stopped going outside to play, wouldn't hang out with my friends — I didn't go anywhere without my sketchpad and a box of colored pencils. Finally, I started getting in trouble in school. That's when my parents enrolled me in a computer camp for the summer and laid down rules about when I could draw." He tenderly replaced the comic book protected by a plastic sleeve back in the bookrack. "Turns out I was pretty good at computer stuff and it became my career, but I'll never forget how that movie fueled my imagination."

Cooper thought she saw a trace of sadness on Nathan's face. She tapped the top of his computer screen. "But now you can create any kind of Web site imaginable, right? So your grown-up job's not that different from being a comic-book artist.

You're just drawing using code, or whatever the word is."

Nathan smiled gratefully. "I never thought of it that way." He walked back into the kitchen and placed a sheet of foil over the warm lasagna. "So you don't think my hobby is totally crazy?"

"Not *totally*," she teased and held the front door open for him. She removed Maggie's stack of Tupperware dishes from Cherry-O and placed them on her lap after climbing into Nathan's BMW sedan. "I don't think I've ever seen a car this shade of green," she told him. "I like it."

Nathan patted the black leather steering wheel fondly. "This is Sweet Pea. It was my mom's car and I bought it from her a few years ago. I'm very fond of this gal, even though she doesn't have nearly enough legroom. She's old and has got her share of scrapes and dents, but she's got all that counts inside." He thumped the dashboard, put the car in gear, and forced its sleepy engine to chug into life. "Come on, Sweet Pea, let's go get Savannah."

Savannah lived in a little white bungalow near the University of Richmond. She must have heard Nathan pulling into her driveway, for she began walking down her short flight of front stairs before he could even turn off the engine, a paper-wrapped parcel tucked under her right arm.

"Thought I'd meet you out here since my cats always try to make a break for it when I go out the front door," Savannah explained as she seated herself in the back. "They're allowed behind the house because I've got a high chain-link fence, but I'm afraid they'd get run over within two minutes on this road." She clucked her tongue. "I swear, those college kids come around this corner on two wheels." She grinned. "Of course I can't *see* them, but judging from their music, they're well on their way to hearing loss."

The threesome talked about their work-weeks as they headed north on Route 1 to Hanover County. Their chatter instantly fell away as Cooper and Nathan caught sight of the Weeks house twenty minutes later.

"Are we here?" Savannah asked as Nathan steered Sweet Pea down a flat gravel drive-way. "What's it like?"

"Well," Nathan began, "it's a gray ranch. But I've never seen a ranch quite this big."

"It's in the shape of the letter *U* and is probably over three thousand square feet — all on one level," Cooper added. "There's almost no trees out front and it's got a three-car garage and two entrances, both with wheelchair ramps."

Nathan parked the car and whispered to Savannah, "This place feels a bit neglected. There are a bunch of dead plants in pots by the front door and a pile of newspapers on the stoop."

Savannah took Nathan's proffered arm. "Then it's a good thing we came. Cooper? Would you gather up the papers and we'll take care of those plants once we introduce ourselves to Eliza."

Cooper rang the bell and opened the door after hearing a woman call out, "Come on in!" in a powerful voice.

Nathan led Savannah into a darkened hallway and turned her in the direction of the voice. "Are you Savannah's friends?" the woman shouted from far down the hall.

"Yes, ma'am," Nathan yelled back.

"All right then! I'm in the TV room." There was a pause as the three friends continued down the hall, passing a dining room table strewn with unopened mail and a filthy kitchen before turning a corner and entering a cavernous room. The ceiling was interrupted by rows of skylights, but there were no windows to interfere with the grouping of soft couches and chairs all positioned to face a mammoth flat-screen TV. Sitting in the center of one of the wide couches was the biggest woman Cooper had ever seen.

Mrs. Eliza Weeks likely weighed over three hundred pounds. Dressed in a sleeveless purple robe, her flesh pushed against the terry cloth in every direction. Her arms, which had a greater circumference than Cooper's thighs, wobbled as she gestured for them to sit. As she adjusted the strained sash of her robe, the multitude of rolls that formed Eliza's torso shifted like a great pile of melting snow. Her feet were tucked into a pair of heelless slippers and her ankles were well hidden beneath folds of fat.

A motorized wheelchair was parked next to Eliza, and Cooper wondered how the poor woman managed to get her formidable bulk in or out of it. Her heart swelled with pity for the obese woman, who clearly suffered from physical afflictions and now faced an emotional one as well. Cooper steered Savannah to a couch and then withdrew to a club chair nearby.

"I know I'm a shocking sight!" Eliza declared unpretentiously. "But I wasn't always like this. Once upon a time I was the queen of the Tomato Festival." She turned slowly to Nathan as though the effort of shifting her thick neck was almost too much to bear. "Do y'all know Jed from church?"

she asked in a conversational tone, as though nothing was wrong whatsoever and her husband would walk in the door at any given moment.

"I've heard of him, ma'am. Everyone talks about what a good man he is," Nathan responded gently and then touched the top of Eliza's hand. "Has there been any word from him?"

Eliza's perky demeanor dissipated like mist burned away by a strong sun. She looked down at her lap and whispered, "No."

"Well, we're here to cheer you up. Just name your desire and we'll see to it," Nathan offered. "We've brought you a meal or two to start with. Could I fix you something to eat?"

"I can't say I wouldn't mind a little plate of somethin'," Eliza answered with a tinge of shame in her voice.

Nathan smiled at her. "Excellent. Do you like lasagna?"

Eliza's eyes shone. "I love it. Can't you tell?" She laughed at herself, but no one else joined in. "That would sure hit the spot, thank you."

After Nathan disappeared into the kitchen, Savannah held out her wrapped parcel. "I don't know if I told you this before, but I'm a folk artist. I thought this silly little painting might make you smile."

"Oh my, you're all too sweet," Eliza gushed as she accepted the package. She opened it delicately, as if cherishing the moment. Finally, the butcher paper fell to the floor and Eliza's eyes widened with delight. "Goodness me! What a wonderful, wonderful picture!" She looked at Cooper. "Have you seen this?"

Cooper shook her head and reached for the piece of folk art. Savannah had painted a white clapboard church situated in the middle of a field of grass. A dirt path led to the front door and picnic tables loaded with an assortment of dishes were set about the lawn. Members of the congregation, dressed in suits and fancy hats, were seated at the tables or carrying out more food from inside the church. Daisies and buttercups bloomed in the foreground and a pair of angels with gilded wings, holding what appeared to be legs of fried chicken, flew overhead. The people's faces were ovals of apricot flesh, completely lacking personalized features such as eyes, noses, or mouths.

"I know what you're going to ask me," Savannah said, smiling. "Why don't my people have faces? First of all, I can't see well enough to paint that kind of detail, and secondly, I like how equal everyone is with the same face."

Cooper handed the painting back to Eliza. "I can practically smell the fried chicken and hear everybody talking as they eat. You can tell the angels are really enjoying their drumsticks, even though they don't have mouths for smiling. This is unique, Savannah. I really love it."

"Speaking of unique, you've got some interestin' eyes, young lady." Eliza leaned her bulk forward to get a clearer look.

Impulsively, Cooper dropped her gaze to the floor. "I had an accident and ended up getting an ocular transplant," she explained.

"You and me both, darling!" Eliza boomed, her body shaking with laughter. "Let's trade sob stories. It'll keep my mind off Jed for five minutes."

After a moment's pause, Cooper told Eliza about her field hockey injury. Eliza and Savannah listened without speaking, though every now and then Eliza made sympathetic clucking noises and put one of her hands over where her heart was cached beneath her enormous bosom.

"That's a better story than mine," she said when Cooper was finished. "I just got in a boring ol' car accident. 'Course it was with an eighteen-wheeler in the dead of night when I was in my prime." She raised her eyes to the ceiling as though still looking for an explanation for her crippled state. "Jed and I had been married two years when it happened. We were just thinking about startin' us a little family. I was workin' as a salesgirl in a lingerie store, of all things, and me and a few of the girls went out for drinks after work and, well, I had a few too many. Crossed the line in more than one way, you might say, and when I came face-to-face with the grille of that truck, I thought I was a goner."

She stopped her narrative and, with a mighty effort, picked up Savannah's painting. Tracing one of the golden angel wings with her finger, she continued. "An angel must have been on the shoulder of that trucker, 'cause his rig rolled around like a hotdog outta the bun, but he ended up without a scratch. Good thing too, seein' as he was a daddy to six kids."

"Seems like you might have had an angel with you that night too," Savannah suggested cautiously. "You made it through, right?"

"*Jed* was my angel," Eliza stated sadly. "All these years, he's stayed with me. I couldn't work, couldn't give him kids, could barely cook or clean the house. He built this whole place around my needs and what did I do by way of thanks? Sat around watching TV and eatin', eatin', eatin'. No wonder he finally flew the coop. How long can one man be tied to a woman like me?" Weeping, Eliza buried her face in her hands.

"Have you called the police?" Savannah asked. "Filed a missing persons report?"

Eliza shook her head, tears flowing down her fleshy cheeks. " 'Course I did. As soon as our neighbors at the river house told me he never showed up. Jed has always been so predictable, but he *was* acting mighty high-strung these last few weeks. I never even thought of another woman until my sister put the notion in my head." She sighed heavily. "I could tell, from the expression on the faces of those two police officers who came to talk to me, that they think Jed's run off on me too. I know what they were thinkin' as they sat here with their pads of paper and their careful words! I've got a mirror!" Suddenly, she uttered a loud cry. "Oh, Jed! I'd forgive anything if you just came back to me!"

Her racking sobs filled the room.

At that moment, Nathan arrived with a tray laden with lasagna, salad, a buttered roll, and a glass of water. Seeing Eliza's distress, Nathan set the tray on the coffee table in front of her and shifted back and forth on his big feet, unsure of what to do. Cooper was also at a loss for words, but thankfully, Savannah moved from her sofa and made her way to Eliza's side. She took Eliza's head and guided it to her own shoulder. Then, holding the distraught woman's hand, she cooed and whispered gentle words until Eliza's tears began to slow.

"Let's go clean up the kitchen," Nathan whispered to Cooper and the pair walked quietly from the room.

Two hours later, they had not only cleaned every inch of the kitchen, but had tidied Eliza's bedroom and done a load of laundry. Eliza's bed sheets were currently in the dryer and, lacking any further areas to scour, they watered all of the house plants. As Cooper tended to the ficus tree in the far corner of the room where Eliza sat, now fully recovered and talking boisterously with Savannah, Nathan walked by with an arm-load of sheets.

"If you aren't the sweetest boy!" Eliza called out. "Could you wait a moment? I've got a favor to ask you."

Nathan sat down with a pile of warm, floral sheets filling his lap.

"Your friend Savannah has convinced me

to look at this situation in another light — that it might be somethin' other than a woman that made Jed run off. She and I have just called my credit card company, and Jed hasn't made a single charge on his card." She gestured at the sheets. "While you're puttin' those on, can you feel behind the headboard for an envelope? It's where we hid our emergency cash. I need to know if that's what Jed's livin' on."

Nodding, Nathan disappeared. Cooper was about to follow him when a thought entered her mind. "This might seem like a strange question, Mrs. Weeks, but does your husband use a Capital City credit card?"

Surprised, Eliza nodded. "Yes. But why?"

Cooper persisted. "Do you happen to know anyone by the name of Hazel?"

Dabbing at her mouth with a paper napkin, Eliza shook her head. "Doesn't sound familiar."

"I'm just wondering what might have made him change his plans to go fishing. It seems like he really doesn't want to be found and I'm just thinking that most creatures go into hiding when they're scared of something." Cooper began pacing the room, trying to think of a reason other than another woman that might have caused Jed Weeks to leave his helpless wife. Maybe the

218

answer lay in his professional dealings. "Mrs. Weeks, what does your husband do for a living?"

"Well, he's mostly retired now, but he's an accountant." Eliza smiled with pride. "He did really special accounting for big companies all over Central Virginia. Now he just takes on a few projects a year. Like the bumper sticker says, he'd rather be fishing."

Cooper tried to process how Jed Weeks could be connected to Brooke Hughes. After all, her death and his disappearance had occurred fairly close together and might not be a matter of coincidence. "Did he ever do work for Capital City?"

Eliza looked perplexed. "I don't know, honey. Probably, but only Jed could tell you for sure. See, he had to keep mum about his work. Lots of times lawyers used his findings in their cases. I guess he was kind of a detective accountant. I forget what the official title is. His business card had all kinds of initials on it."

"Do you happen to have one of his cards?" Cooper inquired.

"Sure thing. Jed's office is down in the other wing. He's got some cards in a dish on his desk." Eliza frowned. "But what's Jed's job got to do with anything?"

"I don't know that it does, Mrs. Weeks,"

219

Cooper confessed. "I'm grasping at straws a bit. Have you ever heard of a woman named Brooke Hughes?"

Eliza furrowed her brow. "Don't think so. Still, I don't know many people, honey, seein' as I don't get out much. I talk to my sister on the phone, but mostly it's just me and Jed." She twisted the sash of her robe in her fingers. "As y'all probably noticed, I don't go to church with Jed. I stopped after the accident. Guess my willingness to be looked at by that big congregation gave out along with my legs."

Clearing his throat, Nathan reentered the room. "There's nothing behind the headboard, ma'am. I even checked under the bed."

"There was over two thousand dollars in that envelope," Eliza told them. "That's not gonna last Jed forever." Tears welled in her eyes again. "If he's livin' on cash, he really didn't want to be found, now did he? Oh, I hope he's all right!"

"There, there," Savannah whispered. "All will be well, you'll see."

The three friends offered words of support and sympathy and promised Eliza they'd visit again soon. On the way out, Cooper darted into Jed's office, took a business card from his desk, and showed it to

Nathan once they were all settled inside Sweet Pea.

"Jed Weeks, CPA, CFE," Nathan read. "I have no earthly idea what a CFE is. I'll have to look it up on the Internet when we get back to my place."

"Or we could call Quinton," Savannah said, brandishing a cell phone. "I've got him on speed dial because he drives me to church most Sundays." She held down a digit and greeted Quinton a few seconds later. After summarizing their visit to Eliza, she asked him about the acronym. "Certified Fraud Examiner?" She then repeated for Cooper and Nathan's benefit. "What exactly do they do?"

She listened for a few minutes, thanked Quinton, and then shut her phone. "Jed is trained as a forensic accountant. According to Quinton, he would have investigated a company's financial practices to prepare documents that could be used as evidence in court. As a CFE, it looks like Jed specialized in fraud auditing."

"A specialist in fraud. Just like Brooke Hughes," Cooper mumbled.

"You might be onto something here, Cooper," Nathan said as he accelerated in order to pass an old pickup truck filled with bales of hay. "Jed might not be off on a romantic getaway with a lover at all. He might be hiding because he's scared of someone."

"But who?" Savannah asked.

Nathan used his wipers to clear stray pieces of hay from his windshield. "Maybe the same person who shot Brooke. It would make sense that he wouldn't tell Eliza anything about his involvement. The less she knows, the safer she is."

"If you're right," Cooper said with a sigh, "we now have to find Jed *and* Hazel."

"This is going to require a whole lot of praying," Savannah said wearily, as she rested her head against the seat and closed her eyes.

10

"You have heard that it was said, 'Love your neighbor and hate your enemy.' But I tell you: Love your enemies and pray for those who persecute you, that you may be sons of your Father in heaven. He causes his sun to rise on the evil and the good, and sends rain on the righteous and the unrighteous."

Matthew 5:43–45 (NIV)

That weekend, on a morning filled with a breeze that coerced fresh dustings of pollen from the groupings of foxglove, snapdragon, and sweet William surrounding the Lees' patio, Cooper woke up unusually early. The spring sunshine had launched an invasion through the cleft in her curtains, prompting her to make the most of the day, so she slipped on a pair of jeans and a Richmond Braves sweatshirt and fixed herself some scrambled eggs and a slice of dark rye toast.

After breakfast, she wandered into her parents' house to see if she could borrow some half-and-half for her second cup of coffee. In the kitchen, her father was contentedly dumping the contents of a Wal-Mart bag onto the counter. He rubbed his hands together and grinned like a little boy.

" 'Mornin'! Look here. I read about these in the paper." He held up a box illustrating a mole covering its ears as it fled from a large spike emanating pulses. "Two batteries is all it takes. We whack this gadget into the ground and it'll cover a whole acre. Scares the moles and the voles by thumpin' steady all day and all night." He handed the box to Cooper. "We can put 'em in the ground this afternoon. What do you think, my girl?"

"Looks cool, Daddy." Cooper smiled as her father began to fit batteries into one of the stakes. "You're firing the first shot of the season, I see."

Earl snorted. "Heck yes, I am. A man's gotta have *some* advantage over the vermin in his own backyard."

One of Earl's favorite activities was to wage war against the creatures attempting to invade the vegetable garden. He and Cooper planned to spend Sunday afternoon after church stringing aluminum pie pans and bars of Irish Spring soap around the perimeter and applying fresh paint on the owl decoys they would fasten to the split-rail fence further bordering the woods.

"You should just move Columbus's cage next to the garden," Grammy advised, shuffling sleepily into the kitchen. "No critter in its right mind would venture in that garden with a hawk nearby."

"But it would be teasin' the poor bird," Earl said. "He'd see all those rodents creepin' around and wouldn't be able to get out of his cage to catch them. No," — he brandished the pie plates — "we'll make do, same as every year. Those folks at the food bank will get their greens from Lee Farm despite the bugs, moles, voles, deer, and rabbits we've got to fight against."

"Speakin' of rabbits . . ." Grammy wiggled her eyebrows up and down suggestively. "You got back a bit late last night, Granddaughter. You must've finally spoke plain about your feelings to that man of yours."

"It was just dinner," Cooper mumbled, as she hid her flushed face inside the fridge and quickly poured some half-and-half into one of her mother's coffee mugs. She then made a show of looking at her watch. "I'd better go get dressed for church. See y'all later."

She scurried up to her apartment and spent several minutes pushing clothes around inside her closet. Finally, she laid an outfit consisting of pressed khakis and a lightweight mocha-colored sweater on top of her bed and started the shower water. It was almost unbearably hot by the time she stepped into the stall, but Cooper preferred it that way. As water streamed through her hair and over her shoulders, she leaned back into the heat, wishing that it had the power to erase the memory of her dinner with Nathan. The evening had gone from being amusing and comfortable to awkward and disconcerting.

At first, everything was perfect. They had dropped Savannah off at her house and then Cooper had washed lettuce and prepared a salad while Nathan decanted a bottle of Italian red wine. As the wine breathed a bit, he set his kitchen table using striped cotton napkins, heavy white dishes, and a copper candleholder. He placed a single unused taper in the holder and then rummaged through every single kitchen drawer in search of matches.

"As you can see, I'm not used to lighting candles," he had said, laughing. "I hope I'm not losing too many points as a host. First, I offer you chicken and pasta that someone else has cooked and now I can't find any matches. Can you tell I'm a bachelor or what?"

Cooper gave Nathan an encouraging smile, removed the candle from the table, and turned on the front burner of Nathan's gas stove. She stuck the wick in the blue-and-orange circle of flame and then handed Nathan the lit candle. He beamed at her as though she had produced fire from a magic wand.

"Okay, I feel a bit stupid now," he said ruefully and poured wine into glass goblets with wide mouths. "I'd be the first one voted off on *Survivor*." Then he shrugged and his good humor returned. "Maybe I'll seem smarter after you've had some wine."

Feeling rather spotlighted by the candle-light and the small table, Cooper fidgeted as Nathan clinked his wineglass against hers. Just as she was wondering if his flirtatious demeanor might morph into something more, Nathan served the food and they settled down to eat. To Cooper's relief, their conversation flowed easily. After all, they had shared an interesting day visiting Eliza Weeks and both of them wanted to rehash their experience and speculate further on Jed's disappearance.

"We sure have had an unusual start,"

Nathan began as he offered Cooper another helping of pasta. She declined on more food but gladly accepted another glass of wine, feeling warmed by the meal, the libation, and the company.

However, as she sipped on the fruity vintage, she mulled over Nathan's last remark. "Start . . . ?" she prompted as he tried to maneuver a slippery piece of noodle onto his fork.

"I mean . . ." Nathan cleared his throat. "Most people become friends because they've got something in common. You know, like a job or a hobby or they went to school together." He took a gulp of wine. "But you and I — our friendship has sprung out of trying to exonerate Wesley Hughes. It's kind of a unique bonding experience, wouldn't you say?"

Nodding, Cooper smiled and, made a bit reckless by the wine, said, "I'm really glad I ran into you in the hall at the high school. If I had gotten the right time for the worship service, we might never have met."

"I'll drink to that." Nathan raised his glass. "Here's to being guided by a greater power."

They gently knocked glasses and stared at one another above the flickering candlelight. Suddenly, something shifted in Nathan's brown eyes and his gaze grew more intense. Cooper felt her entire body grow warm and again experienced a prick of guilt. She tried to push thoughts of her ex-boyfriend away. For once, she didn't want her memories of him to invade the present.

"This is nice," Nathan whispered huskily and pushed his plate off to the side. Just as he made a move to reach for Cooper's hand, the kitchen phone rang, shattering the moment as effectively as someone throwing a rock through the window.

Cooper exhaled loudly. She hadn't realized she'd been holding her breath.

Nathan glanced at his watch. "I'm sorry," he said, standing. "Because I host Web sites on my server, I sometimes get client calls at odd times. The server might be down." He moved to the phone and examined the caller ID box beside it. He cast an apologetic look at Cooper. "I've got to take this call. Excuse me."

Picking up the phone, Nathan offered a quick greeting and then asked the caller to hold as he relocated to his office. Cooper drained the rest of her wine, feeling a strange mixture of disappointment and relief that Nathan's attempt to initiate physical contact had been interrupted.

I like Nathan Dexter, she admitted to

herself. *So why am I so nervous?*

Perplexed, Cooper carried their dinner plates to the sink and, as quietly as possible, began to rinse and load them into the dishwasher. When that task was complete and Nathan's office door still remained closed, she handwashed their wineglasses, wiped off the countertops, and put the leftover chicken and pasta in the fridge. All that remained on the table were the linens and the burning candle, which seemed to cast a poignantly lonely reflection in the bay window.

Cooper suddenly felt tired and had no idea what to do next. Should she sit back down and wait for Nathan or should she knock on his office door and signal that she should be heading home? After several minutes of indecision, she strolled over to where the phone sat and, her curiosity overwhelming her sense of decorum, took a surreptitious glance at the caller ID box. The caller was from RichmondMatchmaker.com.

Instantly, Cooper imagined Nathan holed up in his office, chatting with a potential date while his dinner guest cleaned up his kitchen. She felt a surge of irritation and was half-tempted to swat the candle off the table with the back of her hand.

How dare Nathan try to seduce her, and five minutes later field a phone call from a prospective girlfriend? Annoyed as she might be, however, Cooper didn't possess the nerve to barge into Nathan's office and interrupt his conversation, so she settled for blowing out the candle, turning off all the lights in the kitchen, and leaving a terse note thanking him for dinner.

"My mama raised *me* right," Cooper snarled under her breath as she left Nathan's house.

As she drove Cherry-O above the speed limit around the downtown streets in pursuit of an on-ramp for I-95 North, Cooper's indignation lost its edge. She suddenly felt foolish for having rushed out of Nathan's house without saying good-bye.

"But he was rude!" she exclaimed to the portion of her reflection she could see in the rearview mirror. Still, she knew that it was childish to base her actions on someone else's.

Now here she was the following morning on the brink of being late to Bible study because she had indulged in too long a shower. Forgoing any attempts to re-create the way her hair had looked after being cut and styled at the beauty salon, Cooper shrugged into her clothes, slid into Cherry-O, and found herself speeding most of the way to church.

"It's only a matter of time before I get a ticket," she said as she passed a police cruiser staked out on the opposite side of the highway. "I never drove this fast before I quit smoking and went back to church!"

Cooper was the last one to arrive for Bible study. All of the Sunrise members had eaten their "second breakfasts," and were settled in their places, ready to begin the lesson. Nathan immediately tried to catch Cooper's eye and held out his hand to indicate that she should sit next to him, but she pretended not to notice his gesture and sat next to Jake. As she opened her workbook, she remembered too late that she had been using the song written by Quinton as a placeholder.

"Whatcha got there?" Jake leaned over and tried to read the lyrics.

Cooper slammed her book closed, her neck reddening. "It's not mine," she blurted.

"Hey, *I've* used that line a time or two in my life." Jake chuckled and opened a piece of Fruit Chill–flavored Nicorette gum. "Man, this is sure gonna spoil the taste of your banana muffins, Quinton," he said, and popped the gum in his mouth.

232

Relieved that Jake hadn't been more persistent about the song lyrics, Cooper asked, "How's the whole quitting thing going? I have my worst cravings right after supper. That's when I used to sit out on my steps and smoke while I watched the stars come out. Now I just stuff cookies down my throat."

Jake guffawed. "I hear ya, lady. I'm getting fatter and meaner every day. Least that's what my coworkers tell me." He grew thoughtful. "Still, I can climb stairs up folks' houses now without strugglin' for breath, so I'll take that as a good sign."

"The way you're striving to improve yourself has given me that perfect segue for our study today, Jake, thank you." Savannah cleared her throat and the members grew silent. "In chapter four, Paul urges us to 'live a life worthy of the calling.' Then Paul goes on to list the attributes we should all strive to possess if we want to be the best Christians we can be." She traced her hand along the text in her workbook. "Paul asks us to have humility, gentleness, patience, love, and acceptance of one another."

"That last one's the tough one," Jake muttered.

Savannah smiled. "You are so right, Jake. After all, we're not talking about loving and accepting people you *already* like and admire. Paul knows that we can easily love and accept *them,* so he is most likely referring to the folks that drive you crazy! The people that you'd rather shake by the shoulders than pull into an embrace. Does anyone have a person they could try harder to love and accept?" She wiggled her finger in warning. "No names, please."

"One of my former bosses made it clear that he didn't think I had what it took to become a top Realtor," Trish began, her lacquered lips turning down at the corners. "He said that prime listings were a man's job and I'd better stick to selling the 'modest' homes. He tried to make me concentrate on rentals, which provided almost no commission, and handed all the top listings to a guy nicknamed Slick Mick."

"But you showed him, huh?" Bryant chucked Trish in the arm. "You've got a successful realty business of your own now."

"Thank you. Yes, I am a success," Trish responded with uncharacteristic softness. "But when I see this man at conferences or trade shows, I still feel like I've got something to prove. I still feel insignificant around him. The idea of loving and accepting him, well, that would be a *real* challenge."

"At least you showed him what you're made of, and you can bet he's noticed," Jake commented in admiration. "The person I've got a hard time feelin' love for is my pop. He left when I was four and we haven't heard a peep from him since. I've never had a chance for him to be proud of me for anything."

Savannah reached out and found Jake's trembling hand. She clasped it in her own. "That must have been hard."

Jake's eyes grew glassy, but he shook his head and blinked back the tears. "But he's still my father and I might forgive him, if he ever gave me the chance." Jake chewed furiously on his gum and fell silent.

Savannah shared how it was challenging to accept one of her sons-in-law. "He says nasty things about my work — whispers them into my daughter's ear while I'm in the room — as if I were deaf, not blind." She took a sip of coffee. "I just hope he doesn't belittle her about the work she does."

"That strikes a chord with me," Nathan said quickly. "I've got a bad vibe about this guy my sister's dating. He seems to drink a lot and I've heard him yelling at her in the background while we're talking on the phone."

"Are you concerned about abuse?" Quinton inquired gently.

Nathan shrugged. "I think my sister would tell me if things had turned violent, but she's just such a great kid and deserves much, much better. I'm struggling with loving the man she says she loves. In fact, I wish they'd break up. I know it's not very charitable of me, but it's the truth."

"At least you've got issues with someone from the present," Quinton grumbled. "I'm still trying to get over all the kids who made fun of me for being fat. I mean, we're talking about being taunted in school halls almost twenty years ago." He turned one of the rings on his finger around and around. "I try to imagine meeting one of those kids now that we're grown-ups. I visualize approaching them with an offering of friendship and just letting go of all the bad memories and starting fresh." He smiled and his chubby face folded into a series of charming dimples. "It makes me feel good to imagine that."

Savannah nodded. "That's a terrific example of making an effort to love and accept our less-than-favorite people. You've inspired us, Quinton. Thank you. Anyone else?"

Bryant twiddled his silver pen back and

forth in his right hand. "There's a nurse at my mama's rest home. I do not like the woman. She treats all the residents like they're bothering her and they should all just end their days sitting quietly in front of the TV." He put down the pen. "But listening to you guys made me realize something. This woman may have her own story of hurt or loss. Maybe someone did her a great enough wrong that it's been eating her up, making her a meaner person than she really wants to be. What if I did something nice for her? Brought her flowers? Wrote her a note about how much I appreciated her caring for my mother? It might turn her around a bit. Maybe all she needs is for someone to express some kindness." He thumped his desk enthusiastically. "I'm going to give it a shot!"

The members murmured their approval. Cooper was impressed by Bryant's insight and was once again embarrassed for judging him by how he appeared on television — vain and vapid.

Smoothing a lock of heavily gelled blond hair, Bryant turned to face her. "What about you, Cooper?"

Cooper was ready to tell her friends about her unusual looks. "I've spent a long time letting go of a grudge against the girl who caused my accident." She touched the lid of her green eye and fingered the curved pink scar beneath her brow. "It happened during our field hockey practice. She was showing off for this boy she wanted to impress, so when she hit me, it was because she wasn't paying attention." She looked back at Bryant. "I stopped going to church with my family because I didn't want the folks there who knew me before the accident to see what I looked like afterward. For some reason, I felt like I must have deserved what had happened to me and they'd all recognize that, I don't know . . . I'd been marked. I've only prayed a couple of times out in my greenhouse since then. That is, until I met you all. Now I'm praying like a madwoman."

Cooper smiled and then picked up her pen and examined the silver lettering written along the base, twisting it back and forth beneath the light so that the letters twinkled. "It wasn't until I was in my twenties, after I got used to how I looked, that I started thinking that the young woman whose eye I was given . . . She was in a much more serious accident than me." She dropped her gaze to her workbook and watched the black words blur. "She died," she whispered. "And any time I've stared at myself in the mirror and not liked what I saw, I remember the gift that stranger gave me. It took a while, but eventually I knew that I couldn't be angry at the girl who did this to me. I guess I felt it would be a lousy way of showing my gratitude for having not lost my sight."

For a moment, the room was silent. Quinton took a bite of a glazed cruller and stared at Cooper. "Well, I think you probably see more clearly now that you almost lost your vision. Look how well Savannah sees without her eyes." He sighed. "I wish I had more insight. I've been reading Brooke's document over and over again, looking for more clues, and am coming up dry."

"Cooper found more scraps from Brooke's copier," Nathan announced proudly as the worship music commenced. "We can see if any of the pieces fit after the service."

"I would have brought them to you sooner," Cooper hurriedly added, "but you didn't answer your phone."

"Business trip," Quinton replied with regret. "I'm sorry. I'd much rather have been working to find Brooke's killer."

"It was only a few days," Trish consoled Quinton. "Let's get pizza at Chianti and we'll get right to work. I've been craving a slice of feta, red roasted tomatoes, and kalamata olives all week."

The group agreed and made their way to the chapel. Savannah took Nathan's arm and Cooper trailed along behind the rest of them. As they headed in the direction of the music, Quinton stepped into the men's room. Pretending to have left something behind in their study classroom, Cooper loitered outside the bathroom until he emerged. She then held out the piece of paper bearing his song lyrics.

"I've been looking for the chance to give this back to you," she said hastily. "You dropped it during the service last week and I wanted to return it when you were alone, but . . ." She trailed off, hoping he'd accept her excuse without questioning why she had kept it for so long.

Without looking at her, Quinton accepted the paper, folded it into a small square, and tucked it inside his suit jacket. "Did you read it?" he whispered nervously.

Cooper squeezed his arm and smiled encouragingly. "I thought it was lovely."

Quinton's face glowed. "Really?"

"Really."

"I scribble lyrics all the time. They just pop into my head." He sighed happily. "Someday, I'd love to get them set to music. Who knows, maybe even have one sung at church."

They began to walk down the hall. "Well, I'd sure love to hear those words come to life," Cooper said and then the two of them joined their friends for worship.

Nathan made sure that he pulled into Chianti's parking lot right behind Cooper. As she opened Cherry-O's door, he dashed around Sweet Pea and grabbed her door before she could close it.

"I just wanted to apologize for last night," he said, his breath coming quickly. "It was incredibly rude of me to stay on the phone for so long. It was a client of mine. One of those people you can't interrupt because they talk without stopping for breath." He paused and uttered a goofy chuckle. "Kind of like I'm doing right now. But I'm really sorry. I was having such a great time with you too."

As much as Cooper wanted to avoid any feelings of discomfort with a member of her Bible study, she couldn't help wondering why Nathan was lying to her. How could he call a woman from his Internet dating service a client? She looked at his pleasant face and his smiling eyes and wondered how he could be so duplicitous.

"And thanks for cleaning up," he continued, oblivious to her irritation. "I'd really like to show you how sorry I am by taking you out to dinner. I'll lock my cell phone in the car and you can leave the dishwashing to the restaurant employees. Pick any place you'd like to go. What do you say?"

Before Cooper could give Nathan a negative reply, Quinton heaved himself out of a cream-colored Cadillac. He walked over to Cooper and said, "I stopped by a CVS and picked up some glue. Do you mind if I see if those scraps of paper you found will fit anywhere on our document before we eat?" His cheeks turned a bit pink. "I know it's silly, but I feel like I've got a good shot at making sense of that thing since it's about financial matters."

Cooper handed over the plastic bag containing the minute shreds. "It's all yours."

"Terrific!" Quinton beamed. "Now let's go order. I'm getting their Italian combo pie: mushrooms, pepperoni, sausage, pepper, and onions. That'll fill a man's stomach."

Cooper's belly growled in agreement and the threesome entered the casual eatery. Bryant and Jake pushed two square tables together to form a rectangle. As a group, they ordered four different pies, including the Mediterranean White that Trish had wanted and the Italian pie that Quinton had longed for, along with pitchers of sweet tea and soda.

"I've finally got something worthy to contribute to our investigation," Savannah announced once the waitress had distributed the drinks and plastic tumblers filled with ice. Quinton was too busy gluing to bother looking up from his work.

"That's good news," Trish answered. "I hope you can shed some light on at least one of our two mysteries."

Savannah turned toward Nathan. "When you called me Friday night, you said that Brooke's assistant claimed that Brooke and Wesley had fought just before she was killed, right?"

"Yes," Nathan agreed. "Cindi said that the Hugheses had an argument on the phone, but she didn't know what it was about. Cooper and I didn't believe her, but we couldn't think of how to press her any further."

"That's just fine, because Brooke's librarian friend, Deanna, knew all about their quarrel. The subject of the fight was Caleb, their son."

Trish clucked her tongue. "Parents do tend to argue about their children. Which school should they go to? Which friends should they have? Do they look good in yellow? All sorts of things."

Savannah waited patiently for Trish to stop talking. "Caleb is a graduate student at Georgetown University. At least he was. This is his second year of business school, but he'd been doing so poorly in his classes that he dropped out without telling his parents."

"Oh, man!" Quinton exclaimed. "My folks would have killed me."

"There's more," Savannah continued. "The reason behind his slipping grades was purely alcohol-related. Caleb finally came clean with his daddy and Wesley checked him into a treatment center two days before Brooke was killed. He didn't want to tell Brooke until after their anniversary celebration, but Caleb called Brooke at work and opened up about everything."

"So Brooke was mad at Wesley for trying to protect her from hurtful news? I don't get that. He was trying to keep her from being upset, so why was she ticked off?" Bryant's tone was judgmental.

"Caleb is Brooke's son too!" Trish countered heatedly, narrowing her eyes at Bryant. "No mother wants to be kept from knowing what's going on in her children's lives. Keeping secrets is not the way parenting . . .

or marriages work," she added pointedly.

"All right already!" Nathan declared as their pizzas arrived. Cooper didn't know if he was exclaiming over the sumptuous pies or Bryant and Trish's exchange. "I hope we haven't misjudged Wesley Hughes. I'm surprised he would keep something so serious from his wife."

"We haven't misjudged anyone," Savannah said soothingly. "Deanna said that Brooke and Wesley rarely fought and that they had already patched things up within hours of the argument over the phone. Wesley made a poor choice, but his motives were pure. According to Deanna, the Hugheses were the type of couple that truly never went to bed angry."

"Well, good for them, but what are we gonna do now?" Jake demanded.

"I believe Cindi's an integral part of our investigation." Nathan looked at Cooper for approval. She nodded. "I think she knows who Hazel is, but since she's already involved with a married man, trying to flirt information out of her isn't going to work."

"How about some female bonding?" Bryant suggested.

Trish examined her hands. "You're onto something there, Mr. Weatherman. Did either of you happen to notice whether she was wearing nail polish?"

Nathan shrugged helplessly, but Cooper remembered the pink polish on Cindi's nails. "Yes. Her nails were bubble-gum pink and perfectly even."

"Women talk to women they don't know at nail salons." Trish clicked her own acrylic beauties together. "I've heard some *pretty* intimate details shared between ladies over a full set. If someone else can follow her around for a bit to see when she goes to her regular nail place, then I can drop in on her when she's getting a manicure and start a friendly chat. I'm sure I can think of a way to bring up dear Hazel."

"I can tail her," Nathan volunteered, "since I work on my own schedule. I can catch up on job-related stuff at night."

Jake bit into a slice of grilled chicken pizza. With his mouth stuffed to the brim he muttered, "Lucky dog. Wish I had my own schedule, but backed-up septic systems wait for no man."

"I think you should come too," Trish told Cooper after casting Jake a look of disgust. Cooper noticed that Quinton had barely touched his lunch. He was too busy meticulously gluing the paper scraps into place.

"Count me out on the nail salon detail," Cooper argued. "She's seen me before."

"Only in your uniform, right?" Trish argued. "And if you're getting a pedicure, you can listen in to our talk and signal me if I've missed anything. She'll never know you're there."

Cooper twirled a piece of mozzarella around her finger, thinking how ridiculous it was for her to have her toes polished and painted. Only family members saw her toes if she was wearing a pair of sandals on a summer weekend. With the exception of Ashley, none of the Lee clan would care if she had bunions, warts, hangnails, or electric green polish on her toes. Cooper couldn't think of a bigger waste of time or money and frankly, she didn't relish the idea of someone touching her feet. Wearing work boots and heavy socks five days a week didn't make for soft heels and toes.

"I don't know . . ." she began, but never got to finish her sentence.

"I've got it!" Quinton put down his tube of glue and shot to a standing position. Then, just as quickly, he sat back down, expelling a loud breath. "Hazel's last name is Wharton. Hazel Wharton. Lady, we've found you at last!"

Bryant pushed back his chair. "I'll go ask our waitress for a phone book!"

The Sunrise members were on the edge

of their seats as Bryant traced a long and graceful finger down the list of Whartons in the white pages. "Here she is!" he hollered in jubilation and whipped out his cell phone.

"What are you going to say to her?" Savannah asked, concerned.

Bryant waved her off, forgetting that she probably couldn't see his dismissive gesture. A few seconds passed before he snapped his cell phone closed and his broad shoulders sagged in defeat.

"So much for discovering the riddle called Hazel Wharton." He sank into his chair. "We're at another dead end. Hazel's number's been disconnected."

11

Before a girl's turn came to go in to King Xerxes, she had to complete twelve months of beauty treatments prescribed for the women, six months with oil of myrrh and six with perfumes and cosmetics.

Esther 2:12 (NIV)

"I have been beside myself trying to figure out what your message on my answering machine meant," Ashley declared late Monday afternoon.

Cooper had just returned from exercising Columbus and was surprised to see her younger sister pacing back and forth in front of the hawk's cage, her ice-pick heels clicking on the blue flagstones. Uncrossing her arms over a silky fuchsia crewneck, Ashley whipped off a pair of tortoiseshell sunglasses with oversized lenses and focused her cerulean gaze on her sister.

"Your message said that you had *a mis-*

sion for me. Well?" She flicked her glasses against her hip impatiently. "What is it?"

After settling Columbus back in his aviary, Cooper stripped off her father's leather gloves and motioned for her sister to follow her to her apartment. "Come on up, I've got to wash my hands anyway." Eyeing Ashley's stylish ensemble, Cooper asked, "You going someplace special?"

Ashley smiled. "Lincoln's taking me to dinner, but he had to work late so he's going to meet me at Little Venice, that darling little Italian restaurant we love." She issued a smug sigh. "I relish all these romantic dinners, but I'm going to be at the gym *all* week if I order pasta *and* tiramisu."

Following Cooper over to the sink, Ashley fixed an appraising gaze on her sister's face. "Have you been plucking your own brows?"

Cooper's neck flushed and she ran her fingers over her brows as though she were touching every strand of dark blond hair. "Yes, but how can you tell?"

"How can I *tell*?" Ashley threw her arms out in mock horror. "Probably because it looks like Daddy went after you with a miniature Weed Whacker, that's all!"

Examining her reflection in the toaster, Cooper repeatedly traced her brows with her fingers. "I guess they're a bit uneven, but I was distracted when I was plucking and just kind of kept going."

Ashley sank down at the small kitchen table. "Just leave your brows to the professionals, Coop. Even the best of us can't do a perfect arch." She kept staring at her sister.

Setting two glasses of fresh lemonade on the table, Cooper sat down opposite Ashley. "Speaking of appointments . . . are you planning on having your nails done this week?"

Ashley spread out her graceful fingers and examined the petal-pink polish on her rounded nails. "Probably on Thursday. I like them to look fresh for my tennis league practice on Friday."

Even though Cooper considered the notion of having nice nails in order to prepare for a sporting event rather absurd, she nodded as though she understood completely. "Would you be willing to go to a different nail salon for the sake of aiding us in our investigation?"

Ashley's face grew animated. "Do you have a lead?"

After taking a sip of the tart lemonade, Cooper gave Ashley a summary of meeting Cindi, visiting Eliza, and the possible significance of Hazel Wharton, whose whereabouts were still unknown.

"Seems like you and Nathan are really bonding over this whole detective thing." Ashley winked at her sister. "Seen any action yet?"

Cooper stirred her lemonade. "So far, we've had dinner. That's it. Dinner. But let's not get off subject, Ashley. I need you to 'bump into' Cindi and find out where and when she gets her nails done. Once we know that, Trish is going to try to finagle some info about Hazel from her, though only the Lord knows how she plans to do that." Cooper hesitated. "I can tell you where she works and what her car looks like, so you might have to tail her and it may take more than one try. After all, she's got two kids and might drive straight home from work to be with them."

"If she's got two kids," Ashley argued, "she's got to go to the grocery store. If not there, then Blockbuster or the library, or heck, straight from Capital City to the liquor store. The working moms *I* know seem to be pretty stressed out these days. They've all got a Superwoman complex." Ashley wiped her hand across Cooper's table as though checking for crumbs. "She'll stop somewhere and that's when I'll find out about her salon. You can count on me."

Relieved, Cooper poured her sister more

lemonade. "Are you sure you're not too busy to commit to this?"

Ashley tossed a golden lock behind her shoulder. "I *do* have several important meetings this week, but since I'm the chairwoman of three benefits, I can leave the meetings a little early if necessary." She raised her glass and eyed Cooper over the rim. "I'll trail Cindi in exchange for the answer to two simple questions."

"And what would they be?" Cooper asked suspiciously, handing her sister a piece of paper containing a map of Capital City's campus, a physical description of Cindi, and a photo of an older Honda Civic that Cooper had printed off CarMax's Web site.

Ashley accepted the paper and leaned forward, her gold necklace with its diamond cross pendant clinking against the glass tumbler. "The first question is this: Did Nathan kiss you at the end of your dinner date?"

Cooper shook her head. "It wasn't a date. And he didn't try," she lied, recalling the moment at Nathan's house when he had pushed his plate aside and reached out for her hand. If the phone hadn't rung, it was possible that their clasping of hands might have led to a kiss. Nathan had certainly been looking at her as if he wanted to kiss her.

"Yoo-hoo!" Ashley waved her hands in front of Cooper's face. "I guess I don't need to ask you my second question. I can see the answer to *that* one written all over your face."

Scowling, Cooper removed the tumblers from the table and placed them in the sink. "And what was your *second* question?" she said more sharply than she had intended.

Ashley stood and tucked a banana-shaped purse under her arm. "If you wanted to kiss him. Clearly," she added complacently, "the idea is floating around inside that head of yours."

After reapplying a frosty pink lipstick and checking her flawless complexion in the mirror in Cooper's bathroom, Ashley opened the apartment door. "I'll phone you as soon as I've got the information," she said in a raspy bass voice, and then giggled at her attempt to sound like a tough guy. "By the time I've called you back, I expect to hear that you've been to the salon." She pointed at Cooper's brows. "If you and Nathan are going to start smooching, he's going to see your face *verrrry* close up."

Nathan was relieved that Ashley had agreed

to tail Cindi, as one of his client's Web pages had been invaded by a nasty computer virus and it would take him at least two days to straighten it out.

"Those Trojan horse viruses can be downright malicious," Nathan told Cooper. "They chew up files in the hard drive like a garbage truck. I would never have been able to follow Cindi around and fix this problem. Thank your sister for me."

Cooper promised to do so. "Sounds like you've got your work cut out for you. Is the client going to lose business because of the virus?"

"They already have," Nathan replied, sounding glum. "And it's one of my biggest accounts. In fact, this was the client who interrupted our dinner Saturday night. I had to test the firewall then, because they were already experiencing some glitches on the site."

For once, Cooper sat very still. "Who's the client, if you don't mind me asking?"

"RichmondMatchmaker.com," Nathan said. "But they won't be clients for much longer if I don't get this issue resolved. I'd better run. Good luck with Cindi and call me later if you find anything out. *I'll* be the guy stuck inside on this gorgeous day."

Placing her cell phone on the work van's

dashboard, Cooper sank back against the seat and looked outside at what was truly a glorious afternoon. The creamy white dogwood blossoms lining Make It Work!'s parking lot were giving way to verdant leaves. The meticulously pruned branches of the native trees cast gentle shadows upon clusters of vibrant pink petunias and lush groupings of variegated liriope grass. Landscapers had just finished removing spent daffodils and pansies from the beds and were sprinkling a few inches of dark, rich mulch around the base of the new plants, which stood a better chance of thriving in the hot and humid Virginia summer.

"He didn't lie to me," Cooper said aloud as she turned on the van's engine. She glanced up at the cloudless sky and watched an airplane cut a white swath through the blue. "Lord, when am I going to stop judging people in such haste? Would you please help me work on that one before I alienate all of my new friends?"

Cooper finished her last job repairing a temperamental copier at a pediatrician's office with a feeling of anticipation. Within the next hour, Ashley would be spying on Cindi's Honda Civic in the Capital City parking lot. Cooper hoped that Cindi was still parking near Building F, as she remembered the administrative assistant telling Nathan that she had been relocated to another division. If she had already moved, her car could be anywhere, and Ashley wouldn't drive around endlessly in her white convertible Lexus coupe.

As it was, there was already a good possibility that Ashley was zipping around Capital City with the convertible top retracted, the latest *American Idol* soundtrack booming through the car's powerful speakers, and her blond hair held in check by a costly designer scarf. And since she believed that most women dressed their best every day of their lives (with the exception of her own family members), she wouldn't have the foggiest notion that her beauty would attract unnecessary attention. But Cooper knew that once the Capital City employees clocked out and headed to their cars to enjoy the remainder of the perfect spring day, it would be difficult not to notice a lovely blond in a sleek and expensive sports car.

After parking the van, Cooper went inside the office, spent a few minutes cleaning her tools, and then changed out of her uniform into a pair of jeans and a paprika-colored T-shirt, just in case Cindi should choose to get her nails done that very afternoon. As she was rinsing out her coffee mug in the employee kitchen, Ben limped in, sighing and groaning as though he carried the weight of the world on his shoulders.

"Rough workout at the gym?" Cooper inquired, seeing how he favored his left leg.

Ben blinked, as though surprised not to find himself alone in the room. "You could say that," he muttered and removed a canned protein shake from the fridge. He popped the can open and began to drink in loud, desperate gulps.

While he was drinking, Cooper examined Ben's thin frame. He didn't look like he had put on much weight over the past few months, but his arms did seem more developed than they had over the winter.

"I think you're bulking up a bit, Ben," she complimented him in hopes of making him smile.

It didn't work. He dunked his empty shake can into the garbage with unnecessary force and wiped his lips with a paper towel. Cooper noticed that his hands seemed to be shaking slightly.

"You going to the gym now?" she asked as he turned away.

"Anywhere but home. There's no room for anyone there if his name ain't Jim Beam or Johnnie Walker." And with that, Ben stalked out of the break room.

Cooper was still trying to digest what was behind Ben's remark when her cell phone rang. It was Ashley.

"I did it!" she shouted exuberantly. "Cindi was *so* easy to spot. I mean, she's got good taste in clothes, but she just doesn't know how to put the pieces together! She was wearing chartreuse and black, which is a great combination, but with these beige slingback pumps and an off-white hobo purse. If she had only —"

"Ashley!" Cooper interjected before her sister could launch into an in-depth analysis of Cindi Rolfing's outfit. "Did you get a chance to speak to her?"

"I sure did. She only went to one store, a place called Wine Lovers off Ridgefield. She spent a long while picking out a Pinot Noir. I broke the ice by recommending a bottle of Castle Rock. I remember you telling me she was a single mom so I figured she wouldn't want to spend more than twenty dollars, so I was mighty surprised when she decided on a bottle of Acacia for more than twice the price of the Castle Rock."

Cooper fought to contain her impatience as Ashley rambled on about how Lincoln had helped her develop a more sophisticated palate. "The nails, Ashley?"

"Oh, I'm just having a bit of fun, Cooper." Ashley was capable of injecting a fat-lipped pout into her voice when she wanted to. "I thought you might be interested in the fact that her clothes, her wine, and that two-thousand-dollar Tiffany bracelet she's wearing seem doggone fancy for a secretary."

"I told you about her and the married man," Cooper reminded her.

"Well, *he* must be doing all right, that's for sure," Ashley stated with a trace of admiration. "Anyway, that's the end of my little story. Cindi uses a really nice nail place in Short Pump Mall, right near Macy's. She's got an appointment at five-thirty tomorrow for a full set." She paused. "Go on, tell me that I'm a genius!"

Cooper frowned. "What's a full set? Trish mentioned it the other day and I have no idea what that means."

"Oh, for goodness' sake, Coop. Do you live under a rock beneath a layer of concrete? A full set refers to having acrylic nails applied over your natural nails. They're resilient and polish lasts *much* longer on them." Cooper could hear Ashley's garage door creaking open. "Personally, I prefer to get weekly manicures and show off the healthy state of my own nails, but *I'm* very dedicated when it comes to applying cuticle cream and taking vitamin E and keratin pills every day. *Some* people don't spend as much time as they need to on their appearance."

Annoyed, Cooper took the bait. "*Some* people have jobs." She immediately relented. "Listen, thank you, Ashley. You found out exactly what we needed to know. Now Trish can do her thing."

"You're welcome. And I'd volunteer to come along, but it would look kind of strange if I showed up at the salon when Cindi does. Plus, I've got my Roofs Overhead committee meeting. My committee is holding a black-tie fundraiser to buy a home in Church Hill for a needy family. That means another dress for me!" Ashley turned off her car engine. "I'm home, Coop, but let me give you a teeny piece of advice before you get a pedicure tomorrow."

Cooper's stomach lurched at the thought. "What?"

"Shave your legs," Ashley ordered. "People at the salon are going to see them all the way to your knobby knees, so don't gross them out."

"I shave my legs, Ashley. Regularly, in fact," Cooper responded crossly.

"Small miracles *do* happen," Ashley retorted, giggling. "I can't wait to hear what color you pick. There's a really nice OPI rose shade called Aphrodite's Pink Nightie. Might get you in the right mood for your next encounter with Nathan."

"I think I can handle picking out my own polish, thanks," Cooper muttered, though the last time she had used polish on her toes had to be three summers ago. It had only taken two days for it to chip off beneath her work boots, so she hadn't bothered to paint her toes since, and she had never had a pedicure at a professional nail salon.

Over the phone, Cooper could hear Ashley enter her house and dump her car keys on a table. "If you're really feeling daring, there's the Australia collection. You can get Tasmanian Devil Made Me Do It. Who knows? You might want to drive right over to Nathan's, show him your toes, and some *other* body parts."

"Good-bye, Ashley!" Cooper shouted and hung up to the sound of her sister's laughter.

"Finally, I can *do* something useful to help!" Trish exclaimed when Cooper phoned her at home to tell her about Cindi's nail appointment. "Ever since Wesley was jailed, I've been listening and puzzling, but not performing any *real* service. I can't wait to use my people skills on this little lamb."

"I'd consider Cindi more wolf than sheep," Cooper cautioned. "And I'm glad I won't be in your shoes, 'cause I don't think it's going to be easy to get information out of her."

"Leave it to me," Trish stated with confidence. "I'll expect to see you in one of the pedicure chairs by the time Cindi and I arrive at five-thirty."

Cooper saluted the phone. "Yes, ma'am!"

At five-ten that Wednesday afternoon, Cooper stepped inside the nail salon and was welcomed by the soft instrumental music of flutes blended with recordings of waves breaking. A group of lovely young Asian women immediately looked up from their work and said, "Hello!" while an older woman, who was likely the only worker in the room weighing over one hundred and ten pounds, approached the tidy reception podium and smiled.

"Can I help you?"

Cooper nodded. "I have an appointment for a pedicure for five-fifteen."

The woman traced a crimson nail down the length of an appointment book. Her finger came to rest on an indiscernible scribble. Without asking for Cooper's name, she said, "Yes. Come this way, please."

"Minnie will do your pedicure," the older

Asian woman informed Cooper, pointing to a petite Asian girl who looked no older than seventeen. Minnie gave a low bow and began to fill the pedicure tub with water. She then sprinkled some green powder into the bath and put a hand on a padded leather seat attached to the tub unit, indicating that Cooper should sit down. Slightly embarrassed by her footwear, Cooper removed her work shoes and thick, white ankle socks and climbed into the luxurious chair.

"Water okay?" Minnie asked her.

"Great," Cooper answered, her feet pleasantly shocked by the bubbles churning up the water.

"You pick a color?" Minnie looked around, frowning.

Cooper shook her head. She hadn't realized that she needed to choose a shade before the pedicure began. "Would you choose one for me?"

Minnie nodded, pleased. She gathered her shining cascade of blue-black hair, twisted it fiercely in one hand, and pinned it up with a clip using the other hand. "You soak," she directed, turned off the tap, and then pointed at a neat stack of magazines alongside Cooper's chair. "We got new *People*. All about Katie Holmes and Tom Cruise daughter. She so cute," she added and then walked off toward the chrome wall shelf containing dozens of shades of nail polish.

Cooper decided that having a magazine available to obscure her face from Cindi's view was a good idea, so she selected the most recent edition of *Vogue* from the thick pile of fashion magazines. Taking note of the gorgeous brunette on the cover, modeling one of summer's trendy strapless tank dresses, Cooper flipped the magazine open to a page issuing advice to women on recovering from an unexpected breakup. She read a few lines of the advice, satisfied that she had already followed several of the writer's sensible suggestions, including creating a fresh circle of friends. However, Cooper was too distracted by the perfume ad on the opposite page to read any further.

The ad for Bondage showed a woman draped along the length of a couch clad in a gold dress so clingy and sheer that she might as well have worn nothing at all. She also wore a thick gold necklace resembling a collar, and a bracelet that reminded Cooper of a manacle. Her hair was a glossy dark brown and her eyes were a frosty blue. A white tiger knelt at her feet, wearing a gold collar similar to the model's necklace. Its fangs were bared and its blue eyes were almost the same shade as her mistress's. A man dressed in nothing but a white towel knelt by the woman's head, offering her a bottle of perfume on a gilt tray. His muscular body was hairless and glistened, as though he had rolled in cooking oil before the shoot. He too wore a gold collar that matched the tiger's, but his eyes were closed, as though in a state of worship.

For a moment, Cooper saw the male model as Drew, who offered her a glass of champagne as she lounged on a sofa, listening to him repeatedly beg for forgiveness and profess his love. But Drew's face wavered, only to be replaced by Nathan's. Her pulse immediately quickened and Cooper fantasized about him pulling her body against his for a passionate kiss. With eyes closed, she took a deep sniff of the perfumed strip enclosed in the magazine and instantly recoiled. To her, Bondage smelled like some of the natural pesticides she and her father used in their garden.

"You no like color?" Minnie sounded hurt.

Cooper shut the magazine and flushed. "Sorry. I didn't know you were back." She took the bottle of polish Minnie held out in her childlike hand. It was a brownish pink called Dulce de Leche. "It's perfect," Cooper told Minnie. "Thank you."

Offering a tiny bow and smile, Minnie

returned to her black stool by Cooper's feet and pulled a wheeled tray closer to her side. Nervously, Cooper noted an assortment of sharp metal objects lying on the tray. The only nonthreatening tool she saw was a fat emery board.

Minnie raised a pair of clippers and prepared to clip Cooper's big toe, but the second the metal connected with Cooper's body, she jerked her foot away. Minnie looked up at her in surprise. "You no want cut down?"

"It tickles!" Cooper laughed. "Sorry, this is my first time. I'll try to sit still."

Minnie smiled. "Oh, you like it. It no hurt. I take good care of you."

"I'm sure you will." Relaxing, Cooper reopened the magazine and glanced at her watch. Ten minutes to go until Cindi would appear. Cooper wondered if it had been a good idea to show up five minutes early for her appointment. What if Minnie finished before Cindi and Trish even arrived? Why, she wondered to herself, did the Lees always have to be five minutes early for everything?

Cooper winced as Minnie removed the dead skin around her toes with sharp cuticle nippers. Unintentionally, Cooper's foot twitched and squirmed as the aggressive metal tool took little nibbles of flesh from her toes.

"Is okay." Minnie withheld her tools for a moment. "Nobody likes this part."

Next, Minnie pulled Cooper's foot off the padded bench at the end of the pedicure tub and retrieved another tool that closely resembled a torture device belonging to a dentist or perhaps a government spy. "What's that?" Cooper asked with a trace of alarm as Minnie pivoted the tool and pointed at the razor blade fastened to the handle.

"Take off thick skin. Ah . . . what you call calluses," Minnie explained. "It no hurt." She began to stroke the bottom of Cooper's foot.

Cooper fidgeted in her chair. "That tickles too!" she declared, laughing out loud.

Just as Minnie took a firmer hold of Cooper's foot, Cindi walked through the door. Cooper could see that Trish was only seconds behind the secretary. In fact, Cindi had to hold the door open for her. Trish thanked Cindi and then immediately asked her where she had purchased her handbag. By the time they were seated side-by-side, the two women were in the midst of an animated exchange regarding their favorite Richmond boutiques.

Cooper raised her magazine to partially

block her face and watched Cindi and Trish. She was so absorbed in their instant camaraderie that she barely noticed Minnie scraping away skin from her other foot. Before she knew it, Minnie had rinsed Cooper's feet and pulled the plug in the tub.

As the water disappeared down the drain, Cooper grew worried. Trish hadn't even begun to interrogate Cindi. "Am I done already?"

"No. We at good part now," Minnie said, brandishing a bottle of pink lotion. "You sit back and relax. I turn on chair for you."

Minnie reached for a remote control dangling from the side of Cooper's chair and pressed two buttons. Immediately, the cushions behind Cooper's back began to churn in a soft, motorized purr. Leaning deeper into the chair, Cooper sighed as the padded knobs circled around her back. She watched Minnie as the skilled technician squirted a line of pink lotion on Cooper's left leg and then spread the cream from her kneecap to the tips of her toes. Cooper closed her eyes as Minnie began to rub and knead the muscles of her calf.

The combination of the chair massage and leg rub caused Cooper to slide into a state of deep relaxation. The magazine slipped from her lap and onto the floor and her thoughts began to wander. As her breathing slowed and Minnie pressed her powerful thumbs into the aching arches of Cooper's feet, she suddenly had a vision of Nathan, hard at work at home, surrounded by his beloved Star Wars figures.

He keeps popping into my head! she marveled as her shoulders sagged deeper into the chair.

"It feel good?" Minnie asked, pleased.

Cooper's eyes opened lazily and she suddenly remembered that she was supposed to be listening to the conversation between Trish and Cindi. "Yes, it *really* does. You're very strong, Minnie. I think you've found muscles in my calves I didn't know I had," she told the young technician and reclaimed her magazine from the floor.

The noise of the drills hovering over Cindi and Trish's nails had ceased, and the sound of the women's laughter filled the void. With the exception of a client receiving a manicure, Trish, Cindi, and Cooper were the only patrons in the salon.

"I had the most *annoying* client," Trish was saying loud enough for Cooper to hear. "She called me *all* the time. At home, at work, on my cell. Seriously. I couldn't even get my roots touched up in peace!" Trish flicked her violet eyes in Cooper's direction, as if to alert her conspirator that she was about to get to the heart of the matter with Cindi.

"You're *so* lucky to be an administrative assistant," Trish gushed when she had completed her tirade. "When your day is done, it's done. No one's calling *you* at all hours."

Cindi clearly didn't like being one-upped. She frowned. "Oh, I've had my share of jackasses pesterin' me. This one crazy lady called *every* day for over two months. I'd tell her over and over that there was no problem with her credit card statement, but she wouldn't believe me. Finally, I gave her a number to call my boyfriend over in the IT department and I thought I had finally gotten rid of her."

"What happened?" Trish asked, her fascination only slightly exaggerated.

Cindi looked pleased to have completely captivated Trish's attention with her story. "She actually showed up at my desk with her bill and, get this, an old adding machine! She started adding up her charges right there and then and demanding to see my boss! What a fruitcake!"

Trish uttered a shallow laugh. "She must have been nuts, all right. Did she look like she was *on something?*" Trish lowered her voice. "You know, like *drugs?*"

"Oh no." Cindi waved off the suggestion just as her nail technician tried to apply the first coat of polish. She scowled, but Cindi didn't notice. "She was a tiny, old black woman with glasses as thick as my wrist. I have more designer purses than little ol' Hazel has teeth," she added cruelly.

Trish pretended to shiver at the image, but Cooper knew that the mention of Hazel's name was what had startled her. "What did she want?"

Cindi's face immediately clouded over. "Oh, the usual complaint," she said disinterestedly. "But I know she just didn't want to pay her bill. That's what it always comes down to. I never actually listened to her crazy idea about what was wrong with her statement and I called security as soon as she started yelling at me and shaking her adding machine in my face. Can you imagine?"

"You poor thing!" Trish exclaimed and patted Cindi's thin arm. "And that was that? She never bothered you again?"

Cindi shrugged. "I think she called one more time, but after that she must have given up." She sighed. "What a relief. Her account's closed anyway, so she's got nothing more to complain to *me* about."

"Wow, she must have really gotten mad to have canceled her card. I don't know *what* I'd do without my credit card!" Trish looked horrified by the possibility.

"Me either!" Cindi agreed. "Especially with two kids. They need something *all* the time. New shoes, new coats, sports equipment. More, more, more. They're always asking me to buy something, like I'm some kind of walking ATM."

Trish frowned in bewilderment. "Exactly. So I can't see how that woman could cancel her card. Everyone knows Capital City has the best interest rates."

Smugly, Cindi nodded in agreement. "We *are* the best. But she didn't cancel her card; someone in *our* company canceled it for her. Had to be a bigwig. Lord knows *I* don't have that much power."

Trish and Cooper exchanged glances and then Cooper looked down at her feet. Minnie was applying a topcoat of clear polish over two thick coats of *Dulce de Leche.*

"They're really nice," she told Minnie, surprised at the result. She liked both the shade and the neatness of her evenly filed toenails.

"You have other shoes?" Minnie pointed at Cooper's work boots. "Sandals?"

"I hadn't thought of that," Cooper admitted in dismay. "Will my toes get messed up if I put them back in my shoes?"

Minnie nodded. "We give you some," she assured her client and walked to the back of the salon. By the time she returned with a pair of yellow foam flip-flops, Trish and Cindi had relocated to a new set of chairs stationed at a machine that seemed to dry wet nails using an ultraviolet light.

"Oh, I'm going to my boyfriend's Little League game tomorrow night. He's a coach," Cooper heard Cindi saying as Minnie slipped on the foam flip-flops.

"Me too!" Trish declared. "A good friend of mine is an assistant coach. How funny. Which field is your boyfriend's team playing on?"

"Oh, one of those Tuckahoe fields. There are like twelve of them, so I always have to ask someone where his team is." Cindi abruptly stood up to leave, clearly not wanting to discuss the subject any further. "It was nice chatting with you. I've gotta get my kids from the sitter's."

"We might just run into each other at the baseball field tomorrow. If you see me, don't think I'm stalking you!" Trish teased. "One of my girls has a crush on the pitcher of my friend's team. If I don't bump into you, remember to call me if you have any real estate needs. I'm the best!"

Holding her spread fingers in the air, Cindi smiled and opened the salon door with her hip and exited. Once she was out of sight, Cooper stepped awkwardly down from her pedicure chair and shuffled to the front in order to pay for the service.

"I'll call the Sunrise members," Trish said, joining her. "It's time to learn a bit more about this boyfriend of Cindi's. Maybe *he's* the bigwig who closed Hazel's account."

"I'll call Nathan, Savannah, and Quinton," Cooper offered. "So you're not on the phone all night."

"That's a deal." Touching her shellacked hair, Trish eyed Cooper's toes. "How did you like your pedicure?"

"I can see why women like it so much. Besides, it was a treat to see you in your element," Cooper said. "You did a great job getting Cindi to talk."

Beaming at the compliment, Trish thanked her, said good-bye, and stepped out of the salon, her heels clicking on the brick walkway leading toward the parking lot. Cooper tried to follow at a similar, brisk pace, but could only shuffle carefully on her paper-thin sandals.

Settling herself into Cherry-O, Cooper noticed the mangled state of the foam slippers. She gingerly removed the temporary flip-flops, tossed them on the passenger seat, and cranked up the stereo. Driving home with the windows down and "Lucy in the Sky With Diamonds" blaring out of her speaker, Cooper wiggled her bare feet with pleasure.

12

But may the righteous be glad and rejoice before God; may they be happy and joyful.

Psalm 68:3 (NIV)

Thursday arrived with the full glory of spring. Cooper made a quick breakfast of maple and brown sugar instant oatmeal and a banana. She paused for a moment to admire her attractive toenails before pulling on socks and shoes, then grabbed her travel mug and the gift box she had carefully wrapped in Betty Boop paper the night before.

It was May 8, a famous day in history for Truman fans (he was born in 1884), lovers of aviation (the first transatlantic flight took place), and Beatlemaniacs (The Beatles released their *Let It Be* album in the United Kingdom). May 8 was also Angela's birthday, though she would tell no one what year this auspicious event had occurred. Regardless of her age, Angela's fellow employees of Make It Work! always tried to make her feel special on this day as a way of thanking her for being the heart and soul of their company. Mr. Farmer paid for lunch and often bought Angela flowers or a small gift on behalf of all the employees.

Several birthday celebrations ago, Angela had declared that she would like to be surprised for her next birthday with something unexpected, as no one had ever succeeded in surprising her. After that statement, made over four years ago, her coworkers had steadily failed to live up to the task. Angela always seemed to know that they had reserved a private room for a luncheon at Maggiano's, hired a magician, arranged for the Domino's delivery man to arrive with a large pizza pie — upon which Angela's name was spelled out with pieces of pepperoni — or splurged on a day's worth of spa treatments. This year, the gang had decided to buy Angela gifts to celebrate her love of vintage items and Mr. Farmer had promised to order her a cake that would knock her false eyelashes right off.

Excited for the workday to speed along so that she could feast her eyes on this one-of-a-kind confection, Cooper trotted down her apartment stairs to the backyard. Despite her haste to get into the office, she couldn't help but linger a few moments in the garden. Bursting with green, the young vegetables were thriving.

Cooper touched the silky stalk of a tomato plant and straightened its stake a fraction. As she stood in complete peace on the edge of the garden, a soft wind pushed a strand of hair onto her cheek and toyed with the tin pie pans until they swiveled on a slow axis, exchanging sunlit winks. She inhaled the heavenly scents of dew-moistened soil, wet grass, and a mingling of rosemary and thyme coming from the narrow wooden planters on the patio.

"Blessings are all around me," she whispered to the brightening horizon before hopping into Cherry-O.

Driving to work, Cooper listened to her favorite morning radio show, *Breakfast with the Beatles*. She pulled into a parking space just as the final bars of "Hey Jude" were drifting away and felt confident that it was going to be a marvelous day.

Inside the Make It Work! office, Mr. Farmer was fussing over Angela's desk, where he was apparently trying to decide where to place a gift bag stuffed with colorful tissue paper.

"Good morning," Cooper greeted her boss.

Mr. Farmer gave her a quick wave and then gestured at the present tucked under Cooper's arm. "How are we going to surprise Angela? She always knows everything that goes on around here. I've made all of the phone calls regarding her cake from my car, but I bet that woman knows the very flavor of the frosting without me saying a word."

Cooper watched her boss as he glanced at the date on Angela's calendar. May 8 had been circled with red ink and Angela had written *MY B-DAY!* on the date in large block letters. Mr. Farmer, who rarely left the sanctuary of his office, stared at the calendar in agitation. He rubbed his hands together as sweat speckled his wrinkled brow, causing his mostly bald head to look even shinier than usual. "No offense, sir, but you're not a very good poker player, are you?"

Mr. Farmer nervously scratched the center of his large, round head where there wasn't so much as a trace of hair, and shrugged. "It's me, isn't it? I give it away every time. What should I do different?" He looked so eager to surprise Angela that Cooper took his gift bag from his clammy hand and smiled reassuringly.

"First thing is to hide these presents. The second change we've got to make is for you to leave for the day. You're not supposed to be out of the office and Angela won't expect a sudden absence. She'll be looking for you to be hovering around her desk — something you only do when we're planning some kind of party, sir. Getting you out of Dodge will help with the surprise part."

"I hover? Really?" Mr. Farmer stroked his round cheek in bewilderment. "I could take my laptop to the Starbucks down the road. What else?"

"Well, we always do something to surprise Angela around lunchtime. If we all pretend like today's a regular day, then Angela will think we actually *forgot* her birthday. We'll surprise her this afternoon, before we all go home." She looked at her boss. "Can you set up the cake in the back of a van a few minutes before five?"

Mr. Farmer smiled, his pudgy features transformed with pleasure. "Back of the van. Got it. Good thinking, Cooper. You tell the others the plan. I'd better get out of here before Angela comes in. She's never been late a day in her life," he added with admiration. "And don't tell her you saw me."

As her boss scuttled off, Cooper couldn't help but wonder if her taciturn employer had a soft spot for Angela after all. He was acting more interested in pleasing the office manager than most bosses did. And why not? Cooper thought. He's single. She's single. Perhaps her conspicuous flirting had finally penetrated his hermitlike defenses.

No more than two minutes later, Angela arrived in a cloud of heady perfume and a tight black skirt trimmed with a black ruffle. She wore a frilly, butter-yellow blouse and a necklace of bulbous white beads. Her platinum hair was puffed out even bigger than was customary and her long nails were as red and bright as a clown's nose. Her four-inch heels created a perky staccato as she sauntered to her place behind her desk. "Good morning, Cooper!" her voice sang out. "Gorgeous day, isn't it?" The penciled lines that formed her eyebrows rose up and down suggestively.

"Sure is. What's my first stop today?" Cooper asked as cheerfully as she would on any other morning, but gave no indication that the day was special for any reason.

Angela hesitated, searching Cooper's blank features. She then glanced down at her appointment book. "Short Pump Elementary. Broken copier and laminator."

"Ugh, I hate those laminating machines," Cooper complained. "More trouble than they're worth."

"Don't worry, darlin'." Angela smiled knowingly. "You should be done in time for lunch."

Cooper collected her toolbox and a set of van keys and was just about to exit the office when Angela blocked her path. "Where's Mr. Farmer?" she demanded. "He's never late."

"I'm not sure," Cooper stated. "He mentioned having some work to do off-site, but that's all he said. You know him, doesn't waste words."

Angela flipped through her appointment book. "I don't have any off-site meetings written down! Hrmph. I'll just get him on his cell." The determined click of her heels sounded across the floor as she returned to her desk and tucked the phone receiver under a lock of blond hair.

Hiding her grin, Cooper loaded her tools in the van and reached the elementary school in less than ten minutes despite heavy traffic on Broad Street. She parked in the back lot, gathered her toolbox, and signed the visitors' log in the front office. The secretary, who was grateful Cooper had arrived so quickly, led her to a vestibule outside the principal's office where the malfunctioning laminator and copier sat.

Cooper frowned. She had repaired this copier, a Toshiba e-Studio 28, several times before and knew that it was only a matter of time before the outdated and overused machine finally collapsed. The mechanical dinosaur had been fitted with so many replacement parts that inside it resembled a student science-fair project. Cooper shook her head in sympathy. It was time for the copier to be scrapped, but she suspected the school lacked the funds to purchase a new one.

As she found working on spent machines rather depressing, Cooper decided to tackle the laminator first. She disliked dealing with the persnickety contraption that covered everything fed into its aperture with a slick, plastic coating, but she knew that the teachers at Short Pump Elementary had come to rely on the machine's abilities to create longer-lasting and reusable items for their classrooms. The last time Cooper had been called to fix the laminator, an agitated young teacher had found herself stuck in the middle of a massive project in which she was laminating the shapes of each of the fifty states. The machine started malfunctioning as it was fed North Dakota and refused to budge until Cooper arrived. She had had to disassemble the entire laminator and North Dakota had been destroyed in the process, but the teacher had been so pleased that her favorite piece of equipment was fixed, she didn't seem to mind having to draw a replacement state.

After repairing the laminator this time around, Cooper began work on the tired copier in silence, coaxing belts, levers, knobs, and rollers into action for a little while longer. As her skilled hands worked their magic, she enjoyed hearing the laughter and delighted shrieks of children emanating from the playground. Echoes of a high-pitched song in praise of rainbows drifted down the wide halls and made Cooper smile. As she screwed the back panel onto the machine, an older woman holding the hand of a young boy with enormous brown eyes and a round face covered with freckles appeared next to the copier.

"Oh, thank goodness!" The woman beamed at Cooper. "Is it ready to go?"

Cooper cast a solemn glance at the machine. "For now. It may even make it to the end of the school year, but I can't promise anything."

"Is it sick?" the little boy asked, his small

285

face creasing in concern.

Unsure of what to say, Cooper looked to the teacher for help.

"Just old, Brandon. It's tired and would like a rest. Kind of like me! Now, let's run off these tulip templates so that we can finish our April Showers, May Flowers board, shall we?"

Brandon nodded, staring at Cooper as she put away her tools.

As his teacher released his hand in order to make copies, the boy edged closer to Cooper, walking on his tiptoes as though not to agitate the ailing copier. "Why do you have two different color eyes?" he whispered loudly.

After a brief hesitation, Cooper bent down and allowed the boy to look at her eyes. "I had an accident," she told him gently. "And I got a new green eye to replace the blue one I lost. See?" She pointed at the dazzling emerald iris.

"Cool!" The boy was clearly impressed. "You're like the Bionic Woman. Like a robot!"

"Brandon!" The teacher turned from the machine. "Hush now. You come over here and press the green start button for me. Can you find the green button?"

Brandon was too short to see the keypad,

so his teacher lifted him into the air. As soon as he had pressed the appropriate button and the copier shuddered to life again, the boy returned his focus to Cooper.

"I didn't know girls used tools," Brandon stated as he pointed at Cooper's toolbox. "I'm going to tell my mommy that she can learn to fix stuff. She always makes Daddy do everything. Does your husband fix stuff too?"

The teacher put her arm around her pupil and flashed Cooper an apologetic grin. "Sorry. You know kindergartners. They'll say anything that pops in their heads. No filtering system whatsoever."

Cooper smiled. "That's okay. Bye, Brandon."

She snapped her tool case closed and brushed off the knees of her work pants. As she stood, Brandon broke free from his teacher's arm and seated himself on top of Cooper's toolbox. "Are you somebody's mommy?"

Cooper shook her head. "Not yet, but I hope to be someday." She gazed fondly at the boy's freckled nose and many dimples, but just as suddenly as he had sat down, he sprang up and returned to his teacher's side.

Back in the front office, Cooper signed out in the visitors' log and asked the secretary if they had budgeted for a new copier for the following school year.

"I don't think so," the woman said anxiously. "We were hoping that one would survive one more year."

"It won't last that long. You've got six months tops." Cooper repeatedly smoothed the paperwork attached to her clipboard. "It's given everything it's got. Next time I come back, I'll have to piece it together with duct tape."

The woman sighed. "If only we got a fraction of the budget the government spends on frivolities," she began and then stopped herself. "Thanks for letting me know. How about the laminator?"

"Oh, that's fine. Temperamental, but it's good to go for a few more years or so," Cooper replied.

"That's how most folks would describe me!" The secretary laughed and led Cooper out.

As planned, the Make It Work! employees ordered a takeout lunch from Five Guys Burgers and Fries. In the break room, an expectant Angela nibbled on a grilled cheese while watching Ben pack away a mammoth bacon cheeseburger and a mountain of Cajun fries. Cooper and Stuart each had a cheeseburger with extra pickles but shared an order of fries, as one serving was copious enough to fill both of their stomachs.

"I thought you were trying to gain muscle weight, Ben," Angela teased. "That kind of lunch will only give you a spare tire and a heart attack sometime down the road."

Ben ripped off a chunk of his burger with his front teeth and then, with exaggerated gusto, shoved four fries in his mouth at once. Cooper and Angela exchanged worried glances. Ben seemed to have become more and more moody over the past two months. It was getting to the point that no one knew how to have a conversation with him anymore.

"Hey, what's with you, man?" Stuart asked while drowning a French fry in a paper cup filled with catsup. "You've been, like, all bummed out lately. What gives?"

"I'm just hungry." Ben offered an unconvincing smile and then amended his answer. "It's my wife. I'm worried about her, but I don't want to bring her problems to this table. There's not enough room, so let's change the subject, okay?"

"So," Angela said a bit too brightly and turned her assessing gaze away from Ben. "Where's Mr. Farmer? Off pickin' up a Chippendale dancer for my surprise?"

Her coworkers smirked.

"Now, *that* would be interesting!" Stuart snorted. "Can you see our boss driving over here with a stripper? Trying to make small talk?"

"I could see it happening if the stripper read *Popular Mechanics*," Ben quipped, displaying traits of his old self. "The two of them could talk about nanoprocessors as the dancer slathered himself with oil."

Angela checked her watch. "There's only five minutes left on our lunch break, so y'all have *got* to have somethin' goin' on. And I admit, I really don't know what it is this year."

Cooper got up from the table in the employee kitchen and threw out her trash. "All we've got going on is work. I'm off to service the medical center's machines. Got lenses to clean and toner to change. See you guys."

"See you!" Stuart called back as he scooted the rest of the fries closer.

Angela opened her mouth to speak, but her red lips, still well covered in lipstick despite her having eaten an entire grilled cheese sandwich, closed again into a tight frown.

She's the one who wanted to be surprised, Cooper thought and hoped that Angela's day-long anguish would be quickly alleviated by the late-afternoon celebration.

Cooper had little time to worry about Angela as she serviced fax machines and copiers in a beehive of doctors' offices. Everywhere she went she seemed to meet the curious gaze of one adorable child after another. She couldn't recall a workday in which she had encountered half a dozen kids who only seemed interested in watching her go about her job.

She was so preoccupied with repairs that she was almost late to Angela's party. As prearranged, Stuart, Ben, and Mr. Farmer prepared Angela's birthday surprise in the back of one of the company vans. Cooper screeched into a parking space and joined them, slightly out of breath.

"Tell me what you think." Her boss led her over to another van, which was pulled beneath the shade of a blooming pear tree. Soft, white petals drifted through the air and created a fragrant carpet on top of the warm asphalt. Mr. Farmer had opened both of the rear doors and tied pink balloons to the handles. Inside, on a pink vinyl tablecloth, he had put Angela's one-of-a-kind cake and an enormous bouquet of pink roses on display. Several fat fuchsia candles burned on either side of the cake and

Cooper caught a cotton candy scent.

"Mr. Farmer, that cake is amazing!" Cooper exclaimed after poking her head inside the van. The large sheet cake was covered with a photo of Marilyn Monroe as she appeared in *Gentlemen Prefer Blondes.* Wearing a pink satin dress, pink satin gloves, and chunky diamond necklace, this Marilyn had been given Angela's face. It was beautifully done and impossible to tell where Angela ended and Marilyn began. The photo image, created using edible icing, or so Mr. Farmer assured them, was framed with dozens and dozens of miniature pink roses. It was truly a work of art.

"How can we cut that?" Stuart looked worried. "It would be, like, gross, to eat a piece of Angela's face." He eyed the cake hungrily. "Still, I could polish off a few of those roses." He clapped their boss on the back. "Good work, Mr. Farmer. I only got her an old lunch box."

"I got her a teddy bear dressed like Marilyn." Ben held out the charming bear dressed in a white pleated gown and frowned. " 'Course my wife accused me of cheating on her when she saw this thing in my car, so Angela better like it."

Mr. Farmer shifted uncomfortably. "Ah . . . what did you get her?" he asked

Cooper.

"Some Lucite bracelets from West End Antiques Mall. I just told the saleslady that my friend liked vintage jewelry and she picked them out for me." Cooper heard the noise of Angela's heels coming down the hall. "Here she comes, guys. Let's hide."

Ben and Mr. Farmer ducked behind one of the van's doors. Cooper hid a few feet away, her back pressed against the side of the van.

"Hey, Angela!" Stuart called frantically and gestured for Angela to come closer. "I backed into a car with my van! What am I gonna do? I'm in huge trouble, right?"

Angela's face creased in motherly concern as she hurried over. "Are you okay, Stuart? Because that's all that really matters."

"*I* am, but I don't know if *you're* gonna be, considering you're another year older . . ." Stuart began.

"*Surprise!*" the others shouted as they popped out from behind the van door.

"It's a movie-star themed birthday!" Mr. Farmer exclaimed and handed Angela the gift bag stuffed with colorful tissue. "Those are DVDs. *The Seven Year Itch, Niagara,* and *How to Marry a Millionaire.* I wasn't sure what you had already . . ." He trailed off.

"Oh my stars!" Angela cried joyfully as

she accepted the bag and peered into the van. "Will you get a load of that cake? How did you guys get someone to bake something so absolutely *perfect?*"

"Wasn't us," Ben said. "The boss man took charge of this year's party."

In a rush of gratitude, Angela planted a kiss on Mr. Farmer's lips, leaving a smudge of red lipstick above and below his own compressed lips. Stunned, he cleared his throat and reached into his pocket, but not finding a tissue or whatever he was searching for, issued a command instead. "Open your gifts, Angela."

Still twittering with excitement, Angela tore open packages and squealed in delight over each of her presents. After taking scores of photos of her cake with a digital camera, Angela insisted that everyone consume an inordinately large piece of the lemon pound cake piled with two inches of strawberry butter-cream frosting. After they had all been served, Mr. Farmer produced a bottle of champagne from a cooler on the floor of the van's passenger seat and poured out glasses for his employees.

"Just enough to soak your mustaches," he said. "To the heart of our company. To Angela. Our very own rose."

Tears sprang into Angela's eyes as she

knocked plastic tumblers with her friends. "Y'all did it! You surprised me, all right!" She dabbed at her heavily mascaraed eyes with a pink napkin. "I was actually beginning to think you forgot about me."

"Never!" shouted Stuart and Cooper.

"Not us," added Ben.

Mr. Farmer added a tiny splash to Angela's cup and said, "Impossible, Angela. You're simply unforgettable."

Cooper had never seen Angela so happy.

Driving home, Cooper felt a little glum. She was pleased to have been a part of Angela's joyful moment, but the celebration had also reminded her that she might very well be alone on her next birthday and possibly for many birthdays after that.

"It's time for a Home Depot stop," Cooper declared. "The handle on my screwdriver's cracked, after all."

Strolling down the aisle, Cooper brushed her hands over the gleaming metal of unused power tools. She paused at the section where the drill bits were displayed. This was the exact spot where she had met Drew over five years ago, and despite herself, the memory of their meeting flooded her mind.

"Oh!" he had exclaimed as she reached for the last DeWalt 28-piece drill-bit set that day. "Did you want those?"

"I did," she had said. "But I don't mind getting the Bosch set."

"No, you take the DeWalt. I insist." Drew had gazed at her with those stormy gray-blue eyes and then his handsome mouth creased into a charming smile. "I hope you don't think I'm being nosy, but are the bits for you or someone else?"

"For me," Cooper had answered. "I'm helping my daddy build a garden fence, but I like to use my own tools instead of borrowing his."

"I'm making bookshelves. One of my bits just got ground to dust when I started drilling the concrete floor instead of the screw. That's what I get for watching *SportsCenter* while I'm building." He paused and ran a hand through his wavy hair. "Listen, I don't normally hit on beautiful women in Home Depot, but would you like to grab an Italian sausage with me? There's a kiosk right outside the front door so you can easily ditch me if you want."

Cooper's heart had fluttered inside her chest. This charming, gorgeous man wanted to have lunch with her! "I'd love to," she had answered and that had been the beginning of many meals and endless discussions about tools, building projects, work, and family.

"May I help you, miss?" a Home Depot employee wearing an orange apron inquired helpfully, breaking Cooper from her reverie.

"No thanks." She held up the screwdriver she planned to purchase. "I got what I came for."

As Cooper turned the corner at the end of the aisle, she came face-to-face with the person she had just been daydreaming about. There, right in front of her, was Drew. Only he wasn't alone. A petite red-head with skin like fine porcelain, and wide, ocean-blue eyes held on to his arm as she examined a lamp display.

Drew saw Cooper and at first, his face grew pale. Then, without breaking eye contact, he pulled Anna Lynne toward Cooper and formally introduced them as though the three of them were at a cocktail party.

Cooper mechanically shook hands with Anna Lynne, who seemed utterly sincere when she said, "I've heard wonderful things about you. It's nice to put a face to all of those praises."

Too dumbfounded to respond, Cooper looked back at Drew, who also seemed to be at a loss for words. "Are you doing okay?" he asked after several seconds of awkward silence.

"Yeah, I'm good," she murmured, longing to escape from the one person who had meant the world to her for so many years. She was shocked over how painful it was to see him with Anna Lynne. Yet here she stood, exchanging meaningless small talk while the cracks and fissures in her heart threatened to rend it in two.

"I wanted to tell you before you found out any other way . . . since we ran into each other like this and all." Drew spoke with haste. "Um, Anna Lynne and I are engaged."

"Drew," Anna Lynne cautioned. "No woman wants to hear that about her ex. Not without a lot more time passing." She turned a sympathetic glance toward Cooper. "I'm sorry. We really should get goin' and leave you be, but it sure was nice to have met you."

Anna Lynne began to pull Drew away, though it seemed he wanted to say something further to Cooper. Finally, Anna Lynne murmured briefly into his ear. Looking abashed, he nodded and reached out to squeeze Cooper's shoulder. "I wish you the best, Coop. Be well."

And with that, the happy couple walked

deeper into the electrical aisle and disappeared from sight.

Cooper stood in front of the lamp display for a long time. The encounter had been so unexpected, so unwelcome, and in the end, devastating.

"Engaged?" Cooper posed her question to the air. "Engaged?" she repeated, stroking the silky lampshade closest to her right hand. It was hard to breathe, almost impossible to move. Since she was barely conscious of what she was doing, the back of Cooper's hand brushed against a display of lit bulbs. The bulb burned her skin and she jerked her hand away. The sensation of physical pain seemed to force reality upon her like an electric shock. "He's gone," she muttered. "And he's *never* coming back."

Suddenly, the giant store felt claustrophobic. Tossing the screwdriver she'd meant to purchase at the base of the lamp, Cooper hustled outside, jumped in her truck, and drove home. Once there, she moved listlessly through the vegetable garden, around the balmy interior of her greenhouse, and, finding no comfort in any of those places, crossed the patio toward the hawk's cage.

"You look as low as my pantyhose after the elastic's given out," Grammy said, joining Cooper as she stroked the feathers on

299

Columbus's neck.

Cooper sighed. She hadn't heard her grandmother approach and didn't want to see another human being at the moment.

"You'll feel better if you let it out," Grammy advised. "You hold on to the blues and they'll keep squeezin' you just like one of those blood pressure cuffs. Lord, I hate those things."

Cooper reluctantly told her grandmother about Drew. She then poured out her fear over never finding someone to love as much again, about the possibility of remaining single for the rest of her life. Grammy listened without a single interruption, which was most unusual. She offered no smart-aleck comments or cynical advice. When Cooper was finished talking, Grammy placed a wrinkled hand on her grand-daughter's arm and said, "Come on into my room."

Cooper followed as her grandmother shuffled down the hall toward her bedroom.

"Sit on the bed," Grammy commanded and began sifting through a bureau drawer. Little Boy jumped from his nest on Gram-my's pillow to the top of the chest in order to see if the drawers contained a succulent treat for him. Grammy kissed him on his pink nose and muttered to herself as she removed old jewelry boxes, letters, tissues, postcards, and other sundry items before she found what she was looking for. Placing a yellow handkerchief on the bed, Grammy seated herself next to Cooper.

"I know about feelin' like you're drownin', child. There was a time, before my boys were born, that I almost let those blues take charge of me." She fingered the handkerchief. "Your grandpa traveled a lot, you know, sellin' dental supplies. He was often gone, but we was doin' okay. After only bein' married a year, I found out I was expectin' a baby." Grammy's voice turned to a whisper. "But the child wasn't to be. She came too early, while Earl Senior was in Duluth or Lord knows where."

"Oh, Grammy," Cooper whispered sympathetically.

Steeling herself to continue, Grammy rubbed her bony knees with both hands as she stared, unseeing, out the window. "Folks thought I'd be so mad at Earl Senior, but I was an empty hole of a woman. I didn't yell or cry or anythin'. I was frozen like a piece of ice. Losin' that baby ripped my heart to pieces." She sighed, remembering what may have been the most painful moment of her life. "When I got out of the hospital, your grandpa picked me up, but he didn't drive me home. He drove us straight to Albuquerque and checked us into a hotel. He told me we'd stay until I was ready to go home — to start livin' again."

"How long were you there?"

Grammy chuckled, but there was no humor in the sound. "Two weeks. That was enough for me. I started to miss Southern food, my little house and garden, and my friends. I told Earl I was ready to go and while we were packin' up he gave me this."

She picked up the handkerchief. "He told me that this pin was to remind me that we can get beyond the greatest of hurts if someone loves us. If we just hold on and do our best, God Almighty will answer our prayers and see us through. I wore this every day until I gave birth to Earl Junior. Then I didn't need it so much, so I put it away. Now I want you to have it. Bear your grandpa's words in mind. He was pretty smart at times."

Grammy peeled back the soft folds of cloth to reveal a silver butterfly pin. It had a narrow body and delicate filigree wings. When Cooper held it to the light, it twinkled in the palm of her hand like a living creature. Looking at her grandmother's weathered face, Cooper didn't know whether she was more thankful for the butterfly or for

Grammy's story.

She reached out, put her arms around her grandmother's scrawny shoulders, and squeezed her gently. "Thank you. I'll wear it all the time."

"Or until your most important prayers are answered," Grammy whispered into Cooper's hair. Little Boy leapt onto the bed and mewled. He was jealous of the attention Cooper was receiving. Grammy gathered the enormous tabby into her arms and waved at Cooper with her elbow. "Now go on with you, it's time for me and Little Boy to watch Jerry Springer."

13

For the lips of an adulteress drip honey,
and her speech is smoother than oil;

but in the end she is bitter as gall,
sharp as a double-edged sword.

Her feet go down to death;
her steps lead straight to the grave.

Proverbs 5:3–5 (NIV)

After receiving the butterfly pin, Cooper sprinted upstairs to her apartment and affixed it to a moss-colored long-sleeve T-shirt. Standing in front of the bathroom mirror, the woman in the green top and jeans looked liked someone on a mission. Since running into Drew and Anna Lynne, Cooper had become especially grateful for the new friends in her life and their readiness to accept her, flaws and all. Now, she felt as though she needed to be in their presence on a regular basis, that she might gain strength and hope simply by being near them.

Inspired and reinvigorated by her dialogue with Grammy, Cooper stopped by her parents' kitchen to say hello before heading out to the baseball game.

"Wanna join us for dinner, honey?" Maggie asked while opening the oven door to make sure that the brisket she was cooking was bathing in enough au jus. "I've got plenty of meat here."

"Thanks, Mama." Cooper inhaled the delicious aroma regretfully. "But I've got hot dogs at the Little League game on my menu tonight."

Maggie scooped a few tablespoonfuls of gravy over the top of the brisket and, satisfied with the tenderness of the meat, eased the oven closed. "You still busy sleuthing?"

Cooper nodded. "We are. It's taking longer than I thought to gather clues, though."

"Well, hon." Maggie sponged off the countertop as she talked. "Just think of how the police feel following those kind of twisty, curvy paths every day — knowing that the trail they're on may not ever lead them to the right person. When I think of those who have lost a loved one to violence or about those poor parents that may never see their missing children . . ." She dabbed at the tears pooled in her eyes with the edge of the checkered dishcloth.

"We're not giving up, Mama," Cooper said quickly, before her mother could dwell on the troubles expounded by the evening news reports. "I think about Brooke Hughes all the time. I'm not going to let this go. And her husband was denied bail so I've heard he's mighty down these days, but he's got a son to live for."

Maggie kissed her daughter lightly on the cheek. "I'm glad I get to see you every single day, my sweet girl. Whenever I have my doubts about this world, I just need to look at one of my girls to know that I did something right."

Cooper inhaled the scent of the brisket cooking and her mother's unique buttery, forsythia-tinged fragrance. "You do plenty right, Mama," she assured her mother. "I'm off to meet my Bible study friends at the game, but if there's any brisket left I'd love to make a sandwich with it to take to work tomorrow."

Maggie snorted. "Between your daddy and Grammy, that three-legged dog out back'll be lucky to get any. I don't know how Grammy eats so much meat and stays so skinny. Must be the trick to livin' to a ripe old age." She winked. "But don't worry, I'll fix you up a proper sandwich and put it in your fridge. You go have fun now."

When Cooper arrived at the Tuckahoe Little League fields, she was amazed at the huge number of minivans, SUVs, and other enormous metal boxes on wheels crowding the parking lots around the twelve playing fields. Cooper had no idea where to meet the rest of the Sunrise gang, so she steered Cherry-O around the deepest dips on the dirt road and looked for Nathan's pea-green BMW. Fortunately, she spotted Jake's work van instead.

The Mr. Faucet van was hard to miss. It was painted sky blue with a shiny silver water faucet on each side. Fat water drops with smiling faces dripped from the faucets and a cartoon plumber, wearing white overalls and carrying a wrench, was frozen in the act of waving. The slogan on each side of the van read *Get the drips outta your life.* Cooper grinned as she parked next to the vehicle. She could almost hear Jake suggesting that slogan at an employee meeting. It sounded just like something he would say.

As she approached the first field on the right, Cooper noted that the game was already underway. The Mr. Faucet kids were dressed in sky-blue shirts while the opposing team was wearing black jerseys. Cooper was unsurprised to see the Capital City logo on the back of the jerseys, but she hadn't expected to see a local news team filming snippets of the game. She surveyed the adults on the field, trying to gauge which of the two coaches might be Cindi's boyfriend, but both men were too far away to see clearly.

"Cooper! Over here!" Nathan's voice called out behind her.

Cooper turned to see Nathan hiking over from the direction of the concession building. He was carrying a cardboard tray laden with hot dogs and packets of condiments. "I got you two dogs," he said, his voice breathy from hustling to her side. "But this doesn't count as me treating you to dinner." He smiled. "Are you free tomorrow night? I thought we'd see a matinee and then go someplace to eat afterward."

As Cooper looked into Nathan's kind face, she felt a warmth flood through her. She realized that the best way of letting go of the past was to leap into the future. Despite the pain she felt over Drew's engagement, it was now more than clear that there was nothing left of her old relationship to cling to.

"That sounds great," Cooper replied, gladly accepting Nathan's invitation. She touched the butterfly pinned on her T-shirt right above her left collarbone and said a silent prayer of gratitude. She was going to move on. She was going to pursue happiness until she held it in her hand.

Completely unaware of Cooper's inner dialogue, Nathan munched on his hot dog while leading her toward the bleachers where the Mr. Faucet fans sat waiting. Their team's batter had temporarily suspended game play by tying his shoelaces with excruciating slowness.

As Nathan and Cooper climbed up several rows, Quinton and Bryant slid deeper into the center of the bleachers to make room for their friends and the tray of hot dogs.

"You make a fine waiter, Nathan." Quinton patted the bleacher beside him, greeted Cooper, and then reached for a hot dog. "Nice night for a ball game, huh?"

"It is," Cooper agreed and said hello to Bryant.

"We've got sodas over here." Bryant pointed to the bleachers to the right of his hip. "No diet though. You okay with full-sugar Sprite?"

"I love sugar in all forms," Cooper said

and accepted a hot dog and soda.

Nathan glanced over at her as the batter finally accepted a pitch from a very determined-looking nine-year-old. Though he swung with intensity, the Mr. Faucet batter missed the pitch completely and the ball landed in the catcher's mitt with a resounding *thump.* "I like that butterfly pin. Is it new?" Nathan asked.

"My grandmother gave it to me earlier today." Cooper doctored her hot dog with a generous line of catsup. She then pushed a squiggle of mustard over the catsup and topped it all off with three dollops of sweet relish. "Why is there a news crew here?" she asked Nathan, wanting to avoid going into any details about how Grammy had come to bestow the pin upon her.

He shrugged. "Dunno, but after we eat let's go find out. I saw them interviewing Cindi's boyfriend before the game, so we might be able to learn something about him." He sipped some soda. "And I'm sure it was her boyfriend because she blew him a pretty sexy kiss before sitting down over there. Too bad he's got his baseball cap pulled down so low over his face. Makes it hard to see his features." He gestured at the opposing bleachers. "Savannah's our ears on the other side until Trish arrives. She's sitting right next to Cindi, so when Trish joins Savannah, it won't look like she's there to stalk the secretary — just meeting an old friend at the game."

The foursome watched the action on the field for a while. When one of Jake's players scored a home run, they cheered with so much gusto that he arched an eyebrow in their direction. With their baseball caps pulled down low, it was difficult to distinguish one coach from another. Cooper recognized Jake by the strut in his walk and the tattooed cross on his forearm, but she had no idea which of the two Capital City coaches might be Cindi's boyfriend and Cindi didn't signal to anyone on the field. In fact, she didn't even clap when the Capital City team made a good play.

As the game progressed, Cooper felt extremely relaxed and content. During the bottom of the third inning, she leaned back on the bleachers and stared at the silver clouds as they lazily traversed the night sky. Every now and then a star would reveal itself from behind the cloud cover and echoes of cheers from other fields would drift through the clear air. By the sixth inning, Cooper had drained her Sprite and craved another. After noting that her other friends still had plenty of liquid left in their cups, she told Nathan that she was going to get a soda refill.

He paused in mid-clap as the Mr. Faucet team took the field. "I'll come with you. Hey!" Nathan grabbed Cooper's elbow before she could stand up. "Don't look now, but Trish has arrived and it looks like she brought one of those little dogs of hers."

"It's wearing a doggie baseball cap!" Quinton exclaimed, helping himself to another hot dog. "My nephews would get a kick out of that. It's darn cute."

"I don't think that pooch with the yellow fur tied to the end of the bleacher approves of Trish's fashion choice for her canine. Look," Bryant said, pointing. Cooper spied the large dog right away, as she had never seen a standard poodle with such a shaggy coat. "Both dogs are barking their heads off," Bryant continued. "Whoa! That woman is sure jerking that poodle around!"

They all focused their attention on the poodle's owner. With a haggard face and hair drawn tightly into a ponytail, the middle-aged woman shouted as she tried to pacify her dog. She put a hand on an angular hip and gesticulated at Trish, who scowled but then marched to the other end of the bleachers and plunked down next to Savannah. While pouting and throwing dirty

312

looks at the poodle's unpleasant owner, Trish seemed to be complaining to Savannah and Cindi. She had clearly won Cindi's sympathy, for within moments of Trish being seated, the two women had their heads bent and seemed to be whispering diligently. Trish only hesitated long enough to shoot fierce looks at the other dog owner, but Cindi didn't even glance at the other woman, which Cooper found unusual. Instead, she kept her eyes focused on the game.

Two surly-looking children sat in front of Cindi, throwing popcorn listlessly onto the ground. Cooper wondered if they were Cindi's brood and for a moment, felt a touch of pity for the single mom. When Cindi leaned over to reprimand the preteens and they responded by rolling their eyes and continuing their aimless and irritating activity, Cooper nudged Nathan.

"Seems like Cindi's got her hands full."

Nathan frowned. "It can't be easy for her. Maybe that's why she's after a married guy. He's got a stable job and is obviously good with kids. If she could lure him away from his wife, she'd certainly have more security. Looks like those two could use a father figure."

Cooper eyed Cindi's son and daughter as

they tossed ice cubes into the air and then tried to catch them with their mouths. "Those kids may be the reason Cindi's boyfriend *never* leaves his wife. Not that he *should*," she added hastily.

Nathan and Cooper ceased staring at Trish and made their way toward the refreshment stand. As they walked, Cooper noticed a silver Porsche pulling onto a portion of grass that was clearly not a parking space.

"I want to see what's brought the camera crew out here tonight," Nathan said in a low voice.

The local reporter, a comely brunette with long legs, hustled over to welcome the sports car's driver as he gracefully unfolded his tall frame from the cramped interior of his car.

"Good evening, Mr. Maynard," the reporter trilled. "Thank you so much for giving us the heads-up about your surprise donation and for coming out here straight from the airport. Were you on vacation?"

"Switzerland. On business. And please call me Vance." The soft-spoken man in his late forties extended a tanned arm to the reporter.

The reporter sat up a tad bit straighter. "You'll be taking the field during the seventh inning, correct?" Without waiting for him to answer, she plowed on. "Perhaps I could ask you some questions before you make the announcement?"

"Sure thing." He flashed her a white-toothed smile that seemed well rehearsed to Cooper. It was a politician's smile — the kind that emanated from a mouth of expensive veneers but was not reflected in the eyes. Vance Maynard untied a golf sweater from his shoulders and pulled it over his tanned face, slightly ruffling his salt-and-pepper hair. He was an attractive man and seemed to immediately put both the reporter and her cameraman at ease. He reminded Cooper of Bob Barker, but something about both his name and face seemed familiar. Where had she seen this man before?

"Why don't we have a seat?" Vance indicated a nearby picnic table.

Nathan turned to Cooper. "Maybe the reporter knows the name of Cindi's boyfriend. Let's talk to her when she's done with this Vance guy. We'll buy some ice cream and eat it at the table next to hers."

As they approached the concession stand, the crotchety owner of the poodle mix was there, brushing dog hairs from her mustard-stained tank top while berating the teenage boy running the concession stand over the hue of her hotdog.

"Do you think I want food poisoning on top of all my other problems?" she shrieked. "I know that a public school education doesn't mean much these days, but surely you must be aware that *bright red* is not a natural color for a cooked hotdog!"

"Um," the boy stammered. "Would you like popcorn instead? It'd be on the house."

"Fine." The woman snatched a box of popcorn from the boy's hand. She then made an attempt at smoothing some stray hairs that had broken free from her ponytail and dabbed at her stained shirt with a napkin. As she passed Nathan and Cooper, they heard her mutter, "When am I ever going to catch a freaking break?"

After greeting the concession worker with the friendliest smile she could muster, Cooper bought two Astro Pops and another sprite. She and Nathan both thanked the young man profusely and were relieved to see that he seemed unmoved by the frazzled woman's tirade over the color of her hotdog.

Unwrapping their popsicles, Cooper and Nathan sat down at the picnic table next to Vance just as he was saying, "I don't have kids of my own. My wife died of cancer two years ago. She was the love of my life and I don't plan on remarrying, so kids just aren't in my future. That's why I like to get involved with fine groups like Little League."

"The love of your life." The reporter nodded dreamily and then leaned in toward Vance a fraction. "That's really touching. After all, you're one of Richmond's most sought-after bachelors."

Vance made a dismissive gesture. "I'm just a self-absorbed widower who plays golf every weekend, so I especially admire men like Reed Newcombe who take time from their busy schedules to help our community. Reed's got four kids and heads our IT department at Capital City, but here he is, and with a winning record so far too."

Cooper stared at the executive fixedly. The name Reed Newcombe was familiar too, but from where? If he was the head of IT, did that also mean his vanity plate read HRD DRIV? Shaking her head in annoyance at not having any solid answers, she wiped at a sticky trail of red that had melted from her popsicle onto her hand, and resumed listening to the reporter.

"But it was your idea for Capital City to donate new lights, fencing, and electronic scoreboards for all twelve fields, right?" The reporter uncrossed and crossed her shapely legs as she consulted her notebook.

Vance never took his eyes from her face. "Only when Reed mentioned that the fields could do with some sprucing up. As executive vice president of Capital City, I get the pleasure of writing the check and making the speeches, but Reed's done the real work here."

Though the reporter made a show of consulting her notepad, Cooper believed that the journalist was just trying to stall for time so that she could grill the eligible bachelor a little longer. "And you and Mr. Newcombe were fraternity brothers at UNC, correct?"

"That's right." Again, Vance's mouth smiled, but his eyes remained flat. "He was a whiz with computers back then too. Oh, there's Reed's wife, Lynda, waving at me. I should go and say hello. If you have any further questions, please contact my office." He placed a business card in front of the reporter and issued a small nod before she had time to realize that their interview was over.

The reporter stared after him with a dreamy look in her eyes. "Let's get plenty of photographs of Mr. Maynard and his co-worker," she directed her male assistant, who was leaning against a tree, smoking. He shrugged and eased the lens cap from his camera.

Nathan and Cooper followed at a careful distance behind Vance Maynard as he moved to embrace Lynda Newcombe. They were both surprised to see that the woman who returned his hug with a pleasant smile was the short-tempered owner of the shaggy poodle mix. After making small talk with him for a few moments, she led Vance to where her husband stood, talking to his team as they took a break for the seventh-inning stretch. Reed's small frame, thinning hair, and dark goatee struck a chord in Cooper's brain.

"The newspaper article in Brooke's office!" she whispered aloud and snapped her fingers several times as the memory became clear.

"What are you talking about?" Nathan gave her a funny look.

Cooper pressed her fingers to her lips. "Tell you later."

Reed and Vance shook hands and then Reed escorted his old friend to the pitcher's mound and handed him a microphone. Vance waited patiently for the cameraman to arrange his equipment and then cleared his throat and began his speech. As the crowd of onlookers tittered among themselves, Cooper and Nathan crept, as unobtrusively as possible, to the side of the dugout. The second Reed returned from the infield, Lynda appeared at his side and hissed, "What is your new *secretary* doing here?"

Nonplussed, Reed took a deep drink of water from a paper cup. "I don't know, Lynda. She probably came to see the dedication. She loves her job, that lady."

"Loves her job, huh?" Lynda's stare was so fiery that Cooper could practically feel its heat from where she stood. "And I guess all those meetings you've had after work and on weekends have nothing to do with your secretary *loving her job,* right?"

"Lynda," Reed began, his tone exasperated. "Can we do this some other time, like after the game? And in private?"

"Why don't I just ask her right now if she's having an affair with my husband?" Lynda threatened. "I know who she is. She's sitting with that Realtor with the bad hair and the annoying little dog wearing a *costume.* And your new secretary won't even look at me. I find that a little odd, since I met her just last week at your office. Why do you think she might be uncomfortable looking at me, Reed?"

In the infield, Vance was winding up his announcement.

"Please, Lynda." Reed's voice softened. "Don't make a fool of yourself. There's nothing between Cindi and me."

"Cindi?" Lynda seemed momentarily taken aback. "Last time you hung up the phone when I came in the room I could have sworn you said Hazel."

"I'm sure I did!" Reed retorted heatedly. "She's a client. Or *was* a client. See? You don't have to worry about *her* name coming up in my conversations anymore, *dear*."

Lynda's eyes narrowed. "I am going to be watching you like a hawk, Reed Newcombe. We've got four kids and sixteen years together. You'd better be thinking about that, because if there *is* another woman, I'm going to find out. And, Reed?" She jabbed at his chest with her finger. "If we get divorced, I will fight for your very last cent so that our kids and I can live the kind of life we deserve. I will wring you dry. Keep that in mind next time you have an *emergency meeting*." She turned away from her husband.

Cooper and Nathan beat a hasty retreat to the bleachers where Quinton and Bryant waited in anticipation.

"What's going on?" Bryant asked. "Anything interesting?"

"Oh yeah!" Nathan answered. "Apparently the Little League assistant coach for Capital City is also the head of their IT department. He has four kids, an angry and suspicious wife, and is sleeping with Cindi, his new secretary." Nathan turned to Cooper. "Would you like to tell them the most interesting tidbit of all?"

"Please do!" Quinton rubbed his hands together in anticipation.

"Reed knows Hazel," Cooper replied. "In fact, I think he's the one who *dealt* with her when Hazel got on Cindi's nerves."

Quinton pulled nervously at one of his loose jowls. His excitement was replaced by solemn concern. "So you're saying that that man" — he pointed toward the field, where Reed had his arm around one of his players — "is capable of a serious act of violence?"

"We know he's capable of betraying his wife and the mother of his children," Bryant said quickly and then looked at Cooper. "Do you think that Reed might have . . . gotten rid of Hazel? Didn't Cindi tell Trish over their manicure that Hazel had been trying to reach Brooke about a problem with her credit card statement?"

"Yes!" Cooper remembered. "And Cindi tried to get rid of her by telling her to call her *boyfriend* at the IT department. Reed is the head of IT. Maybe Hazel knew about their affair." She looked to the bleacher seat Cindi had occupied, but the single mother and her two kids were gone.

Bryant stroked his chin. "In other words, she might have complained to Brooke or tried to hold Reed's affair over his head to try to get her issues with Capital City straightened out?"

"Maybe. Reed may have felt threatened by Hazel *and* Brooke. He might have decided to silence *both* women!" Cooper replied angrily. "Let's head over to where Trish and Savannah are sitting. We've got to figure out *exactly* what he's done."

"Am I missing something?" Nathan asked her as all four of them began to walk. The announcer called out the final game score and the Capital City bench cheered. "Why do you suspect Reed?"

"Because if his bad-boy behavior came out, he might lose his job, his wife, his position in the community. Who knows what lengths he'd go to in order to protect those things?" Cooper glanced across the field at the other bleachers. The game was over and the players had just finished shaking hands with one another. Several of the boys picked up equipment from the dugouts, but the rest quickly gathered around their parents, tired but animated by their evening of physical exertion.

Lynda Newcombe embraced a young boy wearing a black Capital City jersey, handed him the poodle's leash, and then whistled to gain the attention of three other children hanging out near the concession stand. As all four kids raced toward the parking lot, Reed approached his wife. She barked something at him and then turned away to follow their children.

Looking angry, Reed marched back toward the field, where he paused to whisper a few words in Vance Maynard's ear. Cooper and her friends weren't close enough to hear what was being said, but they could see the deep scowl that appeared on Vance's tanned face. However, the intense frown was immediately replaced by Vance's practiced smile and he whispered something briefly in return, clapped his friend on the back, and then headed for his Porsche.

"Cindi must have gone home," Quinton remarked. "No sign of her or her kids."

"Oh, she's still here all right." Bryant snorted. "She just dragged Reed near that big oak tree over there. See?"

Sure enough, Cindi's white blouse glowed in the spring darkness as she stood with

Reed in a copse of trees lining the parking lot. Her two kids loitered nearby, kicking at the dirt in a display of boredom. As the Bible study members watched, Reed shouted something at Cindi and her face crumpled. She called back to him, her eyes and outstretched arms full of pleading, but Reed turned his back and walked off. Cindi put her face in her hands and her shoulders shook.

"Oh goodness, did we just witness a breakup?" Trish said, leading Savannah over to where the group stood.

Jake joined them, a bat bag slung over his shoulder. "What'd I miss?"

"Cooper thinks Reed Newcombe, the assistant coach for the Capital City team, may be the villain we've been looking for," Quinton answered.

Several of her friends spoke at once, begging Cooper to explain her reasoning. Cooper turned to Nathan. "Do you remember when you called that shipping store? The place where the threatening faxes were sent from?"

"Yeah," Nathan nodded. "But they didn't know what the guy looked like, so it wasn't much help."

"But Jessica remembered that the man who sent the faxes had blond dog hairs on his sleeve," Cooper persisted.

Trish got what Cooper was implying immediately. "The Newcombes' dog! It's a goldendoodle, you know. A cross between a golden retriever and a standard poodle. That's why it has that unique kind of fur. Curly, red-blond, and apparently untrimmed. Goldendoodles aren't exactly a common breed!"

"Cockapoo. Goldendoodle. What happened to beagles and boxers?" Jake demanded. "I've never heard of these wacko dog breeds."

"So," Savannah whispered as though Jake hadn't spoken, her face a sketch of worry. "Based on the dog fur on his jacket sleeve, we have reason to suspect that Reed sent the 'Forget about Hazel' faxes."

"Hey! If he can cheat on his wife and send a pile of nasty letters to that nice Brooke lady, there's no tellin' what that S.O.B. is capable of," Jake snarled.

Savannah touched Jake's arm, just below his tattoo. "Though I'd prefer us not to pass judgment on Reed, I think it's time to tell the police of our suspicions. This man could be dangerous."

"I agree," Nathan said. "I don't think Reed's going to confess anything to us and maybe the police need to poke around in

Reed's life and find enough evidence to get him thrown in jail."

"Well, I hope they find something on him and that Wesley is set free, don't you, Donald?" Trish sighed and then accepted a barrage of kisses from her tiny dog. "But I have my doubts about Reed being caught. That man strikes me as being rather shifty. I think he's learned how to hide his wickedness."

"So there's nothin' else *we* can do?" Jake looked disappointed.

"If there is, God will let us know," Savannah answered.

Donald barked in agreement.

14

That is why snares are all around you,
why sudden peril terrifies you,

why it is so dark you cannot see,
and why a flood of water covers you.

Job 22:10–11 (NIV)

After the game, Cooper went right to bed,
but sleep was slow in coming and not as
restorative as usual. Images of angry faces,
including Lynda's, Cindi's, and Reed's,
flashed through her mind throughout the
night. It was as though she was viewing
these people beneath the rapid, fractured
light of a strobe.

In her dream, the Little League crowd
watched Vance Maynard walk to the pitcher's mound to make his announcement during the seventh inning, but instead of donat-
ing lights and scoreboards, his mouth
opened into an inhuman yawn and released

a deep-throated snarl. He bared his fangs and curled his lip like a threatened wolf while the Newcombes' Goldendoodle and Trish's Cockapoo commenced a chorus of frenzied barking.

At ten past six, Cooper jerked awake and lay unmoving beneath the shadows from the poplar tree outside her window that fell on her ceiling. She heard a dog whining, and the crazed barking from her dream returned to her. After checking to make sure that the complaining canine in the yard below was Grammy's three-legged stray and not Vance Maynard in werewolf form, Cooper pulled on yesterday's pair of socks, which she had discarded on the floor next to her bed, and shuffled into the kitchen to make coffee.

Just as she was opening the fridge to remove a carton of half-and-half, the phone rang. Cooper blinked at it for a moment, still spooked by her strange dream. *Who would be calling at this hour?*

"Hello?" she croaked.

"Cooper," Nathan whispered. "I'm sorry to call so early, but do you have the morning news on?"

"I don't watch TV in the morning. I'm more of a *Breakfast With The Beatles* kind of girl," Cooper answered, speaking too rapidly to disguise her bewilderment. "Am I

329

missing something?"

"You'd better switch on channel six." He waited for her to turn on her set. "I got up before my usual time to catch up on work, and I always put on the local news while the coffee's brewing," Nathan explained. "This morning, I heard one of the anchors mention Reed Newcombe's name and something about him being found in the James River. The full story is coming up next."

Cooper sank down on her couch. "His body? Does that mean — ?"

"Shh!" Nathan commanded. "This is it."

"A Richmond man was allegedly pushed from the Willey Bridge overpass late last night." A photograph of Reed Newcombe appeared in the graphic box to the upper right of an agreeable-looking anchorwoman with solemn blue eyes and a layered puff of brunette hair.

"The man has been identified as Reed Newcombe, a department head at Capital City. Newcombe's wife, Lynda, told a CBS 6 reporter that her husband often worked late so she was not concerned when he did not follow the family home after the Little League game they all attended a few hours before the incident.

"Newcombe, one of the coaches at last

330

night's game, was discovered by two high school students who decided to sneak out for a midnight kayak trip on the James. It was fortunate for Newcombe that the young men broke their parents' strict rules against kayaking after dark, for both boys are certified lifeguards. They witnessed Newcombe's fall from the bridge and immediately pulled him from the river. The Godwin High School seniors then took turns performing CPR on Newcombe until paramedics arrived."

The screen switched to a high school boy with a pinched face and lively eyes. He was dressed in an orange life vest, a damp white T-shirt that clung to his muscular upper arms, and a University of Virginia baseball cap. "We were paddling downstream of the Willey when we saw two shapes near the cement wall above us. We both thought that was weird 'cause you can't stop your car on that bridge just to hang out. It was hard to see much, but the moon was pretty bright and it looked like one guy was kind of supporting a second guy. All of a sudden, we see the one guy lean the second guy against the edge of the wall and — bam! — the second guy is falling through the air!" He shook his head in disbelief. "Guy didn't make a sound — just hit the water like a freakin' cannonball. That's the part that tripped us out. He didn't scream. It was like he was already dead."

The boy removed his cap, raked his hands through his blond hair, and then replaced the cap and glanced over at his friend. "Connor and I busted our asses to reach him. We figured no way he survived that fall, but we had to see if we could do anything."

The reporter, who looked as though he had been up for hours and had already consumed several pots of coffee, jammed the microphone beneath the nose of the second boy. "I understand you're both trained in lifesaving techniques. How would you describe Mr. Newcombe's condition when you pulled him from the water?" he asked, his eyes bright with purported interest.

In a gesture identical to his friend's, the boy named Connor ran his hand through a tousled nest of dark hair. He seemed reluctant to look at the camera. "First we had to get him to shore. He was floating face down when we got to him so I flipped him over, ditched my kayak, and swam him to the bank. Man, he didn't look good. He was cold and his lips were kinda blue," he added glumly, then brightened. "But Neil and I had him breathin' by the time the ambulance came."

"How were you able to alert the authorities?" the reporter asked with wide-eyed intensity.

Connor smirked. "Neil had his cell in a Ziploc. He's totally whipped by his girlfriend and never goes anywhere without it in case she calls."

Neil jostled his friend's shoulder with his fist and the screen switched back to the studio and the impassive anchorwoman.

"Newcombe was taken to CJW Medical Center where he remains in critical condition. Authorities received an anonymous tip that a dark-colored SUV was seen crossing the bridge seconds after Newcombe was pushed into the river. If you have any information regarding the vehicle or any other details relating to this incident, please call Crime Stoppers at the number below."

A band of white numbers on a blue field sprang up beneath the anchorwoman's red suit jacket. After a few seconds, the numbers disappeared and a commercial for the new line of Ford vehicles roared onto the screen. Cooper turned off the television.

"Someone tried to kill Reed Newcombe," Nathan said numbly.

Cooper had almost forgotten that she had the phone pressed to her ear. Shutting her gaping mouth, she tried to digest the information. "This keeps getting worse!" she finally spluttered.

"I know," Nathan replied softly. "Reed must have known something Brooke's killer found threatening. We've been following the right trail. Just too slowly." He sighed. "We couldn't make enough sense of this mess to keep someone from being pushed off a bridge."

Cooper's stomach turned. She fought back the wave of nausea that rose in her throat and moved into the kitchen, where she put the phone down on the counter and drank quickly from the sink tap.

". . . to talk to the police this morning," Nathan was saying when she gripped the receiver once again. "Cooper? Are you there?"

Cooper wiped her mouth with a dish towel. "Yes, sorry. Just give me a sec. It's a bit of a shock . . . this news." She turned the tap on cold, put the cloth under the stream, and pressed it to her forehead. "We saw three people who were mighty unhappy with Reed at last night's game. Lynda, Cindi, and briefly, Vance Maynard." Cooper struggled to think straight. "Did you just say something about the police?"

"Yeah. I'm going in today to tell them

everything we know, even though I bet they're going to be pretty ticked at us for conducting our own investigation."

Cooper's gut constricted again. "Ugh," she groaned, reaching for the coffee carafe. Coffee always settled her stomach. "I am so ready to pass the buck to them. In the beginning, I thought we were doing Wesley a service, but now I feel like we haven't helped anyone. And we still don't know what's happened to Hazel!"

"I know. I'm sorry, Cooper," Nathan apologized, as though he had forced her to investigate Brooke's murder in the first place. "I'll call you after the police are done with me."

The workday dragged by. Cooper did her job mechanically, her hands as adept as always, but her mind drifted from one worry to another. She wasn't surprised when Nathan called to inform her that she would need to make an official statement to the authorities as soon as possible and that she should prepare herself for a stern berating from the officer in charge.

Nathan was right. All seven members of the Sunrise Bible Study group were directed to appear before Investigator McNamara at the police headquarters at six o'clock sharp.

They did as they were told, even though Bryant grumbled about missing one of his live weather reports, and provided explicit statements on their confusing findings, which they then signed. However, none of the group was allowed to leave the small conference room where they had been herded until Investigator McNamara, the officer in charge of the Hughes case, gave them a sharp rebuke.

When McNamara was finished dressing them down, he signaled for them to leave. He remained seated at the head of the table, sifting through their statements. Trish pushed back her chair, hesitated, and then raised her hand. "Officer? Sir?"

"What is it, Ms. Tyler?" The officer looked weary.

"Will you be checking on Hazel Wharton? We're all deeply concerned about her well-being. Her name has come up time and time again in our. . . . We're just afraid for her."

Nathan and Quinton nodded in agreement.

"Please," Savannah added gently, also standing. "We truly meant no harm. We were seeking to aid our friend Wesley. He's been in our church family for a long time and has done many good things for our community. We are certain he is innocent." She reached out, her fingers fumbling against the backs of several chairs as she made her way to the police officer. As she approached the end of the row, her hands lingered helplessly in the air. Automatically, McNamara stood and stretched his arm forward so that Savannah could grasp it. "If he was your friend," Savannah continued, "I believe you would do the same."

Cooper was afraid to breathe lest the officer look away from Savannah's blind but searching stare.

"Ma'am, we're doin' our best," the officer answered, passing Savannah's hand to Jake. "I know you've got your hearts in the right place, but your heads are all mixed up. If your friend *is* innocent, and I mean *if,* you're chasin' after a cold and calculating killer. Now, forgive me if I question your ability to handle the situation if you should come face-to-face with this person." He yanked authoritatively on his gun holster, reminding Cooper of a cowboy preparing for a quick draw. "Job said, *I get my knowledge from afar; I will ascribe justice to my Maker.* Trust your Maker, folks. And trust us. We'll check on Hazel and dozens of other issues related to this case. That's all, ya hear?"

"Investigator McNamara quotes Scripture." Savannah smiled as the lawman strutted off. "I find that most comforting."

"Personally, I'd find Dairy Queen comforting right about now," Quinton mumbled, rubbing his temples.

Nathan slung an arm around his chubby friend. "Me too. A cherry dip cone would sure hit the spot."

"What about dinner?" Trish sounded shocked.

"If you get a banana split, it'll be big enough to count as both dinner *and* dessert," Jake assured her.

"Well, I'm not in the mood for a treat," Trish sulked. "I feel like a little girl in trouble and my parents have told me how disappointed they are by my behavior. I always lost my appetite when I'd been naughty, and I've lost it now!"

Bryant grabbed Trish's hand and began pulling her toward the exit. "Come on, lady. I'll buy you a Diet Coke. I'm sure you can manage to swallow that." He waved his hand toward the police department building. "This was all show and bluster and it worked. We've been chastised and we'll stay out of things now. Except for praying for Wesley and Hazel and now Reed, that's all we can do."

Murmuring in agreement, the group of

friends headed for their cars. Nathan caught Cooper's elbow as she opened Cherry-O's door.

"Are you still up for dinner and a movie on Saturday?" he asked, his face doleful. "I mean, if you change your mind because this whole thing has made you sorry you ever bumped into me that fateful Sunday, I'd understand." He dropped his eyes and stared at his big feet.

Cooper moved a fraction closer, enjoying the feeling of his hand on her arm. Despite her plans to take things slow with Nathan, she knew that she wanted something more from him than a casual relationship. The proximity of his body, the scent of his after-shave, and the sincerity in his voice forced her to recognize that she was attracted to him — that she wanted to spend time alone with him, and soon. Above all else, she wanted him to kiss her, to claim her as his own.

"No matter what, I'd never regret running into you," she murmured. "And yes, we're still on for Saturday." She smiled up at him.

The heaviness evaporated from Nathan's eyes and his hand slid down Cooper's arm, sending jolts of warmth through the right side of her body. His fingertips closed around hers and then he suddenly leaned forward, his mouth parted, and he grazed her lips with his. Drawing back, he winked at her. "Last one to the Dairy Queen buys the popcorn Saturday!" He then squeezed her hand and hopped into Sweet Pea.

Cooper got into her car, brushed her butterfly pin with her right hand, and tried to slow the thumping of her heart. Though she had desired that kiss, she had been completely unprepared for her wish to be granted that very moment.

What a day, she thought and allowed thoughts of Reed Newcombe and the visit to the police department to be replaced by fantasies of a caramel sundae and the possibility of another, more lingering, kiss.

"I know we planned on a movie," Nathan began nervously as he opened the front door of his Fan district row house. "Oh, you look nice!" he said, interrupting himself as he noticed her pale yellow sundress. "And you've got lovely feet, too."

Cooper flushed, embarrassed at her vanity over her polished toes. She had bought two pairs of summer sandals, one in a straw brown and another in black. In her room, she had slipped on the straw-colored sandals, pivoting her feet this way and that in the wall-length mirror attached to the inside of her closet door as she admired her new shoes and still-pristine pedicure.

"Well, it *is* Saturday," she answered, fidgeting with her purse. "No work boots required. Now what were you going to say about the movie?"

Nathan gestured to his porch swing. They both sat down, steadying themselves as it lurched a bit, making them laugh.

Brandishing a slip of paper, Nathan immediately grew serious. "I haven't been able to stop thinking about our investigation," he began sheepishly. "I know we've entrusted our information to the authorities and that should be that, but I can't shake the feeling that Hazel's still in danger. What if the police haven't been to see her?"

Cooper shrugged. "I'm sure they've checked on her. Investigator McNamara seemed sincere *and* pretty darn capable of handling this muddle."

Nathan nodded and twisted the paper in his hands nervously. "I don't know why I didn't think of this before, but late last night, while I was playing a civilization-building game on the computer, it hit me! I could do a reverse lookup using Hazel's home phone number in order to find her address."

"Come again?"

"All the major search engines have them." Nathan waved his hands in animation. "It's the online version of the white and yellow pages, but you can do more creative searches too. I looked up Hazel's phone number online and then typed it in the reverse search box along with the city and state. Only one address result popped up." He offered Cooper the paper. "This is it."

Cooper opened her hand, but didn't even glance at the address scrawled in his nearly illegible writing. Instead, she stared into Nathan's kind eyes. She longed to reach up and stroke his chin and have him kiss her again as he had in the parking lot the other day. However, she could see that he was deeply troubled and was unlikely to enjoy himself on their date until they visited Hazel Wharton. She looked at the address.

"She's close by — in Church Hill. So let's skip the movie and pay her a visit," she suggested.

Nathan beamed. "Hazel's still the key to this whole puzzle," he reminded Cooper. "I'd sleep better at night if I knew she was keeping an eye out for bad guys." He took Cooper's hand and pulled her gently out of the porch swing. "Besides, I wouldn't mind finding out what was wrong with that famous Capital City statement of hers. Seems like a whole lot of evil originated with that document."

"Nathan," Cooper warned. "It sounds like you're going to stir the pot again. We're not supposed to be investigating."

Opening Sweet Pea's passenger door, Nathan gave her a boyish grin. "I won't get us into trouble. I promise. And afterward, we'll go to an early dinner at Strawberry Street Café."

"That's the place that has the soup and salad bar set up in a claw-foot bathtub, isn't it?"

"One and the same," he answered, shutting her door. As he slipped into his seat and gunned Sweet Pea's sleepy engine, he glanced at Hazel's address again and said, "But I'm not wasting my appetite on salad. I'm having chicken potpie followed by a slice of chocolate truffle cake. Hey?" he wondered aloud. "Maybe Hazel would like to join us!"

Cooper sighed. Somehow she couldn't see events leading to the three of them sitting down to a jolly meal together. As Nathan wound through the maze of downtown streets and headed east toward Church Hill, she absently rubbed the butterfly pin, which was attached to the thin white sweater she wore over the sundress, and prayed that they wouldn't discover anything horrible at Hazel Wharton's house.

Fifteen minutes later, Nathan pulled up in front of a dilapidated row house standing at the end of a long line of homes in a similar state of disrepair. Sagging porches, peeling paint, and cracked cement had robbed the once-charming houses of their former dignity. Cars with no tires or utterly rusted bodies had come to their decisive ends on either side of the street, and tiny lawns overrun by weeds formed most of the greenery in the neighborhood. Despite the somewhat bleak environment, children of all skin tones played in the street or sat on decrepit front steps as they chatted with one another.

Nathan told Cooper to stay in the car, but she joined him as he knocked on Hazel's front door. As they waited, Cooper glanced at the two plastic chairs on the porch and at the dead fern on the simple wood table positioned precisely between the chairs. Cooper spied a metal watering can below one of the dirt-streaked front windows. In spite of all the visible signs of poverty around her, the brown and wilted leaves of the fern affected her the most, because the plant indicated that for some reason, its owner had stopped caring for it and had allowed it to die.

"I don't think she's here anymore," Cooper whispered.

Nathan rubbed a clean circle in the glass of the front window and peered inside. Next, he took his sunglasses from his pocket and opened the mail slot. Angling his mirrored lenses into the slot, he shook his head.

"Then where's her mail?" he asked Cooper without looking away from the house's shadowy interior. "If she's not collecting it, then it would be piled all over the floor." He stood and brushed off his pants. "I'm going to check around back and then ask the next-door neighbor if Hazel's been around lately. Do you want to wait here?"

Cooper cast a final glance at the fern. "No."

The backyard yielded no further information. The little lot was enclosed by a rusty chain-link fence whose main purpose seemed to be to act as a divider between the tall grass and scraggly bushes in Hazel's lot and the identical grass and shrubs growing next door. Cooper spied more potted plants on Hazel's back stoop and examined them. Two geraniums, a marigold, and a tomato plant had succumbed to thirst. Cooper plunged her finger into the soil and absently rubbed the dry dirt between her fingertips. She noted a bottle of plant food

345

on a junk-cluttered table by the back door.

"Hazel cared for these plants," she said, fingering the crackly, brown-spotted leaves of the geranium. "The only reason she'd suddenly stop watering them . . ."

Nathan stood on his tiptoes and stared into the small window of the back door. "It's the kitchen. No dishes in the sink. The dish towel's folded on the counter. Two placemats on the table. Salt and pepper shakers. Napkin holder, half full." He stepped away from the window. "Someone lives here all right, but where is she?"

Cooper had to trot to keep up with Nathan's determined stride as he walked to the house to the right of Hazel's. Hazel's squat, eggshell-colored house was at the end of the row, and the house adjoining hers was slightly larger and noticeably cleaner. The porch was free of dirt and dust, and a new rubber welcome mat sat askew in front of the door. Cooper noted that the doorbell glowed, indicating that, unlike Hazel's, it was operational. An old wicker sofa was the only piece of furniture on the porch and the fabric showed faded sunflowers on a field of lusterless blue.

Nathan pressed the doorbell and several seconds later, a hand pulled back the curtains covering the bay window and a pale and wrinkled face appeared. Through the glass, a short, elderly woman holding a crying infant shouted, "We're not buyin'!" and released the curtain again. Without hesitation, Nathan knocked on the window and the woman's face reappeared, frowning.

"We're looking for Hazel Wharton," Nathan called to her.

The woman's frown morphed into a glower. "Why? You ain't no friends of hers."

"No, ma'am, but we've come in the name of friendship," Nathan said hurriedly, his voice pleading. "We're worried that she might be in danger, ma'am. Please. All I ask is five minutes of your time."

The curtain fell back in place and Nathan's shoulders sagged in defeat. But suddenly, locks clicked on the front door and the woman motioned for Nathan and Cooper to step inside the house. Looking up and down the street with more curiosity than alarm, the woman shifted the still-wailing infant to her other arm and closed the door.

"I can tell about folks," she informed Nathan over the baby's complaints. "You two ain't up to no devilment. Here." She pushed the child, who was clad only in a diaper, into Cooper's arms. "I gotta get this chile some milk 'fore she kills me with all that carryin' on."

The woman disappeared from the room and Cooper stared at the baby in astonishment. She whispered, "Shush," and tried to make comforting rocking motions, but her awkward attempts to silence the child were ineffectual. In fact, the tiny girl's face grew crimson with rage and she redoubled the force of her howls.

"Got none of your own, I reckon," the old woman said upon her return, amused by Cooper's discomfort. "I watch this one for my daughter. My name's Rose. Now, sit on down and tell me why you're frettin' about ol' Hazel." She sat and pushed a bottle into the baby's mouth. Mercifully, the crying ceased.

Nathan eased himself onto a side chair covered in plastic sheeting. It made a squeaking noise as his body weight forced creases into the stiff material. "She complained to her credit card company about something being wrong with her bill, ma'am," Nathan replied simply. "And now some folks from that same company have been hurt. Hazel's name has been connected to these people and we're worried about her safety."

Rose nodded, satisfied with Nathan's explanation. "You tellin' the truth all right.

I always knows." She angled the bottle slightly higher and the infant sucked hungrily. "Look here. Hazel's just fine. It's her sister who ain't. Got a bad heart and had surgery. Hazel's gone off to Danville to lend a hand." Rose eyed her visitors over the baby's head. "You're not the first to look for her, you hear? Cops pokin' around yesterday. Same as you all. They knocked, waited a bit, then left." She shrugged. "I didn't pay *them* no mind."

"There were others looking for Hazel?" Nathan squeezed the arms of the chair as he abruptly sat forward and the plastic whined in protest.

"Them first folks was bad." Rose gazed tenderly at the baby in her arms. "It was dark, so I didn't see them good. Two of them knocking on Hazel's door. Next they went round back and I didn't see 'em again for a while. When they headed back to their big black car, they were hissing at each other. 'Minded me of a pair of snakes."

Cooper stared at the child, who had reached up to touch her grandmother's face. "Do you know if these 'visitors' were men or women?" she asked Rose.

"Naw. They both walked like folks who are up to no good. Kind of slinkin'. Like they was more serpent than regular folk."

She stared at Cooper, studying the blue eye first and then, for a bit longer, the green one. The baby finished drinking and drifted quickly to sleep. Cooper swallowed beneath Rose's scrutiny. Finally, the old woman pointed at a brass cross hanging on the wall behind her. "The Lord gave you two ways of seein', girl," she said to Cooper. "The way things is and the way they could be. I hope you don't waste His gifts."

As Cooper tried to fathom the meaning of Rose's odd comment, the older woman shifted the baby to her shoulder and began to pat her firmly on the back. "Them folks came at night — they meant Hazel harm, I just knows it. But Hazel was two days gone already. She left the day after Easter. Hasn't been back since."

"Are you collecting her mail?" Nathan inquired.

Rose nodded. "Got it all in a grocery bag. Them bills'll wait. I think Hazel's gonna move down to Danville anyhow. Her sister's got a nice place and Hazel ain't got anyone left here since her man died a year back."

Nathan drew a business card from his wallet. "Ma'am, could you give this to Hazel when she comes back? Will you tell her to call me and warn her that she's in danger?"

"G'faw," Rose snorted. "Look around,

boy. There's plenty of danger in this place 'sides those folks came lookin' for her." She stared at Cooper again and then, after several moments in which Cooper's neck turned bright red, Rose smiled. "Yessir. I'll tell her. Shoot, she can even stay with me if she wants. Lord knows I could use some help with this chile. Some company too."

Cooper tried to imagine what it was like for Rose to raise an infant at her age and with so few resources. "Do you like cookies?" she asked Rose.

Rose displayed a nearly toothless grin. "Sure enough. Where you think all my teeth got to?"

"My mama makes really good ones. I'll bring you some."

"Bless you, chile. I sure would like me a treat." Rose reached over and clasped Nathan's hand. "You a good man. You try to make wrong things right. I can see that. I'll watch out for ol' Hazel." She stood. "Now, you'd best get goin.' Your car ain't new, but plenty of folks round here would like to help themselves to those rims and maybe your radio too."

Nathan's face was mournful as he squeezed Rose's hand. She cupped his cheek in her weathered palm. "Aw, they's plenty of good folks here as well, boy. Don't you look so down. One day, I'm gonna take my place at the mighty feast with Abraham, Isaac, and Jacob in the kingdom of heaven. Till that glorious moment, my girls and my faith keep me goin'."

Back in the car, Cooper rubbed her butterfly pin for comfort. "Remember the day in Bible study when Bryant was talking about heaven? He was wondering if angels were already living all around us?"

Nathan looked over at her. "Yeah, I remember. And I think he's onto something." He smiled and sighed happily. "I'm so glad we came here. Hazel's okay and now the cops can locate her and talk to her. We can finally step aside and feel like the dark clouds are beginning to part." His smile turned shy. "Um, thanks for standing alongside me today."

"Anytime," Cooper replied sincerely, wondering if all their future dates would be this exciting.

15

"Can anyone hide in secret places
so that I cannot see him?"
declares the LORD.
"Do not I fill heaven and earth?"
declares the LORD.

Jeremiah 23:24 (NIV)

Cooper stood in front of her open closet, comparing the charming hue and feminine cut of the sundress she had worn on her date with Nathan with the rest of her rather tomboyish wardrobe. The Weather Channel hinted at a warm day, with temperatures rising into the nineties, despite the fact that the official start of summer was still weeks away. Cooper wanted to look especially pretty today, for Nathan to look at her the way he had last night on his front porch, when he put his arms around her and kissed her.

It wasn't a long kiss, because Nathan's

neighbors had returned home from an evening out and their energetic pooch had sprung from their car and headed straight for Nathan. Still, it was enough of a physical connection to make Cooper's legs feel boneless. She had leaned into his embrace, caught up in his scent of Irish Spring soap and a hint of earthy aftershave, while her mind emptied of all thoughts but the fullness of his lips.

"I like you, Cooper Lee," Nathan had whispered. Instead of replying, Cooper had pressed her head against his chest and listened to the steady drumming of his heart, feeling as though she could linger there for the rest of the night.

As the neighbors pretended not to watch, the couple had said goodnight and then Cooper had driven home. She was too restless to sleep, so she meandered around the backyard, stroking the three-legged dog and sniffing her mother's herbs, smiling ridiculously at the green tomatoes on the vine, and spinning around in a patch of moonlit grass like a little girl trying out a new party dress.

Cooper was not a woman whose closet was stuffed with frilly dresses, patent leather shoes, or fun jewelry. She and Drew had always opted for comfort over fashion.

Therefore, Cooper's clothes mostly included jeans and plain T-shirts, and these would fail to coordinate with the flush of happiness on her cheeks or the twinkle infusing both her flat blue eye and the dazzling green one.

At least her butterfly pin glinted gaily on her blue blouse. She had washed and polished her treasure before attaching it above her left collarbone. Ever since Grammy had bestowed the pin upon her, Cooper had worn it every day, even to work. The one day she forgot to put it on, she kept reaching toward her left shoulder to touch it, only to meet with the fabric of her uniform shirt. She felt as though something were missing and wondered if the sensation was similar to what married people felt when they left the house without wearing a wedding ring.

Cooper looked down at her bare left hand and tried to dismiss the unbidden vision of Drew wearing a gold band on his ring finger. Instead, she ruminated on how Ashley often paused to twist her gigantic diamond ring so that the stone caught the light. A little smile played at the corners of Ashley's mouth when she admired her own ring, and Cooper was always curious as to the thoughts swimming around in her sister's mind when she smiled like that.

Pulling into the high school parking lot, Cooper shook off the fantasy of having a ring on her own finger one day. After all, she and Nathan had just had their first official date, and she wasn't ready to think of him as more than someone she was just getting to know. Cooper suddenly faced the unpleasant realization that he might still be searching for the perfect woman on RichmondMatchmaker.com. She decided that the next time they were alone together, she would muster up the courage to find out whether theirs was an exclusive dating relationship or not.

Outside the classroom where the Sunrise members gathered, she paused.

Maybe I should wait until he makes it clear what he's looking for, she thought glumly. *What does a kiss mean these days? After all, I thought I knew where I stood with Drew and look what happened there! Maybe I shouldn't even like another guy until I can think about Drew without his very name giving me heartburn.*

Lost in these confusing thoughts, Cooper didn't hear Jake strutting down the hall until he had almost reached the classroom door.

" 'Mornin', Cooper. Mind gettin' that for me?" He gestured with his chin at the door, his arms filled by a box from the liquor store. "It's my turn to bring in food but I didn't remember till it was too late to get anything decent."

"So we're having Wild Turkey for breakfast?" she teased.

Jake grinned and returned the jibe. "Hey, I can only kick one habit at a time, lady."

The rest of the group clapped as Jake set down his burden and pulled out two boxes of Krispy Kreme doughnuts. "They're still warm," he announced triumphantly. He then produced a 107-ounce can of Del Monte tropical fruit salad and waved a can opener in the air. "I know it ain't fancy, but I'm a bachelor with no skill in the kitchen —unless ya need me to fix your sink."

"What are we supposed to use for bowls?" Trish asked, eyeing the fruit salad with disdain.

"Cool your jets, lady." Jake elbowed Trish playfully. "I brought Dixie cups and helped myself to a few plastic forks from the 7-Eleven while I was gettin' gas. See? You won't have to get corn syrup on your fingers."

"You're quite chipper today," Savannah said to Jake as she accepted a cup of fruit from him. Cooper noticed that Jake had picked out several cherries and piled them into Savannah's cup. It was the kind of overture a grade-school boy might do to express a crush on a cute classmate.

Jake then placed a box of doughnuts under Savannah's nose. "Chocolate glazed. Take a whiff." As Savannah inhaled blissfully, he placed a paper towel on her desk. "I'm *chipper* 'cause I haven't had a cigarette in almost a month, so I'm feeling like I really might've quit for good this time."

After receiving words of praise from the other group members, Jake opened his study workbook and folded his hands together. "Cooper's doin' great too, and she doesn't even use the patches."

"I told you," Cooper argued good-naturedly, "that I've been eating way too many cookies to numb the cravings."

Jake gave her a sideways smile and continued, "But I gotta make a confession. I almost had a smoke after that Little League game last week and again after findin' out about Reed gettin' pushed off a bridge. I mean, it's all I could think about. I was even gonna mooch one off the mailman. I was *that* freaked out."

"I know what you mean," Bryant agreed. "I'm afraid I had a few more glasses of merlot that night than usual. The image of someone falling through the air toward the dark water . . ." He trailed off.

"And we've just got to sit back and hope things work out for the best," Quinton muttered, as he neatly broke up a glazed doughnut into bite-sized pieces.

"Today's lesson topic makes it seem even harder to give up our cause," Nathan added. "In Ephesians Six, Paul tells us that we are going to have to deal with spiritual struggles and that mankind has faced these struggles since the Fall. Well, I've got to admit, *my* spiritual struggle is that I don't want to simply *pray* and *believe* that good will triumph over evil, I want to *act!*"

Savannah gestured at her Bible. "Paul details our weapons, friends. Our armor, our shields, our swords are comprised of faith, truth, righteousness, and peace. We won't help anyone without God at our side, and we fight using the Word and with a commitment to prayer."

"I also understand how Nathan feels," Trish countered softly. "I think I've been seeing our involvement in Brooke's murder as some kind of test. The test that Paul talks about right here." She thumped her workbook. "Our call is to fight against darkness, against evil. I felt energized by fighting for good, in trying to bring a murderer to justice, but now I feel a little lost."

Savannah nodded. "I hear you, Trish, but

I think Paul is telling us that we can't fight against evil without putting our faith first, before all other things."

Bryant sloshed some fruit salad around in his Dixie cup. "When I read the words 'you can stand against the tactics of the Devil,' in verse eleven, I thought about how this killer, this person who has brought darkness into the lives of the Hugheses, the Newcombes, to Hazel, and who knows who else, has *got* to be stopped!"

"Actually, Hazel is okay," Nathan stated somewhat guiltily and then went on to explain how he and Cooper discovered Hazel's address and found out that she was out of harm's way in Danville.

"Well, thank goodness *she's* safe and sound." Trish exhaled in relief. "And despite Investigator McNamara's warning, I haven't been able to stop mulling things over in my mind. Personally, I think Lynda Newcombe has a hurt and angry soul, and seems perfectly capable of pushing her husband off a bridge."

"She may have harmed Reed, but why would she kill Brooke?" Bryant immediately argued. "I think our villain is Cindi. Reed broke up with her at the game. You all saw how upset she was!"

"But Brooke's murder was about money,

remember?" Quinton disagreed. "I think Reed was involved in something illegal at Capital City. Brooke found out and he killed her."

Quinton threw out his arms. "Then who shoved him into the river?"

"What about Vance Maynard?" Cooper piped up. "There was a moment at the game where he didn't look too pleased with Reed."

"Yeah, that guy has the cat-who's-caught-a-canary look about him," Jake grumbled. "Too slick for his own good."

Savannah had listened to these tangents with genuine patience, but she finally grew exasperated. "Friends!" she spoke firmly. "We're doing a fair amount of judging and finger-pointing here with no evidence to back up our statements." She tapped on her Bible. "It is not our purpose to decide someone's guilt based on how they look or even how they act. Can we see inside their hearts? There is only *one* who can." Savannah drew in a breath. "Now, let's get back to the lesson, please."

Looking abashed, Quinton pulled out several sheets of paper from his workbook. "Sorry, Savannah. I'm afraid my pride has taken precedence during this whole investigation. I think we all need to do exactly as

Paul counsels us. Perhaps now, more than ever, when we're feeling so low." He stood and shyly placed one of the papers taken from his workbook in front of each group member. "I wrote this song because I was inspired by Paul's final lines of Ephesians. In verse twenty-four he says, 'Grace to all who love our Lord Jesus Christ with an undying love.' "

Quinton drew in a deep breath and continued. "I was really moved by Paul's prayer, which was meant for all of us. I want to be worthy of grace and hope that my humble song will serve as a reminder of my Christian role — that my main purpose is to practice love and kindness and charity. And to pray." He bowed his head as though emphasizing his point.

"Even Jesus took time out to pray and, like Paul says, we have to commit to prayer." Quinton sat back down and stared at his hands. "My song is a kind of prayer. It's called 'Let Me Wash Your Feet, Lord.' I've written songs for years, but you're the only group of people I feel comfortable sharing one with."

Cooper looked down at the paper Quinton handed her and read:

Let me wash the dirt from your feet, Lord,

You've walked so many miles.
Let me wash the dirt from your feet, Lord,
I long to earn your smile.

Let me wipe the dust from your hands,
    Lord,
You've healed so many souls.
Let me wipe the dust from your hands,
    Lord,
All Your glory was foretold.

Let me clean the blood from your wrists,
    Lord,
Those who hurt You don't understand.
You've already risen above them
Son of God and King of Man.

Let me fetch You some water,
Drip it on Your loving brow,
You've given everything to save us,
Let me do the giving now.

You've given everything to save us,
Let me do the giving now.

Let me clean the blood from your side,
    Lord,
Those who hurt You don't understand.
You've already risen above them,
Son of God and King of Man,

Son of God and King of Man,
Son of God and King of Man.

Several seconds passed before anyone spoke, but then Trish, her face covered with rivulets of mascara-streaked tears, covered Quinton's plump hand with her own and whispered, "This is beautiful."

"It really is, Quinton," agreed Nathan as the other members nodded their heads and murmured their compliments. They had all clearly been moved by the song's lyrics.

"You got any more of this stuff?" Jake demanded, his eyes aglow. "We could set it to music, make one of those demo tape things. You've got a gift, man."

Quinton blushed. "Can you write music, Jake?"

Jake fidgeted with his coffee mug. "Yeah, a bit."

"Well, folks." Savannah stood and held out a clipboard for Bryant to take. "Before we head to worship, I asked the church secretary to make us a sign-up sheet to help us accomplish some of the goals Paul set before us. Like Jake mentioned, let's begin by living a life of prayer and then continue by spreading love. I've got open time slots to visit Wesley, Eliza, and Lynda New-combe. I'm sure she could use some casseroles, with a husband in the hospital and four kids to feed."

Cooper spoke up quickly, before Bryant had a chance to volunteer his time. "Could I add someone to this list?"

"Of course," Savannah answered.

"Her name is Rose." Cooper told the Sunrise members about Hazel's next-door neighbor. "She could use baby gear for her granddaughter and some company. When Hazel gets back into town, Rose is going to put her up. She's a giving person and could do with a little taking for a change. I'd also like to ask that my coworker, Ben, be added to our group prayer list. I think his wife's got an alcohol problem, and he seems pretty lost. I don't know how to help either."

"I've got a brochure you can give him," Savannah said, passing Cooper her bag. "It's a telephone hotline for loved ones of alcoholics. Just get that brochure into his hands and trust in God to do the rest."

"Thanks." Cooper removed the brochure from Savannah's leather tote.

Bryant then added Rose's name to the chart and everyone filled in spaces until there were no blanks left. Then they clasped one another's hands and prayed for all of the people on the list.

■ ■ ■ ■

Cooper had signed up to visit Eliza Weeks on Wednesday afternoon. Savannah also chose to visit Eliza and asked Cooper to be her chauffeur. Cooper was slightly disappointed that she and Nathan wouldn't be heading to the Weekses' home together, but Jake was markedly dejected as he eyed the list and noted that Savannah would be accompanying Cooper one day and Bryant the next, leaving him no opportunity to spend time alone with her.

"Why don't you just ask her to dinner?" Cooper felt like advising Jake, but she kept her mouth shut. After all, she'd learned that Savannah's husband had passed away a long time ago, but perhaps that man had been the love of her life. And what did Cooper know about romance? Though Nathan had smiled warmly at her and had sat beside her during church service, he hadn't mentioned getting together in the near future. As a result, Cooper spent the first three days of the workweek preoccupied by doubts concerning her date with Nathan. Was she a bad kisser? Had there been too much garlic on her Strawberry Street Café chicken breast? Had he found someone online that

366

he wanted to meet in person?

"You're kind of quiet today," Savannah commented once she and Cooper had been in the car together for ten minutes and had barely spoken a word.

"Sorry. I'm just spacing out a bit." Cooper sniffed the air. "What did you cook? It smells delicious."

"Pearl, the woman who helps me with household chores, is an excellent cook. She whipped up this Greek spaghetti in no time flat." Savannah smiled sadly. "It's one of my few regrets about not being able to see clearly. Cooking takes a certain amount of finesse that my blurred vision can't produce."

"Well, you make up for it with your paintings," Cooper assured her friend.

Savannah nodded at the compliment. "How about you? Did you bake something? I smell cinnamon."

"I made an iced cinnamon-raisin loaf and picked up a basket of strawberries from a farm stand near my house. I thought it might make a nice afternoon snack for Eliza and her sister."

Savannah closed her eyes and allowed the sun streaming through the windshield to wash over her lovely face. She stayed in this position of repose until Cooper exited off

I-95 and headed for the country roads of Hanover County. Traffic dwindled and the foliage bordering the roads grew thick and verdant.

"Eliza says there's been no word of Jed at all." Savannah finally broke the silence. "Poor thing. I hope she's doing all right. She must have imagined all kinds of awful scenarios by this point. And the police have had no luck tracking Jed down."

"It must be taking every ounce of strength she's got to hold herself together," Cooper replied. As she steered Cherry-O down the Weekses' gravel drive, she immediately noticed that someone had tidied up the property. "The grass has been trimmed," she informed Savannah. "And those planters out front have been repotted and filled with daylilies and purple verbena." She parked the car and turned off the engine. "Walk's been swept and it looks like the windows have been washed. Eliza's sister has certainly been busy."

Placing Savannah's hand on her forearm, Cooper led her friend up the walk. A woman with liberal curves, the same pale hair as Eliza, and a generous smile opened the front door.

"I'm Ellie, Eliza's sister." She hugged them both. "It is so nice of y'all to visit," she said with the accent of one who has lived her entire life in the Deep South. "Eliza's in a real tizzy today, so I'm hopin' y'all can distract her. She keeps declarin' that someone's been sneakin' things outta the house, and this Alabama gal can't talk her out of believin' her wild notions."

Eliza was ensconced on her favorite sofa, the television turned to HGTV. A home makeover show played on the screen while Eliza flipped listlessly through a *Good Housekeeping* magazine.

"I heard that, Ellie." Eliza pouted and turned to her visitors in appeal. "Some of Jed's clothes are missing from his closet. And there's food gone from the pantry and a whole package of toilet paper from the bathroom in the hall!"

"I keep tellin' her that they must've been taken . . . before," Ellie argued gently. "We've had lots of things to distract us lately, what with gettin' the house and the yard in order. And we've been cookin' like two tornadoes in the kitchen, so it's no wonder she's gettin' mixed up."

Eliza gave her sister a fond look. "It's Ellie that's been workin' like a slave. I just point to where the ingredients are and she comes up with dishes that are near divine." She crossed her arms over her chest. "But I know what I know. Things are disappearing."

Cooper led Savannah to a chair and seated herself opposite Eliza. "Have you both been out of the house recently?"

Eliza flushed. "Ellie, bless her heart and her powerful arms, has driven me to Wal-Mart twice over the last week. Got me right up to the front door and into one of those automatic carts, just like Jed used to do." Her lip trembled and she began to weep soundlessly.

"Hush, now," Ellie stroked her sister's hair and Cooper's heart swelled at the sight of such tenderness. She thought of Ashley and was ashamed that she couldn't remember the last time she had made an attempt to spend time alone with her sister. Ashley was constantly trying to help her; albeit her aid was often in the form of beauty advice. Perhaps it was the only way she knew how to reach out. Cooper resolved to call Ashley and plan a girls' night as soon as she got back home. Until then, she was determined to discover the answer to Eliza's riddle.

"Does your property border on other houses?" she asked Eliza.

Eliza nodded. "We've got ten acres, and the closest house is miles away back in the woods. It's a big farm. They'll be startin' up their strawberry pickin' days before long."

"There are no buildings around here?" Cooper thought of all the dilapidated barns and old outbuildings that were scattered throughout every part of the Virginia countryside. She had seen several such structures on the roads that led them to Eliza's house. "Not even a tree house?" she partially joked.

Ellie sat down next to her sister and took Eliza's hand. "You thinkin' there's someone out there?" Her eyes grew wide.

Eliza jerked, her flesh shifting as she moved. She leaned toward Cooper. "There's a tobacco-drying shed on the far side of our property. It used to belong to the farm, back when their family owned all the land round here. Lord, I've never set eyes on the thing, but Jed told me about it. Said it's right near the blind curve in the road you take to get to the farm. Jed said you could see it clear as day from the road in wintertime. He always thought it made a pretty picture with the snow on its roof and the icicles drippin' off it."

Cooper grew excited. "Do you have any binoculars? Maybe I can see it from the road."

Eliza pointed to a cabinet across the room. "Ellie? Would you, dear?"

Ellie jumped up and sifted through all

three drawers. "There's nothin' here."

"Then that's another thing gone." Eliza shivered. "Do you think someone's watching us? Using the binoculars?" Her voice was tiny and frightened.

"I'm going to check out that shed," Cooper said, standing. "If there's no one there, then its less likely someone's been spying on you."

Savannah frowned. "By yourself? Is that a good idea?"

"I'll go with her," Ellie offered. "I'll carry my cell phone and if she doesn't come out of the woods in fifteen minutes, I'll holler for Johnny Law quick as you can blink."

Eliza twisted her hands with worry. "Oh, be careful, you two."

Cooper turned right from the end of the Weekses' gravel drive. Cherry-O bounced so roughly on the uneven dirt road as they headed west on Happy Hanover Farm Road that Cooper felt as though her teeth were in danger of becoming separated from her gums.

"Have you been to the farm before?" Cooper inquired of Ellie, her voice wobbly as they rounded a particularly jarring bend.

Ellie grinned and steadied herself against the dashboard. "If you're worried 'bout missin' that blind curve, don't be. You practically gotta come to a full stop to get around it."

After a few more minutes of jostling, they followed a gentle curve and immediately afterward, the road turned so sharply to the left that all Cooper could see were tree trunks. She slowed down dramatically and whistled. "Wow. You could really get clobbered here."

"Funny enough." Ellie shrugged. "They bus school kids out here all the time for pumpkin and strawberry pickin' and hay rides. Nobody's ever been hurt. I don't know how a bus driver could finagle one of those big school buses over this road, but they do. Jed says the kids love being bounced about like pinballs. The ride to the farm is practically like bein' on a roller coaster to them." She grasped her generous bosom. "But it makes me wish I was wearin' two bras!"

Laughing, Cooper looked for a break in the woods once she maneuvered around the curve and pulled Cherry-O gently off to the side. She left the engine running and glanced at her watch. "Fifteen minutes?" she confirmed with Ellie, swallowing hard. Trying to appear as brave as possible, she waved and then turned toward the woods.

She walked straight in for a few moments and then looked back over her shoulder. She could see the red glint of her beloved truck through a break in the trees. Casting her eyes left and right, Cooper kept walking.

Only a minute or two passed by the time she spied the old tobacco-drying shed. She hesitated, bending her fingers one by one and wondering if there really was someone inside. If there was a person in there, were they a killer? She imagined a dark shape huddled within the shed, holding a gleaming chopping knife and waiting very, very patiently for her to become the next victim.

Shoving such thoughts aside, Cooper plodded forward through a thick blanket of leaves. She stepped on sticks and pinecones as she progressed, and if someone was indeed hiding within the shed, that person would certainly be aware that an intruder was approaching.

Pausing once more, Cooper stooped to retrieve a heavy stick. She snapped off the end so that it formed a point and held her makeshift spear in her right hand, poised to strike, and pressed her body against the back of the shed. Her heart was thundering in her chest, making it difficult to listen for sounds coming from inside the building.

Cooper took her time examining the

condition of the old structure from the outside, noting that new pieces of plywood had been nailed over the larger holes in the weathered brown boards. Steeling herself, she eased back the crooked door to the shed and peered inside. Without entering, she was able to see a sleeping bag, a Coleman camping stove, two kerosene lanterns, and a group of Hefty bags stuffed with what appeared to be clothes, unopened food packages, and garbage. Next to the sleeping bag, a milk crate, which served as a nightstand, held a stack of paperbacks. Cooper thought that the book titles might reveal something about the shed's occupant, but she was too afraid to set foot inside the lair of the person who had blatantly pilfered items from Eliza's house.

Behind her, a twig snapped and Cooper drew in a sharp breath. She raised her pointed stick and prepared to swivel around and meet her attacker face-on, but before she had a chance to flex a single muscle, the metal mouth of a gun barrel was pressed harshly into the small of her back.

"Don't move," a man's voice growled.

Wincing, Cooper began to pray that her fifteen minutes were up.

16

He did not say this because he cared
about the poor but because he was a thief;
as keeper of the money bag, he used to
help himself to what was put into it.

John 12:6 (NIV)

Cooper's assailant tried to get a glimpse of
her face without removing the gun barrel
from the middle of her back. She could
sense him angling his body forward in order
to look at her and she tried not to grimace
at the pungent smell emanating from his
body.

"Why don't you tell me why you're tres-
passing on private property?" the man demanded.

Could this be Jed? Feeling a glimmer of
hope, Cooper spoke as calmly as she could.
"Is this your property . . . sir?" Her voice
trembled as every fiber of her being focused
on the feel of the metal pressed against her

thin shirt. She could sense the cold hardness of the weapon — its powerful and indifferent ability to end her life within a matter of seconds. She closed her eyes and prayed desperately as she waited for the gunman to answer her question, knock her out with a blow to head, or squeeze the trigger. She braced herself, too fearful of the possibility of pain to do anything else.

The force of the gun barrel eased a fraction. "I'm asking the questions," the man grumbled, but the malice in his tone had lessened. "Who are you and what's your business in these woods?"

Cooper swallowed, "I'm a friend of Eliza's," she answered. "A recent friend, but I suspect you know that already."

The man uttered an unintelligible sound and slung the gun over his shoulder. Cooper cautiously turned around and faced him. She saw a man in his mid-sixties, with unruly gray hair and a wild beard, both peppered with bits of leaves. His blue eyes were puffy and looked bruised from lack of sleep, and his frame was rather gaunt. He had the ripe odor of someone who was no longer maintaining a regular hygiene routine. Cooper noted his long and ragged fingernails, the assortment of stains on his jeans, and the sweat marks on his shirt.

He narrowed his eyes and appraised her in turn. "What do you mean by that remark?"

"You've been watching Eliza," Cooper said very gently, concerned about the man's state of mental health. If she voiced her suspicions, would she be in greater danger than before?

As she tried to decide how to explain her statement, the man shifted the gun from his shoulder into his hands and she quickly held out her own in supplication.

"It's okay!" she said quickly, stepping back a pace. "I know you're just looking out for her. I'm concerned about her safety too . . . and for yours." She let her hands fall slowly to her side. "You're Jed Weeks, aren't you?"

The man's shoulders sagged. He let the gun slip from his fingers and fall softly onto the bed of leaves, but immediately, he squatted down and picked it up again, his face filled with distrust.

"I go to Hope Street, Mr. Weeks," Cooper hastily assured the frazzled man. "Savannah Knapp sent us to check on Eliza. I was here once before, a week or so after you first disappeared. At that time, your wife thought you were having an affair." She spoke softly, as though coaxing a skittish animal to take food from her hand. "Now she's concerned about your safety, Mr. Weeks. More than concerned. She's terribly upset."

Jed looked stricken. He held out his dirt-encrusted hands and touched the gold wedding band on his ring finger.

"I guess you never left for that fishing trip at all," Cooper continued. "This is all tied to the murder of Brooke Hughes, isn't it?"

Jed nodded. He removed two shells from the shotgun and met Cooper's stare. "Yes," he whispered, as though it was an effort to form words. He spoke again, his voice slowly gaining strength. "Brooke hired me to investigate a case of fraud against her own company. My findings were confidential and meant for her eyes alone. When I heard she'd been killed, I knew it was because of what I'd discovered."

His eyes darted around the woods. "I was sure the murderer would come after me next. Only Brooke and I knew the truth, so I wanted to get away from Eliza so she'd be safe." His eyes darted around the woods. "I figured it was only a matter of time before the killer came to the house. I figured I could stop them and that it would be best if Eliza genuinely believed I had run off."

"You've been hiding in these woods this whole time?" Cooper asked in astonishment. Then, without waiting for his reply, she glanced at her watch. "Shoot!" She glanced at the shotgun, berating herself for her choice of words. "Mr. Weeks! Please! We've got to get back to my truck before Ellie calls the police! She was going to call if I didn't return in fifteen minutes. Come on!"

Without checking to see whether Jed was behind her, Cooper raced toward the road. Branches scratched her face and neck but she didn't slow down. Breathing hard, she burst out of the woods and waved at Ellie, who had her red fingernails poised over the keypad of her phone.

Ellie put her window down a few inches and frowned. "What in the *world* is goin' on? Do you know how *close* I was to callin' for help?" She fanned her flushed face. "It's gotta be a thousand degrees in this here truck. I've never been so —"

"I found Jed," Cooper interrupted. Ellie's jaw dropped.

"I think he's gone a bit soft," Cooper said, lowering her voice. "He's been roughing it out here for all these weeks." She turned and scanned the break in the trees for a sign of Jed's blue pants and green shirt.

"For heaven's sake, what was the man thinkin'?" Ellie's voice grew shrill. "Does he know what kind of fiery hell he has put my

380

sister through?"

"I'm sorry," Jed said from afar as he stepped warily out of the woods. He no longer carried his weapon. He looked at Cooper. "And I apologize for pointing my gun at you. I didn't mean to scare you like that."

"Lord have mercy!" Ellie opened the door, slid out of the car, and put her hands on her curvy hips. "You look like you've been shipwrecked! Come on now, you're goin' home. I don't know what Eliza's gonna make of her man lookin' like *Castaway* Tom Hanks, 'cept you've got a bit more gray to your hair than ol' Tom, but I suspect she'll recover from the fright eventually."

Jed shook his head. "I can't go back, Ellie. I've been reading the paper pretty regularly because I ride my bike to the library in town every couple of days. Brooke's killer is still out there, and now someone's tried to bump off Reed Newcombe. It's not safe for me to be around Eliza. Can you just get her out of the house for a few hours so I can take a shower and get some fresh clothes and food?" he pleaded.

"I *cannot* do that to her, Jed. No sir." Ellie clasped her hands together. "I can see that you're in some kinda fix, but we'll think of somethin'. There ain't no way you're goin' back to that shed. My sister is sittin' in that big ol' house with her heart breakin' into little pieces. You're comin' back with me if I gotta carry you myself." She flicked her eyes over his lean figure. "Skinny as you've gotten, that should be no trouble at all."

"Ellie's right, Mr. Weeks," Cooper said gently. "Not only is Eliza suffering, but your fellow churchgoer, Wesley Hughes, is in jail for a crime he didn't commit. You need to tell the authorities what you know. Your information could break the case wide open!"

Jed rubbed his filthy hands together, indecision playing across his haggard face.

"I'll call the officer in charge of the case. He's a good guy," Cooper assured him. "He can come out here and talk to you without anyone being the wiser. Then you *and* Eliza can go away somewhere."

"We're not gonna keep chewin' the fat on this dirt road. Git in the truck, Jedediah Weeks." Ellie pointed at the car, her eyes steely.

Jed didn't dare refuse her. He climbed into the cab seat like a penitent child.

The threesome rode back to the house in silence. Cooper was dying to ask Jed a dozen different questions, but he had put his head against the seat back and immediately closed his eyes. Even though she disagreed with his decision to hide in the woods behind his property instead of contacting the authorities, Cooper felt a rush of sympathy for him. Ellie was the only person who seemed delighted by the outcome of their foray to the tobacco shed. She hummed cheerfully as Cherry-O bounced up and down among the deep divots and churned up a wake of dust.

As Cooper pulled in front of Jed's house, he opened his eyes, leaned forward in his seat, and touched Ellie on the shoulder. "Give me a minute alone with her, okay?"

Ellie pivoted in her seat and nodded. "Of course, honey. You just hold her tight and tell her it's all gonna be right as rain." She raised her finger and wiggled it at him. "But don't you dare go tellin' her all the details till I'm back inside. I've earned the right to know just what has happened."

Jed's exhaled wearily, but his eyes were alight with anticipation. "Yes, you certainly have, and I will spend many days expressing how grateful I am for the comfort you've given Eliza. Aside from my wife, you're one of this world's finest ladies, Ellie May. God bless you for your strength and loyalty."

Tears sprang into Ellie's eyes. She pivoted and wordlessly pressed her hand into Jed's.

She and Cooper watched as Jed strode into his house, his anxiety over reuniting with his abandoned wife revealed in the twitching of his fingers. The door opened and he entered his home.

For a while, the two women sat in the car and watched the windows in the wing where Eliza sat waiting, as though the curtains would be pulled aside and they could witness Eliza's face when she realized that her husband was alive and standing before her. The curtains remained still, however, while Cooper and Ellie made small talk and shifted impatiently in their seats.

"I can't take this much longer!" Ellie declared after ten minutes of waiting. "Maybe we'd best check on Jed. My sister's got a mean left hook, and if she's real angry . . ." She trailed off as the front door opened and Jed waved at them to come inside.

Ellie jumped out of the car and hustled as fast as her fleshy legs would carry her up the steps, down the hall, and into the room where Eliza sat fanning herself on the sofa. Cooper was right behind an out-of-breath Ellie. Savannah was still settled in the chair across from Eliza, her face infused with a range of emotions. As Cooper watched her friend, Savannah dabbed at her nose with a tissue.

"My fool of a husband would like to take a shower," Eliza began, her voice trembling as she gazed at Jed adoringly. "But he's gonna have to stink to high heaven a tad longer while he tells us all *exactly* why he's been livin' in that ol' shed like some kind of fugitive."

Jed sat on the floor near his wife's feet, clearly reluctant to soil the upholstery of the creamy white couch. He gulped down a glass of water and opened his mouth to speak.

"Hold that thought, Jed. I'll be right back," Ellie ordered and bustled out of the room. She returned with a plate laden with Greek spaghetti. She thrust the plate into Jed's hands and dumped a napkin and silverware onto the coffee table next to him.

"Thank you kindly." He smiled at Ellie and then hungrily twirled a thick wad of noodles covered in feta and mozzarella cheese onto his fork and pushed them into his mouth. When he had chewed and swallowed, he set the plate gingerly on his lap.

"I've known Brooke Hughes for years," he began. "We served on several Leadership Committees at Hope Street Church together, and I knew her as a woman with a kind heart and sound judgment." He loaded his fork again, but this time with careful deliberation. Cooper thought he showed incredible restraint considering how famished he must be. "Therefore, when she asked me to investigate a possible case of internal fraud at Capital City, I was pleased to oblige. Brooke told me that her suspicions of internal fraud were aroused after an elderly African American woman named Hazel Wharton complained that her Capital City statements were inaccurate by a total of three cents and they'd been off for the past four months."

"Three cents?" Cooper asked.

Jed nodded. "Every month, she had been overcharged on her bill by three cents, and whenever she called customer service, she received a runaround. There were no records of an overcharge according to Capital City. Customer service representatives checked, but insisted that Hazel was talking nonsense. Eventually, Ms. Wharton contacted Brooke Hughes, who offered to meet with her."

Smiling thinly, Jed recalled Brooke's story of Hazel arriving with an old-fashioned adding machine and a pile of statements and receipts.

"Brooke told me that Ms. Wharton was

old and frail, and looked like a little owl, due to her diminutive size and enormous glasses. Brooke said that Hazel was sharp as a tack. She counted each penny she spent and kept every receipt — no matter how small the purchase. And Capital City had indeed been overcharging her for the past four months, but the overcharge was only reflected on Hazel's statements."

"All the hubbub was over, what, twelve cents?" Ellie sounded dubious.

Jed ate a few more mouthfuls of spaghetti. "Hmm. Delicious." Eliza touched him on the shoulder and he tore his gaze from the food and continued his narrative. "Brooke began to examine random customer statements from the same time period. She actually stopped by their houses and reviewed their statements. It seems that other customers had also been overcharged. *A lot* of other customers."

Savannah raised her brows. "So now it's more than just twelve cents from one person. It's twelve cents times lots of people."

"Yes. Brooke assumed it was thousands and thousands, in fact." Jed ripped a piece of bread in two but didn't lift it to his mouth. "I discovered that she was right. Someone inside Capital City had created a monumental scam, which was to run for six months and charge each customer three cents extra per statement. The person or people involved in this scam were looking at walking away with almost two million dollars."

Cooper frowned. "But if you only had one charge on your bill, surely you'd notice that your total payment due to Capital City was off by three cents."

"I wouldn't!" Ellie declared. "I just look at the bottom line and pay the bill."

"That's how most folks are," Jed said, looking at his sister-in-law. "But whoever wrote the computer program was smart enough to make sure that statements with single items weren't included in the scam. Plus, the extra money only appeared on the person's bill, but not on the electronic balance sheets at Capital City. This devious computer whiz, who I now suspect may have been Reed Newcombe, had to also write a second program to filter the extra money to a private bank account." Jed's expression turned sheepish. "Brooke was killed before I could investigate the fraud any further, but I'd be willing to bet there's a whole pile of money in someone's secret bank account and that Reed wasn't the only fellow at Capital City with dirty hands."

"So Brooke was killed after you gave her

your written report," Cooper stated. "That's what was jammed in her copier the day I met her. She was very agitated and said that she really needed copies of that document. Now I see why she was upset and frightened." She sighed. "That poor woman."

"But Jed!" Eliza's eyes filled with tears. "If you were pickin' up newspapers over the last few weeks, you knew Brooke's husband was arrested for murder. How could you let him sit in jail when you *knew* he was innocent!" Her voice was anguished.

Jed's face was filled with shame. "I figured the evidence against him was circumstantial and all I could think about was that the killer might come looking for me and hurt you." He turned and took both of Eliza's hands in his own. "I was just trying to buy time, my love. If I took you away with me, we'd be easier to track. I'd have to take the van and . . ."

"People notice me because I'm big and I'm in a wheelchair," his wife finished Jed's thought. There was no bitterness in her tone, but Cooper saw Jed look away, his face etched with agony.

"I couldn't risk you, Eliza," he whispered softly. "You're my everything. I've been out there, twisting my mind into knots trying to think of a way to clear this up. I even mailed

Brooke's boss a copy of my report the day I heard about Brooke's murder on the news, but I guess *he* was too scared to show it to anyone."

Cooper started. "Who's her boss?"

"She reports directly to Vance Maynard," Jed said. "I figured he'd want to know if someone was stealing millions right out from under his nose."

"Unless he was sharing in those millions," Savannah suggested quickly.

"But wouldn't someone get wise to that much money comin' into a bank account?" Ellie asked. "My bank would notice if I started wirin' them truckloads of cash."

All the women looked at Jed. He shrugged. "The money could have gone to an offshore account or to a Swiss bank account. Even in this day and age, you can hide money obtained by illicit means and still look squeaky clean."

Unintentionally, Cooper grabbed Jed's arm. "Vance Maynard just got back from a trip to Switzerland!" She immediately released her grip and returned to her own space, but her voice tripped from her mouth rapid-fire. "And when Nathan and I were searching Brooke's home office, she was reading a book about offshore investing. The chapter she had marked was on *Swiss bank accounts.*"

Jed instantly grew alarmed. "Vance was Brooke's mentor. She would have invited him into her house without giving it a second thought. He could have shot her and no one would ever suspect him. After all, he's a charming widower. But good Lord, doesn't the man have enough money?" He glanced forlornly at the women in the room. "Oh, no! What have I done? I should have sent the report to the police! But I was so worried they wouldn't catch the person responsible and then they'd come looking for me. And you, Eliza."

Eliza took her husband's face and cradled it in her hands. "It's not too late, darlin'. Cooper has the number of the man in charge of the case and you'll call him right now. Then you'll take a nice hot shower, put on some clean clothes, and eat some of Cooper's homemade raisin bread along with a nice cup of coffee. While we're waitin' on the investigator, you, me, and Ellie will figure out how to make ourselves scarce until there's enough proof to put the real criminal behind bars and get Wesley Hughes set free."

"All right, Eliza. We'll tell the cops, but then we're leaving." Jed turned to Ellie. "Do you still have that little cabin in North

Carolina?"

Ellie nodded. "I was rentin' it for a while, but it's empty as my pocketbook right now."

"Not for long. I'm going to call that investigator from my office. Eliza, you think about what you want to pack."

Once Jed had left the room, Cooper tried to organize the multitude of varied thoughts swirling around in her brain. She tried to form a picture of Vance Maynard, the handsome philanthropist executive, killing Brooke and then shoving Reed Newcombe off a bridge. She found that she was able to envision Vance in the role of villain with greater ease than she expected, especially when she recounted his false smile and his smooth talking the night of the Little League game. She also remembered the brief but intense anger on Vance's face when he had spoken to Reed before driving off in his Porsche.

Savannah suddenly stood and cleared her throat. Cooper ceased thinking about Vance and took her friend's arm. "Are you all right?"

"Yes," Savannah answered. "But we should get a move on." She turned toward Eliza. "We shouldn't be here when Investigator McNamara arrives. He specifically asked us to stay out of this affair and I doubt he'd be pleased to see us here when he comes to speak with you and Jed."

"She's right," Cooper added. "Hopefully, Jed's information will put an end to the entire investigation anyhow." She smiled at Eliza. "I can't wait to let the other Sunrise members know that Jed's safe at home. They've been so worried about you."

Eliza held out her hands in supplication. "Please don't tell the folks at Hope Street about Jed just yet. I'd like some time to organize ourselves for a long stay in a small cabin with only a battery-powered TV before it gets out that my husband didn't actually run off with some piece of two-bit trash." She grinned. "It'll wound my pride somethin' awful for folks to think that he's been cheatin' on me, but it's better than facin' a cold-blooded killer." She plucked at a loose thread on her sleeve. "It's not that I don't have faith in the police, but we're not brave like you folks. We're gonna crawl under a North Carolina rock until this storm blows over."

"It won't be easy, but we'll keep the happy news about Jed's return to ourselves for now," Savannah promised Eliza.

Jed reentered the room and immediately went to his wife's side. "I've called in the cavalry." He kissed her round cheek and then backed away. "Forgive me, dear. I must smell like a barnyard. I'm going to get cleaned up and then I'll accept your offer of coffee. I'm too full for raisin bread, I'm afraid. The investigator will be here in thirty minutes." He looked at Ellie in appeal. "Think you can brew us a fresh pot in that time?"

"Do I?" Ellie squealed. "I've got more in mind for you than just coffee, Jed Weeks. I'd like to put ten pounds back on your bones 'fore that cop steps foot in this house, but I reckon we should let you ease back into it, so we'll just start with liquids. Go get some soap on your skin. I'll meet you in the kitchen." She gave Cooper and Savannah brief hugs. "I'm mighty grateful that Eliza's made such fine friends as a result of this mess," she said, and then hurried off to start the coffee maker.

"Ellie's right!" Eliza exclaimed. "How can I ever thank you both? You came to bring me comfort and you end up finding my husband — and that poor dear man had clearly lost his way." Eliza put her hands over her heart as she spoke. "And please don't tell me what you did was nothing. You brought my Jed — my best friend, my truest love — back to me. You've taken the darkness from my life and brought me light."

Savannah smiled. "That wasn't our doing, Eliza. We were guided by a power greater than ourselves." She embraced the larger woman. "Anytime you want to come to church, you've got a group of friends to sit beside you. You hear?"

"Thank you," Eliza whispered and then turned to Cooper. "Can't I express my gratitude in some way? Please think of something. I'm beggin' you."

Cooper paused and then an idea came to her. "How do you feel about dogs?"

"I love them," Eliza answered, somewhat perplexed. "Jed and I were thinking of adopting one . . . well, before things got all turned around, that is."

"I know of a sweet dog that really needs a home, but he's missing a leg. Are you okay with that?"

Eliza thumped her own useless limbs and laughed. "Are you kiddin'? He sounds perfect! We'll pick him up on the way to North Carolina. I hear there's a forest filled with squirrels and rabbits where we're headed." She winked playfully. "And if that dog's bum leg keeps him from catchin' furry creatures, Jed will just shoot 'em in the leg — even things up a bit."

Cooper laughed uneasily, uncertain whether Eliza was joking or not.

17

So man lies down and does not rise;
till the heavens are no more, men will not
   awake
or be roused from their sleep.

If only you would hide me in the grave
and conceal me till your anger has
   passed!
If only you would set me a time
and then remember me!

Job 14:12–13 (NIV)

Cooper hadn't spoken to Nathan since they had exchanged banal chitchat during the Sunrise Bible Study meeting. The evening after discovering Jed Weeks in the woods behind his house, she wanted to call and tell Nathan about her exciting day, but when she actually picked up the phone, doubt assailed her before she could dial his number. After her experience with Drew, she wanted to be certain Nathan cared for her before she trusted him completely. Cooper decided to wait for him to contact her for a second date, and if he did call, she'd assure him that Eliza was well, as she had promised to keep mum about Jed.

When she returned from work the next day, the only new message on her answering machine was from Trish, asking Cooper to take her place Saturday morning in visiting Lynda Newcombe at Reed's room in the critical care unit at Henrico Doctors' Hospital. Apparently, Trish needed to show a couple from out of town half a dozen houses in a single day. In exchange for Cooper taking over her hospital duties, Trish offered to pay a visit to Rose instead.

"And I'll stop by Babies 'R' Us on the way and bring that little granddaughter of hers a whole shopping cart full of goodies," Trish added as extra incentive.

Cooper returned the call and left a message on Trish's voicemail saying she'd be glad to visit Lynda, though in truth, she hated hospitals and hadn't been to one since her high school field hockey accident.

Next, Cooper went through her mail, which was comprised of bills, catalogues, and coupons for services she would never need, such as outdoor lighting or garage organization. At least her Visa bill was shrinking, though with agonizing slowness.

Glancing outside her window, Cooper surveyed the sun-bleached garden and Grammy's comforter hanging heavily on the laundry line. The three-legged dog, soon to be adopted by Eliza and Jed, slumbered in a small circle of shade on the patio. Cooper sighed. The evening stretched before her, feeling more lonely than usual.

In search of distraction, she phoned her sister.

"I was just going to call you." Ashley seemed pleased that Cooper had contacted her first. "When do you want to go shopping?"

Cooper frowned. Her interest in revitalizing her wardrobe had waned a little following Nathan's lack of follow-up since their date Saturday night. "I dunno. Maybe I'll wait awhile."

"For what?" Ashley demanded. "Your clothes are *never* going to be in style. They're too androgynous. You need some color and some shape in your wardrobe," she insisted. "And don't worry, I'm just going to make suggestions. I won't be pushy, I promise."

"Yeah, right," Cooper responded uncharitably and then regretted taking her dating woes out on her sister. She thought about the camaraderie between Eliza and Ellie and how she had vowed to spend more time with Ashley. "I'm sorry. I know you've got good intentions. Let's go this weekend. We can have lunch. I've got to see someone in the morning, but I'm free after that."

"Let's add a pedicure to our outing." Ashley giggled. "Mama's told me all about how vain you've gotten about your *purty* toes. Oh, now don't get your hackles up," she added when Cooper didn't respond. "I'm just so thrilled that you're primping like a *real* girl. How are things with Nathan?"

Cooper confessed that she had no idea where she stood with her fellow Bible study member.

"Don't you fret," Ashley commanded. "When you show up for church on Sunday, you'll be in an outfit that'll knock his socks off."

"It might take more than a new dress to figure out how he feels," Cooper argued woefully.

"It won't be the clothes he notices, Coop. It'll be your confidence," she explained. "When you feel beautiful on the inside, it shines through. That boy is going to be *totally* blinded by you! Oh, here comes Lincoln. He's home early. See you Saturday."

As it turned out, Cooper saw Nathan earlier than she had anticipated. He called shortly after Ashley hung up, just as Cooper was dumping a fistful of uncooked linguine noodles into a pot of boiling water. Reaching for the phone with one hand, she up-ended a small jar of Ragu into a saucepan and set the gas flame on low with the other.

"Hey, you," Nathan greeted her. "Sorry I haven't caught up with you in a few days, but I just got a new client — Virginia Credit Union — and have been burning the midnight oil this week. How did things go with Eliza?"

Stirring the meat sauce with a wooden spoon, Cooper reported that Eliza was holding things together with the help of her sweet sister, Ellie. As she elaborated on Ellie's culinary skills and how clean and organized the Weekses' house had become, Cooper added some minced garlic as well as fresh basil and oregano from her mother's herb garden to the pan. She inhaled the aroma contentedly as Nathan talked about his day. Seeing her own smile reflected in the toaster, Cooper knew that the flush on her cheeks had little to do with the fact that she was standing over a pot of bubbling tomato sauce.

"By the way, I switched my volunteer day

with Quinton," Nathan said. "His nephews are in a karate tournament on Saturday so he couldn't make it to see the Newcombes in the hospital. Maybe we could catch a movie once I'm done there."

Cooper looked toward the ceiling of her apartment and mouthed, *Thank you, Lord.* She then told Nathan that she was taking Trish's place on Saturday.

"Perfect," said Nathan. "Now we can go to that matinee we missed last weekend. You still game for that flick about the international espionage ring?"

"Sounds great. I love action movies," Cooper replied. After hanging up with Nathan, she transferred the steaming noodles from the pot to the colander, then feverishly dialed Ashley's number.

"I hope you're free on Friday," she hurriedly told her sister. "How about I take you out for a girls' night instead of our Saturday lunch date?"

"Only if there's a good reason." Ashley pretended to pout. "You're going to drag me to one of those burger joints, I just know it. You eat more red meat than a lion."

"We can eat wherever you want. And I *do* have a good reason." Cooper told her sister about her previous phone calls.

"Sweet mercy!" Ashley declared. "I've got

to form a plan of attack. You'd better leave Thursday *and* Friday open. We'll do nails, clothes shopping, find you some decent perfume, and get you waxed again. Maybe you should get your legs done this time. A girl can never be too prepared." She paused for breath. "And don't worry about Saturday. I've got the *most* adorable new pink and green argyle golf sweater that I'm just dying to wear to the club. Now I'll have the chance to show it off at the Eighteen Holes for Autism Awareness Benefit Game."

After digesting the complicated event title, Cooper said, "I didn't know you played golf. I thought tennis was your game."

Ashley snorted. "I'm not *playing,* silly. I'm just driving around a golf cart filled with coolers of champagne. It's going to be hot out there, you know, and people'll write bigger checks after they've had a few."

"That's a pretty shirt," Nathan complimented Cooper after meeting her in the hospital hobby.

Smiling, Cooper repeatedly smoothed down the fabric of her green floral tie-back tank top. She was unaccustomed to wearing such a form-fitting shirt and had almost refused to purchase it, but Ashley insisted. Her stylish sister said that it was the perfect

403

accompaniment for the pair of white capris she had convinced Cooper to buy, claiming that their stretch fabric accentuated Cooper's trim legs.

"I wish I had a sweater," Cooper mentioned as she and Nathan boarded the elevator for the critical care unit on the fifth floor. "Why are hospitals always so cold?"

"Maybe they're trying to prevent the germs from multiplying," Nathan said as he pressed the already lit elevator button for the third time. "I've got to tell you, Cooper. I'm not very comfortable in hospitals. I never know what to say, and the second I visit someone here, I'm already thinking about when I can leave."

"I don't think anyone likes to come here. I mean, unless you're having a baby, you're not really at the hospital to celebrate anything."

Nathan touched her shoulder. "I'm sorry. I forgot that you lost an eye in a place like this. I'm so used to your two different colors that I don't really notice anymore. I guess I just see you."

Cooper's neck grew warm. "That's one of the nicest things anyone has ever said to me, Nathan Dexter." She reached over and squeezed his hand. Nathan smiled and raised her hand to his lips. He brushed her palm with the faintest of kisses, sending a flutter of heat through Cooper's arm. As the elevator doors opened, he reluctantly released her.

They paused to check in at the nurses' station where a soft-spoken nurse with white-blond hair and a sincere smile gave them directions to Reed's room.

"Did you ever wear colored contacts?" Nathan asked tentatively while stepping around a cart stacked high with folded linens. "To try to match one of the eye colors?"

"I did wear a green contact for a long time because Dre—" She cut herself short. "Because my ex-boyfriend bought it for me," she admitted. "But it never felt quite right. I didn't really want to cover up the green eye because it was a gift and I didn't want to cover my blue eye either because, well, that's mine. It's part of me. When I covered up my eye, it was like hiding part of myself away, so I stopped wearing the contact."

Nathan squeezed her shoulder in understanding and then abruptly stopped walking. They had reached Reed's room.

It seemed impossible that Reed Newcombe was the immobile figure in the bed. Tubes came out of his mouth, an IV line from his arm, and black wires attached to monitoring equipment formed a spiderweb around his upper body. Electric green waves and repetitive bleeps from two of the machines added to the gentle, repetitive noise of the respirator. Cooper reflected that the room seemed oddly peaceful. Lynda Newcombe sat in an upholstered chair by the room's only window, her head slumped forward and her mouth agape in sleep.

As Nathan knocked quietly on the open door, Cooper took a step closer to Reed under the pretense of placing a fruit basket on the table next to his bed. Reed was a small man in stature, but he seemed even more shrunken in the hospital bed. White sheets were tucked tightly around his frame like a shroud, and his closed eyes and expressionless face made him look closer to death than to the world of the living. Cooper was surprised to feel a tear tickle the surface of her cheek.

"Mrs. Newcombe?" Nathan whispered and Lynda opened her eyes slowly, as though reluctant to return to reality. "I'm Nathan Dexter. We're from Hope Street Church. I believe you've met some of the other members of our Bible study." He hesitated. "Um, we've brought dinner for you and your family."

Lynda said nothing and her fixed gaze was not unfriendly, just tired. Nathan shifted on his feet and pointed at Cooper. "This is my friend, Cooper. We were also at your husband's most recent Little League game, though we were rooting for the other team, I'm afraid."

Giving Nathan a weak smile, Lynda accepted the brown grocery bag with quiet thanks.

"We can only take credit for the delivery," Cooper said lamely, not knowing what else to say to Lynda. "My mama insisted on making every dish."

When Maggie heard about Cooper's errand and the fact that Lynda had four boys, she had wasted no time fixing the Newcombe family a hearty supper. As a result of her kindness, Lynda received a meal consisting of chicken dumplings, onion rolls, salad, green beans, and a pie made with fresh peaches from a local farm.

"This is very nice of you," Lynda muttered. "Lots of people I don't ever know have been so kind to us since this happened. I'm very grateful, but it feels strange too."

"How is your husband, ma'am?" Cooper whispered.

"You don't have to keep your voice down," Lynda answered instead. "He can't hear you and I'm tired of acting like we're already at the funeral. Truth be told," she glanced sideways at Reed, "there are moments when I'm not sure I want him to wake up."

Neither Nathan nor Cooper replied.

"I know how that must sound to you churchgoing folks, but Reed hasn't exactly been good to me or to my boys for quite a while." She sighed and ran her fingers through her disheveled hair. "There have been other women, a lot of overtime at the office, and recently, a whole bunch of expensive purchases we can't afford." She took a sip of water from the glass by her side. "I don't know why I'm telling you all this. My parents took my boys to Kings Dominion today to get their minds off their father, and this is the first real sleep I've had in days. I'm just babbling. Don't pay me any mind."

"We're sorry to have disturbed you," Cooper said, and started backing toward the door.

"No, please stay. I could use some adult company," Lynda beseeched them. "It's been just me and the boys for a long time now. Reed's paid the bills and done his public bit, like the Little League stuff, but he hasn't been *home* with us for years."

"But you're here, by his side," Nathan

pointed out. "That's what really matters, Mrs. Newcombe. What is Reed's prognosis?"

Lynda looked at the inert figure of her husband. "He's suffered oxygen deprivation and had some bleeding in his brain, probably due to the force of the impact when he hit the water." She swallowed. "They've got him in a medically induced coma to help bring down the swelling in his brain. They say it's a miracle he survived at all, but that he may never be the same after what he's been through." She shook her head, fighting back emotion, though Cooper couldn't tell if it was anger or grief.

"Who would do this to him?" She raised her voice, still staring at Reed. "It was no accident, that's certain. Someone pumped him full of morphine so that they could shove him off the bridge with him offering up no resistance."

"Morphine?" Nathan's face creased in thought.

"Yeah." Lynda chuckled without humor. "And I had nothing to tell the cops except that I suspected that Reed was screwing around on me, and maybe his girlfriend got really mad at him. I couldn't even tell them who the latest bimbo was. Some woman named Hazel? His new secretary? The waitress at our favorite Italian restaurant? Who knows?" She got up and began to pace. "I almost laughed out loud when the cops asked me where *I* was Saturday night. Supermom Lynda was hosting a sleepover with half the Little League team. I would have *loved* to have been out on a bridge in the moonlight instead of telling my son and his friends to be quiet every ten minutes." She snorted ruefully.

At this opportune moment, there was a brisk tap on the door and a doctor wearing a white lab coat over blue scrubs entered the room. "Hello." He smiled at Cooper and Nathan and then made his way over to Lynda's side. "How are you, Mrs. Newcombe?"

"Hanging in there," she replied, smirking. "Actually, I'm a bit better today, Dr. Palmantiers. These two brought me dinner to feed the boys tonight, so that's one less thing I have to worry about."

Nathan cleared his throat. "Doctor? Mrs. Newcombe mentioned that Reed had morphine in his system. You need a prescription for that drug, correct?"

"Yes," the doctor answered and then began examining Reed's chart.

"Why would someone be given a prescription for morphine?" Nathan persisted.

The doctor turned a pair of bright blue

eyes in Nathan's direction. "Primarily for pain control," he replied, and then, seeing that Nathan had opened his mouth to ask another question, elaborated further. "For example, I've written prescriptions for patients with severe pain resulting from a variety of medical conditions from kidney stones to chronic back pain. However, I most commonly prescribe morphine to my patients who have cancer and are suffering from constant pain."

Cooper stared at Nathan. Why was he suddenly so curious about morphine? Doctor Palmantiers told them that he'd like to have a word with Lynda about Reed's condition, so Nathan and Cooper wished Lynda well, shook the doctor's strong, warm hand, and exited the room.

"Vance's wife had cancer!" Nathan announced as soon as they were out of earshot. "What if *he* gave the morphine to Reed? It obviously wasn't Lynda since a bunch of kids saw her all night long, so that leaves Cindi and Vance as the primary suspects. Cindi was clearly upset over being dumped, but what was Vance angry about that night?" He rubbed his long chin. "How are we ever going to find out?"

Cooper thought about Vance's recent trip to Switzerland and about the report Jed

411

Weeks had mailed to the executive right after Brooke's death. "We should call McNamara and tell him that Vance's late wife died of cancer and might have had a prescription for morphine," she suggested. "Maybe then he'll poke around into Mr. Executive Vice President's life a little deeper. As for us," — she held out her hands helplessly — "short of driving to Vance's house, knocking on the door, and asking him why he had words with Reed at a Little League game, we're not going to be able to find out."

"Maybe that's exactly what we should do." Nathan entered the elevator and stood inside the car, so lost in thought that he forgot to press the button that would take them back to the lobby.

"I doubt he'd tell us anything," Cooper said. "We have no excuse to interrogate Vance, McNamara would probably toss us out on our ears."

"Or arses," Nathan mumbled.

"The only reason I can think of for approaching him at home is to pretend to ask for a donation to a charity," Cooper suggested. "We'd need to come up with a genuine charity, though, in case he actually gives us a check."

"That's a great idea! Hope Street has been

collecting funds for the women's shelter. Maybe he'll let us in if I tell him about the project." Nathan beamed at Cooper. "Let's drive out to his place right now! I'll call McNamara about the morphine theory en route."

"Wait a second." Cooper followed him down the long tile hall, which smelled of a nauseating mixture of lemon disinfectant and fried chicken. "Do you even know where Vance lives?"

Nathan's cheeks grew warm. "Uh, yes. I like to Google people when I'm bored. I've Googled *all* of the major players of this drama and I remember where Maynard's place is. He's on a pretty parcel out in Goochland, right near Hermitage Country Club. The house looks so big from the aerial view that I don't think we can miss it."

There goes our matinee again, Cooper thought. And then, *Computer maps show aerial views?*

"Do you mind driving?" Nathan asked once they had reached the parking deck. "Sweet Pea has been acting up today and I don't want to break down out in the country."

Cooper knew that this adventure could lead to something messy, but she wanted to spend more time with Nathan and, truth be

413

told, she enjoyed the excitement of playing detective.

"We can take my truck, on one condition." She patted her stomach. "We can go to the Sunset Grill Café for lunch first. Believe it or not, the smell of that fried chicken made me hungry, even if it was mixed with Pine-Sol."

"Deal." Nathan hopped into Cherry-O. "It's too bad we don't know some society person. I mean, Trish knows rich people, but we need someone from the blue-blood, country club set to give us the inside scoop on Vance."

Cooper immediately thought of Ashley. "I'm related to someone who travels in that circle. She's no blueblood, but she'd sure like to be."

"Can you call her?" Nathan's eyes gleamed.

Knowing full well that they were not supposed to investigate any longer, Cooper recalled how recklessly she had entered the woods in search of Eliza's stalker, and how favorable that outcome had been. "Okay, wait till we get off the highway and I'll call her. In the meantime, call McNamara."

Nathan complied and then began speaking rapidly into his cell phone. A few seconds later, he slipped his phone back into his front pocket. "I left a message on his voicemail. Your turn."

Cooper dialed while the truck was stopped at a red light, but Ashley didn't answer her phone. Cooper had an image of her sister whizzing zealously around a putting green in her golf cart as champagne sloshed onto the trimmed turf. She left Ashley a message and pulled into Sunset Grill's parking lot. As usual, the eatery was crowded and they had to settle for a table near the bar. Though tempted to choose the daily fish special, Cooper ordered the more humble cheese and asparagus quiche and a tossed salad while Nathan opted for chicken wings.

After the waitress had served them both sweet tea with lemon, the pair exchanged anecdotes about their workweeks. Cooper shared how Make It Work! had landed two new accounts: the new Bon Secours medical office center as well as all of the State Farm Insurance branches. The increase in business meant that Mr. Farmer would be forced to hurriedly hire another full-time employee.

"The poor person Mr. Farmer brings on will have to take full responsibility for the shredding business," Cooper said as she drizzled blue cheese dressing on her salad. "The rest of us are thrilled. No one really likes driving around all day and emptying those bins. I already feel sorry for the new guy . . . or girl."

Nathan told of a frustrating day in which one of his clients made him change the design of their Web site three times before finally agreeing to the initial design. As he mimicked the client's whiny voice, their waitress came by to deliver the check. Cooper reached for it, but Nathan covered her hand with his own.

"I'm an old-fashioned guy. We're on a date so I'll take care of this." He placed a twenty on the table and held on to Cooper's chair as she stood.

"Okay, but if we ever *do* make it to a movie," Cooper replied as they headed out to her truck, "I'm going to buy the tickets."

Nathan told her that Vance Maynard's house was quite close to the Sunset Grill. In fact, it took less than five minutes for Cooper to reach the curvaceous driveway marking the entrance into the exclusive property. Just as she was going to ask Nathan what to do next, her cell phone chirped. She pulled onto the shoulder just past one of the stone pillars flanking Vance's driveway and flipped her phone open.

"It's so funny you asked about Vance Maynard," Ashley trilled. "He's here at the golf benefit today!"

"Is he standing close by?" Cooper felt paranoid. She didn't want harm to come to her sister.

"No, he's throwing back some g and t's with the other boys inside the clubhouse. I'm out here cleaning up after their first nine holes," Ashley stated petulantly.

Cooper searched for a way to pep up her sister or, in Ashley's current state of sulk, she wouldn't feel like gossiping about Vance. "How'd your sweater work out?"

"Just peachy!" Cooper could sense some preening on the other end of the line. "I know I'll be in the next club newsletter. Too bad it's in black and white. Anyway, what do you want to know about Vance? I could tell you that he looks mighty sharp in a tuxedo."

"When did you see him wearing one?"

"Last week. Saturday night was the Red Ribbon Gala. It was a dinner dance to raise money for cancer research. Vance's wife died of cancer, so he's very involved in the cause."

Cooper was glad she was no longer driving, as she might have swerved off the road after hearing that remark.

"Ashley?" Cooper tried not to sound too eager. "Do you know what time Vance left the gala?"

"He was still there when Lincoln and I snuck out before the stroke of midnight. I was turning into a pumpkin 'cause I just couldn't dance in my Marc Jacobs pumps for another second."

Cooper tuned out as Ashley droned on about which women wore the skimpiest dresses, who ate their neighbor's portion of lemon cream cake, and which members of Richmond society most likely wrote the biggest checks.

"*I* wouldn't wear a strapless gown and let my dance partner dip me like that!" Ashley jabbered on. "Now we all know that she *did* go to a plastic surgeon last July instead of *relaxing* at her beach house like she said."

A car suddenly appeared in Cooper's rear-view mirror. It was exiting Vance's driveway. Cooper accidentally loosed her grip on the phone as she recognized Cindi's old Honda. The phone skittered across the seat, though Ashley's perky jabbering continued unabated.

Nathan scooped the phone off the seat and handed it back to Cooper. "Ashley, I gotta go! Talk to you later!" She cut her sister off and turned the car around.

"What's going on?" Nathan was bewildered. "Isn't that Cindi's car?"

"Yes." Cooper sped up in order to keep an eye on the Honda as it disappeared around the numerous bends in the road. "We've got to speak to her, Nathan. If she's involved with Vance somehow, we need to warn her — tell her about our suspicions."

"If she is involved with Vance, maybe we shouldn't trust her either."

Cooper frowned. "Cindi's got two kids, Nathan. She's probably just looking for a new boyfriend. After all, Vance could easily afford to take care of her kids, and I don't mean to sound callous here, but Reed's no good to her as a provider anymore." She eased off the accelerator as the road took a sharp turn. "If Vance is our bad guy, then there's no way Cindi knows about it. I doubt she'd deliberately put her kids in harm's way. Besides, she drives a Honda Civic, and the person who pushed Reed off the bridge drove an SUV, remember?"

"You're right." Nathan nodded. "I've got to stop searching for the worst in everybody and try to concentrate on what's motivating them instead. Cindi's after money, I'm sure of that, and she's only acting this way to provide a better life for her kids. Even so, she doesn't know that this sugar daddy has a dark side worse than Darth Vader's. We've got to convince her to get as far away from

Vance as she can."

"Good thing we came here today." Cooper was pleased.

"Oh, man. McNamara is going to wish he had locked us up when he had the chance," Nathan groaned, but then his mouth turned upward in a mischievous grin.

18

They eat the bread of wickedness
and drink the wine of violence.

Proverbs 4:17 (NIV)

Cindi drove her Honda as though she were late for an important appointment. Cherry-O shook noisily as Cooper roared up the on-ramp of I-64, trying to keep the silver sedan in sight.

"I don't like driving this fast," Cooper said as they blew past an eighteen-wheeler piled high with logs. "I feel like I'm in tryouts for the NASCAR circuit."

"Just stay within nine miles of the speed limit and we should be okay," Nathan suggested. "I've heard that's how to drive fast without getting a ticket."

Cooper eyed her speedometer. She was doing seventy-five in a sixty-five-mile-per-hour zone. "Someone should tell Cindi about the nine-mile thing. She's doing at least eighty."

The pair watched Cindi switch lanes without signaling as she maneuvered the Honda around slower traffic. Approaching the split for I-95 South and I-195 toward downtown, Cindi positioned herself in the middle lane and hugged the bumper of a FedEx truck.

"I can't tell which highway she's going to take." Cooper stared fixedly through her windshield as the cars in the two right lanes began to slow down. Within seconds, Cindi, Cooper, and the rest of traffic had eased to a complete stop. Finally relaxing a bit, Cooper scanned through the AM radio channels until one of the disc jockeys announced that there was a major accident on I-95.

"Nothing new here, folks," the disc jockey scoffed in his deep, smooth voice. "The section of 95 as it cuts through Richmond is the worst scrap of asphalt in the nation, but you all keep voting against the road repair bills, so enjoy sitting there while you inhale the sweet-smellin' exhaust from all those tractor trailers. Or find yourself an alternate route, because two of the three southbound lanes are closed. And now for the weather."

"Look!" Nathan pointed at Cindi's car, which suddenly slid behind a white van traveling in the exit-only lane for the Downtown Expressway. Cooper, who was firmly wedged between two cars in the middle lane, looked over her right shoulder to see if she could also pull into the moving stream of traffic. She knew she should wait for an open space of road to present itself, but if Cindi's car disappeared around the bend, they'd lose sight of her. As the log truck began to bear down upon them, Cooper stomped down on the accelerator. The driver of the log truck blared his horn as Cherry-O shot in front of him.

Nathan's face was a bit pale as he said, "Now that's aggressive driving."

As they headed south, Cooper didn't release her tight grip on the wheel. There was no sign of Cindi.

"I think I've lost her," Cooper moaned as they passed the Cary Street exit.

Nathan checked the off-ramp as they shot by, and shook his head. "Not there. We'll catch her at the toll." He shook a fistful of change. "Take the exact-change lane."

The tollbooths lay ahead on a downward slope in the road. After a few seconds of scanning the area, Nathan spied Cindi's car pulling out on the other side of the tolls.

"There!" He pointed as Cooper put down her window. "Hurry! Dump the money in!"

Frazzled, Cooper threw the change in the metal basket and then almost clipped the gate as it lifted in agonizing slowness. She cut off a minivan in order to follow the Honda as it exited at 7th Street. The minivan driver, a man wearing a baseball hat and sunglasses, rolled down his window, shouted an expletive, and gave Cooper the finger. Her neck turned bright red as she gave him a peace sign in return.

"Why did you do that?" Nathan asked.

Cooper shrugged. "I guess I was trying to tell him I deserved that gesture."

Cindi's car merged onto East Byrd Street and then continued heading east half a dozen blocks. Just past Virginia Avenue, she pulled into the basement parking lot of one of the newest luxury condominium high-rises that were sprouting up all over the waterfront.

"I wonder who lives here," Cooper said as Cindi's car disappeared in the shadows. Not knowing where else to go, Cooper headed for a section of parking spaces set aside for visitors and turned off the truck.

Just then, Nathan shouted, "She's getting in the elevator!" He pointed toward the dimly lit elevator bay as the brass doors slid closed.

He and Cooper hastened to the elevator,

but it was already moving upward. By the time it returned to the parking garage, it was empty except for a beautifully dressed elderly woman. Emerging from the elevator, the woman withdrew a large ring of keys from her purse and in doing so, dislodged a white envelope, which fluttered to the ground. The woman, who was unaware of having dropped what appeared to be a cash envelope from the bank, nodded politely at Cooper and Nathan, and walked by.

"Ma'am! Something fell out of your bag!" Nathan grabbed the thick envelope, and, without so much as glancing at the hundred-dollar bill that protruded from inside, he handed it back to her.

She beamed at him. "Oh my. How careless of me. Thank you ever so much!" She tucked the money envelope back into her bag. "And people say there are no gentlemen left. Pfahh!"

"Thank you." Nathan issued a soft bow. "Um, could I beg a favor, ma'am?"

"Of course, my dear," she responded warmly.

"We're looking for a friend of ours. We were wondering if you were a resident here and might by chance know her."

The woman raised her chin proudly. "As a matter of fact, I'm in charge of the new neighbor welcome baskets, so I know all the residents."

Nathan smiled. "It's awfully lucky we ran into you then. Our friend is Cindi Rolfing. Does the name sound familiar?"

The woman's pleasant smile evaporated instantly, to be replaced by a fierce scowl. "If you're a friend of that tramp's then I have nothing further to say to you."

Nathan stared at the woman in mute bafflement.

"Wait!" Cooper pleaded as the woman turned away. "We're actually concerned for her children."

"What children?" The woman's scowl turned into a sneer. "You mean that pair of brats who run wild all around the grounds *completely* unsupervised? *If* they are, in fact, her progeny, then she certainly hasn't raised them correctly."

Cooper gaped. What did she mean "if"?

The woman narrowed her eyes. "Why not tell me the truth? You can hardly be friends of *Ms.* Rolfing's if you don't know which floor she lives on." She waggled a finger at them. "I'd bet my prize orchid that you weren't even certain she lived here. Can't say I blame you on that score. After all, look how she dresses." Her gaze grew steely. "Come on, out with it or I'll call security."

Panicking, Cooper glanced at Nathan, but he was clearly at a loss for words.

"We work for the law firm of Winters & Winters," Cooper quickly lied. "We represent the wife of one of Ms. Rolfing's . . ." She floundered about, wondering what to call Cindi's men.

"Paramours?" the older woman swiftly guessed, her white eyebrows raised and her blue eyes lit with curiosity.

"Yes, ma'am. We're building a divorce case against her husband."

"Which one? The tart's got two boyfriends," the woman stated acidly. "A little man, not much bigger than today's television actors, has been there the most, but I've seen her with another man as well. I've never seen *that* one's face, but he's taller. *Both* men come at night and don't leave until morning." She brushed a fleck of dust from her sleeve. "And *I* should know. I live next door."

"I guess that explains how she can afford the rent," Nathan murmured.

The woman snorted. "There's no rent, young man. *Someone* has bought the premium condo she resides in. At close to five hundred thousand dollars, *Ms.* Rolfing must be *very* persuasive between the sheets." Disgusted, the woman put a hand on her hip. "Your *friend* is in 6A. It is my sincere hope that once this divorce case is over and the husband is sued to the ears by his poor wife that our resident hooker will find herself out on the street!" She shouldered her purse. "Now if you'll excuse me, I'm late for my hair appointment."

Exchanging stunned glances, Nathan and Cooper got into the elevator as though they were walking through a thick fog.

"Two boyfriends?" Cooper repeated in bewilderment.

"I guess so," Nathan replied and shook his head. "Reed *and* Vance? At the same time? Now *that* requires some juggling."

They rode up to the sixth floor while trying to make sense of Cindi's behavior. "What are we doing?" Cooper whispered as the doors opened. "What if she's involved in this mess?"

Nathan waved off her suggestion and stepped in front of the door marked *A* with a shiny brass letter. "Like you said before, she probably wouldn't put her kids in jeopardy. There must be some logical explanation for her to have been at Maynard's house."

"I'm sure money had something to do with it," Cooper muttered cynically.

"Maybe," Nathan agreed. "Or maybe

she's trying to build a case against him too. After all, she obviously cared for Reed or she wouldn't have been so upset about him breaking up with her." He lowered his voice to a whisper. "Cindi may actually be able to provide *us* with some answers."

Cooper wasn't sure she agreed with this line of logic, but before she could protest, he rang the doorbell to 6A.

There was a slight noise directly on the interior side of the door, as if Cindi were leaning against it as she looked through the peephole. Since Cooper wasn't standing alongside Nathan, it was likely that his was the only face Cindi would see as she gazed out into the hall. After several tedious seconds, the door opened.

Cindi was wearing a pleated black skirt and a black-and-white polka-dot silk blouse. A thick leather belt encased her narrow waist and a white headband secured her dark hair. She was barefoot and Cooper couldn't help but notice that her stubby toes were painted an unattractive shade of orange. Her eyes were bloodshot and puffy with unshed tears.

"Aren't you the Xerox people?" Cindy asked derisively. "What on earth are y'all doin' here?"

Cooper thought it was a fair question, but

before she could think of an answer, Cindi passed her manicured hands over her face in a gesture of fatigue and resignation and mumbled, "Look. Whatever the reason, this isn't a good time."

Nathan's arm shot out to prevent Cindi from closing the door. Her eyes widened in surprise.

"We came to warn you." Nathan spoke gently. "We think the person responsible for Brooke Hughes's death is . . ." — he fumbled for words — "someone you might be friends with."

Clearly disturbed by this pronouncement, Cindi took a step back into the shelter of her apartment. "How do you know anything about my personal life?"

"We're from the church Brooke attended," Nathan explained simply. "And we've been trying to get her husband Wesley released from jail by finding her real killer." He stole a quick glance at Cooper. "Now we think we know who he is."

Cindi paused, her face a mixture of fear and a desire to hear him out. "I'm not sure I like the sound of this, but you'd better come in."

Cooper had just crossed the threshold when Cindi blocked her way and pointed at her rubber-soled sandals. "Please take off your shoes," she said with distaste. "I don't like the floor to get scuffed."

Quickly complying with her request, Nathan and Cooper removed their shoes and lined them up alongside Cindi's sexy black sandals. Eyeing the sharp heels, Cooper could see how they might pose a threat to the blond wood that ran the length of the great room.

"This place is beautiful," Nathan said, awestruck.

Cooper moved slowly past a small marble fountain that gurgled hypnotically before she glanced into the kitchen, which was all gleaming granite and polished chrome. An enormous glass vase stood on the center island. It was filled with clear marbles and several calla lilies placed with such precision, that Cooper wondered if the flowers weren't in fact glued to the base of the vase.

Cindi smiled. "Mighty nice, isn't it? My boyfriend hired some fancy decorator to make this apartment look like a magazine picture."

Pivoting around, Cooper took in the white shag carpet, the voluminous white sofas with matching side chairs, and the glass and chrome accent tables. The coffee table, which was made entirely of glass that sparkled beneath the soft overhead lights, held no books. Instead, two crystal glasses and a sleek decanter half-filled with amber liquor decorated the piece. Dozens of beige and brown pillows made with expensive-looking fabrics were carefully scattered on the sofas, and several large floor pillows were stacked in front of a fireplace whose mantel bore a collection of modern chrome vases. Each vase was filled with a single gerbera daisy the color of a ripe orange. Lush silk curtains in a camel hue flanked enormous windows that overlooked the historic canal to the south and the James River to the west.

"This view!" Cooper breathed and then turned away from the window in an effort to break free from the apartment's spell. It was easy to forget about the outside world in such a lush and hedonistic setting.

Nathan also tore his eyes from the breathtaking view. "Where are your kids?"

Cindi's face immediately grew guarded. "With their father. Why?"

"Just trying to be friendly," Nathan answered kindly. "I know they must mean the world to you."

Cooper reflected on how Cindi's neighbor had said, *If they are her progeny* . . .

Making an obvious show of shifting back and forth on her feet as though she was in a state of discomfort, Cooper cleared her throat in embarrassment. "Nathan, you fill Ms. Rolfing in on all we know. Ma'am, I had an awful lot of sweet tea for lunch. Would you mind if I used your bathroom?"

Hesitating fractionally, Cindi nodded and then said, "This way." She walked several feet ahead of Cooper and hastily closed the doors leading to two of the three rooms off the hallway. One of the doors had a sign reading BEWARE OF KIDS: STAY OUT! hanging from the knob. Gesturing to the only remaining open door, Cindi flicked on the light to a bathroom painted in bold crimson.

In case Cindi was standing right outside, Cooper used the bathroom. Afterward, she washed her hands and then opened the door a crack. No one was in the hall, and she could hear Nathan's voice in the other room. Flushing again, Cooper pulled the door shut behind her and as quietly as possible, eased open the door across from the bathroom.

A speedy glance confirmed that the room was a media center. A large flat-screen television dominated one wall while a U-shaped sofa in black leather took up the remaining space. The only accents in the room were the square, red pillows on the sofa and the black-and-white photographs on the wall. As Cooper looked at one of them more closely, she gasped. It was a nude photograph of Cindi, lying on her stomach with one of the square pillows propped beneath her arms. There were a dozen shots altogether, each showing Cindi revealing parts of her body that should only be seen by a doctor or a lover.

Cooper closed the door and dashed back into the bathroom where she turned on the faucet and splashed her face with cold water.

"Are you okay in there?" Cindi's voice echoed down the short hall.

"Ye-es." Cooper struggled to control her astonishment. "I'll be right out."

She wiped her hands and face on a black hand towel embroidered with the letter C in gold thread. Then, turning on the tap once again, she snuck out of the bathroom and opened the door with the sign hanging from the doorknob. Having already spent far too long pretending to be using the facilities, Cooper only took the time to peek at a single object inside the bedroom. One look within the family album was all she needed to cause her heart to skip several beats. She ducked into the bathroom, turned off the water, and reentered the white, beige, and chrome living room.

"Sorry," she said, avoiding Cindi's gaze. Instead, she locked eyes with Nathan, taking comfort in the kind, familiar face. "My lunch doesn't seem to be settling too well."

"Let me get you some ginger ale," Cindi offered and walked into the kitchen.

Nathan got up from where he had sunk into the cushions of one of the white sofas and took Cooper's elbow. "You don't look so good." He searched her face as the sound of an icemaker depositing ice into an empty glass resonated from the kitchen.

Cooper didn't reply, but gestured in the direction of the kitchen and then made a pair of horns on either side of her temple using her pointer fingers. Nathan frowned and shrugged.

"She and Vance —" Cooper began.

Cindi came back into the room carrying a highball glass filled with ice in one hand and a gun in the other.

"Sit down," she commanded with a flick of the gun as she made her way over to the coffee table. Utterly relaxed, Cindi perched at the end of the sofa across from her guests and poured herself a drink from the crystal carafe. "I'd offer y'all some whiskey, but it's the good stuff."

"You don't have kids, do you?" Cooper blurted out as she stared at the gun held so nonchalantly in Cindi's hand.

Cindi drank a slug of whiskey and licked her lips. "Nope. I can't have babies. There's somethin' wrong with my plumbing." She put a hand on her flat stomach and grinned wickedly. "My job was to seduce Reed Newcombe and convince him to make up a computer program to steal money from Capital City customers. Well, Reed loves kids, and I knew he wouldn't wanna be with me unless I put on the helpless little mommy act, so I borrowed my sister's kids a couple of times." She looked up, her eyes dark and defiant. "I've been good to those snotty brats too! Bought 'em all kinds of stuff, though I'd like to have killed 'em a dozen times over."

Nathan looked around wildly, clearly searching for some way to distract Cindi and buy them some precious time. "But Reed has four kids of his own. How could he afford this place?"

Cindi polished off the whiskey. "Ever since our scam got goin', Reed's had plenty of cash, but it turns out he didn't plan to share it with me after all." She poured herself another splash of whiskey and laughed condescendingly. "He actually wanted to patch things up nice and pretty with his sow of a wife. 'Course he didn't get a chance to

436

tell *her* that!" She smirked.

Cooper thought back to the brief exchange between Reed and Vance on the pitcher's mound. "Is that what Reed told Vance at the Little League game? That he was planning on quitting his job at Capital City? Vance looked angry, and then he wiped the emotion from his face and pretended to be supportive."

"Reed wasn't supposed to quit. He was supposed to get caught, but he let Vance down by turning into a prissy Boy Scout at the last second." Cindi crossed her legs and allowed her back to rest against the plump cushions. "I was gonna get rid of Reed sooner or later. Vance and I just needed someone to pin the blame on, so that boy's days were numbered from our first kiss. He made it easier by makin' both me and Vance mad. Can you believe that he actually broke up with me?" She uttered a deranged giggle.

"We thought Vance pushed him off the bridge, but it was you, wasn't it?" Cooper tried to control her shaking hands. "I saw all the pictures of the two of you in the *kids'* bedroom. Vance has been your boyfriend for years, right?"

Cindi pretended to clap using her free hand against her glass. "Vance's got the brains, I've got the balls . . . so to speak. I

437

borrowed his SUV and dead wife's morphine, and gave Reed a little push. Whoopsie!" She giggled, and the sound was eerie in the atmosphere of palpable tension. Cindi began counting on her fingers. "Brooke was first, then Reed, and I'd hunt down that weasel accountant if I had the time, but I don't. Now it looks like I'll be holdin' up two more fingers by the end of the day."

Her face slowly transformed. Gone was her expression of smug pride and a cruel and calculating mask fell over her features like a curtain. Impatiently pushing a strand of black hair off her forehead, Cindi stood and waved the gun at Cooper and Nathan. "That's enough chitchat. I'm not gonna sit here and tell you all the hows and whys. We wanted money. Loads of it. Vance came up with a way for us to get enough to buy a whole island for ourselves. Just think of us as Bonnie and Clyde, but with nicer clothes."

"Did you send Brooke those threatening faxes?" Nathan couldn't rip his eyes away from the gun.

"No. Reed did that. Went to some mailing place south of the river so he couldn't be traced." For a moment, she looked at him as though hoping to be entertained. "How did you find out about those?"

438

"We found them in Brooke's office at home. The woman who owns the mailing place remembers that the man who sent the faxes had curly, light-colored dog hair all over the sleeve of his coat. When we saw the Newcombe family dog at the Little League game —"

"You must have thought you had it all figured out, huh, Mr. Smartie?" she said with a sneer and then, glancing around the room, located a voluminous black leather purse and placed the pistol inside the bag. "I can shoot y'all easy through this bag. The leather's as thin as paper. Now stand up."

As Cooper and Nathan rose from their seated positions, Cindi stepped directly in front of them. "And don't even think about tryin' any hero stunts! Vance is on his way. I called him when I was gettin' your ginger ale." She smiled sinisterly at Cooper and opened her apartment door. "He's gonna decide what to do with y'all, but just so you know, I've got no problem blowin' either of your churchgoin' brains out before he gets here. That's probably what it's gonna come down to in the end anyhow. Now get in that elevator."

Inside the elevator, Nathan immediately put his arm around Cooper's shoulder. "Hit the garage button and then keep your hands out in front of you, Xerox boy!" Cindi snapped from behind them.

"Hazel Wharton was right." Nathan's voice was filled with ire. "You three were all going to get rich by ripping off Capital City clients. Did you stop to think that every penny mattered to some of those clients?"

Cindi snorted. "Poor folks shouldn't charge stuff they can't pay for. They should just do without. *I* did, growin' up in a trailer park. My daddy drank away every dime he got, but the one thing he did right was teach me how to shoot."

The elevator paused at the lobby level. Seconds before the doors slid open, Cindi rammed her purse against Cooper's back. "Don't say a word," she hissed.

An elderly gentleman in a seersucker suit put a single shiny loafer inside the elevator and then immediately stepped back out. "Goodness, I forgot my glasses again," he declared. "My apologies for delaying you."

Cooper longed to grab the man by the sleeve, and though she prayed with all her might he would turn around and discover the terror in their faces, the last they saw of him was the fabric of his suit as the brass doors closed and the elevator resumed its downward journey.

"You oughta put some meat on your

bones," Cindi whispered behind Cooper, still pressing the gun against her back. "Men like a little somethin' to hold on to."

Anger surged through Cooper. This made two times in a matter of weeks that someone had jabbed a gun barrel into her flesh, and she didn't enjoy the feeling.

Cooper's anger swelled as an image of the Hughes family photographs came into her mind. "I can't believe you shot Brooke Hughes!" she exclaimed with fury. "She kept you on as her assistant because she felt sorry for you, and you repaid her by showing up at her house and shooting her point-blank! What kind of person does that?"

The elevator stopped at the garage level. Cindi pushed Cooper forward and then slid behind Nathan, her right hand inside her bag and her free arm draped possessively on his left arm. "I *told* her I would handle Hazel, but Brooke wouldn't trust me with one of her precious clients — 'specially an old, upset, black lady. If my saint of a boss hadn't hired that nosy accountant, she'd still be alive." Cindi's eyes darted around the dim parking lot. "Reed could have lived too, but he got too greedy. After all, he just made up a computer program. Vance is the one who thought of the whole penny-stealing bit."

"Reed might still live," Cooper stated rashly, knowing that it was unwise to taunt a woman who held a gun and had already committed murder with no signs of remorse.

Cindi shrugged. "Lucky him. He'll have to take the fall for the whole dang scam. Vance has got everything laid out all nice and tidy for the finger to point right at Reed. He's left a paper trail even you two could follow." She laughed, delighted by this notion. "That ol' bat Hazel and that dumb accountant don't know how lucky *they* are. We're not gonna waste any more time tryin' to find them. Once you two are taken care of, Vance and I are outta the country. Ah," she cackled zealously, "here's my ticket to the good life now."

A dark-colored SUV pulled to an abrupt stop in front of them and a sound indicating that the doors were automatically being unlocked made Cooper feel weak in the knees. She darted a desperate look at Nathan, whose face was grim and fearful. "If we get in that car, we're going to die," she whispered urgently to him.

Overhearing, Cindi laughed with mirth and then opened the back door of the SUV. She pulled the gun from her bag and her finger moved to the trigger. Smiling crookedly, her dark eyes flashed. "You're gonna die anyway." She trained the gun on Cooper, but stared at Nathan, her expression filled with a crazed elation. "Get in, copy boy, or I shoot her right here and now."

Nathan hesitated, looking around for anything that would serve as a weapon, but there was nothing. With a defeated slump to his shoulders, he got into the SUV.

"You with the freaky eyes," Cindi came so close that Cooper could feel Cindi's breath on her face. "Your turn. Since you and Brooke went to church together, then you must be a *good* Christian girl. So let's see if all your *songs* and your *faith* and your *Bible thumpin'* can save you now. Go on," she commanded viciously. "Start prayin'."

Cooper closed her eyes and felt her knees buckling as she began to do just as Cindi ordered. Eyes squeezed shut, she heard voices shouting all around the garage. There were men's voices and then Cindi was yelling — her high-pitched screams filled with surprised rage. The exchanged shouts escalated until the boom of a gunshot eclipsed all other sound.

19

The LORD loves righteousness and
   justice;
the earth is full of his unfailing love.
                     Psalm 33:5 (NIV)

"Do you need a drink of water?" Investigator McNamara asked patiently as he waited for Cooper to finish her statement.

She sat up straighter in bed, wincing at the pain that flared along the length of her left arm. "I'm okay, but I don't have much more to add. After Cindi told me to pray, that's exactly what I did." She raised her eyes and looked at the police officer. "I heard you yell 'Put your hands in the air' to Cindi and then, I think you shouted 'Get down' to me."

"That's exactly what I said. I was trying to get you out of the line of fire." His steely eyes softened. "But you were already falling to your knees when I yelled."

From where she sat in the corner of the hospital room, Trish clamped her hand on Quinton's forearm. "This whole thing sounds just like a movie scene!"

"Yeah, 'cept in the movies, the cops are decked out in bulletproof vests and get to shoot people without fair warnin'. The real good guys gotta practically recite the Gettysburg Address before they're allowed to take down a wacko like Cindi Rolfing," Jake scoffed and bit into a Butterfinger. "I've gotta quit eatin' this junk. May as well go back to smoking. Least I was skinnier."

Looking tired but amused, McNamara turned his attention to Nathan, who had seated himself in a chair directly next to Cooper's bed. "At what point did Vance Maynard pull a gun on you?"

"Right after Cindi fired her pistol at you and your men. One of the bullets from the return fire grazed Cooper just below the shoulder. That's when Maynard decided to bolt." His eyes fell on Cooper's bandaged arm. "I wish I was the one standing in that spot," he said mournfully.

"What was Mr. Maynard's reaction?" the lawman prompted. "Would you mind telling me again, for the record?"

Nathan nodded, his face etched with shame. "He pointed a gun right at my forehead and told me to get out of the car. As soon as I did, he sped away." He glanced at Cooper again. "He could have run you over!"

"I'm fine," Cooper assured him as she smoothed the wrinkles in her blanket. "In fact, I'm not going to stay here overnight. There's nothing wrong with me except for a little cut."

"You're as bruised and stitched as a prize-fighter," Savannah pointed out gently. "Hit your head on that cement ground too. It would be best to take it easy, dear."

McNamara flipped through his notepad and cleared his throat. "Ms. Lee, you mentioned that Cindi Rolfing claimed that she didn't have time to track down Hazel Wharton and Jed Weeks. What do you think she meant by that?"

"I think she was getting ready to leave the country," Cooper answered. "She had two suitcases open on her bed and she mentioned making enough money to buy an island."

"And Vance had two duffel bags on the front seat of the SUV," Nathan added.

"Well, she won't be going anywhere fast," McNamara said, rising. "And I hope you all have learned your lesson about snooping. As you can see," — he gestured at Cooper's arm — "those on the wrong side of the law can inflict *real* injuries. It's not a game out there. If me and my men hadn't come along, we might be pulling you and your boyfriend out of the James River right now instead of taking your statements."

"Yessir," Cooper muttered, her face burning because of the reprimand, not to mention McNamara's use of the term *boyfriend*.

"What brought the police out to Cindi's place, if you don't mind me asking?" Quinton inquired. "Something about her must have raised some red flags."

"Financial red flags," McNamara answered. "In murder cases, we always look at the financial angle. The fact that Brooke Hughes was in charge of the Fraud department, with full access to the inner workings of the entire Capital City system, kept nagging at me as being significant. Despite the evidence, what most folks saw as Wesley's motive for killing her was weak from the get-go."

He threw out his arms as if to embrace everyone in the room. "All couples argue, but very few of those arguments end violently, so what would cause a man to shoot his wife in cold blood? Another woman? Drug or alcohol abuse? Sometimes folks just go plumb crazy, but most of the time, murder is about money. Wesley Hughes wasn't interested in money. He was perfectly content with his life and *that* interested me. I was lookin' for someone with a financial motive."

"You thought Wesley was innocent all along?" Savannah spluttered.

"I felt he might be, yes, Mrs. Knapp." The officer was solemn. "But what I think doesn't matter without evidence to back it up. Luckily, Ms. Lee stumbled across Jed Weeks, and the information he provided allowed us to crack the case." He eyed the Sunrise Bible Study members one at a time. "We were at Ms. Rolfing's apartment to question her about Brooke's murder. One of the Hugheses' neighbors recently remembered seeing a silver Honda sedan parked down the street from their house the morning the murder occurred. This woman was also able to recall two of the letters in the license plate, both of which appear on the plate of Ms. Rolfing's car."

"Will she live?" Cooper whispered. "Is Cindi going to stand trial?"

McNamara closed his eyes and finally issued the slightest of nods. "She's still in surgery, but the doctors are confident she'll pull through. On a more positive note, Mr. Newcombe's condition has improved remarkably and he's been completely co-operative with us." He lowered his voice and winked. "I think he'd do anything to please the missus at this juncture, but she says she's going to stick by him no matter what happens."

"We'll have to pray for their marriage, my friends," Savannah said to her friends.

Glancing at her in approval, McNamara placed his hands on his hips. "Mr. New-combe's agreed to see a counselor with Mrs. Newcombe, so between the prayers and the professional, they might just pull through." He paused and seemed to lose himself in thought for a moment. "I'll see to the release of your friend Wesley personally, folks. Perhaps Ms. Rolfing will provide us with a confession and make things all nice and tidy."

"I doubt it. And what about that rat, May-nard?" Jake demanded, balling his hands into fists so that the cross tattoo on his arm rippled. "How'd he get away with his part in all this?"

The officer sighed. "Unfortunately, Mr. Maynard had been seen at public events during the time period that Mrs. Hughes was killed and again when Mr. Newcombe was pushed from the bridge. During the afternoon Mrs. Hughes was murdered, Mr.

Maynard was playing in a charity tennis match and when Mr. Newcombe was injured, Mr. Maynard was attending a charity ball until close to two in the morning."

"But what if he gets away?" Cooper whispered.

McNamara put his warm palm over Cooper's right hand and stared sternly into her eyes, making it clear that the possibility for further discussion on the subject of Vance Maynard was now closed. "I'll be in touch, Ms. Lee. Please take care and listen to the doctors' advice. I'm posting a man outside your door, so don't you lose sleep thinkin' anyone's comin' in here that you don't want to see."

"Thank you, Investigator." Cooper gave the lawman a grateful smile. Nathan stood, shook the police officer's hand and they all watched as he left the room, his posture firm and his mouth set in a thin line. He was a man with a purpose.

"I can't believe that Vance character! Leaving his own girlfriend behind to face the firing squad. What a coward." Trish gazed at Cooper in remorse. "I know she's committed horrible, evil deeds, but she must be a tormented soul to have done the things she's done."

Jake smirked. "She's gonna be real mad at

that Vance guy for a long time. And it sounds like she'll have a few decades in prison to think about that island they bought."

Nathan slumped in his chair. "That's what I worry about. What if Vance got away and is headed for that locale as we speak?"

The friends exchanged anxious glances. Cooper agreed with Nathan. Vance Maynard was crafty enough to come up with the entire Capital City scam, so it was likely that he had an escape plan in place from the moment Brooke Hughes began to suspect that someone in her company was involved in criminal pursuits.

"Hey, where's Bryant?" Quinton asked in an attempt to lift the gloom that had descended upon the group.

"Fending off the news crews," Nathan replied.

Trish shot out of her chair. "He's going to get all the prime camera time! Where are they? Outside?" She was practically salivating as she feverishly dug in her purse for business cards.

Cooper smiled as she gazed at her friends. Her family had been by earlier and between her mother's anxiety and the investigator's pointed questions, Cooper was suddenly feeling tired. In fact, the idea of spending the night in the hospital didn't seem so bad. The nurse on duty had informed her that macaroni and cheese with green beans and garlic bread was on the menu for dinner and that she could check out first thing in the morning after the doctor assigned to her case completed his rounds.

Taking a drink from her plastic cup, Cooper thought about how the media would be trying to contact her at home, demanding to have their questions answered and their curiosity sated. Instead of unplugging her phone and asking her parents to deal with visitors to the house, she could simply stay here, spending a blessedly uneventful evening watching a rerun of *Extreme Makeover: Home Edition*. Then she could return home in the morning, feeling completely refreshed. She'd still refuse to talk to the press, but at least she'd feel strong enough to turn them away.

"Why don't you help Bryant make a statement on behalf of me and Nathan?" Cooper suggested wearily to Trish.

Savannah lifted her nose in the air as if tracking a scent. "Your voice sounds tired, Cooper. I think it's time for us to get going."

"Call me if you need anything!" Trish trilled and was out the door in a frantic clicking of heels.

"Oh, before I forget," Nathan said to Cooper as Savannah, accepted Jake's arm. "Your boss called. He says to take the rest of the week off."

For some reason, Cooper found Mr. Farmer's offer extremely touching. He already had too much work for his current employees to handle and yet he was willing to put off some of their clients in order to give Cooper an entire week of rest. She closed her eyes and struggled to keep from crying, but as soon as she shut out the light, the sounds of gunfire echoed through her mind. Trembling, she tried to block out the shouting, the roar of Cindi's gun being discharged above her, and the searing pain of the bullet lacerating the soft flesh of her arm.

Cooper felt a hand covering her own and she opened her eyes again. "Do you want me to stay awhile?" Nathan asked tenderly, though his face pinched with fatigue.

"You've been through a shock as well," Savannah spoke from the doorway. "You both need rest."

"Come on, my friend," Quinton took Nathan's elbow. "I'll give you a lift home."

Nathan cast one last look over his wide shoulders at Cooper. She gave him a weak

453

smile and for a moment, his face became effused with its customary animation. "I'm glad you're okay," he whispered, his voice breaking slightly. "If something had happened to you because I got in the car . . ." He trailed off, miserable with guilt once again.

"We're *both* okay," Cooper assured him warmly. "Good night, Nathan."

As the room emptied, Cooper released a mouthful of air that she hadn't realized she had been holding in. She laid her cheek against her pillow and thought she could smell traces of gunpowder in her hair. Envisioning Cindi's demented smile as she ordered Cooper to pray, tears sprung into her eyes and trickled down onto the pillowcase. She could still taste the fear in her mouth. It was an acid, metallic taste, and she longed to wash it away with something wholesome, like a glass of milk and a few of her mother's cookies.

Magically, Cooper's nurse bustled into the room carrying a small tray. "All your visitors gone?" she asked as she placed the tray next to Cooper's bed and gave her patient a brief examination. "Oh, honey, you're shakin' like a leaf! Are you cold?"

Cooper looked down at the goose bumps on her unbandaged arm in surprise. The nurse examined her patient's tear-streaked cheeks.

"Sweetheart, you've had a right awful shock. Now, you just tell me what to do to make you feel better, and I'll do it."

"Thank you. There is something that would make me feel better. I'd really, really like to take a shower." Cooper sniffed the ends of her hair again. "Everything that's ha-happened today . . ." She choked back a sob. "I just want to wash it all away."

The nurse took Cooper's hand. "Your mama brought a pair of your pajamas along with a bag of those cookies with the jelly in the middle. My nana used to call them thimble cookies and you've got enough here to feed the whole ward. Why don't you take a nice, hot shower — but you keep that left arm from gettin' wet, ya hear? — and then have yourself some milk and cookies? I'll bet you'll be asleep before the mac and cheese even gets here. You look like laundry that's been wrung out and hung to dry."

The nurse was right. Every inch of Cooper's body felt exhausted and she longed to be able to focus her thoughts on something other than the day's events. She stood under a scalding stream of water for a long time, dried her hair, and then put on her pajamas. After hungrily eating five of her mother's thimble cookies, she phoned her parents to tell them that she would be home in the morning, and thanked her mother for her foresight.

"Baby," Maggie's voice quivered and Cooper knew she had been crying. "You just sleep tight. Let your body and your mind shut down for a while and when you come on home tomorrow I'll fix you a brunch that'll make you feel like a new woman." She sniffed back tears. "After that, your daddy wants you to sit awhile with him in the garden. He says lookin' at the new crop of Better Boy tomatoes will heal you faster than any medicine."

Cooper said goodnight, eased her bed to a flat position, and pictured her father's vegetable garden. She could see the sun shining on the red curves of the tomatoes and the glossy surfaces of the cucumbers slick with dew. In her vision, bean plants were tickled by a breeze and bumblebees hovered over the bed of coneflowers that bordered the garden. Cooper could almost smell the fragrant honeysuckle, which grew in a tangled mass across the length of the back fence. The last thing that passed through her mind as she sank toward sleep was an image of herself at home, leaning against the fence as Columbus soared overhead, circling ever higher toward the comforting expanse of sky.

The congregation filed into Hope Street's chapel. Chatter buzzed around the room, punctuated by laughter and the hungry cries of several infants. Soon, the opening praise hymn boomed joyfully throughout the large space and the worshipers leapt to their feet, singing and clapping in harmony with the drummer up on stage. Two more songs followed, before the offertory was given and several announcements were made. Then, as it was the first Sunday of a new month, it was time for Communion.

As the minister prepared the table with the bread and wine he and the elders would give to the congregation, the side door to the auditorium opened and a middle-aged man entered the room. His arms were wrapped around the shoulders of a handsome young man, and the two walked confidently to a pair of empty seats in the front row.

Behind them, people began to mumble. Toward the back of the room, parishioners craned their necks to see what the fuss was about, and when they recognized their fellow worshipers, their faces broke into wide smiles.

The minister welcomed his flock to come forward, and as each man, woman, and child came to partake of Communion, they paused before approaching the altar in order to hug, kiss, or shake hands with Wesley and Caleb Hughes.

Father and son had been overwhelmed by the letters of encouragement in the mailbox, the piles of food delivered regularly by women of all ages, and the hundreds of phone calls and emails offering help and comfort. Now, sitting among their friends, they received whispers of sympathy, gracious prayers, and the physical touches and tearful smiles of every single person in the room. Young or old, close friend or distant acquaintance, each churchgoer made it a point to reach out to the two men and bless them.

When the minister stood to offer a Communion prayer, he did so with his hands resting on the crowns of the Hughes men's heads. Tears wet his cheeks but his voice was made powerful with joy.

"Thank you, Lord!" He lifted his face as he began his prayer. "For bringing these men home to us."

Outside Gold's Gym, Cooper's coworker, Ben, slung his workout bag onto the passenger seat and sank down into the driver's seat with a heavy sigh. He placed the keys in the ignition, but did not start his car. He just sat there, weary in mind and body, as the sun winked off his plastic water bottle and scattered star-shaped rainbows across the backs of his hands. Ben stared at them, and then lifted the bottle to his lips, drinking deeply. After wiping his lips onto his right shoulder, he held the bottle against his heart. The rainbows fluttered, shifted, and came to rest on the corner of the alcoholism brochure someone had placed inside his locker.

Ben withdrew the paper from his bag, powered up his cell phone, and dialed. When the sound of a woman's voice answered, he didn't know what to say. He cradled the phone against his ear, but couldn't begin to speak the words he needed to say. The woman prodded him gently, reassuringly, until at last, he began to talk. Suddenly, it all came pouring out of him, in a rapid tumble of pain and grief.

The stranger listened, and in her compassionate silence, Ben distinctly heard the sound of hope.

Ashley arrived at the hospital at the same time the Hope Street service was being held and Ben was dialing the hotline number. Dressed in jeans and a T-shirt instead of one of her chic Sunday suits, she entered the room just as Cooper's doctor departed, saying that she had no sign of a concussion and was free to leave.

"We're having a family day at home. Mama's making one of her famous million-calorie brunches," Ashley informed Cooper after hugging her gently. "I brought you a change of clothes. Mama says your shirt was fairly ruined." She dumped a shopping bag on the bed. "I simply cannot believe that Vance Maynard's girlfriend is a murderer! And how greedy could Vance be? He had plenty of money already!"

"From the photos I saw in Cindi's bedroom, Vance and Cindi have been together for a long time." Cooper fastened her watchband and dusted some dirt from the glass face. "They've been putting on an act that they were simply acquaintances. I bet they used that act a lot."

Ashley handed Cooper a set of clothes. "As in, like, when Vance was still with his wife?"

Cooper nodded, sadly. "I'm afraid so."

"Do you think he had anything to do with his wife's death?" Ashley whispered dramatically.

Tired of the subject of murder, Cooper only answered by saying, "The police are looking into that." As she headed off to the bathroom to change, she added, "Can we talk about other things, Ashley?"

"Sure! How about my idea to throw you a *fabulous* birthday bash?"

"I don't like the sound of *bash*. Reminds me of your country club parties. How about something small, like a barbeque at home?" Cooper shouted through the closed door as she ran a brush through her hair.

Ashley's voice grew closer. "Not what I had in mind, but okay. A party will take your mind off all the *nasty* stuff you've been through, and it would be a great way for the family to meet all your Bible study friends and especially Nathan."

Cooper emerged from the bathroom. "I'm ready to go home," she stated firmly. "This whole mess has taught me a thing or two. I've been sitting back too much, letting life happen to me instead of *making* things happen. If I can give up cigarettes, charging things on my Visa, and pining away for Drew, then I can do a lot of things."

Eyeing her reflection in the mirrored closet door, Cooper squared her shoulders and adopted an expression of determination. "I've got a busy summer ahead of me,

Ashley, starting with that barbeque. After that, I'm going to start a new exercise routine, like running or biking, and I'm going to grow bushels of vegetables for the Food Bank. *And,* most importantly, I'm going to make sure Nathan Dexter takes me to that movie he owes me. Shoot, I might even get my hair highlighted." Cooper gestured impatiently at her startled sister. "Are you coming?" she asked, and then marched purposefully down the hall, forcing Ashley to carry her bag.

Ashley spent the drive home casting sidelong glances at her sister, marveling at how different Cooper had become since the morning she had stumbled into the Sunrise Bible Study. Pleased that her older sister seemed to have discovered a new inner strength, Ashley relaxed at the wheel and launched into feverish chatter about an upcoming benefit while Cooper leaned against the passenger window and delighted in the sunlight falling upon her face.

As soon as Cooper got out of Ashley's convertible, her parents ran out of the house and welcomed her with cautious hugs and kisses on the cheek. Even Grammy was careful when she planted a dry kiss on her granddaughter's neck.

"I'm not going to break, y'all!" Cooper

chided them happily. It had never felt so good to be embraced by her loved ones.

The tension from yesterday's events drained steadily away as Cooper sat at her parents' kitchen table, drinking Southern pecan coffee and watching her mother fry bacon. Grammy began to nag Ashley about producing great-grandchildren while Earl unfolded the Sunday paper. He filled in a Jumble word puzzle with one hand while holding Cooper's uninjured hand possessively in the other.

"Oh, a friend of yours dropped a box off here early this morning," Maggie said casually as she transferred six strips of bacon to a stack of paper towels. "It's on the hall table."

Cooper finished her coffee and retrieved the shoebox. Pushing the top off with her right hand, she picked up the note sitting on top of a pile of tissue and read:

Dear Cooper,
I truly hope you've had some rest and are feeling better today. I got up early to spend the day with my sister. I am bringing her to Hope Street Church this morning and her boyfriend actually wants to come too!
Your shirt from yesterday was pretty

trashed so your nurse put it in a bag in the closet of your hospital room. I was afraid something might happen to your pin and as I know how much it means to you, I brought it home with me. It was a little bent, so I hammered out the dings (very gently, I promise) and polished it. Now it looks as good as new.

When you've recovered, I hope you'll put your pin on and join me for a movie. Here's a gift certificate to the theater on Broad Street — just to show you that I haven't forgotten about that matinee I owe you. Give me a call when you're ready to eat a very large tub of buttered popcorn and one of those giant boxes of Milk Duds. 'Cause I like sugar too.

Yours,
Nathan

Cooper reread the note and then quickly unfolded the tissue. There was her butterfly pin, carefully nestled in a single sheet of bubble wrap. Cooper held it to the light and it shimmered as though the wings were moving and it was poised to lift in flight.

She turned back toward the kitchen and saw her mother removing a pan of cinnamon rolls from the oven. Grammy hastily identified the roll with the most icing and directed that it be put on her plate while Earl helped himself to a pile of crisp bacon. Ashley refilled her sister's coffee cup before pouring more into her own. Encased by the comforting warmth of this scene, Cooper's heart swelled. She glanced at Nathan's words once more and then tucked the note and the gift certificate into the pocket of her pants.

"Thank you for all of these gifts," she said in a whispered prayer as she gazed lovingly into the kitchen. Caressing the butterfly pin in her right hand, Cooper rejoined her family as they sat down to say grace.

Magnolia's Marvels: *Butterscotch Cheesecake Squares*

Crust:
3/4 cup butterscotch chips
1/3 cup butter, room temperature
2 cups graham cracker crumbs

Filling:
8 oz cream cheese, room temperature
1 can sweetened condensed milk (14 oz)
1 egg
1 teaspoon vanilla extract

Drizzle: (optional)
1/4 cup semi-sweet morsels
2 teaspoons shortening

1. Preheat oven to 350 degrees. Lightly grease a 13 × 9 baking pan.
2. Crust: Combine butter and butterscotch morsels in a saucepan and, stirring con-

stantly, cook over low heat. Once blended, add graham cracker crumbs.

3. Pack crust evenly onto bottom of baking pan.

4. Filling: Beat cream cheese and condensed milk in a small bowl. Beat in egg and vanilla extract. (Maggie likes to use an electric mixer on medium for 2 minutes. Make sure all the chunks of cream cheese have been beaten smooth.) Pour over crust.

5. Bake for 25–30 minutes until knife inserted into the center comes out clean. Cool in pan and then cut into squares.

6. Chocolate drizzle: For fancier squares, melt 1/4 semi-sweet chocolate morsels with 2 teaspoons shortening and drizzle over bars with a fork.

MAGNOLIA'S MARVELS: DARK CHOCOLATE RASPBERRY BARS

1 cup butter, softened
2 cups all-purpose flour
1/2 cup brown sugar
1/4 teaspoon salt
1 package (12 oz) bittersweet morsels
1 can (14 oz) sweetened condensed milk
1/2 cup seedless raspberry jam

1. Preheat oven to 350 degrees.

2. Grease 13 × 9 inch baking pan.
3. Cream butter and add in sugar and flour until crumbly. Press 1 3/4 crumb mixture into bottom of pan.
4. Bake for 10 minutes or until edges are golden brown.
5. In microwave-safe bowl, microwave 1 cup morsels and can of sweetened condensed milk for one minute or until chips are all melted. This may require frequent stirring.
6. Spread over hot crust.
7. Drop small teaspoonfuls of jam over crumb mixture. Sprinkle remaining bitter-sweet morsels on the very top.
8. Bake for 30 minutes or until set. Cool in pan or wire rack.

MAGNOLIA'S MARVELS: *THIMBLE COOKIES*

1/2 cup butter, softened
1/3 cup sugar
1 egg yolk
1 cup sifted flour
1/4 baking soda
pinch salt
your choice of jelly

1. Preheat oven to 350 degrees.
2. Cream butter and sugar.
3. Add egg yolk.
4. Mix in flour, baking powder, and salt.

5. Roll into small balls and place on baking sheet, about one inch apart.
6. Press thimble into dough and fill hole with jam (Maggie likes seedless raspberry, strawberry, or apricot best).
7. Bake for 15 minutes.